Wandsworth

— Booklist

Winner of Northern Ireland Book Award 2011
Shortlisted for Independent Booksellers Book Awards 2011 and 2012

Chris Bradford likes to fly through the air. He has thrown himself over Victoria Falls on a bungee cord, out of an aeroplane in New Zealand and off a French mountain on a paraglider, but he has always managed to land safely – something he learnt from his martial arts . . .

Chris joined a judo club aged seven where his love of throwing people over his shoulder, punching the air and bowing lots started. Since those early years, he has trained in karate, kickboxing, samurai swordsmanship and has earned his black belt in *taijutsu*, the secret fighting art of the ninja.

Before writing the Young Samurai series, Chris was a professional musician and songwriter. He's even performed to HRH Queen Elizabeth II (but he suspects she found his band a bit noisy).

Chris lives in a village on the South Downs with his wife, Sarah, his son, Zach, and two cats called Tigger and Rhubarb.

To discover more about Chris go to *www.youngsamurai.com*

Books by Chris Bradford:

The Young Samurai series (in reading order)
THE WAY OF THE WARRIOR
THE WAY OF THE SWORD
THE WAY OF THE DRAGON
THE RING OF EARTH
THE RING OF WATER
THE RING OF FIRE
THE RING OF WIND
THE RING OF SKY

Available as eBook
THE WAY OF FIRE

THE RING OF SKY

CHRIS BRADFORD

PUFFIN

Disclaimer: *Young Samurai: The Ring of Sky* is a work of fiction, and while based on real historical figures, events and locations, the book does not profess to be accurate in this regard. *Young Samurai: The Ring of Sky* is more an echo of the times than a re-enactment of history.

Warning: Do not attempt any of the techniques described within this book without the supervision of a qualified martial arts instructor. These can be highly dangerous moves and result in fatal injuries. The author and publisher take no responsibility for any injuries resulting from attempting these techniques.

PUFFIN BOOKS

Published by the Penguin Group
Penguin Books Ltd, 80 Strand, London WC2R ORL, England
Penguin Group (USA) Inc., 375 Hudson Street, New York, New York 10014, USA
Penguin Group (Canada), 90 Eglinton Avenue East, Suite 700, Toronto, Ontario, Canada M4P 2Y3
(a division of Pearson Penguin Canada Inc.)
Penguin Ireland, 25 St Stephen's Green, Dublin 2, Ireland (a division of Penguin Books Ltd)
Penguin Group (Australia), 250 Camberwell Road, Camberwell, Victoria 3124, Australia
(a division of Pearson Australia Group Pty Ltd)
Penguin Books India Pvt Ltd, 11 Community Centre, Panchsheel Park, New Delhi – 110 017, India
Penguin Group (NZ), 67 Apollo Drive, Rosedale, Auckland 0632, New Zealand
(a division of Pearson New Zealand Ltd)
Penguin Books (South Africa) (Pty) Ltd, Block D, Rosebank Office Park, 181 Jan Smuts Avenue,
Parktown North, Gauteng 2193, South Africa

Penguin Books Ltd, Registered Offices: 80 Strand, London WC2R ORL, England

puffinbooks.com

First published 2012
005

Text copyright © Chris Bradford, 2012
Cover illustration copyright © Paul Young, 2012
Map copyright © Robert Nelmes, 2008
Enso symbol by Andy Lin
All rights reserved

The moral right of the author and illustrators has been asserted

Set in Bembo by Palimpsest Book Production Limited, Falkirk, Stirlingshire
Made and printed in Great Britain by Clays Ltd, St Ives plc

British Library Cataloguing in Publication Data
A CIP catalogue record for this book is available from the British Library

ISBN: 978-0141-33972-6

www.greenpenguin.co.uk

Penguin Books is committed to a sustainable future for our business, our readers and our planet. This book is made from Forest Stewardship Council™ certified paper.

Dedicated to all Young Samurai fans,
may you follow the Way of the Warrior in life . . .

CONTENTS

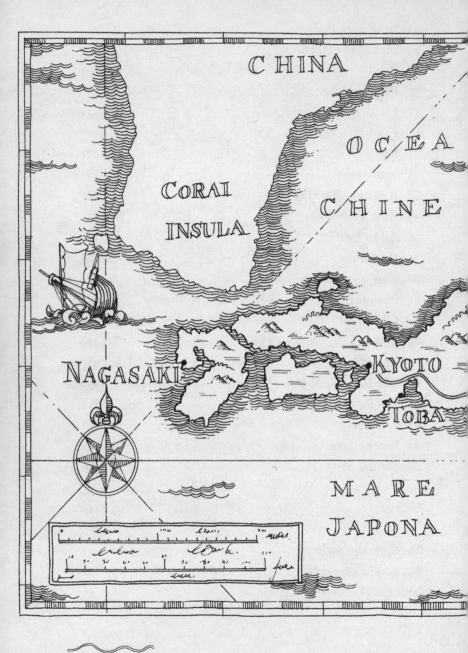

CHINA

OCEA

CHINE

CORAI

INSULA

NAGASAKI

KYOTO

TOBA

MARE

JAPONA

TOKAIDO ROAD

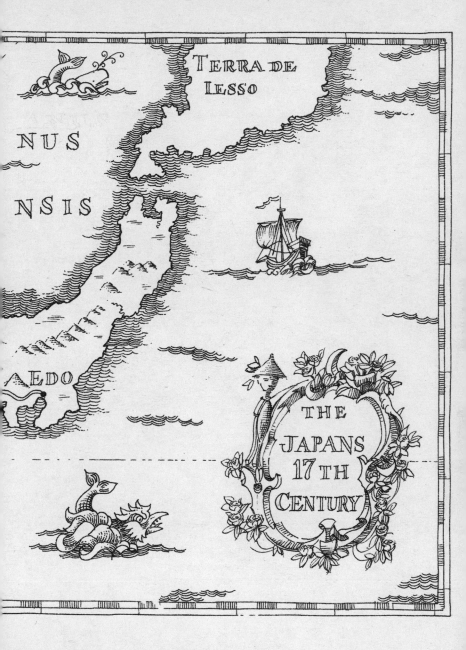

TERRA DE
IESSO

NUS

NSIS

AEDO

THE
JAPANS
17 TH
CENTURY

THE LETTER

Japan, 1614

My dearest Jess,

I hope this letter reaches you one day. You must believe I've been lost at sea all these years. But you'll be glad to know that I am alive and in good health.

Father and I reached the Japans in August 1611, but I am sad to tell you he was killed in an attack upon our ship, the Alexandria. I alone survived.

For these past three years, I've been living in the care of a Japanese warrior, Masamoto Takeshi, at his samurai school in Kyoto. He has been very kind to me, but life has not been easy.

An assassin, a ninja known as Dragon Eye, was hired to steal our father's rutter (you no doubt remember how important this navigational logbook was to our father?). The ninja was successful in his mission. However, with the help of my samurai friends, I've managed to get it back.

This same ninja was the one who murdered our father. And, while it may not bring you much comfort, I can assure you the assassin is now dead. Justice has been delivered. But the ninja's death doesn't bring back our father — I miss him so much and could do with his guidance and protection at this time.

Japan has been split by civil war and foreigners like myself are no longer welcome. I am a fugitive. On the run for my life. I now journey south through this strange and exotic land to the port of Nagasaki in the hope that I may find a ship bound for England.

The Tokaido Road upon which I travel, however, is fraught with danger and I have many enemies on my trail. But do not fear for my safety. Masamoto has trained me as a samurai warrior and I will fight to return home to you.

One day I do hope I can tell you about my adventures in person . . .

Until then, dear sister, may God keep you safe.

Your brother, Jack

P.S. Since first writing this letter at the end of spring, I've been kidnapped by ninja. But I discovered that they were not the enemy I thought they were. In fact, they saved my life and taught me about the Five Rings: the five great elements of the universe — Earth, Water, Fire, Wind and Sky. I now know ninjutsu skills that go beyond anything I learnt as a samurai. But, because of the circumstances of our father's death, I still struggle to fully embrace the Way of the Ninja . . .

1

FOOTPRINTS

Japan, summer 1615

Spluttering and choking, Jack hacked up a lungful of salt water. His fingers gripped the wet sand as another wave broke over him, threatening to drag him back into the chill sea. The constant roll of breakers was like the restless breathing of a great dragon that, having had its fill, spat him out on to the shore.

With the last of his strength, Jack clawed his way up the beach. Once clear of the waves, he rolled on to his back, gasping from the effort, and opened his eyes. The sky was a wide expanse of crystal blue, not a cloud in sight, no trace of the storm that had raged the previous night. The early morning sun shone down in warming golden rays from the east, hinting at the fine summer day to come.

Jack had no idea how long he lay there recovering, but when he opened his eyes again the salt water had cracked his lips and his kimono was bone dry. His mind whirled like the churning ocean and his entire body felt sore and bruised, having been pummelled by waves, rocks and the reef in his desperate bid for land. So far as he could tell no bones were broken, although every muscle ached and there was a painful throb in his left side. But, to his relief, he discovered this was just the hilt of his sword jammed against his ribs.

He sat up groggily. By some miracle, he still possessed both his *katana* and the shorter *wakizashi*. A samurai warrior's sword was considered to be his soul. And Jack – trained in the ways of the samurai and the ninja – was thankful not to have lost his. For in a country that now deemed foreigners and Christians to be the enemy of the state, these weapons were his lifeline.

His pack was also tied round his waist. Bedraggled and misshapen, its contents looked to be in a sorry state. He emptied it on to the sand. A cracked gourd fell out, along with a couple of crushed rice balls and three slim iron *shuriken*. The ninja throwing stars were followed by the heavy thump of a book – his father's *rutter*, a priceless navigational logbook that offered the only means of safely crossing the world's oceans. Jack was reassured to find the *rutter* still protected within its waterproof oilskin cover. But the sight of the broken gourd *was* cause for concern. Having spent much of the night battling for his life, Jack was weakened by hunger and thirst. Snatching up the gourd with a trembling hand, he poured the last dregs of fresh water into his parched mouth. Then, without bothering to brush the sand off, he consumed the cold rice balls in a few ravenous bites. Meagre and salty as they were, the rice revived him enough to clear his head and take stock of his situation.

Glancing round, Jack discovered he'd washed up in a sheltered bay. The beach was bounded by craggy headlands to the north and south, while behind, a small cliff rose westwards to a scrub-lined ridge. On first inspection the bay appeared to be deserted. Then Jack spied a piece of wreckage bobbing at the shoreline. With a sinking heart, he recognized it instantly. Sprawled out like a huge drowned moth was the broken mast of the skiff, its tattered sail rippling in the waves.

Only now did the realization hit Jack that his friends were missing.

Scrambling to his feet, he ran down to the shore and frantically searched for any sign of them. Finding no bodies on the beach or in the shallows, he scanned the bay and horizon for their boat. But the little skiff was nowhere to be seen. With a growing sense of despair, Jack feared Yori, Saburo and Miyuki were lost at sea. Then Jack spotted two sets of footprints in the sand and a spark of hope was rekindled.

Dropping to one knee, he inspected the prints and applied his ninja tracking skills. Grandmaster Soke had taught him how to identify tracks by their size, shape, depth and pattern. Immediately – and with a sigh of dismay – Jack could tell these didn't belong to any of his friends. They were too large. Made by an adult and facing opposite directions, it was evident that the two sets belonged to the same individual. Both prints possessed a similar uneven pattern, indicating the person either had a limp or an odd gait. Jack also noted the approach had been hurried, but the departure *urgent* – the sand being more heavily displaced and the prints wider apart, signalling a change of pace into a run.

Whoever it was, their presence was unlikely to be favourable for Jack.

He caught the distant sound of voices to the north. Hastily

gathering up his belongings, Jack fled the opposite way. He ran along the beach towards the southern headland, all the time keeping his eye out for the slightest proof his friends had survived. Approaching the rocky outcrop, he noticed the opening to a cave and made directly for it. Just as he entered its cool darkness, he heard a shout.

'The *gaijin*'s over here!'

Jack glanced back to see an old fisherman with bandy legs leading a patrol of armed samurai on to the beach. Hiding inside the cave's entrance, Jack observed the fisherman totter over to where the mast lay.

'Where is he then?' demanded the leader of the patrol, a sour-faced man with a topknot of black hair and a thick moustache.

'I promise you,' the fisherman protested, pointing a gnarly finger at the marks in the sand. 'I saw him with my own eyes. A foreigner washed up on this beach *and* he had samurai swords.'

The leader bent down to examine the evidence. His eyes followed Jack's tracks along the beach.

'He can't have got far,' snarled the man, drawing his *katana*. 'We'll hunt this *gaijin* samurai down like a dog!'

2

STUCK

Jack plunged deeper into the cave to avoid being spotted. The headland was a honeycomb of rock with passages breaking off in different directions. The cold wet stone closed in around him and the sunlight receded to little more than a reflected gleam. He could hear the sea surging deep within like a primeval heartbeat. Jack took the most obvious route along the widest passage, hoping this would lead to a way out. He stumbled through the darkness and damp. His fingers groped for handholds on the bare rock as he followed the curving wall to his right. But this turned out to be a dead end and he had to double back.

As Jack tried the next passage, a wave boomed, rolling like thunder, and the previous night's storm flashed before his eyes. White lightning and black clouds. Torrential rain and monumental waves. Their boat tossed like a cork from crest to trough. His friends clinging on in sheer terror, their faces pale and drawn. Jack still couldn't fathom how their good fortune had turned ill so quickly. They'd escaped Pirate Island with their lives, and been blessed with a well-stocked boat, an accurate sea chart and a fair wind. It should have been plain sailing to the port of Nagasaki. After no more than two weeks' voyage, he should have been standing upon the deck of an English galleon, preparing to sail home to his sister, Jess.

But the Seto Sea had other plans. During the middle of the third night, a tempest erupted out of nowhere. Taken by surprise, Jack had been unable to avoid its perilous path. His seafaring skills were tested to the limit as he fought to keep their little boat afloat. But the storm worsened. In danger of all being washed overboard, he'd instructed his friends to tie themselves to the skiff. Then suddenly his pack, with its precious cargo, became dislodged. Fearful of losing his father's *rutter* to the depths, Jack had dived to rescue it. He'd caught hold of its strap just as an almighty wave engulfed the boat. There was a horrendous crack, like a bone breaking, and the mast was snapped in two. The boat keeled over, throwing its young crew into the wild foaming sea.

Jack swam hard to be reunited with his friends, but he was dragged away with the current. Weighed down by his pack and swords, he only managed to keep his head above water by grasping on to the broken mast. His friends, tethered to their capsized skiff, cried out to him. But their shouts were carried away on the howling wind as they drifted further and further apart, until the mountainous waves overwhelmed their little boat.

That was the last time he saw Yori, Saburo and Miyuki alive. Jack had to face the bleak truth – his friends had perished in the storm. Drowned. Dead. Gone forever.

But he had no time to grieve their loss as a man's gruff voice echoed through the cave. 'The tracks lead this way.'

Jack fled down another passage. Tighter than the previous

ones, he had to keep his head low to avoid hitting the jagged rocks. After twenty or so paces, he noticed a glimmer of light and held out hope that he would escape.

He entered a gloomy cavern. But, everywhere he turned, he met with solid rock. The sunlight he'd spotted was filtering in through a crack high in the ceiling. Jack desperately sought for handholds to pull himself up. But the sea had worn the rock smooth, and even with his climbing skills he had no chance of reaching the tiny gap. Jack had struck another dead end and this time he couldn't turn back.

A voice worryingly close by said, 'Let's try this one.'

'Don't take any chances,' warned the leader. 'Kill the *gaijin* on sight.'

Jack heard the samurai entering the passage to the cavern. Weakened from the storm, Jack had wished to avoid a fight. But, cornered as he was, he now drew his swords and prepared to make a stand. He felt water slosh over his feet then disappear. Looking down, he discovered a narrow opening in the cavern floor. Jack's luck had finally returned. If the sea was flowing in, there was every chance of a way out.

'I've found him!' cried a samurai.

Dropping to all fours, Jack shoved his swords and pack into the gap and squeezed through after them. Hands grabbed at his ankles and he was yanked backwards. Jack kicked out hard, breaking the samurai's grip. He disappeared down the hole like a rabbit into a warren. The gap widened into a descending passageway. He scrambled along, knees and elbows scraping against the rough rock.

'Don't let him get away!' cried their leader. 'There's a price on his head.'

'It's too narrow,' the samurai protested.

The leader swore in frustration. 'Stay here in case he doubles back. The rest of you come with me. We'll catch him on the other side . . . if he gets out alive.'

3

NINJA BREATHING

Jack furiously crawled, pushed and pulled his way down the passage. It was pitch-black and growing ever tighter. As the sides closed in, he couldn't help thinking of the immense weight and pressure of the headland bearing down on him. He began to perspire. His hands trembled uncontrollably as claustrophobia took hold. His shoulders became jammed between two rocks and he panicked. He twisted and turned, but couldn't free himself. All of a sudden he had trouble breathing. There didn't seem to be enough oxygen in the air.

Then he heard the ominous roar of a wave.

A rush of wind preceded the unseen wall of water as the sea funnelled into the confines of the passage and hurtled towards Jack. Snatching a last breath, he braced himself. The wave hit him with the impact of a stampeding horse. Water flooded the passageway and he was submerged beneath a bubbling roar.

Fighting to control his panic, Jack knew his only chance of survival lay in a ninja breath-suppression technique. There'd been no time to perform the requisite deep-breathing exercise, so he had to rely on the other elements being enough. With practised skill, he relaxed his muscles and focused his mind. Summoning up a joyous moment in his life as a means of *zazen* meditation, Jack pictured Akiko, his closest friend, sitting with him beneath the *sakura* tree in Toba. The turbulent wave buffeted him as he dropped into a meditative state and his heartbeat slowed dramatically. At half the rate, his body's demand for oxygen fell and he was able to suppress his natural need to breathe.

But only for so long . . . a few minutes at the most.

The sea surged through the passageway, threatening to hold him in its watery embrace forever. Then his shoulders broke free, the pressure of the wave dislodging him. A moment later, the flow reversed direction and Jack was pulled along in its wake. As he struggled in its wild current, his heart rate shot up and his lungs burned for oxygen. Jack had reached his limit and his mouth involuntarily opened to suck in water where it expected air . . .

On the brink of drowning, Jack was saved at the last second when the wave finally receded. His head broke the surface and he gasped for air. Coughing and spluttering, he groped in the darkness for his swords and pack. His hands clasped round the handles and strap, then he scrambled as fast as he could along the gradually widening passageway. But, before he could reach the sea entrance, another wave flooded in.

Jack was more prepared this time. Bracing himself against the walls, he took three deep breaths before holding the last and re-entering his meditative state. The sea tore past him and his kimono felt as if it would be ripped from his back. But Jack held firm. He counted time, waiting for the turn of the current. The wave rolled on and on, a seemingly endless surge.

Then he felt the shift in direction. All the while his need to breathe intensified. The water took far longer to disperse than he'd anticipated. His lungs were on the point of bursting . . . then the passage emptied of water. As he gulped in precious air, he could already hear another wave approaching and realized the tide must be coming in.

Lucky to have survived the first two waves, Jack knew the third would be the end of him.

He crawled along the passageway, dragging his pack and swords behind. The wave thundered closer. He scrabbled over some rocks and came to a fork in the darkness. With no time to hesitate, a gleam of light convinced him to go left. The slope inclined upwards to a large hole. Behind, the sea pursued him like a foaming monster. With a final burst of effort, Jack clambered out and rolled on to a patch of sand, a spray of seawater shooting out of the blowhole after him.

Jack lay for several moments on his back, recovering from his narrow escape. He found himself in a large cave with rock pools and stalactites. Bright welcome sunlight poured through the cave's craggy opening. Beyond stretched a beach of glistening black sand.

Wasting no more time, Jack secured his swords and shouldered his pack. Cautiously, he made his way to the entrance and peered out. Apart from a few seagulls, the beach was deserted. It appeared the samurai patrol hadn't yet managed to climb over the headland. Leaving the shelter of the cave, he dashed across the beach towards what looked like a trail winding its way up the opposite cliff face.

The sand was hot beneath his feet as he ran. By midday, Jack guessed it would become unbearable. He was halfway along the beach when he spied an object among the pecking seagulls on the sand. As he drew closer, the seagulls flew off and Jack was sickened to discover that it was a human head.

He shouldn't have been so shocked. The samurai were well known for decapitating their victims. After a battle, it was the tradition for warriors to present the heads of their conquered enemies to their generals for inspection. Heads were also cut off as part of *seppuku*, ritual suicide. Or, in less honourable circumstances, as a brutal form of capital punishment. In this case, the unfortunate victim was a boy and appeared to be a peasant or common criminal – the head didn't sport the shaved pate and topknot of the ruling samurai class. Instead, wayward black hair shot up as if still in shock from its owner's sudden demise.

Jack offered the head a pitying look and ran on, keenly aware that the same fate awaited him if he didn't escape.

'Hey, *nanban!*'

Unsheathing his *katana*, Jack spun to face the samurai patrol. But there was no one chasing him.

'Are you blind? Down here!'

Jack stopped in his tracks. The decapitated head was *talking* to him.

4

HEAD IN THE SAND

'Stop gawping and help me,' it demanded, squinting against the bright sunlight.

'Y . . . you're still alive!' Jack exclaimed in disbelieving horror.

'Of course, *nanban*. Now stand in front of the sun.'

Sword still drawn, Jack warily approached and positioned his shadow across the head's face. On his journey through Japan, he'd experienced many strange encounters – from shape-shifting monks to fortune-telling witches to warrior spirits – but this undead head was beyond all reasonable explanation. Then he realized the young man was buried up to his neck in the sand. A year or so older than Jack, the disembodied boy possessed a flattened brow, snub nose and large ears that stuck out like jug handles. The thick lips were sunburnt and the reddened cheeks glistened with sweat. Several bloody peck marks dotted the forehead beneath the wild forest of black hair.

Once shaded from the sun's glare, the boy sighed with relief. Then he scrunched up his face and began twitching manically. 'Scratch my nose, will you?'

Jack reached out a tentative hand and rubbed the boy's nose with a fingernail.

'A little lower . . . ah, that's better! An itch is torture. Now, are you going to help me or not?'

'I'm not sure there's much more I can do.'

'Are all *nanban* so simple-minded?' said the boy in exasperation. 'How about digging me out?'

Before leaping to his aid, Jack took a moment to glance over his shoulder. Although there was still no sign of the patrol, he couldn't afford to linger on the beach digging this person up . . .

'What are you waiting for?' complained the head. 'I'm dying here!'

But neither could he abandon the victim to certain death. The sun was already scorching and the tide was coming in. Within hours the young man would be killed by the blistering heat or drowned beneath the waves. Forgetting his own fate for a moment, Jack hastily sheathed his sword, dropped to his knees and began scooping up handfuls of sand. Then he hesitated again.

'Don't stop!' cried the head.

'Why are you buried in the first place?' asked Jack, suddenly aware he could be unearthing more trouble for himself.

'My friends did it for a joke,' the head replied, giving him a hearty smile.

'Some joke.'

The head could see Jack wasn't convinced. 'I'm not a murderer if that's what you're thinking, *nanban*. You of all people must know what it's like in Japan with the new shogun. The innocent are guilty . . . unless they're samurai!'

Jack did understand. Since his arrival in Japan, he'd witnessed a deaf tea merchant lose his head for simply not bowing and Christian priests hung by their necks solely for their beliefs. Race, religion or lowly status provided enough reason for a death sentence under Shogun Kamakura's ruthless reign. Whatever crime this young man had committed, he was unlikely to deserve such a cruel punishment.

Jack resumed his digging. 'So who are you?'

'Benkei the Great!' proclaimed the head.

Jack raised an eyebrow at such a grandiose title, but made no comment. 'I'm Jack Fletcher from England.'

'A *nanban* who speaks fluent Japanese,' remarked Benkei, impressed. 'Nor have I ever met a southern barbarian with samurai swords before. Who did you kill to acquire those? Or did you steal them from a battlefield?'

'They were a gift from a close friend,' Jack stated, working hard to shift the wet sand trapping Benkei's chest.

Benkei shared a conspiratorial wink with him. 'Whatever you say, *nanban*.'

Jack ignored his cynicism and asked, 'How long have you been buried like this?'

'Oh, a day or so.'

'I'm surprised you're still alive.'

'I caught a couple of sand crabs in my mouth,' Benkei explained. 'A bit crunchy for *sashimi*, to be honest. And they fight back!' He stuck out his tongue to show a red pincer mark. 'Then last night when the heavens opened, I had more than enough to drink. Actually, I almost *drowned*.'

Jack stopped digging again and asked tentatively, 'Have you seen anyone else along this beach?'

Benkei considered this for a moment. 'Maybe. Who are you looking for?'

'Three friends. A small monk by the name of Yori, carrying a Buddhist ringed staff. A young samurai called Saburo. He's a lot larger, particularly round the middle. And Miyuki, a slim girl with spiky dark hair and eyes black as midnight.'

'Aren't we all looking for a girl like that?' Benkei replied with a mischievous grin.

'This one could kill you,' warned Jack, and the grin died on Benkei's face. 'So have you seen any of them?'

'Finish digging me out and I'll tell you who I saw.'

Encouraged by this, Jack furiously shovelled sand until Benkei's arms were free. Then between them they created a hole large enough for Jack to pull him out.

'That's the last time I go to the beach,' said Benkei, brushing the sand from his brightly coloured kimono, a motley patchwork of red, green and yellow silks. He shook his gangly legs and a bewildered crab dropped from his undergarments. '*That* was really uncomfortable.'

'So who did you see?' Jack urged, eager for news of his friends.

Benkei shrugged apologetically. 'No one fitting those descriptions, I'm afraid.'

Jack felt cheated. 'But you said –'

'Thanks for digging me out, *nanban*,' he interrupted, his eyes flicking to the headland, before sprinting off in the opposite direction. 'Nice to meet you!'

Hearing a shout from behind, Jack turned to find the samurai patrol charging along the beach towards him. Beginning to regret his decision to stop and help, Jack ran after Benkei.

ONSEN

'They're after *me*, not you!' cried Jack as they reached the top of the cliff.

'That may be true, *nanban*, but I'm not exactly popular with the samurai in these parts either,' said Benkei, not breaking his stride.

The trail cut through shrubland to a crossroads beside a lone tree. A well-used dirt road followed the coastline, while a smaller track headed inland towards a rugged mountain range.

'Which way? I've no idea where I am,' Jack admitted.

Benkei raised an eyebrow in surprise. 'This is Kyushu Island. North takes you to Shimonoseki, south to Funai through the town of Beppu, and that way –' he pointed along the track – 'leads to the Kuju range. But I'd avoid that route if I were you. Unless you want to get *really* lost!'

Below, they heard the shouts of the patrol drawing closer and, to their alarm, saw two more samurai tearing along the road from the direction of the headland.

'Your best chance of escape lies in Beppu. Follow me, if you want,' said Benkei, dashing off towards the town.

With little alternative, Jack hurried along in his wake. Flee-ing south, they crested a rise and Jack was greeted by a remarkable sight. The town of Beppu lay at the foot of a mountainous slope, whose curving sides embraced a broad inlet of the Seto Sea. But what stunned Jack were the clouds of steam billowing skywards from the surrounding land. It was as if Beppu had been constructed atop a smouldering bonfire.

Catching Jack's astonished expression, Benkei breathlessly explained, 'Beppu sits . . . in the shadow of . . . Mount Tsurumi.' He pointed to a towering volcanic peak in the distance. 'What you see is the breath of the mountain's dragon.'

They entered the outskirts of town. The two samurai were close on their heels, the rest of the patrol not much further behind. Double-storey wooden buildings with *washi* paper walls and sliding *shoji* doors bordered the streets on either side. Many appeared to be inns offering accommodation.

'That's why Beppu's such a popular spa town,' Benkei continued, leading Jack through the maze of steaming streets. 'The *onsens* here are truly magnificent . . . some of the best in Japan . . .'

Startled residents and visitors exclaimed their annoyance and alarm at Benkei's haste as he upset a vegetable cart to slow the samurai's pursuit. Then several people cried out at the unexpected sight of a blond-haired, blue-eyed foreigner running headlong through their spa town.

'Noblemen, samurai, merchants . . . they travel miles to rejuvenate themselves in these waters –' Benkei bowled into a passer-by, sending the man reeling on to his backside. '*Sumimasen!*' he apologized, then sprinted on as the man cursed him.

They cut down a side alley, hoping to lose the patrol. But the samurai were familiar with the town's layout and, despite his best efforts, Benkei was having great difficulty shaking them off. At the same time, Jack was struggling to keep up, his pack bouncing off his back and his swords rattling on his hip. The angry shouts of the patrol relentlessly trailed them through the streets. *Shoji* slid open on all sides as curious residents peered out to see what all the commotion was about.

'The *onsen* owners claim the baths work wonders on the body and spirit,' explained Benkei. 'Let me show you one.' He suddenly switched right towards a large wooden building with a thatched bamboo roof and barged through a set of double doors.

Baffled by his companion's mid-chase tour, Jack nonetheless followed him inside. They skidded on the polished wooden floor of the reception area and knocked over a display of perfectly arranged flowers.

'This way!' cried Benkei, ignoring the protests of the bath attendants.

He led Jack down a corridor into a room clouded with steam. Several bathers were relaxing in a sunken pool fed by a natural hot spring. Shocked by the sudden intrusion, they sat gaping like wide-mouthed frogs in the milky water.

'Where now?' said Jack, unable to spot a way out.

'Wrong turn!' Benkei cried apologetically, racing back to the door.

The first samurai entered the *onsen*. Benkei snatched up a wooden bucket full of hot water and threw it over the warrior. The samurai gasped in surprise but kept coming, so Benkei threw the bucket itself. It struck the warrior in the head, stunning him. Jack finished him off with Fall Down Fist, as the second samurai charged in, sword drawn. Benkei grabbed a towel from a terrified bather. Twirling it, he threw the towel into the samurai's face. The momentary distraction gave Jack the opportunity to side-kick the samurai into the steaming bath. He landed with an almighty splash among the dumbstruck bathers.

'Impressive kick, *nanban!*' said Benkei. 'Let's get out of here.'

Returning to the corridor, they ran down to the last door. Screams filled the air as female guests grabbed their robes.

'*Sumimasen!*' apologized Benkei, pretending to cover his eyes. 'Just passing through.'

Jack respectfully averted his gaze as they dashed to the opposite side of the *onsen*. Sliding open a door, they emerged into a well-tended garden with rock pools and waterfalls. Steam rose from a number of natural stone *rotenburo* where more bathers soaked in the super-heated waters.

'Pity we can't stay,' remarked Benkei. 'I could do with a bath.'

Leaping over a bubbling pool of pink-fleshed guests, Benkei and Jack ran through the garden as cries of outrage and alarm followed them. They clambered over a stone wall and dropped into a backstreet, before quickly ducking into a deserted alleyway. From behind the shelter of a woodpile, they peered out.

'I think . . . we've lost them,' said Benkei, wiping the sweat from his brow.

Jack started to nod his agreement, when there was a bellow from the other end of the alley.

'Stop right there, *gaijin*!' snarled the sour-faced samurai. 'And you, Benkei.'

The rest of the patrol, their swords drawn, stood in formation behind their leader.

'Then again, maybe not!' admitted Benkei, holding up his hands in surrender.

6

NINE HELLS OF BEPPU

'By order of the Shogun, you're under arrest for treason,' declared the patrol leader, striding down the alley towards them.

'*What?*' exclaimed Benkei in genuine shock. 'I only hoodwinked the local magistrate.'

'Not you, idiot. The *gaijin*. But don't think you'll escape punishment. You're an accomplice now.'

'You'd best arm yourself, Benkei,' Jack suggested, unsheathing his *katana* as the patrol advanced.

'You're the one with the swords. You fight them.' Benkei began to back away. 'My mother always said, when in trouble . . . *run!*'

Hightailing it up the street, Benkei left Jack to fend for himself. Outnumbered ten to one, Jack decided that Benkei's mother might be right in this instance. Cutting the ropes binding the woodpile, he shoved his shoulder into it with all his might. The logs rolled and clattered their way down the alley. They caught the feet of the approaching samurai, causing them to stumble and sprawl on the ground. In the confusion, Jack took off after Benkei.

He finally caught up with him near the outskirts of town.

'They're still after us,' cried Jack.

'Of course they are,' replied Benkei, rolling his eyes. 'You're charged with *treason* against the Shogun himself! I was better off buried up to my neck in sand!'

'And I'd be long gone if I hadn't stopped to save your life,' retorted Jack.

Benkei sighed. 'Fair point, *nanban*. But don't start thinking I owe you any life debt. I don't believe in any of that *bushido* nonsense.'

'There they are!' came a shout as the samurai patrol made a reappearance further down the road.

'Here we go again,' sighed Benkei in exasperation. 'We'll have to risk the Nine Hells of Beppu.'

'*Nine* hells?' Jack wasn't reassured by the sinister-sounding name.

'It's our only hope,' Benkei replied gravely, scrambling up a trail into the forested hillside. 'The nine *jigoku* are home to the demons of the volcano. No one goes near, unless they have to.'

The path wound its way through the trees and bushes, before passing beneath several red *torii* gates. As they progressed deeper, the trees became sickly, their leaves blotched and limp, their trunks bleached white as bone. Wisps of steam swirled amid the skeletal branches, lending the forest an eerie and unearthly atmosphere. Jack felt as if he'd entered another world, one of spirits, demons and dragons. The air was humid and thick with the tang of sulphur. A ferocious hissing, like an angry nest of serpents, issued from within the veils of mist.

'Careful where you tread,' warned Benkei, pointing to a

small fissure in the ground through which scorching vapour whistled out. 'The heat will as soon cook you as it'll cook rice!'

Jack kept close to Benkei as he guided him across a hellish landscape. Through the swirls of roaring steam, Jack spied noxious pools of bubbling mud and shimmering lakes in lurid hues. A pond, bright blue as a cobalt sea, simmered like a giant's cooking pot. Another flowed white like sour milk. A third seethed with waters yellow as molten gold.

'Fall into a *jigoku* and you'll be boiled alive!' warned Benkei, holding a hand to his mouth against the egg-like stench that filled their nostrils.

As they negotiated their way round the different Hell ponds, they heard an argument break out among the samurai patrol.

'I don't care what demons or dragons dwell in this place!' barked the leader, his voice strangely disembodied amid the steam. 'The Shogun signed this *gaijin*'s arrest warrant *personally*. Now spread out and find them – or I'll throw each of you into a Hell!'

Hidden by the same mist, Jack and Benkei silently made their escape. They passed a pool of hiccupping grey mud, large bubbles rising like the bald pates of Buddhist monks until they burst with a *pop*.

All of a sudden the air cleared and Benkei found himself face to face with a steely-eyed samurai. He barely managed to duck as a blade sliced towards his neck. Jack withdrew his *katana* in a flash, blocking a second strike aimed at Benkei's midriff, and pushed him out of harm's way.

The samurai now swung his sword with deadly intent at

Jack. Deflecting the blade easily, Jack countered with a rising cut. The tip sliced within a hair's breadth of the samurai's chin and would have made contact if Jack hadn't been seized from behind. A second larger samurai wrapped a forearm round Jack's throat and began to strangle him. Anticipating an easy kill, the first samurai charged forward to skewer their foreign captive through the stomach. But Jack still had his sword arm free and managed to fend off the attack. The samurai struck again. Jack deflected it – and the next strike – much to the warrior's frustration. But the other samurai was fast choking the life out of Jack. Black spots were clouding his vision and Jack knew he was fighting on borrowed time.

Where's Benkei when I need him?

Blocking another deadly sword thrust, he front-kicked the first samurai in the chest, sending him staggering backwards. Then he elbowed his captor hard in the gut, loosening the man's grip. Dropping to one knee, Jack threw him using *ippon seoinage*, a one-arm shoulder throw. The samurai flew through the air just as the other warrior charged forward again, the tip of his sword targeted at Jack's chest. The two samurai collided. The blade impaled the second samurai, while the first was knocked off his feet by the impact. As his companion clutched his bleeding stomach, the first samurai teetered on the lip of the boiling mud pit.

'Help!' he cried, his arms flailing to regain his balance.

Barely recovered from his throttling, Jack staggered forward to save the man, but was too late. A horrendous scream escaped the samurai's lips as he plunged into the bubbling *jigoku*. Covered head to foot in scalding mud, only the whites of his eyes visible, the warrior floundered in the Hell like some primordial monster. He clawed for the bank, but quickly disappeared beneath the surface, the pit sucking him into its foul depths.

Rejoining Jack near the edge, Benkei stared into the mud pond with a mix of fascination and horror. 'You can see where the name comes from now. That really is one hellish way to die!'

7

TORNADO HELL

'Where were you?' gasped Jack, massaging his bruised throat. 'Why didn't you help me?'

Benkei patted him on the back affectionately. 'You looked to be doing fine on your own.'

Jack was about to protest this, when the rest of the patrol materialized out of the mist on the other side of the pond.

'Let's go,' said Benkei, racing off towards the remaining Hells.

Running virtually blind through the steam, they weaved in between the deadly pools. A samurai cut across and blocked their path. They switched directions. In his haste, Jack landed on one of the steaming vents. Crying out in shock and pain, he stumbled and pitched forward. Directly ahead was a blood-red Hell – its crimson waters waiting to strip the skin from his flesh. At the last second, Benkei grabbed his arm and pulled him back from the brink. 'This is no time for a bath!'

Eventually they reached a rocky slope at the edge of the Nine Hells, only to be faced with a roaring wall of white-hot steam. The blast subsided, then roared again as if it were the pulse of the volcano.

'Mountain Hell,' explained Benkei. 'We'll have to go round it.'

They skirted the Hell until they came to a boulder-strewn patch of ground at the base of a small cliff. As they searched for a route up the rock face, the samurai patrol caught up and surrounded them.

'Nowhere to run this time,' declared the leader with a triumphant grin. 'Surrender or die.'

'Not much of a choice,' remarked Jack, turning to face them, 'when the punishment for treason is death anyway!'

'True,' agreed the leader, giving the command to attack.

Jack unsheathed his *wakizashi*, raising it over his head while keeping his *katana* poised in a front guard. Despite the impossible odds of battling eight samurai at once, Jack realized their only chance of survival lay in the Two Heavens – a devastating double sword technique that his samurai guardian, Masamoto, had taught him.

Unfazed by the threat of a *gaijin* wielding two swords, the samurai patrol continued to advance.

'I could do with some help this time,' said Jack out of the corner of his mouth to Benkei.

'Don't worry, I'm right behind you,' replied Benkei reassuringly.

Jack glanced back to see his companion *literally* shielding himself behind Jack's own body.

The first two samurai attacked, their blades arcing for Jack's neck from either side. Jack blocked both sword strikes before side-kicking the warrior to his left. He then spun round, slicing his *katana* across the other's chest. The samurai barely managed to leap away in time, his kimono left in tatters by the sword's razor-sharp *kissaki*.

Witnessing Jack's deadly defence, four warriors now charged at him. Jack's *katana* and *wakizashi* became a blur of steel as he fended off strike after strike. He ducked beneath a vicious sword swipe for his head, then leapt over another blade. Quickly rolling between two samurai, he cross-blocked a lethal attempt to cleave him in half by the leader himself.

'So the rumours are true!' spat the leader, with something approaching respect. 'You have mastered the Two Heavens.'

His heart pounding and his lungs burning, Jack fought like a warrior possessed. The samurai patrol couldn't lay a single blade upon him. But, with Benkei left unprotected, the attention of one of the patrol was turned on him.

Benkei picked up a rock to arm himself – and immediately dropped it.

'Oww!' he cried, blowing on his fingers. 'That's red hot.'

The samurai laughed at his misfortune. But his gloating was his downfall. Benkei hurriedly wrapped his hand in a piece of cloth torn from his motley kimono. Then he snatched up another rock and hurled it at his attacker. The missile struck the samurai square in the face, searing his flesh. The samurai reeled away in agony.

Meanwhile, Jack fought his way back to Benkei and they held off the patrol with a combination of sword and rocks. But the demands of battling so many opponents rapidly drained Jack's strength.

'I've run out of rocks!' exclaimed Benkei.

The patrol closed in for the kill.

As Jack prepared to make a final stand, the ground started

to tremble. A rumbling noise deep below the earth grew louder and louder.

'The dragon awakes!' cried a terrified samurai, turning on his heel and sprinting off through the mist.

The next moment, scalding steam erupted into the sky, followed by a jet of super-heated water. Beads of blistering rain pelted the samurai and they fled in all directions.

Shielding himself with his pack, Jack grabbed Benkei and ran too.

'They're getting away!' shouted the leader in fury.

'I forgot about . . . that last Hell,' Benkei panted as they dodged the thundering geyser. '*Tatsumaki Jigoku.*'

Tornado Hell, how appropriate, thought Jack, recalling his violent encounter with the Pirate Queen of the same name.

He stopped before Mountain Hell and caught a glimpse of the forested slopes beyond. The wall of steam continued to throb in blasting waves. 'If we time it right, we can make it through.'

'Are you completely mad?' exclaimed Benkei, eyeing the scalding barrier.

'Do you know the Heart Sutra?' Jack asked with all seriousness.

'Of course, everyone's heard of that Buddhist scripture. But what's that got to do with anything?'

'I was taught how to use one of its mantras to walk across a fire pit,' Jack hurriedly explained, remembering Sensei Yamada's lesson during the *gasshuku* training camp in Koyasan. 'Essentially, by emptying your mind, you empty your body of all sensation, all pain and all suffering. Have you ever meditated?'

'Well . . . once or twice,' blustered Benkei.

'Good, then recite this and it will help protect you from the heat: *Om gate gate paragate parasamgate bodhi svaha . . .*'

Jack chanted the mantra until they were both repeating the incantation in unison. A sense of calm amid the storm descended upon them and Jack felt a familiar tingle spread throughout his limbs.

'There they are!' came a cry.

Unable to wait for a lull in the blasts, Jack grabbed Benkei's arm.

'No! Stop!' shouted Benkei. 'Didn't you say the mantra was for fire?'

But Jack had already dived head first into Mountain Hell, dragging Benkei through the steam along with him.

8

GRIEF

'I'm red as a lobster!' complained Benkei, inspecting his raw blistered skin as he stood cooling beneath a waterfall on the upper slopes of Mount Tsurumi.

'At least you're a live one,' replied Jack, his legs dangling in a rock pool.

'No thanks to that mantra of yours. I've got burns in places I can't even see!'

'You'd be a lot worse without its protection,' said Jack, who'd escaped Mountain Hell with little more than scalded feet. 'Besides, we lost the patrol, so the gamble was worth it.'

Benkei shook his head in astonishment. 'You're the craziest *nanban* I've ever met! And the deadliest. Where did you learn to fight like that?'

'I trained at the *Niten Ichi Ryū* in Kyoto . . . until the school was closed by the Shogun.' Having only just met Benkei, Jack decided to omit his time spent training as a ninja. Discretion at this stage in their relationship was wiser and far safer.

'And that's another thing — why's the Shogun so desperate to kill you?' asked Benkei. 'I realize you're a foreigner, but that patrol leader said the order was *personal*.'

'Kamakura has borne a grudge against me, ever since I made him lose face by defeating his sword school in a *Taryu-Jiai* contest,' admitted Jack. 'Then I fought against him during the Battle of Osaka Castle.'

Benkei whistled through his teeth. 'No wonder you're in trouble! I'd heard rumours that they were hunting samurai who'd taken up arms against the Shogun. A *foreign* samurai, though, is ten times worse.'

While this was true, Jack knew that was only half the reason. The other was Kamakura's desire to get his hands on the *rutter*. The Shogun knew that the logbook could be used to control the trade routes between nations, making it a very powerful political tool as well as extremely lucrative. He intended to use it for his own gain. But Jack had vowed to his father never to let the *rutter* fall into the wrong hands.

'So what are you going to do now?' asked Benkei.

Jack hadn't thought about that. He'd been too busy *running* to worry about his next move.

'I was headed to Nagasaki until . . .' From his vantage point at the edge of the rock pool, Jack gazed out across the wide expanse of Beppu Bay. Clouds of steam rose into the evening sky before scattering like departing spirits. The fading sun glimmered off the rippling waters of the Seto Sea and his eyes searched for a mast-less skiff, adrift somewhere in the bay or beyond. But it was futile. He was too far from the coast to see such things. And, in his heart of hearts, he knew that the skiff could never have survived the storm and, in all likelihood, now lay rotting on the seabed.

A tear rolled down his cheek and he felt his throat tighten.

Jack wanted to cry out in anguish and anger at losing his friends. But he clenched his fists in frustrated fury instead, banging them against the rock. Since his arrival in Japan all he seemed to have known was *loss*: the loss of his father at the hands of the murderous ninja Dragon Eye; the courageous sacrifice of his samurai brother Yamato; the banishment of his guardian Masamoto; of leaving his best friend Akiko time and time again . . . and now the tragic loss of his loyal friends, Yori, Saburo and Miyuki.

Feeling heavy with grief, Jack bowed his head. He thought of giving up there and then – sitting upon that rock until cold, hunger or the samurai patrol took him. But he couldn't allow all that suffering and loss to come to nothing.

When it is dark enough, you can see the stars, his Zen master Sensei Yamada had once said.

And there was one glimmer of light in his black funereal sky. Jack realized the only way to bring meaning to their deaths was to reach Nagasaki, return home and reunite with the sole family he had left – his sister, Jess.

'Have you listened to anything I've just said?' asked Benkei, plonking himself down next to Jack.

Jack glanced up, quickly wiping his eyes with the back of his hand. 'Sorry?'

'I said, I'll be your guide, *nanban*.'

'To where?'

'Nagasaki, of course.' Benkei gave him a concerned look. 'Are you all right?'

Jack nodded. 'Why risk your life to be my guide? I'm a fugitive. There's no need for you to be one too.'

Benkei laughed. 'My mother always said, *Dip your toe in the water and you're likely to fall in*. I'm already up to my neck in this! Besides, who wouldn't want to be chased, beaten and boiled alive in a day?' He clapped Jack on the back. 'Just imagine what excitement awaits us on the road to Nagasaki.'

9

THE SHELL GAME

The morning sun was a welcome relief to the cold night spent on the mountain. Its warmth banished the stiffness from Jack's bones as he foraged for food among the bushes. Thanks to the fieldcraft he'd learnt as a ninja, he knew what to look for and where, and had soon gathered a good handful of nuts, berries and edible roots. Returning to the waterfall, he found Benkei still fast asleep. His patchwork kimono made him look like a forsaken court jester and Jack wondered who his new companion *really* was. So far he knew nothing of the young man's history – not even why he'd been buried alive on the beach, although Jack guessed that had something to do with the magistrate. Until he learnt more, he needed to be on his guard with Benkei. Nevertheless, he was grateful to have a willing guide.

Jack nudged him with his foot. 'Rise and shine!'

'Hey, *nanban* . . .' Benkei groaned, rubbing his eyes. 'Why did you have to wake me? I was having a wonderful dream about a banquet served by beautiful *geisha* –' He yawned loudly.

'Well, you've got me serving you instead,' replied Jack, laying out the rations on a flat rock.

'And I thought dreams never came true!' Benkei shot him a wry smile. He rose, stretched and dunked his head in the pool, before taking several long draughts of the crystal-clear mountain water. Running his fingers through his unruly hair, he joined Jack beside the rock and sat down. Together they tucked into the modest meal.

'Thanks,' said Benkei, munching on a nut. 'But we can't live like squirrels all the way to Nagasaki. We need supplies. Have you got any money?'

Jack shook his head.

There was a brief sigh of disappointment, then Benkei said, 'Not to worry. We'll acquire some.'

Jack became wary. 'You're not going to steal, are you? I don't wish to attract any more trouble.'

Benkei looked almost offended. 'I'm no thief! We'll win it.'

He produced three shells from inside his kimono and placed them in a row upon the rock. Taking a small nut from their breakfast pile, he hid it under the middle shell.

'Follow the nut,' he instructed Jack.

Benkei started to slide the three shells around, switching their places. Jack's eyes remained fixed upon the one with the nut inside. Benkei made several more moves before asking, 'Where's the nut?'

Jack smiled. This was too easy. He pointed to the shell on the left.

'Are you certain?' asked Benkei with a sly grin. 'Would you bet on it?'

Jack nodded.

'Then you'd lose,' he said, lifting the shell on the right to reveal the nut.

'Impossible!' exclaimed Jack. 'I watched your every move.'

'Try again. Let's bet that last juicy berry on the outcome.'

Agreeing, Jack closely studied Benkei as he put the shell over the nut and shuffled their places around. He did a couple of back-switches, but these were easy enough to follow. Without hesitation, Jack selected the middle shell.

'Wrong again,' said Benkei, uncovering the end shell to show the nut. With a triumphant expression, he popped his prize into his mouth.

Jack was dumbfounded. There was simply no way he'd made a mistake. His eyes had never left the nut-containing shell.

'Third time lucky. Do you want to bet your swords this time?' suggested Benkei.

Jack shook his head. He'd never risk gambling his weapons. The red-handled *katana* and *wakizashi* were forged by Shizu, one of the greatest swordsmiths to have lived. Moreover, these swords were an heirloom from Akiko's father as well as Jack's last link to Akiko herself. He treasured them almost as much as he treasured their friendship.

'Wise decision,' said Benkei. 'You see, this shell game is our moneymaker. Merchants and greedy samurai love to gamble!'

'But what if you lose?' said Jack, doubtful Benkei's luck would hold.

'That will never happen.'

Jack gave him a sceptical look.

'You see, I'm not a gambler. I'm a conjuror!' revealed

Benkei with obvious pride. 'That's why my friends call me Benkei the Great.' He jumped to his feet with a flurry of his multicoloured kimono and bowed. 'I'm the *greatest* trickster in Kyushu.'

Jack looked uneasy at the idea.

'Don't worry, *nanban*. Your noble conscience will be safe. We'll only take from those who can afford it – *not* like the *daimyo* and their samurai, who take all they can from the poor farmers.'

Picking up his three shells and the nut, Benkei strode off towards a treelined ridge heading west.

'First stop, Yufuin. It's the nearest spa town from here. There'll be lots of rich merchants and dumb samurai who need their purses lightening.'

10

LOOKOUT

As they descended a rocky mountainside later that afternoon, Jack could see why Yufuin was such a popular destination for travellers and *onsen* seekers. The small provincial town sat in a picturesque green valley, with a sparkling river weaving its way like a silver thread into a crystal-blue lake. A magnificent double-headed volcano reared up behind the town, providing a stunning backdrop for the hot springs. Serving the visitors' every need, numerous thatched-roof inns, temples and *onsen* lined the streets and winding alleyways. Even from a distance, Jack could hear the tranquil flow of water and the meditative chime of temple bells.

'A genuine heaven on earth, don't you think?' remarked Benkei.

Jack was inclined to agree and felt a sudden urge to stop running. He wished he could do what his heart really desired and return to Akiko in Toba. Ever since he'd made that fateful decision to leave her, his life had been like a cork tossed on the ocean waves. But however much he longed for those precious times he was duty-bound to his orphaned sister in England.

And there was no turning back. The Shogun had made certain of that.

Avoiding the main road, they approached Yufuin from the east, using the trees for cover. The town's terraced paddy fields had turned golden in the late afternoon sun, their shallow waters still as dew ponds now that the farmers had finished working for the day. Benkei and Jack trotted along the mudbanks, skirting the fields until they came to a group of farm buildings. An old farmer emerged from a nearby cottage and Jack and Benkei quickly ducked inside a barn.

'I can't go into town like this,' said Jack, indicating his blond hair and foreign looks.

'You're right, *nanban*,' replied Benkei, studying him intently. 'We should put a bag on your head. That would make you easier on the eye!'

Jack baulked at the idea, unsure whether he was being serious or not.

Benkei laughed at Jack's offended expression. 'Only joking! Here, wear this.'

He'd found a straw hat discarded upon a pile of rotting hay. The hat was old and tattered, but its rim was broad enough to cover Jack's face and hair.

'It stinks of dung,' said Jack, trying not to grimace as he put it on.

'Beggars can't be choosers,' smirked Benkei and held his nose against the reek. 'At least no one will go near you!'

After the farmer had gone back inside, they slipped out of the barn and entered town. Keeping to the backstreets and alleys, they passed walled gardens, several bubbling *onsen* and a noisy kitchen. The inviting smell of cooked rice wafted under Jack's nostrils, and his mouth began to water and his stomach tighten. He suddenly realized how critical it was that Benkei succeeded in his scheme.

Forcing all thoughts of hunger aside, Jack followed Benkei down a narrow alleyway. They heard the clack of wood, followed by the rattle of rolling dice and several disappointed groans. Through a gap in the boards, Jack spied a group of men sitting cross-legged beside varying piles of wooden tokens. With an almost desperate excitement, the men began slapping down the tokens and calling out 'odd' and 'even'.

'It appears Yufuin isn't just about soaking in hot springs,' whispered Benkei, raising his eyebrows knowingly. 'All the better for us.'

They continued to make their way through the backstreets until they reached a small square in the centre of town. A steady flow of foot traffic passed along the two roads leading off from it. Kimono-clad women, sword-bearing samurai and finely dressed merchants browsed shops, frequented tea houses and entered the numerous *onsen* establishments.

Remaining in the shadows of the alley, Benkei turned to Jack.

'This spot is ideal. Now your job is to act as lookout,' he explained. 'If you see any *dōshin* or patrols coming along, whistle twice like this.' He put his fingers in his mouth and sounded two high-pitched notes like a cuckoo. 'Got that?'

Jack nodded.

'Wish me luck!' he said, brushing his wild hair up into spikes. 'Not that I need it,' he added with a wink.

Benkei marched out as if he were an actor taking to the stage. He strode across the square, his colourful garb drawing the attention of passers-by. Setting himself up on a flat bench by a street corner, he quickly gathered a small crowd.

Jack remained hidden in the alleyway, from where he had a clear view of Benkei and the main thoroughfare.

'*Double your money!*' Benkei promised the intrigued onlookers, beckoning them closer.

A merchant laid a confident bet upon a shell. With a flourish, Benkei revealed the actual location of the nut and the merchant cursed his misfortune. Benkei claimed his winnings. Another bet was made and promptly lost, and the crowd gasped in astonishment, many convinced they'd known where the nut was. Benkei pocketed his takings. After a third round was lost by a portly samurai, mutterings of disgruntlement arose and a few people drifted away. Then a cry of delight went up as an old woman won a small bet on the shell she'd chosen. Immediately there was a flurry of gambling.

Jack had to admit Benkei was good. His artful skills made winning appear possible, enticing people to lay bigger bets. But, as Jack knew from experience, they had no chance – unless Benkei wanted them to.

'People's greed is their downfall,' he'd said, and he was right.

As the crowd grew bigger and the money rolled in, Jack noticed two men dressed in black *haori* jackets, tight-fitting trousers and dark-blue *tabi* socks heading down the road. They each wore thin white *hachimaki* across their foreheads and carried a *jutte* in their belts. The distinctive iron truncheons were the trademark weapon of the *dōshin* – the Shogun's recently appointed enforcement officers.

Jack whistled twice and Benkei looked up in alarm.

All of a sudden Jack felt a hand clamp on to his shoulder.

The fingers dug in, pain rocketing through his body as pressure was applied. His legs were kicked out from under him and he buckled to his knees. Struggling to break free from the grip, Jack twisted away. At the same time, he grabbed his attacker's wrist and wrenched the arm into *sankyo*. This powerful wrist-lock would dislocate his attacker's arm, or at the very least throw the person to the ground. But his assailant swiftly countered by flipping through the air and turning the lock back on to Jack's own wrist.

'How dare you resist me!' exclaimed his attacker.

In a white-out of pain, Jack was driven into the earth. His head struck the side of the building and his hat fell off. Unable to roll away, his ligaments were stretched to their limit, the agonizing force of the lock threatening to break his arm. But at the last second the attack was halted.

Still immobilized by pain, Jack managed to twist his head for a glimpse of his attacker. His eyes widened in disbelief.

11

BUGYŌ

A diminutive man with black specks for eyes glared down at Jack. He had a pudgy nose – broken many times in battle – and a thin unsmiling mouth, above which sat a greying tuft of a moustache. In spite of his tiny stature and age, every muscle was toned as hard as granite beneath his crisp *dōshin* uniform.

'Sensei Kyuzo,' gasped Jack, both shocked and relieved to see his old *taijutsu* master again.

But Sensei Kyuzo didn't release the excruciating wristlock and his expression remained inscrutable.

'It's me! Jack!'

'I know who you are, *gaijin*,' he hissed, 'but you *don't* know me.'

'But, Sensei –' Jack's wrist flared once more in agony.

Sensei Kyuzo forced Jack's face into the dirt as the two *dōshin* came running over.

'Did you get the other one?' he barked.

'No . . . he disappeared into the crowd,' explained one of the officers sheepishly.

'Idiots! How could you lose a suspect dressed like a clown fish?'

48

'Sorry, Renzo. He was too slippery.'

Renzo? thought Jack. *Have I mistaken the man?*

Spitting dirt from his mouth, Jack tried to catch another glimpse of his captor. The man certainly looked like his *taijutsu* master. His voice had the same rough edge to it. And his attitude was as harsh and unforgiving as ever. Then there was the wristlock he had him in: *tekubi gatamae*. It was classic Sensei Kyuzo, and Jack could never forget the distinctive pain his teacher was capable of inflicting. Always selected as his *uke*, demonstration partner, at the *Niten Ichi Ryū*, Jack had suffered many agonizing sessions being locked, thrown, grappled, kicked and punched by his teacher – all for the purposes of *authentic* technique. Pinned helpless to the ground now, Jack was left in no doubt that this *dōshin* was Sensei Kyuzo.

The other two officers stared in astonishment at their prisoner.

'You've captured the *gaijin* samurai!' cried the *dōshin* in unison.

'Yes,' snapped Sensei Kyuzo impatiently. 'Now quit gawping and hand me your *hayanawa*.'

The *dōshin* obediently passed him a short rope with a small loop on one end. Snatching it from the officer's grasp, Sensei Kyuzo dropped his full weight on top of Jack. With a knee pressed painfully into the small of his back, Jack was swiftly relieved of his swords and pack. Then, in a matter of seconds, he was trussed up with the *hayanawa*. His hands were bound behind him and the rope secured round his neck, so that if he struggled the *hayanawa* would choke him. Although still able to walk, Jack was otherwise powerless to fight back.

Sensei Kyuzo dragged him to his feet.

'Let's go, *gaijin*!' he ordered, shoving Jack down the road.

'Where are you taking me, Sen—'

Sensei Kyuzo jabbed his thumbtip between Jack's ribs, sending a shockwave of pain through him.

'Less talking and more walking.'

As Jack recovered his breath and hobbled on, he finally figured out why his teacher was being so brutal in silencing him. Benkei had mentioned that certain samurai warriors who'd opposed the Shogun were being hunted down. Sensei Kyuzo must be trying to keep his past identity secret. Realizing he'd almost given the deception away twice, Jack now held his tongue. Besides, he had to trust Sensei Kyuzo. His *taijutsu* master was his sole hope of escaping this predicament alive. And, until he discovered what the plan was, he had no choice but to follow his teacher's lead.

Sensei Kyuzo and the two *dōshin* escorted him along the main street to a large white building with a curving tiled roof. Steps led up to the entrance beside which a wooden sign read:

大分地區の奉行

Thanks to Akiko's patient teaching, Jack was able to translate the Japanese script. The sign proclaimed: *Bugyō of Oita District*. Jack knew *bugyō* meant magistrate. Above, a long golden banner hung from a rafter. Emblazoned in the centre was the circular *mon* of three hollyhock leaves – the family crest of the Shogun.

Jack's blood ran cold at the sight. Not only had Sensei Kyuzo arrested him but he was now turning him over to an official of their mutual enemy. *Had he been wrong to trust in his* taijutsu *master?* It was true that they'd never seen eye to eye. From his very first lesson at the *Niten Ichi Ryū*, Sensei Kyuzo had objected to teaching a foreigner the secrets of their martial arts. And he'd made little attempt to hide his personal hatred of Jack, bullying him at every opportunity. But, in spite of the bad blood between them, Sensei Kyuzo had ultimately proven to be loyal. During the Battle of Osaka Castle, he'd fought a group of ninja single-handedly – sacrificing himself while Jack and Akiko had made their escape. Sensei Kyuzo was a true samurai. He would not break the code of *bushido*. Jack was certain of that.

A guard at the entrance waved them through. He stared open-mouthed at the appearance of the infamous *gaijin* samurai.

Slipping off their wooden *geta* at the top of the steps, Sensei Kyuzo led Jack down a corridor to a double set of *fusuma* doors. The two *dōshin* followed close behind, their hands on their *jutte* at all times. After knocking respectfully, Sensei Kyuzo slid back the panel doors to reveal a stark white rectangular room with dark wooden ceiling beams. A *shoji* to their right was left ajar, through which the setting sun shone and gleamed off the polished woodblock floor. A cool evening breeze wafted in from the stone Zen garden outside, where a wind chime tinkled softly.

At the far end of the room, a portly man sat behind a desk studying some papers. Dressed in an ink-blue *kataginu* jacket with stiffened shoulders like wings, he exuded an air of authority and Jack assumed this was the *bugyō*. Although the magistrate didn't look up, Jack noticed his jowls hung loose, seeming to merge with his neck. And his thinning hair was overly oiled and tied into a sparse topknot. A *katana* and *waki-zashi* sat upon a display rack behind him, their *sayas* brightly polished and silk handles unblemished. At his side, an Akita hunting dog sat obediently to attention, regarding Jack with hungry eyes.

The magistrate didn't bother to acknowledge their entrance as Sensei Kyuzo marched Jack into the room. Halfway down, Jack was forced to his knees and made to bow his respects. Still the magistrate barely glanced up as he selected a fresh piece of paper and dipped a fine brush into an inkstone.

'Name?'

Encouraged by a rough prod from a *jutte*, he declared, 'Jack Fletcher.'

The magistrate started to inscribe the *kanji* characters before the foreign name fully registered. The *bugyō* almost dropped his brush when he realized the Shogun's most wanted fugitive knelt before him.

12

TRIAL

'How on earth did you catch the *gaijin*?' enquired the *bugyō*.

'He was an accomplice to an illegal betting scam,' stated Sensei Kyuzo.

The *bugyō* raised his pencil-thin eyebrows in surprise. 'So where are the other perpetrators?'

Sensei Kyuzo glared at the two *dōshin*. 'There was only one other and he got away.'

The magistrate tutted disapprovingly. 'I don't like loose ends, but I suppose it's of little consequence at a moment like *this*.'

He wet his ink brush again and finished writing Jack's name on the paper.

'Was the *gaijin* carrying any belongings?'

Sensei Kyuzo nodded and one of the *dōshin* presented the magistrate with Jack's swords and pack. The *bugyō* inspected the weapons, then laid out the pack's contents on the table, making a meticulous inventory of all that he found. To Jack's consternation, the magistrate took particular interest in the *rutter*. Then with surprising care he repacked the bag and instructed the *dōshin* to store the property in his private office.

Recharging his brush from the inkstone, the *bugyō* now fixed his bulbous eyes on Jack.

'Before we attend to the greater matter at hand, we must first deal with your crime here,' he declared. He inscribed several more characters on the paper. 'Jack Fletcher, you've been arrested on the charge of illegal gambling.'

To his astonishment, Jack realized he was on trial. Already accused of high treason against the Shogun, he stood little chance of a fair hearing from this magistrate. He glanced up at Sensei Kyuzo, again wondering what his plan was.

Sensei Kyuzo stepped forward. 'Is it really worth trying the *gaijin* when he's already been sentenced to death by the Shogun?'

A flicker of annoyance passed across the magistrate's face. 'I'm the *bugyō* for this town and it's my responsibility to see that law and order is maintained. This recent plague of gambling needs to be stamped out. We must set an example to all lawbreakers. *None* should escape the consequences of their crimes, including this *gaijin*. Now, are there any witnesses to the offence?'

The two *dōshin* both bowed in acknowledgement.

'He whistled a warning,' stated one of them.

The magistrate made a note of this on the paper and seemed satisfied.

Without offering Jack the opportunity to plead his case, he declared, 'In my authority as *bugyō* of Oita District, I pronounce you, Jack Fletcher, guilty as charged. In respect of the severity of your crime, you're sentenced to *yubitsume*.'

Jack had never heard this term before, but it didn't sound pleasant and a rising sense of panic gripped him.

'Is that wise?' interjected Sensei Kyuzo. 'The Shogun signed the warrant for the *gaijin*'s arrest himself. He should be the one to administer the punishment. This judgment could have an adverse effect on the reward for his capture.'

'I, of all people, am aware of the reward, Renzo,' said the *bugyō* firmly. 'Yet the Shogun would surely respect my duty to uphold *his* law. And I intend to carry it out to the letter. Besides, the *gaijin* will still be in one piece . . . my mistake, two pieces!'

The *bugyō* allowed himself a small grunt of laughter.

'But —'

'Don't question my authority again,' said the *bugyō* tersely, cutting off Sensei Kyuzo. 'Do as I say or I'll charge you with contempt. Carry out the punishment forthwith.'

Sensei Kyuzo fumed. Nonetheless, he submitted to his superior's will with a curt bow of the head. He gave instructions to the two *dōshin* to bring in the block.

'If the *gaijin* wishes to act like a samurai, then he should be punished like one,' stated the *bugyō*. 'Finger shortening is a fitting penance and one that would meet the Shogun's approval, I'm sure.'

Jack realized he was to be mutilated. Sensei Kyuzo's attempt at defence had failed. He *had* to escape, but, bound helpless, he was unable to avoid the imminent *yubitsume*.

The *bugyō* settled back to watch the proceedings, giving his dog an affectionate pat on the head as a wooden chopping block was brought in and placed before Jack. One of the *dōshin* laid a ceremonial white square of cloth on top and smoothed it flat.

Jack silently willed his teacher to make his move.

Without a word, Sensei Kyuzo unbound Jack's left hand and strapped it to the block, palm down.

'Hold him tight,' he ordered the two *dōshin*.

Jack struggled, helpless in their grip. His throat went dry and his heart began to pound as Sensei Kyuzo unsheathed a razor-sharp *tantō*. The lethal blade caught the last rays of the dying sun, burnishing the steel an ominous blood-red.

'Cut off the little finger,' instructed the *bugyō*, his eyes bulging in cruel anticipation.

Sensei Kyuzo approached the block, his knife raised. Whatever his *taijutsu* master's plan, Jack knew this was the final chance to execute it. As the blade hovered over Jack's finger, Sensei Kyuzo caught his eye and grinned. Taking this as the signal, Jack readied himself for his *taijutsu* master to cut his bonds and for them to fight their way out.

The knife sliced down.

13

CELL

Crouched in the darkened cell, Jack clutched his wounded hand to his chest. The stump of his little finger throbbed like wildfire. Although the bleeding had stopped, Jack was pale and shaken from the experience.

He simply couldn't comprehend what Sensei Kyuzo had done to him. He'd watched in disbelief as his *taijutsu* master brought down the knife, the keen blade slicing through flesh and bone like butter, severing the tip of his little finger. Bizarrely, he could recall the steel feeling cool to the touch, before the nail and first knuckle were separated and dropped to the floor. For a moment, Jack felt nothing but numbing shock. Then a raging fire ignited in his hand as the pain registered and blood spurted across the white cloth. He'd screamed to block out the agony. But it shook him in wave after fierce wave.

'Stop whining, *gaijin*!' Sensei Kyuzo had snarled, wiping clean his knife. 'Show some samurai backbone.'

Somehow Jack managed to stifle his cries. But what had hurt him the most was that his teacher had done the deed with a *smile* on his face. Sensei Kyuzo had even wrapped the severed portion of the fingertip in the cloth and presented it to the *bugyō* for inspection. Indifferent to Jack's suffering, the magistrate had merely logged an account of the punishment before sealing the court document for his records. He then put his brush aside and tossed Jack's fingertip into the expectant mouth of his hunting dog.

Sickened to the pit of his stomach, Jack barely heard the *bugyō* as he determined his fate. The magistrate decided that Jack should be held in prison until the Shogun's samurai came for him. He then wrote a message and summoned a *hikyaku* to deliver it. The 'flying feet' courier was running before he even got out of the door. Only when the *bugyō* noticed blood staining his highly prized woodblock floor did he send Jack to his prison cell.

Before they threw him in, one of the *dōshin* bandaged his hand and tied a tourniquet round the stump of his little finger. Jack mumbled his thanks, but the *dōshin* had just snorted, 'We don't want our "reward" dying on us from gangrene now, do we?'

Jack looked up at a small barred window. The silvery light of a waning moon cast its deathly pallor on to the dirt floor. The few stars he could spy seemed more distant than ever – but still not as far away as England and his sister now felt.

His journey was over.

His hopes of reaching Nagasaki had been brought to a swift and agonizing end by his old *taijutsu* master. Jack couldn't believe Sensei Kyuzo would go to such lengths just to keep his identity hidden. But Jack had to face the hard truth. Sensei Kyuzo *wasn't* on his side. He'd been wrong to trust in the *bushido* code of loyalty. Sensei Kyuzo had never had any intention of saving him – in fact, he seemed determined to be rid of him once and for all.

In the darkness, Jack heard the hunting dog scrabbling at the earth outside, no doubt lured by the prospect of a larger bone to gnaw on. In his injured state, Jack didn't hold out much hope of fighting his way out before the Shogun's samurai arrived. Although he wasn't crippled by any means, he'd be unable to control a sword properly. Until his hand had healed, he was like a tiger whose teeth had been pulled.

From the direction of the Zen garden, the jingle of the wind chime drifted into his cell. Aware that he had to do something positive to stop himself lapsing into despair, Jack focused his mind on the delicate sound. He meditated until the throbbing in his hand subsided. Then, under his breath, he began to chant the mantra for *Sha*:

'*On haya baishiraman taya sowaka . . .*'

Sha was one of the nine rituals of *kuji-in*, the art of ninja magic. Combined with a secret hand sign and focused meditation, it would speed up the healing process. But Jack was under no illusion. *Kuji-in* couldn't bring his fingertip back. He'd be scarred for life. But at least it might mean he could grip a weapon far sooner.

With one hand out of action, Jack couldn't form the complete sign required for the ritual, so he just extended the thumb and forefinger of his right hand and held the palm over the bandaged wound. As he chanted, he sensed a tingle of warmth. But his stump was such a confusion of pain and numbness that he wasn't certain this was the result of *kuji-in*.

How he wished Miyuki was with him now. She was an expert healer, having tended to his injuries many times. Loyal, dependable and resourceful, she would have completed the healing and already be planning their way out of the cell.

If Saburo was here, Jack knew he'd be making some joke. Lightening the mood and keeping everyone's spirits up.

Then there was Yori. What Jack would do to hear some wise and comforting words from his dear friend. He'd probably say something like, '*Pain is inevitable, but suffering is optional.*'

A sad smile passed across Jack's face at the memory of his friends. He keenly felt their absence. They'd each played a crucial part in his life. Together they'd been a team — strong, courageous and seemingly invincible. Now he sat alone in a dark prison cell, injured and without hope.

But he daren't give up. His friends wouldn't have wanted him to.

Outside the dog stopped digging.

'*Hey! Nanban!*' whispered a voice from the barred window.

Jack glanced up to see a wild-haired silhouette against the moonlight.

'Benkei!' said Jack, amazed. 'You've come back?'

'Of course,' replied Benkei. 'I've got your half of the winnings here!'

14

AN OLD SCORE

Jack heard more scrabbling and realized the noise hadn't been the dog. A chink of moonlight shone through a crack in the cell's plaster wall. Then the iron tip of a leaf-shaped blade appeared and the gap widened.

'Give it a kick,' hissed Benkei from the other side.

Sitting on the floor, Jack thrust his heel at the loose plaster. It fell away to reveal a hole gouged into the wattle-and-daub wall. The opening was barely big enough for Jack. But, with Benkei's help, he scrambled through and soon stood next to him in the courtyard.

'What happened to you?' asked Benkei, noticing Jack's bloody bandage.

'I had a run-in with an old sensei,' said Jack, brushing the plaster from his kimono with his good hand. 'So how did you get away?'

'A quick costume change,' replied Benkei, who was now dressed in an unassuming brown kimono. With a flourish, he revealed his jacket's multicoloured interior. 'I simply turned it inside out and hid in the barn until nightfall. That's where I found this *kunai*.'

He held up the farmer's digging tool – a blunt broad-bladed knife with twine wrapped round the shaft for grip.

'We should keep that,' said Jack. 'A *kunai* makes a good weapon.'

'Then you have it,' said Benkei, passing him the tool. 'I'm no fighter.'

With an accepting nod, Jack slipped the *kunai* into his belt.

From an outbuilding came the sound of raucous laughter and drunken singing.

'The *dōshin* are celebrating your capture,' sniggered Benkei, picking up a large bag and heading out of the yard. 'Let's go! I've already bought our supplies.'

Jack shook his head. 'I have to get my swords and pack first.'

Benkei gave him an exasperated look. 'How many fingers do you want to lose?'

'I won't leave without my belongings,' insisted Jack.

Realizing he wouldn't be swayed, Benkei resigned himself to the situation. 'I'll wait for you in the barn until sunrise . . . then I'm going.'

'I understand,' replied Jack, grasping his shoulder in friendship. 'You've done more than enough helping me to escape.'

'And all that effort will be wasted if you get yourself caught again!' Benkei muttered, before disappearing down a backstreet.

Jack skirted the courtyard, keeping to the shadows and steering clear of the celebration. Entering the Zen garden, he noticed the outline of the *bugyō*'s dog on the veranda to the courtroom. The Akita lay with his muzzle between his paws, apparently asleep. Jack had the unsettling vision of his fingertip disappearing down the dog's throat and shuddered.

Using his ninja stealth-walking skills, Jack crossed the pebbled path. Step by cautious step, he drew closer to the veranda without making a sound. But, as he climbed up, the dog stirred. Jack froze, still as a statue. The dog snuffled and turned its head, before settling back down, the soft pant of sleep flaring its nostrils.

With great care, Jack continued and slid open the *shoji* to the *bugyō*'s courtroom. He let his eyes adjust to the dark. The pale moon shone in, giving Jack just enough light to see that the place was deserted. The door to the *bugyō*'s private office was on the opposite side of the room. Checking the dog was still asleep, he stepped inside. Jack crept round the edge, avoiding the centre of the wooden floor in case it creaked. As he reached out for the handle, he prayed that his belongings would still be there.

'You were never one to give up easily, were you, *gaijin*?'

Jack spun to see Sensei Kyuzo emerge from a hidden alcove beside the *fusuma* doors.

'*Seven times down, eight times up!*' mocked his teacher, recalling the proverb that had been Jack's winning mantra during the *Taryu-Jiai* match three years ago. 'Well, you won't be getting up this time.'

Sensei Kyuzo stalked towards him.

Jack held up his bandaged hand as a sign of peace. 'You're supposed to be my sensei, not my enemy. How could you have cut my fingertip off! Have you lost all respect for *bushido*?'

Sensei Kyuzo snorted. 'Think yourself lucky. I could have severed the whole finger!'

The *taijutsu* master glared at him, his expression one of bitterness and hate.

'Since the war ended, I've been on the run. Forced to hide

63

for fear of reprisal. I've lost all status because of *gaijin* like you. And now I've no choice but to work as a lowly *dōshin*.' He tugged at his uniform in disgust. 'I have to take orders from that potbellied *bugyō*. A man not even of samurai class. He's a bureaucrat, little more than a pumped-up clerk who likes to think he's a warrior. He hasn't fought in a war, let alone held a sword in combat! Yet *I* must bow to him.'

'If you despise him so, then why arrest me?' argued Jack. 'Or is it that you wanted the ten *koban* reward?'

'I'm not interested in the *money*,' spat Sensei Kyuzo, offended to the core by such a suggestion. 'You're my guarantee to redeem my status. To become a *respected* samurai once more.'

Jack was aghast. His *taijutsu* master's vendetta was about personal loss of face. 'You claim to be a samurai, yet you violate the very code of *bushido* – rectitude, honour and loyalty. By turning me in, you're betraying Masamoto-sama, my guardian and *your* friend.'

Sensei Kyuzo's face contorted as a battle of emotions played out – fury, guilt, sorrow, loathing – before they all hardened into pure anger. 'I owe *him* no allegiance. Not since he surrendered and went into exile. He should have committed *seppuku*. Died with honour.'

'Masamoto never surrendered!' shot back Jack. 'And if defeat is so shameful, then why didn't *you* commit *seppuku*?'

Sensei Kyuzo stopped in his tracks and fixed Jack with his beady eyes.

'Because I've an old score to settle first,' he revealed, cracking his knuckles.

15

A FINAL LESSON

Sensei Kyuzo dropped into a fighting stance and beckoned Jack to engage.

Even uninjured, Jack had been no match for the hand-to-hand combat skills of his *taijutsu* master. And with one limb incapacitated he was as good as dead.

So Jack reached for the *kunai* in his belt.

Sensei Kyuzo was unperturbed by the appearance of the weapon. 'At least it'll make the fight a bit more *challenging*,' he mocked.

They circled the woodblock floor, their bare feet scuffing across its polished surface. Sensei Kyuzo waited patiently for Jack to make his move.

'You can have first strike,' he promised, narrowing his eyes in anticipation.

Sensei Kyuzo's confidence in his own combat skills had turned to arrogance. Still, Jack knew this opening attack might be the only chance he'd get. He had to find a gap in his *taijutsu* master's defence before committing to any strike.

At first glance there was no obvious weakness, his sensei's stance being near perfect. Then Jack noticed the lead left hand was a little low. To a trained warrior, this was an open door inviting a full-on assault. On the other hand, when dealing with an opponent as cunning as Sensei Kyuzo, Jack knew such a defensive error could equally be a trap.

He decided to feign an attack at the supposed opening, then switch to a low thrust to the ribs.

As the *kunai* jabbed high, Sensei Kyuzo shifted his arm to block the attack. Tricked by the bluff, his left-hand side was now exposed and Jack changed the *kunai*'s trajectory. But Sensei Kyuzo had been ready for it. His right fist shot across, the knuckles targeting the back of Jack's right wrist. They struck a nerve point, causing Jack's hand to spasm, and he lost grip on the *kunai*. The weapon flew across the room and clattered into the darkness.

Before Jack could retreat out of range, Sensei Kyuzo countered with disconcerting speed. His left fist targeted Jack's lower ribs. Jack buckled under the paralysing blow. A right hook caught his eye. Then a left uppercut to the jaw floored him. Seeing stars and his head ringing with pain, Jack writhed on the ground, an easy target. But his *taijutsu* master made no attempt to finish him off.

'Get up!' snarled Sensei Kyuzo, a malicious glint in his eyes.

As he recovered from the hammer-like blows, Jack realized the old man intended to extend and *enjoy* the fight. While he had no wish to give his teacher such pleasure, neither could he allow himself to be defeated so easily. Wiping blood from a split lower lip, Jack pulled himself to his feet.

'Have you not learnt anything I've taught you?' said Sensei Kyuzo in a disappointed tone. 'Not that I ever wanted to teach scum like you.'

With brutal force, he front-kicked Jack in the chest and sent him skidding across the floor. This time Sensei Kyuzo had hit Jack's solar plexus. Feeling as if his lungs had imploded, Jack found himself fighting for every snatch of breath. Sensei Kyuzo approached unhurried, relishing Jack's suffering. He flexed his fingers in readiness for the next barrage of blows.

Despite being half-crippled from the after-effects of the kick, Jack rose again. All the *taijutsu* lessons in which he'd been *uke* for Sensei Kyuzo were now paying off. Over time he'd built up a tolerance to the pain his teacher could inflict – a resilience in the face of constant punishment. Jack also *knew* his opponent. He realized he could see the telltale signs of each technique – and had been taught the counters to each of his teacher's attacks. But, more significantly, Jack had one big advantage that Sensei Kyuzo had no idea about: his *ninjutsu* training.

The ninja's hand-to-hand fighting style was specifically developed to counter the samurai arts. And one of those techniques was to feign weakness and defeat.

Half-bent over, he gave Sensei Kyuzo the target of his head. His *taijutsu* master went to roundhouse-kick him there, but Jack suddenly leapt into action. Avoiding his sensei's foot and stepping inside the arc of the kick, he trapped the leg with his left arm and drove an Extended Knuckle Fist strike at the mid-point of the inner thigh. Sensei Kyuzo grunted with pain as the unexpected attack hit a *kyusho* point. The nerve was struck with such force that it paralysed his teacher's entire leg.

Jack then brought his head up, using Demon Horn Fist to ram Sensei Kyuzo under the jaw. His *taijutsu* master staggered backwards. Jack heel-struck Sensei Kyuzo's left ankle and swept him off his feet. Sensei Kyuzo tried to correct his fall with his right leg, but the immobilized limb simply gave way beneath him. He crashed to the ground, his face contorted in shock, anger and pain at being beaten.

Jack didn't hesitate now. He rushed forward to finish him off. But Sensei Kyuzo lashed out with his still-mobile left foot. He targeted Jack's injured hand. Jack cried out as a searing stab of pain almost caused him to pass out. Sensei Kyuzo kicked him again, then rolled out of harm's way. By the time Jack was able to focus on something other than sheer agony, Sensei Kyuzo was standing and furiously massaging his leg back to life.

'This will be your *final* lesson, *gaijin*,' snarled Sensei Kyuzo, his near defeat having brought his cruel game to a swift end.

As his *taijutsu* master limped determinedly towards him, a deep-throated growl emanated from behind Jack. Glancing over his shoulder, he caught a glimpse of the Akita hunting dog at the open *shoji*. It leapt for his back. On instinct, Jack dived aside. He felt the dog's claws rake his neck as it flew past to collide with Sensei Kyuzo instead. As dog and teacher both tumbled to the ground, the Akita tore its teeth into Sensei Kyuzo's right shoulder. While the *taijutsu* master wrestled the ferocious beast in his arms, Jack scrambled away and headed for the *bugyō*'s office.

A crack, like a branch breaking, abruptly ended the snarls and gnashing of teeth. Sensei Kyuzo shoved the Akita to one side, its body slumping lifeless to the floor.

'I never did like that dog,' spat the sensei, inspecting his ravaged shoulder. Blood dripped down his arm, which now hung limp at his side.

'Your superior,' said Jack, emphasizing the *bugyō*'s status, 'won't be happy you killed his dog.'

Sensei Kyuzo glared at him. 'I'll simply blame it on you, *gaijin*.'

Jack ran for the door and his swords, but Sensei Kyuzo pounced on him in a miraculous leap. With his one good arm, he grabbed Jack and executed *Yama Arashi*. The Mountain Storm throw tossed Jack high in the air before bringing him smashing into the wooden floor. Sensei Kyuzo then dropped beside him and wrapped his legs round Jack's neck.

'This is *Yoko Sankaku Jime*,' explained Sensei Kyuzo, as if he was instructing Jack in a class. 'It's a triangular choke. The technique gets its power from the pressure exerted by the legs.'

Sensei Kyuzo began to squeeze. Jack spluttered as his airway was instantly cut off.

'The top leg also imparts direct force on your carotid artery, blocking the blood to your brain.'

Jack felt a horrendous pressure starting to build in his head.

'The second leg working in conjunction with the arms optimizes the choke.'

Jack felt as if he was gripped in a human vice.

'Within a matter of seconds, you'll pass out,' revealed Sensei Kyuzo with evident glee. 'But if I then keep the choke on . . . brain damage is certain . . . followed by death.'

The throbbing in Jack's head grew thunderous. Out of the corner of his eye, he spotted the dull sheen of an iron blade beside the office door. Jack desperately reached for the twine handle. Blackness was seeping into his vision. He had mere seconds to live.

His fingers clasped round the *kunai*.

As the curtain fell over his vision, he drove the iron tip into Sensei Kyuzo's right leg. His *taijutsu* master yelled in agony and the pressure was instantly released. Jack pulled away, taking the *kunai* with him. All sensation returned in a flood.

He then leapt on his wounded *taijutsu* master. His rage boiled over at the sensei who'd made his life hell at the *Niten Ichi Ryū* – the teacher who'd publicly humiliated and tortured him in front of the entire class. Now this man had arrested him and cut off his finger . . . and had been determined to murder him.

'Go on, kill me!' goaded Sensei Kyuzo, blood pouring from the laceration in his leg.

Jack raised the *kunai* and brought it down hard. He struck his *taijutsu* master in the temple with the blunt end of the handle.

'No, I follow the code of *bushido*, unlike you,' said Jack as Sensei Kyuzo slumped unconscious on the floor. 'And I still *respect* my sensei.'

16

PRAYER FLAGS

'You look terrible!' exclaimed Benkei as Jack limped into the barn with a black eye, split lip, bruised jaw and swollen throat.

'You should see the loser,' rasped Jack.

'Well, I hope the damage was worth it.'

Jack nodded and patted his treasured swords.

'We should go,' said Benkei, grabbing their bag of supplies. 'As soon as the sun rises, they'll come after us. And I don't want to end up looking like you!'

Jack didn't argue. He shouldered his pack – all the contents still there – and followed Benkei out into the night.

They darted across the moonlit paddy fields to the cover of the trees. Heading west, they climbed the valley and up the steep slope of the double-headed volcano. Trees gave way to hardy bushes, then to a barren rocky landscape. Following animal tracks, they traversed the mountainside and reached the first peak just as dawn was breaking.

Like a newborn phoenix, the sun rose out of the glistening Seto Sea in the far distance. Its warming rays were a welcome sight for Jack and Benkei, who were cold and fatigued from the ascent. Hearing the flapping of a flock of birds, Jack looked up but couldn't spot any flying overhead. Then, as they crested a small ridge, he discovered the sound was made by hundreds of prayer flags fluttering in the wind. At their heart was a solitary shrine perched atop an outcrop of rock. Adorning its wooden eaves were streams of brightly coloured silk banners.

Jack and Benkei passed through a grey stone *torii* gateway and up steps hewn into the rock. They entered the shrine.

'I feel so drab compared to these flags,' remarked Benkei, dumping their supplies in a sheltered corner and disappearing behind the altar.

Exhausted, Jack sat down at the shrine's entrance and gazed at the rippling prayer flags. The constant flutter of silk was like an unending mantra to the gods, the yellow, green, red, white and blue hues forming an undulating rainbow against the cloudless sky. He recalled Yori once explaining the significance of these colours for a Buddhist monk. To his surprise, they'd corresponded to the Five Rings of the Ninja . . .

Earth was yellow.

Water denoted by green.

Fire symbolized by red.

Wind represented by white.

Sky signified by blue.

These five great elements of the universe, which were the spiritual touchstone of Buddhist monks, also formed the basis of the ninja's philosophy to life and combat. Both groups channelled the energy and wisdom of the Five Rings: the monks for peace and the ninja for protection.

The most powerful of these was Sky.

His ninja Grandmaster had explained that this element was the source of *mikkyō*, their secret teachings of meditation, mind control and *kuji-in* magic. He'd demonstrated to Jack how to invoke the power of Sky to connect to the energy of the universe. When attuned to this element on a mission, a ninja was able to sense the surroundings and respond without thinking – without even using any *physical* senses.

Master the Five Rings, the Grandmaster had told him. *Learn to endure like the Earth, to flow like Water, to strike like Fire, to run like the Wind and be all-seeing like the Sky. Then you'll be a ninja.*

But it wasn't a simple task to tap into the Ring of Sky. It took immense focus and concentration. Jack was quite adept at the healing aspect – even helping to save Saburo's life on one occasion – but that was just a small part of the secret teachings for Sky. With true mastery, a ninja could draw upon great strength in times of crisis, sense another person's thoughts, foretell of imminent danger and even control the elements of nature itself.

At first Jack had been sceptical of such claims. But, after witnessing the old Grandmaster lift a tree trunk above his head and another ninja, Zenjubo, invoke a mist during a mission, he quickly became a believer. But in his own *kuji-in* training he'd only once managed a true connection to the Ring of Sky – and that had been luck. And Jack knew he needed more than luck if he was to survive the journey to come.

A sudden gust of wind whipped the flags into a flurry, their faded tatters galloping on the breeze.

Wind horses.

That was what Yori called the prayer flags. Upon the silk were potent symbols, inscriptions and mantras that the wind supposedly bore away into the world to ease mankind's suffering.

Just as a drop of water can permeate the ocean, Yori had explained, *prayers released to the wind disperse and fill the sky.*

As Jack sat within the mountain shrine, he sensed Yori's spirit close by. Silently reassuring him. Jack whispered a heartfelt prayer – for Yori, his lost friends, Akiko and his distant sister – hoping that his blessing would also be carried on the wind.

'That's much better,' announced Benkei, slumping down on the steps, having reversed his kimono back to its motley-coloured glory.

He rummaged through the supply bag and produced a length of clean cloth.

'I thought you could use this,' he said, indicating the blood-soaked bandage on Jack's hand.

'Thanks,' replied Jack. Tearing off a strip, he began re-dressing his wound. He bit his tongue against the pain as he unwrapped the old bandage to reveal his mutilated finger.

Benkei grimaced at the sight of the raw and bloody stump. 'We should rest a while,' he suggested. 'From here on, it's tough going. The Kuju range is just mountains and rock and . . . more mountains.'

He took a swig from a water gourd, then offered it to Jack. After a couple of mouthfuls, Jack poured some over his wound to clean it.

'Don't use too much,' warned Benkei. 'Not all streams are fit to drink in this volcanic region.'

Putting back the stopper, Jack returned the gourd. Then, after tucking into a *mochi* rice cake, Benkei settled down for a nap while Jack focused on healing himself. But his body hurt so much he almost didn't know where to start – his hand, his head, his jaw or his throat. If the battles kept coming at this rate, Jack realized it would take a miracle to reach Nagasaki in one piece . . . let alone alive.

17

CALDERA

The sky stretched out like a boundless kingdom above their heads, volcanic peaks competing with one another to claim the horizon. Graced by fair weather, Jack and Benkei made good progress on their journey across the rugged Kuju range. With each passing day Jack felt stronger and fitter, his healing sessions seeming to be enhanced by their proximity to the heavens. By the third day, his throat was no longer swollen and his eye was turning into a healthy yet colourful purple patch. He changed dressings regularly, ensuring that his wound didn't become infected. And, although his finger was still in trauma and throbbed painfully, he forced himself to open and close his hand to maintain the flexibility and strength he'd need to wield a sword.

As they hiked along majestic ridges, through gullies and across gorges, they encountered no one, apart from the odd startled deer and hunting hawk. In the crystal-clear mountain air and the wild barren landscape, Jack could almost believe they'd eluded their pursuers. But he knew that would be a foolhardy assumption and they both pressed on.

At such altitude the nights were cold but spectacular with

their starry display of constellations that glittered like cut diamonds in the black sky. By contrast, the summer days were hot and stifling, the only relief a mouthful of water and the breeze that blew across the grassy ridges. With no tree cover, Jack tied a bandanna round his head to combat the sun's fierce rays and stop the sweat streaming into his eyes.

'You could fry noodles in this heat!' remarked Benkei, mopping his brow with a red handkerchief.

Jack noticed the symbol of a horse and an inscription on the silk cloth. 'You stole a prayer flag!'

Benkei nodded. 'There were hundreds,' he replied by way of defence. 'Who's going to miss *one*?'

Jack shook his head in dismay. 'The flags repeat the same pattern of colours over and over. A good tracker will soon spot a break in the line.'

Benkei gave a contrite shrug. 'Sorry, *nanban*, I . . . didn't realize.'

He guiltily threw away the flag.

'No!' cried Jack. But it was too late.

The flag caught in an updraught and sailed out of reach. Benkei ran after it, but the wind horse twirled high over a sheer cliff.

'Now we've left another marker,' sighed Jack.

Benkei offered him an apologetic smile. 'Perhaps if it flies far enough, the flag could send them off course.'

'Let's hope so,' replied Jack, trying his best to sound optimistic.

They walked on in silence, leaving their fate to the wind.

★

'I think we're home free, *nanban*!' announced Benkei cheerily.

It was their fifth day of hiking and there'd been no sight or sound of a patrol.

Jack was inclined to agree. If any *dōshin* or samurai from Yufuin were on their trail, they would have seen them by now. Reassured, he allowed himself to relax a little.

'Now we're friends, you can call me Jack if you want.'

An affable smile graced Benkei's lips. 'It's *because* we're friends that I call you *nanban*. I wouldn't dare insult you by using the term *gaijin*. You're certainly not a barbarian, but you must be from the south – that's where all the other foreigners came from.'

'Actually, I was shipwrecked on the eastern shore, near Toba.'

Benkei raised his eyebrows in surprise. 'That may be the case, but *azuma no yaban hito* doesn't exactly trip off the tongue.' He gave Jack a rueful grin of apology. 'Anyway, how's the finger, *nanban*?'

Accepting that his nickname was to remain, Jack replied, 'Healing well.'

He held up his hand, the bandage neatly wrapped and no longer bloodstained.

'Still, that's a brutal wound. How could a sensei do that to one of their own students?'

'You've not met Sensei Kyuzo. His favourite expression was: *Pain is the best teacher and that's why you're in my class!*'

Benkei laughed. 'Well, I'm glad I never went to samurai school!'

'Not all the teachers were that harsh,' said Jack, remembering his kindly Zen master, Sensei Yamada. 'In fact, I owe one my life. When I washed up on these shores, half-drowned and orphaned, I was taken in by Masamoto Takeshi, the head of the *Niten Ichi Ryū*. He treated me as his own son. Fed, clothed and sheltered me. Taught me how to fight with a sword. Made me a samurai. If it wasn't for his kindness, I'd have been dead a long time ago.'

'It must be good to have someone care for you like that,' said Benkei wistfully. Then his expression hardened. 'But where is he now, when you need his protection most?'

Jack sighed, saddened at the memory. 'The Shogun forced him into exile, banishing him to a remote temple on Mount Iawo for the rest of his life.'

Benkei studied Jack, clearly feeling his pain and loss. 'And you've not seen him since?'

Jack shook his head. Upset at the thought of his imprisoned guardian, he tried to move the conversation on. 'So you never went to school?'

Benkei snorted. 'My mother always wanted me to become a monk, so I could learn to read and write.'

'Did you?'

'Of course not! I'd have had to shave off all my hair!'

On the seventh day, they emerged from the Kuju range to be faced by a formidable wall of rock. The escarpment rose before them like a gigantic tidal wave, stretching north and south as far as the eye could see.

'Welcome to the Aso caldera,' announced Benkei, noting the disbelief on Jack's face. 'We could go round it, but that would take days.'

'Then we've no choice but to go over it,' accepted Jack.

Benkei led the way up the precipitous slope. Traversing back and forth, they made painstakingly slow progress towards the summit. The sun beat down and with every step their legs grew heavy as lead weights.

Eventually, after a whole morning of relentless climbing, they breached the wall to be greeted by an awe-inspiring sight. The caldera was a single giant collapsed volcano, its crater wide as a sea and equally as long. The opposite side was little more than a hazy mountain ridge on the distant horizon. Over the centuries, the fertile soil of the vast inner plateau had been farmed into a carpet of green paddy fields, laid out like *tatami* mats for the gods. At the heart of the ancient crater was a group of smouldering peaks, a potent reminder that the massive volcano was still very much alive.

'Aso-san's five peaks . . . are supposed to look like . . . a sleeping Buddha,' gasped Benkei, struggling to get his breath back. With an exhausted wave of the hand, he indicated the eastern peak to be the head and a steaming vent on another to be the Buddha's navel.

Although Jack couldn't quite see the resemblance, standing on the lip of the caldera he felt as if he was on top of the world. The sky above was a cloudless blue dome, while the bowl of the crater dropped away into forested slopes to meet the patchwork plateau far below.

Before they began their descent, Jack stole one final look at the Kuju mountain range behind. Upon a far ridge, he caught the sun glinting off something. Calling for Benkei to wait, he shielded his eyes and looked again. He now wished he possessed Miyuki's eagle sight, but his eyes were good enough to spot more reflected gleams moving rapidly in their direction.

Jack turned to Benkei to deliver the bad news. 'We have company.'

18

NAKA-DAKE

'Those samurai don't give up easily, do they?' panted Benkei, as they weaved in between the shimmering fields of rice.

'Focus on your breathing,' said Jack, not breaking his stride.

He'd taught Benkei the art of Dragon Breathing, the secret to the ninja's ability to run like the wind. This special cyclic pattern of inhales and exhales ensured that maximum oxygen reached the lungs. *Inhale – exhale – exhale – inhale – exhale – inhale – inhale – exhale*. The rhythm focused the mind, while the increased breaths improved efficiency, allowing the body to sustain its pace over long distances. Propelled by this extra energy, the two of them raced across the plateau.

But however fast they ran the samurai had one distinct advantage – they were on horseback.

Jack had spotted the mounted patrol crest the caldera at the same time as he and Benkei reached the crater basin. Still too far away to make out any details, he did glimpse a flash of golden armour. With a heavy heart, he realized this was no ordinary patrol. It could only be the Shogun's elite samurai.

'We should hide,' said Benkei, panic seizing his voice.

'*Where* exactly?' replied Jack, indicating the wide-open terrain before them.

Beyond the forested slopes, there was minimal cover to conceal their escape. The plateau was just rice field after rice field, with a few villages and farmhouses dotted here and there.

The handful of workers tending the fields watched wide-eyed as the two fugitives shot past.

'They're bound to catch us . . . if we just keep running,' said Benkei.

Jack realized he was right. Even Dragon Breathing was no match for a galloping horse.

'Maybe we can lose them among Aso-san's peaks,' he suggested, pointing to the five smouldering mountains that divided the caldera basin.

'But they're active volcanoes!' exclaimed Benkei.

'Exactly,' replied Jack. 'The horses won't want to go anywhere near.'

'Nor do I!'

But Jack headed towards them nonetheless. 'Just think of them as a bigger version of the Nine Hells of Beppu.'

'That's reassuring!' cried Benkei, reluctantly following. 'You almost broiled me alive there.'

With their heads down, they sprinted for the slopes of Mount Taka, the highest of Aso-san's five summits. Their plan was to cross from here to Naka-dake, the volcanic offshoot of this peak, lose the samurai amid the sulphurous vents and escape west.

As they ran the last stretch, the Shogun's samurai emerged from the forest. Paying little regard to the farmers or their crops, the patrol thundered in a direct line across the paddy fields. Their horses trampled rice under their hooves, breaking apart bunds and scattering the workers in their wake.

Jack and Benkei scrambled up the mountainside through the treeline to the craggy heights. But the steep slope slowed their pace and the patrol rapidly gained ground.

'Faster!' urged Jack, almost pushing Benkei up the volcano.

They were barely halfway when the Shogun's samurai began their ascent. The horses struggled on the rough terrain, but their riders spurred them on.

As Jack and Benkei passed the last traces of vegetation, they were confronted by a forbidding sight. Swirls of black and grey lava stone scarred a desolate landscape. Craters the size of islands pockmarked the surface and the volcanic ash under foot was dangerously unstable. Clouds of sulphurous gas pumped out of gaping vents, creating a billowing blinding fog.

'Now this *is* Hell!' wheezed Benkei, coughing and spluttering from the acrid air.

Jack pulled his bandanna over his mouth and nose, then offered a spare bandage for Benkei to do the same.

'Stay close,' warned Jack as a steam cloud enveloped them. 'We only want to lose the samurai, not each other!'

The going was arduous and disorientating, and Jack wondered if he'd made a fatal mistake heading into the heart of a volcano. But as they neared the summit he heard the samurai's horses whinnying in protest. Through a brief gap in the sulphurous clouds, he spotted the patrol dismounting lower down the slope and continuing their chase on foot. Jack's strategy was paying off.

All of a sudden Benkei stopped.

The ground ahead sheered away into seeming oblivion. They'd reached the jagged lip of the main crater. Far below, amid the turbulent steam, a seething green-grey lake boiled and bubbled.

'Which way now?' asked Benkei, gagging on the sulphuric reek of rotten eggs.

'Your guess is as good as mine,' replied Jack, his eyes red and streaming.

They decided to head right, skirting the crater rim. As the steam swirled around them, they caught further glimpses of the samurai. The patrol had been forced to split up to increase its chances of capturing them.

Jack and Benkei hurried on. When they finally reached the far side of the crater, they discovered a lava field leading across to Naka-dake. Running as fast as the treacherous rock-strewn ground allowed, they almost tumbled head first into a chasm. It yawned like a jagged mouth between the two peaks, dropping dizzily into a grey graveyard of boulders, rocks and rubble.

'Look, there!' cried Jack, pointing to an old rope bridge strung across the chasm.

They darted over, but Benkei halted at the foot of the bridge and refused to go any further.

'I can't cross *that*,' he yelled, visibly trembling.

Somewhere in the mist the shouts of the samurai drew closer.

'If one sees with the eyes of the heart, rather than the eyes of the head, there is nothing to fear,' said Jack, recalling the lesson of his blind *bōjutsu* master, Sensei Kano, when they were asked to cross a similarly dangerous gorge.

'What's that supposed to mean?'

'If the height scares you, simply don't look. Become blind to your fear.'

'I'm not scared of heights,' replied Benkei. 'I'm scared of the bridge!'

Jack now saw that the construction was on the verge of falling apart. The ropes were frayed, the wooden planks pitted and rotten from the acidic atmosphere. The bridge was only wide enough for one person to cross at a time, but the gaps between the planks were equally wide enough for a person to fall through.

The shouts of the samurai were closing in.

'We've no choice but to risk it,' said Jack.

'Then we go one at a time,' said Benkei.

Jack nodded his agreement. 'You go first. I'll hold off any samurai.'

'I'm not sure which is more dangerous,' muttered Benkei, taking a deep breath and stepping on to the rickety bridge.

It creaked loudly, the ropes becoming taut. But it held his weight. Step by cautious step, Benkei began crossing the swaying bridge. Below, piles of sharp rock and jagged boulders promised to impale him if it collapsed . . . or he lost his footing.

Benkei was barely halfway when a figure emerged out of the fog behind them.

Jack turned to face the samurai. The warrior was dressed in black leather armour adorned with gold fastenings and a red sun *kamon* emblazoned on the breastplate. He wore an ornate golden helmet with a fearsome *menpō* covering his face.

'I vowed I'd hunt you down, *gaijin*.'

With a black-gloved hand, the samurai removed his mask to reveal a young handsome face with dark hooded eyes and high imperious cheekbones.

Jack instinctively drew his sword. 'Kazuki!'

19

ROPE BRIDGE

'That's no way to greet an old schoolfriend!' remarked Kazuki, eyeing Jack's *katana* and keeping his distance.

'*Friend?* You've no idea what friendship means,' replied Jack, feeling his blood boil at his rival's arrogance. 'You betrayed *everyone* at the *Niten Ichi Ryū*.'

'I was being *loyal* to my family and the future Shogun,' shot back Kazuki. 'That is true *bushido*.'

Jack regarded him with contempt. 'You know nothing of Respect, Rectitude or Honesty. Without those, you're no more than a common mercenary. And it's obvious you've been well rewarded for your treachery.'

'This?' said Kazuki, patting his golden helmet and grinning. 'This is my promotion for capturing Sensei Kano.'

Jack was too stunned to reply. He'd thought their *bōjutsu* master had managed to disappear after leading the surviving *Niten Ichi Ryū* samurai to safety during the Battle of Osaka Castle.

Kazuki laughed cruelly. 'No one escapes the Shogun's wrath, *gaijin*. After sustaining some injuries in the flood during our last encounter, I was recommended to a blind healer.

Imagine my surprise when he turned out to be Sensei Kano!'

'You handed him over, when he was *helping* you?' exclaimed Jack, aghast.

'No, *after* he'd helped me,' corrected Kazuki, without a flicker of remorse.

'You're the lowest of the low, Kazuki!' Jack couldn't stand his rival's bragging any more. He shot a glance in Benkei's direction. His friend was almost to the other side of the bridge. Jack could make a run for it . . . or confront his enemy. A showdown was long overdue and, fuelled with outrage at Sensei Kano's fate, Jack raised his *katana* to attack. But as he gripped the handle with both hands, an agonizing fire shot through the stump of his little finger and he winced.

'Missing something?' smirked Kazuki.

'Thanks to Sensei Kyuzo,' seethed Jack, clenching his teeth against the pain.

Kazuki nodded approvingly. 'He was always my favourite teacher. That's why I didn't turn him in when I recognized him in Yufuin.' He held up his gloved right hand, his fingers curled into an impotent claw. 'At least we're more evenly matched now – although *yubitsume* is hardly enough punishment for Akiko's arrow through my hand.'

Jack bristled at the implied threat. 'You vowed to leave her alone!'

Kazuki smirked at his impassioned reaction. 'Don't worry, I haven't gone near your beloved friend . . . yet.'

Struggling to keep his temper in check, Jack advanced on Kazuki. But, rather than going for his sword, his rival retreated.

Jack pursued him into the mist.

'*Nanban*, it's this way!' cried Benkei, stopping several planks short of the end.

Chasing after shadows, Jack realized too late that Kazuki had baited him on purpose. Out of the steam materialized the rest of the patrol. And Jack recognized them all.

The samurai were the four key members of Kazuki's Scorpion Gang, the unit established in honour of *daimyo* Kamakura's campaign to rid Japan of foreigners – and Jack was the *gaijin* at the very top of their death list.

Nobu stomped towards him, a solid wall of muscle and flesh like the bulbous body of a walrus. While no match for Jack's sword skill, he possessed the sheer brute force of a sumo wrestling champion.

Hiroto, on the other hand, was as skinny as a bamboo stalk and had eyes that sat too close together aside a pinched nose. Limping slightly, he wielded a lethal barbed spear and wore thick body armour, clearly worried that Jack would wound him in the stomach for a third time.

A greater threat was Goro, a muscular hardened warrior with devastating sword skills and total lack of honour. The boy slashed the air threateningly with his *katana*, the blade whistling as it cut through the mist.

Finally, a giant stepped out. A good head taller than everyone else, Raiden was like a tree trunk with legs – and just as thick. What he boasted in pure strength, he lacked in brain. Jack had beaten him once in a *taijutsu* match, but the fight had almost been the end of him. On this occasion, Raiden brandished a formidable *nodachi* sword, its blade twice the length of Jack's *katana*. Such a weapon could cleave him in half.

The last gang member was missing: Toru.

'If you're looking for my brother,' grunted Raiden, 'he drowned in the flood . . . and it's *your* fault.'

Kazuki reappeared, his mask back on, his *katana* unsheathed in his left hand.

'I've promised Raiden that he can cut off your head, once *I've* finished with you.'

Kazuki's eyes fixed on Jack – his unwavering stare certain of victory.

Jack cursed himself for letting his rival trick him so easily. With only a single *katana* at his disposal against five opponents, he didn't have a hope of defeating the Scorpion Gang all at once.

Divide and conquer.

That had been one of Masamoto's key strategies in combat training. Somehow Jack had to reduce the gang's combined fighting strength. The bridge was the answer. Crossing it, they'd be forced to engage him one at a time. But first he had to reach there alive.

Jack's foot found a loose rock on the lava field. As Kazuki advanced on him, he flicked it into his face and caused his rival to flinch. Then, with lightning speed, he leapt at Hiroto and cut down. The *katana* blade sliced the barbed spear in two as if it were no thicker than a chopstick. Left with a useless stump of wood, Hiroto's eyes widened in terror as he stood defence-less against Jack's sword.

'Not *again*!' he wailed, trying to protect his stomach.

But a sudden thrust from Goro's sword forced Jack on the retreat and he had to resort to front-kicking Hiroto in the face instead. The boy crashed on to the lava field, clasping his broken nose and howling. Jack fled from the encircling

Scorpions. As he sprinted away, a blade swiped past his ear, missing his neck by a fraction.

'After him!' yelled Kazuki in frustration.

Jack had no idea which direction he was heading. He just ran, the sulphurous steam swirling around him like ghosts.

Then his heart leapt into his throat as the chasm lurched into view. Jack skidded to a halt, his feet almost slipping into the abyss. Through a break in the steam he spotted the rope bridge. Benkei was still there, uncertain whether to flee or await his return.

'Run, Benkei!' cried Jack.

As he dashed along the chasm edge towards the bridge, he heard a clatter of rocks and a scream.

'Help!' came a cry.

Jack glanced back to see Nobu clinging to the lip of the gorge. But Kazuki ran past, blatantly ignoring his friend's peril.

'Leave him,' he snarled to Raiden and Goro. 'Get the *gaijin* first.'

Jack reached the foot of the bridge at the same time as Kazuki caught up with him. Their swords clashed and they became locked in combat. As the other Scorpions caught up, Jack shoved Kazuki away and leapt on to the bridge. He heard the *whoosh* of a blade and ducked. Kazuki's sword sliced through thin air, then straight through one of the supporting ropes.

The bridge shuddered as the tension in the rope pinged loose.

Benkei dived for the safety of the other side, while Jack struggled to keep his footing on the warped planks.

Unfazed, Kazuki forced Jack further on to the swaying bridge. Consumed with bloodlust, he was relentless in his attack. Jack could barely deflect the barrage of strikes as they rained down on him one after the other. With every impact, a spasm of pain rocketed through his arm. He felt his grip weaken on the *katana* and his defences rapidly crumbling.

As he retreated from Kazuki's onslaught, a plank cracked beneath his foot. Feeling himself drop into the chasm, he threw his weight backwards and managed to land on the plank behind. But he'd now left himself exposed to a killing strike.

Kazuki brought his sword high up to spear Jack through the heart.

'Now I *will* have my revenge, *gaijin*.'

20

COLLAPSE

In moments of death, a warrior's perception is heightened and Jack saw everything with crystal-clear clarity. The gleaming point of Kazuki's blade. The triumphant grin on his rival's face. The wisp of steam that rose like a spirit from the depths of the chasm. He felt the coarse grain of the plank beneath his back. The smooth silk of his *katana*'s handle. The latent heat of the volcano. He heard the protesting creak of the bridge. The cry of alarm from Benkei. Even the beat of his own heart.

Jack knew he had no chance of avoiding Kazuki's death blow. But if he was to die he decided his rival must too. He couldn't allow Kazuki to survive and go on to harm Akiko.

As the sword came down, Jack didn't attempt to block it. Instead he slashed at the bridge with his *katana*, his blade scything through another supporting rope. Already on the brink of collapse, the bridge now tore itself apart. Like a writhing serpent, it buckled and twisted. More ropes snapped and planks twirled away into the abyss.

Kazuki's expression turned from triumph to horror as the bridge disintegrated beneath them. In the chaos his sword missed its target and, screaming, he plummeted into the chasm alongside Jack.

The bridge having ripped in two, Jack wrapped his arm round a plank and clung on for dear life as it swung across the abyss. He smashed into the chasm wall. His whole body jarred on impact, his arm almost wrenched out of its socket as he was slammed repeatedly against the rock face.

Eventually the battering subsided and Jack hung there, limp as a rag doll. Blood dripped from multiple cuts and grazes on his arms, legs and face.

'*Nanban!*'

Jack groaned and looked up. Benkei's shock of black hair peered over the lip of the chasm.

'You're alive!' he cried in disbelief.

Not for much longer, thought Jack, as he swung precariously above the jagged rocks that were waiting to break his fall – and his body.

'Climb up!' urged Benkei.

Jack didn't know whether he had the strength to . . . or the will. His body was so tired of the continual running and fighting that it was tempting just to wait until the bridge collapsed entirely and they both tumbled into the chasm depths.

He blinked away the blood dripping off his brow and his sister's face flashed before his eyes: smiling and expectant of his return. For a moment, he imagined he heard her infectious giggle on the breeze and in that instant his resolve to reunite with his family burned brighter than ever.

The body can keep going as long as the mind is strong.

Jack had learnt that during the ritual challenges of the Circle of Three. Deep in his heart, he felt the fire that had driven him on all these years. The motivation that had helped him overcome every trial and obstacle in his path. He *had* to survive and return home, if only for his sister's sake.

Clamping his *katana* between his teeth, he began to haul himself up the tattered remains of the rope bridge. His weakened hand flared each time he gripped the wood. Light-headed and trembling, he ignored the pain and fought his way up, plank by plank.

'Nearly there!' encouraged Benkei.

Wheezing from the acrid air, Jack focused on Benkei's face as he reached up to grasp the last plank. But it failed to take his weight.

'Got you!' cried Benkei, grabbing Jack's outstretched wrist before he plunged into the abyss.

With a grunt of superhuman effort, he dragged Jack over the lip and to safety. They collapsed side by side on the ash-covered ground.

'You're truly mad, *nanban*,' said Benkei. 'You must have a death wish!'

Jack shook his head. 'I just don't fear death any more.'

Benkei shot him a dubious look.

But that was the truth, Jack realized. Having stared death in the face so many times, he was no longer frightened by the prospect. Although that didn't mean he wanted to die. As Yori might have said, *a deer runs from the lion, not through fear but for love of life.*

'*GAIJIN!*'

Jack sat bolt upright. On the opposite side of the chasm, an equally battered Kazuki clung to the other half of the bridge. Raiden was slowly pulling him up on a rope.

As he swung above the chasm, Kazuki vented his fury at Jack.

'I'll block every road, every crossing, every pass. I'll turn all *ronin* against you. There'll be no place you can run or hide. I'll hunt you down and destroy you, *gaijin*, if it's the very last thing I do!'

21

OX AND CART

'We must have lost them . . . by now,' panted Benkei, collapsing against a tree.

Jack sat down next to him, trying to recover his breath too. After surviving the chasm, they'd climbed Naka-dake's summit and descended its far slopes, leaving Kazuki and his Scorpion Gang to backtrack and find another route. Determined to maintain their lead, Jack and Benkei hadn't stopped for a day and a night as they raced across the plateau. They'd passed between the peaks of Kishima and Eboshi and were now heading for a wide gorge in the caldera's western wall.

Even though there was no sign of pursuit, Jack disagreed with Benkei's statement and reluctantly shook his head.

'Why ever not?' said Benkei. 'They've no idea which direction we've gone in.'

Jack gave his companion an awkward look. 'Kazuki *knows* I'm heading to Nagasaki.'

Benkei rolled his eyes in exasperation. 'So why are we even bothering to run?'

'We have to get there first. If I can board an English or Dutch ship, I'll be safe.'

'Well, let's hope there's one waiting for you,' replied Benkei, opening their supply bag and taking out two rice cakes. 'I've heard it's mostly the Portuguese trading out of Nagasaki.'

Jack felt as if he'd been slapped in the face. He'd imagined Nagasaki as a thriving port, like London, with numerous trading vessels from around the world – not just ships manned by England's dreaded enemy. But thinking about it now, out of the hundreds of expeditions that set sail each year from England, only a handful were ever destined for the Far East. Of those, perhaps one or two would strike out for the fabled Japans – his own ship, the *Alexandria*, being one such vessel. The realization dawned on him that now Japan had closed its doors to foreigners the chances of a friendly ship awaiting his arrival were even more remote.

Jack bit morosely into his rice cake as he realized he could be chasing a ghost ship.

Benkei took a swig from their water gourd, then handed it to Jack. 'So what does this Kazuki have against you in the first place? He isn't just following the Shogun's orders. He's out for revenge.'

Jack sighed heavily, thinking of the long-running feud between him and Kazuki. From their first confrontation in the *Niten Ichi Ryū* courtyard, through their bitter class rivalry and escalating fights, to their battle at Osaka Castle and duel upon Kizu Bridge, Kazuki had harboured nothing but pure hatred towards him.

'He lost his mother to an illness caught from a foreign priest,' Jack explained. 'Kazuki blames all *gaijin* for her death . . . especially me.'

'But you had nothing to do with it,' snorted Benkei in disbelief.

'I'm not just any *gaijin*; I'm the first foreign samurai. In his eyes, that's even more reason to despise me. Just like the Shogun and Sensei Kyuzo, he thinks I'm a disease that needs to be wiped out.'

'Samurai! They're so arrogant. I never even knew my mother . . . but I don't go round blaming other samurai for that.'

Jack was puzzled. 'I don't understand. You're always talking about your mother.'

Benkei contemplated the remains of his rice cake and his expression darkened. 'That's the good mother . . . the one I wish I'd had,' he admitted. 'The *real* one abandoned me when I was a baby. *Mabiki*, the farmers call it, weeding out the weaker rice seedlings. My mother was a samurai, my father a lowly farmworker. Their love was forbidden. And I was the unwanted fruit.'

'So you're actually a samurai!' said Jack, both amazed and saddened at this news.

'No!' replied Benkei firmly. 'And I'm not a farmer either. I don't fit anywhere in Japanese society.'

He swallowed the last of his rice cake, then held up his hands to show they were empty. He forced a grin on to his face. 'But I survived to become a fine conjuror!'

With a flick of his wrist, he produced a *mikan* out of thin air and presented the small orange fruit to Jack. He then took another out of their supply bag and began to peel it. For a while, they both sat in silence.

Jack regarded his friend in a new light. Despite his outward exuberance and carefree attitude, Benkei was a lonely soul inside. Perhaps that explained why he was so willing to help Jack. He recognized a fellow outcast and survivor. But at least Jack was fortunate enough to have family left that loved him. He vowed to himself that if there was the *slightest* chance of a hospitable ship bound for a foreign port he would board it and strive to find his way home to his sister. He'd come too far, fought too hard and lost too much to turn back now.

'We need to keep moving,' said Jack, getting back to his feet. He offered his hand. 'Is Benkei the Great still willing to be my guide?'

'Of course, *nanban*!' replied Benkei, grasping his hand in friendship. 'You've got a boat to catch.'

By late afternoon they reached a confluence of two fast-flowing rivers. Their turbulent waters coursed across the final stretch of the plateau and into the treelined gorge that formed the only break in the caldera's wall.

As the two of them made their way along a dirt track towards the gorge, Benkei explained, 'Legend says the god Takei-watatsu saw his people starving and kicked this opening in the western wall to drain the mighty lake inside. Since then, the Aso caldera has become the rice bowl of Kyushu.'

Looking at the perilous way ahead, Jack asked, 'Do you think this same god could stop the river so we can cross it?'

Benkei laughed. 'I don't know about that, but there's a bridge a bit further down.'

Keeping to the trees to avoid being spotted, they found the main track and followed it to the crossing point. As they drew closer, Jack became aware of more and more foot traffic. The majority were farmers carrying their goods to market, along with a few travelling merchants and the occasional wandering samurai. All of them were converging on a checkpoint beside the bridge.

Ducking behind a bush, Jack and Benkei considered their options. Jack counted at least eight guards patrolling the crossing, as well as two officials checking travel documents.

'It never used to be like this,' said Benkei. 'Now the Shogun's in power, every traveller is under suspicion.'

'We'll have to find another place to cross,' said Jack, realizing that to fight their way through would be both foolhardy and dangerous.

'There isn't one, unless you fancy your chances swimming the rapids,' replied Benkei. 'This is the *only* gap in the caldera wall. Otherwise, we'd be forced to climb again and your old schoolfriend is bound to catch us up.'

'But I can't simply stroll through like you,' said Jack.

Benkei considered this for a moment, then, grinning, pointed to a solitary farmer leading an ox and cart down the track. 'We'll hitch a ride across!'

The rickety wooden cart was piled high with rice straw and baskets of fresh vegetables.

To hide is the best defence, thought Jack. That had been the Grandmaster Soke's final piece of advice to him. And this was the perfect opportunity to put that lesson into practice. He nodded his agreement to Benkei's plan.

As the farmer passed by, they darted out and leapt on to the back of the cart. Hurriedly, they buried themselves beneath the bundles of rice straw before anyone spotted them. Huddled next to one another, they tried not to cough in the musty dust-laden air.

The farmer trundled his cart up to the checkpoint.

'Halt!' ordered a bridge guard.

Hidden under the straw, Jack and Benkei exchanged worried looks.

'Travel permit,' demanded the official.

They heard the farmer pull out a piece of paper.

'I've permission to visit the market in Ōzu,' explained the farmer, his voice low and deferential.

'I'll be the judge of that,' snapped the official. 'What are you selling?'

'Straw, rice, vegetables —'

'*Saké?*' interrupted the official.

'No . . . no . . . not at all.'

'You realize it's *illegal* for a farmer to sell rice wine.'

'Of course,' replied the farmer, alarmed at the accusation.

But, despite his protests of innocence, the official ordered, 'Check the cart.'

22

SPEARED

Jack and Benkei held their breath as they heard a pair of wooden sandals clunk across the bridge and approach the cart. A moment later, the wicker baskets were noisily rummaged through. The search drew nearer and Jack's hand reached for his sword.

'Just vegetables,' said the guard, his tone disappointed.

'What about the straw bales?' asked the official.

The steel tip of a spear suddenly appeared in front of Jack and Benkei's startled faces. It disappeared. Then it shot through the straw to land between Jack's legs. It withdrew and Jack gave a nervous swallow at his very narrow escape. The guard thrust again. This time the spear struck Benkei's thigh. The blade cut deep, piercing skin and flesh. Benkei bit down hard on his lip to stop himself from screaming.

As the samurai tugged on the shaft, Jack snatched the bandanna from his head and wrapped it round the blade. If the samurai removed his spear and saw blood, their presence would be instantly discovered. The bandanna wiped the tip clean as it exited the wound. Several more jabs were made further down the cart.

'There's nothing here but straw,' said the guard.

'You're clear to go then,' declared the official irritably.

The farmer urged on his ox and the cart bumped across the bridge.

Beneath the bales, Jack frantically tied the bandanna round Benkei's thigh to stem the flow. But blood still poured out of the wound, soaking the straw and dripping between the rough wooden planks. Benkei's face had gone pale with shock. Jack tried to silently reassure him, but they both knew the injury was serious.

The cart left the bridge and continued down the gorge road. Jack pulled out the last bandage from his pack and tried to tend to the wound. But, with every rut and rock jolting the cart, this proved impossible. Staunching the bleeding as best he could, he whispered, 'I'll finish off the bandage as soon as the farmer stops.'

Benkei nodded, grimacing each time the cart juddered on its journey.

Eventually the farmer brought his ox to a halt. Peering between the straw bales, Jack saw that they'd reached a small village. The gorge had widened into a forested valley, the powerful river snaking away across the plain. Dusk was not far off.

The farmer tethered his ox to a stable pillar, then walked over and greeted the owner of the village's sole inn.

'Are you in need of new bedding straw?' asked the farmer, bowing humbly.

Smiling agreeably, the innkeeper invited the farmer inside to discuss the sale.

'We have to get off,' Jack whispered to Benkei. 'Can you move?'

Benkei put on a brave face. 'I'll hop if I have to.'

Parting the straw bales, Jack checked the way was clear, then helped him down. With Benkei's arm over his shoulder, Jack carried him into the stable barn. Carefully lowering him into an empty stall, he began dressing the wound. But it was apparent his friend had lost a great deal of blood. His face was ghostly white, his breathing rapid and his skin cool to the touch. Jack immediately set to work on the *Sha* healing ritual. But no sooner had he begun than he heard the sound of horses' hooves pounding down the road.

Forced to leave Benkei a moment, Jack peered through a gap in the stable door. The horses were at the far end of the village. The setting sun glinted off a golden helmet on the lead rider.

'That must be the cart!' yelled Kazuki.

His Scorpion Gang rode over, dismounted and began tearing the goods off it.

'Stop! Stop!' cried the farmer, bursting out of the inn. 'That's all I own.'

Nobu shoved the man to the ground as the rest of the Scorpion Gang continued unloading, trampling the straw in the dirt and discarding the vegetables.

'Look what I've found,' said Hiroto, grinning in satisfaction. He held up Benkei's supply bag that Jack had forgotten in his haste.

'And there's *fresh* blood too,' Goro added.

'Someone must have wounded him,' exclaimed Kazuki with evident glee. He began to scan the village. 'He's bleeding badly, so he can't have got far.'

'How can you be certain it's the *gaijin*?' asked Raiden.

Kazuki shot him an annoyed look. 'Who else is going to hide in a cart? Spread out and look for blood trails.'

Jack rushed back to Benkei's side. He took his arm.

'Leave me, *nanban*,' murmured Benkei, his eyes sunken and dark. 'I'm just . . . a weed.'

Jack hauled him to his feet. 'I *never* leave friends behind.'

Stumbling to the rear of the stables, Jack kicked open the back door. Moving as fast as he could, he took a track up the slope into the forest.

'Where . . . are we going?' groaned Benkei, barely able to stand.

Jack honestly had no idea. They simply needed to get away and find a place to hide. If they could last until nightfall, they might have a chance. The track took them past a Shinto shrine, but it was too small to offer them any refuge.

Back in the village, Jack heard Hiroto shout, 'The *gaijin*'s gone this way!'

They hobbled on in full knowledge that Kazuki and his Scorpion Gang were hot on their trail. Like a baying pack of wolves, they could be heard bursting from the stable and into the forest. Jack was now dragging Benkei along the track, his friend almost a dead weight in his arms.

The shouts of pursuit were drawing ever closer.

As Jack headed deeper into the forest, they came to a junction of paths. One track ran alongside a high wall, but Jack couldn't see any way of clambering over it with the half-conscious Benkei. Their only hope lay in the onset of dusk concealing their escape or Kazuki taking the wrong path. But his Scorpion Gang were almost on top of them and darkness would likely come too late.

Suddenly a gate opened in the wall, and a hand beckoned Jack and Benkei inside.

'This way!' urged a voice.

Desperate and with little alternative, Jack dived through the entrance. An old man, with a grandfatherly face and a full head of shiny black hair, hurriedly escorted them through a garden and into the hall of the secluded house.

'Hide in here,' instructed the old man, sliding back a panel in the wall to reveal a secret alcove. 'And don't make a sound.'

Trusting his and Benkei's life to the old man, Jack carried his friend into the recess. The panel slid shut with a click. Almost immediately, Jack heard furious banging on the gate. After a pause, the old man hollered, 'Patience! My door isn't a drum!'

The old man crunched down the gravel path back to the gate. Jack strained to listen to what was happening, but the alcove dampened the noise outside. He wondered who the old man was and why he'd come to their rescue . . . *if* indeed he had. They were now trapped inside a stranger's house, and for all Jack knew the old man was claiming the credit as well as the reward for capturing them.

23

SHIRYU

Without warning, the panel shot open. Prepared to face a gloating Kazuki, Jack was surprised to discover the old man alone.

'They're gone,' he declared.

Almost unable to believe their good fortune, Jack's sense of relief was cut short when Benkei slumped unconscious to the floor.

'Let's tend to his wound, then we can talk,' said the old man.

He helped Jack carry Benkei into an adjacent room and settle him on a *futon*. With great care, the old man cleansed and re-dressed the spear wound, applying a potent-smelling paste. Reviving him with smelling salts, he then gave Benkei a herbal concoction to drink. The medicine eased Benkei's pain and his shallow breathing soon turned to one of deep sleep.

With Benkei out of immediate danger, the old man showed Jack through to the reception room of his house.

'You must be hungry,' said the old man, disappearing into the kitchen.

While he waited in the reception room, Jack's eyes were drawn to a large scroll hanging upon the wall. Two black *kanji* characters were inked on the paper's surface as if the calligrapher had attacked it in a fit of fury. Raging and brimming with intense energy, the scroll was one of only two pieces of decoration in the *tatami*-matted room – the other being a single white lily displayed in an alcove.

'*Fierce Frog*,' said the old man from behind, translating the *kanji*.

Jack looked over his shoulder to see that the old man had returned with a bowl of fresh noodles and a pot of steaming green tea. He knelt and handed Jack the bowl and a pair of chopsticks. With a grateful bow, Jack tucked into the simple yet welcome meal.

Pouring the tea, the old man explained the meaning of the scroll. 'Many years ago, a *daimyo* was leading his troops to battle when he noticed a tiny frog on the road puff up in readiness to attack the intruders on his territory. Impressed by the frog's fighting spirit against such odds, the *daimyo* urged his men to display similar courage in facing their foes. That same determination and strength is represented in the brush-strokes of this calligraphy.'

Jack took the tea that was offered to him. 'That's one brave frog,' he agreed.

'Brave as you are,' stated the old man, toasting him with his own cup. 'My name is Shiryu and you're welcome in my home.'

Jack bowed. 'I can't thank you enough for saving us, Shiryu. My injured friend is Benkei and I'm –'

'I know who you are,' he said with a kindly smile. 'The

shouts of your pursuers made that clear enough. Jack Fletcher, the *gaijin* samurai. Why do you think I opened the gate in the first place?'

Jack was taken aback. 'So you know by sheltering me you're defying the Shogun?'

Shiryu nodded without concern. 'I owe the Shogun no allegiance. Not since the death of my wife.'

'I'm sorry to hear of your loss,' said Jack. He put down his tea, wondering how many more lives the Shogun's rule would destroy. 'What happened?'

Shiryu's gaze fell upon the white lily in the alcove. 'My precious Yuri was burned at the stake for her Christian beliefs,' he explained, his voice subdued with sorrow. 'Her spirit lives on, though. And, while I'm not of that faith, I consider it my duty as her husband to help her fellow Christians.'

'I appreciate the risk you're taking,' said Jack, thinking how awful it must have been for Shiryu to watch his wife die in such a gruesome way. 'If we can just rest tonight, we'll move on tomorrow.'

'I won't hear of it,' Shiryu insisted. 'You must stay until your friend is healed.'

'But my enemy doesn't give up that easily. Once Kazuki can't find me in the forest, he'll come back *here*.'

Shiryu shook his head confidently. 'I sent them north to the caves. In that region, there are many ways you could have escaped. Besides, I'm well known and respected in these parts. No one will question my word.'

Shiryu finished his tea, then showed Jack to a spare room. 'Sleep soundly, Jack Fletcher. You're safe in my house.'

★

Jack woke to fierce shouting. Fearing the worst, he snatched up his swords and burst from his room to fend off the intruders. The hallway and reception room were deserted. Another battle cry issued forth from the garden. Throwing open the *shoji*, Jack charged out into the bright morning sunlight. Expecting to confront Kazuki and his Scorpion Gang, he was surprised to discover the garden empty and undisturbed.

Lovingly tended, the walled garden was a miniature landscape of pruned trees, bushes and ornate rocks. A trickling stream flowed into a pond filled with a circulating rainbow of koi carp. In the centre stood an open-sided pavilion with a simple arched roof of green tiles. Only now did Jack spot Shiryu kneeling inside, an ink brush in his hand. With a terrific shout, the old man launched himself at the paper scroll spread over a low table. Black ink flew as high as the ceiling as he wielded the brush like a sword. He moved with grace and fluidity, each stroke executed with complete commitment and certainty. Once finished, Shiryu knelt back to regard his work.

Relieved to discover the old man was the cause of the disturbance, Jack resheathed his swords and made his way over a narrow stone bridge to the pavilion. Shiryu smiled at his approach and held up the finished scroll. A powerful scrawl of ink marked the surface, two energetic *kanji* characters joined by a single straight line.

'Stillness in motion,' he translated.

The calligraphy looked impressive, but Jack didn't understand the title's contradiction.

'Observe the pond,' said Shiryu, noting his puzzlement. 'The koi are active this morning, yet the surface of the pond remains calm. *Dochu no sei*. Stillness in motion. The lesson being: no matter how fast the movement, it must originate from a calm and quiet centre. This is the essence of *Shodo*, the path of writing.'

He laid the scroll back on the table.

'Like the koi-filled pond, the *kanji* sit in repose on the paper, but appear as if they are moving.'

Jack nodded in agreement. There was a definite dynamism to Shiryu's calligraphy, like the imperceptible stirring of leaves on a tree or the reflection of oneself in the water.

'For an artist to create such work, the brush has to flow in a free and easy manner. As you may already know, each *kanji* has a set number of strokes that must be inked in a precise order. The brush has to move smoothly from one stroke to the next. This creates a "rhythm" in the calligraphy, a flow of concentration that must not be broken if the character is to take on a dynamic appearance.'

'So what's all the shouting for?' asked Jack. 'I thought *Shodo* was meant to be meditative.'

'That's to focus my *ki*,' explained Shiryu. '*Shodo* is rooted in the heart. One must let life flow into the brush. By doing so, you produce a vivid movement in the brushstroke that reveals your *ki*, your inner energy, in the form of the jet-black ink.'

He directed Jack's gaze to two scrolls hanging in the pavilion. One bore a dynamically inked *kanji*; the other, a more gentle inscription:

勇　　和

'The need for a shout depends entirely upon the subject. Certain words like "Courage" require the additional emphasis of a *kiai*,' he explained, pointing to the first *kanji*. 'While others, such as "Harmony", call for a more graceful and balanced approach, the *ki* generated silently within.'

Shiryu selected a fresh sheet of rice paper and loaded his brush from the inkstone.

'Whatever the subject, an artist must never go back to touch up a character, so the completion of each stroke has to be performed with the *full* force of one's mind, body and spirit, as if one's very life depended upon it.'

Shiryu held his brush above the paper and, in a single silent sweep, prescribed a large circle.

'This is *ensō*. It symbolizes absolute enlightenment, for a circle is empty yet full at the same time. Zen Buddhists believe that the character of the artist is revealed in how they draw an *ensō*. Only a person who is mentally and spiritually complete can create the perfect *ensō*.'

He offered Jack the brush.

'Would you like to try?'

24

ENSŌ

Jack knelt before the table, shaded from the morning sun by the pavilion's roof. A crisp sheet of rice paper lay in front of him, blank as the sky. Beside it was a small rectangular black stick, the solid lump of ink decorated in the form of lotus leaves and flowers. Its end was shiny and wet, having been rubbed and mixed with water in the well of a large square inkstone. Jack picked up the bamboo brush, grasping its shaft midway between his thumb, index and middle fingers. Akiko had taught him how to hold a calligraphy brush and write the most commonly used *kanji*. But with tens of thousands of characters to master, compared to the mere twenty-six of his own alphabet, Jack was still very much a novice.

'Sit up straight, not too close to the table,' advised Shiryu. 'Arm out, brush perpendicular to the paper. Left hand rests on the table, keeping the paper still. As in Zen meditation, remember to breathe steadily and on the *push* of the stroke. Your aim is to become one with the brush, ink and paper. Think of yourself as a *single* wave of motion.'

Heeding Shiryu's advice, Jack dipped the white goat-hair tip of the brush in the inkstone, then boldly drew upon the rice paper in one unbroken movement. The resulting circle was roughly symmetrical – but at the end of his stroke he lifted the brush too early and left a gap.

'Wonderful!' proclaimed Shiryu, much to Jack's surprise. 'Many *Shodo* beginners lack the spiritual strength to paint an *ensō* so decisively. To do so reflects the samurai swordsman in you.'

'But I didn't complete it,' said Jack, considering the praise to be polite rather than truthful.

'That is telling in itself.' Shiryu looked him in the eye as if assessing his soul. 'An *ensō* is the expressive movement of the spirit at a *particular* moment in time. The opening left in your circle suggests your spirit is not separate but part of something greater. That it requires something, or someone, to complete it.'

Jack felt Shiryu touch upon a truth. His thoughts immediately turned to Akiko . . . then Yori, Saburo and Miyuki . . . and finally Jess. He realized that without his friends and family, he was like an incomplete *ensō*. Yet that was one circle that could never be whole again – *unless* he managed to get home.

'I should check on Benkei,' said Jack, not wishing the old man to sense his sadness.

Shiryu nodded sagely. 'I understand. We'll continue the lesson later. You show *great* potential.'

'Please don't cut my leg off,' groaned Benkei, his forehead perspiring and his eyes bulging fearfully. 'I know it smells like rotting fish, but I'm quite attached to it.'

Jack smiled reassuringly and mopped his friend's brow with a cool cloth. 'That's just the medicine that stinks.'

Benkei breathed a sigh of relief. 'For a moment, I thought my dancing days were over!'

Jack helped him drink some soup. 'Shiryu made this especially for you. It contains herbs to reduce the pain.'

'Shiryu!' said Benkei, his eyes widening. 'I've heard of him . . . he's the most famous *Shodo* master in all of Kyushu.'

'Well, he's also a talented herbalist,' replied Jack, lifting the bowl to his friend's lips. 'He says your wound will heal within a week. And you'll be back on your feet the week after.'

'But . . . we can't risk staying that long!' spluttered Benkei. 'They're sure to find us.'

'Shiryu says there are many samurai patrols scouring the forest and caves, so lying low is the best plan for now. Besides, I need the time to practise my sword work.'

Benkei managed a laugh. 'You? Need practice? Not from what I've seen!'

Jack put down the empty soup bowl. 'I was lucky to have survived my fight with Kazuki. Before I lost my finger, we were an equal match, but now . . .'

He trailed off, the reality biting hard. Kazuki had defeated him with disturbing ease. Unless he could resolve the problem of his weakened grip, their next confrontation would end in death. *His* death.

That afternoon Jack devoted himself to Two Heavens practice in the garden. As if he was training at the *Niten Ichi Ryū*, he limbered up, stretching his muscles and flexing his joints. Then he worked his way through the different sword *kata* that Masamoto had taught him. Each prescribed set of moves focused on a particular combat technique: Flint-and-Spark,

Lacquer-and-Glue, the strike of Running Water, Monkey's Body, Autumn Leaf strike and so on. The goal was to internalize the movements of each *kata* so that the techniques could be executed under any circumstance, without thought or hesitation.

Jack had practised these *kata* so many times they were second nature to him . . . at least they should have been.

Rather than flowing in a natural, reflex-like manner, his *kata* were flawed and uneven. The weakness in his left hand, combined with his diminished grip, unbalanced his moves – only marginally, but enough for him to miss his intended target at crucial times. He noticed that the blade of his *waki-zashi* often wavered rather than cutting in a straight line. Much to his annoyance, he even dropped it on two occasions.

With every *kata*, Jack grew increasingly frustrated. He felt like a beginner again. He'd lost the fine control that he'd spent the past four years honing – the control that meant the difference between life and death in a duel. When he lost grip on the *wakizashi* a third time, Jack wearily turned his back on it and left the sword where it fell, the steel blade mocking him like a silver snake in the grass. Finding a rock beside the edge of the pond, he sat down and gazed at the koi carp gliding past without really looking. He massaged his throbbing left hand. The tip of his little finger itched wildly, although there was nothing there to scratch.

How could the loss of something so small have such an impact on his sword skills?

Jack knew the little finger was crucial for grip on the handle. It also helped him judge the delicate balance of the sword and to execute *ten-uchi* correctly – this was the twisting technique upon the handle, like the wringing of a towel, that caused the blade to strike its target with a sharp snapping force that broke any initial resistance. Without *ten-uchi*, the attack was only half as powerful. But Jack didn't have a clue where to begin adjusting his overall technique. He desperately needed Masamoto's expert advice. His guardian would know how to compensate for the lack of a fingertip. But with Masamoto banished to a remote Buddhist temple on Mount Iawo there was no hope of gaining his wisdom. Jack was on his own and at a loss for ideas.

'A samurai without belief has lost the battle before it has begun,' said Shiryu, who had been watching Jack's struggle from the pavilion. 'Maybe I can be of assistance?'

'I appreciate your offer,' said Jack, bowing his head. 'But, with respect, what would a *Shodo* master know about the way of the sword?'

Shiryu smiled. 'Everything.'

25

REVERSE GRIP

'The way of the sword and the way of the brush are one and the same,' explained Shiryu, picking up Jack's discarded *wakizashi*. 'Yuri's priest told me that in the West you say "the pen is mightier than the sword". But in Japan we say *bunbu ichi* – the pen and sword in accord.'

He held the brush beside the blade, uniting the tools of art and war.

'If you think of the paper as your opponent and the brush as your sword, then the connection becomes clear. In *Shodo*, each stroke must be delivered like the slash of a samurai sword, yet the brush must be held in a relaxed manner and manoeuvred without loss of controlled calmness. The same is true for a warrior and his sword in a duel. Without a focused mind and a complete commitment of spirit, the fight is over before the blade has been drawn.'

He returned Jack his *wakizashi*.

'Why not grip the sword like one holds the brush?' Shiryu suggested.

Jack stared at the old *Shodo* master, perplexed at the idea. They were totally opposite techniques. A samurai sword was gripped primarily by the middle, fourth and little fingers, whereas a brush was held between the thumb, fore and middle fingers. The shift, while apparently small, represented a major alteration of technique.

Disheartened though he was, Jack realized it was worth a try. He reminded himself that Kazuki had overcome his own hand injury to return a stronger fighter. If his rival could manage such a feat, then he was determined to do so too.

Jack stood and retook his position in the garden. Holding his *katana* in his right hand and the *wakizashi* in his left, using the new grip, he resumed his practice. Working through the first *kata*, it became immediately apparent that the imbalance of the *wakizashi* was a problem. He stopped and slid his hand down the handle.

'In *Shodo*, the little finger is required to do nothing, just lie naturally,' explained Shiryu, helping Jack to position his fingers correctly. 'So don't concern yourself about the missing tip.'

With the sword now evenly weighted, Jack tried again. He understood the new technique would take time to master, but the first few moves passed with surprising fluidity. Gaining confidence from such progress, Jack sped up . . . then in the middle of an overhead strike, the *wakizashi* flew from his grasp. It spun through the air, whipping past Shiryu's startled face to pierce a pillar of the pavilion.

Jack hung his head, both embarrassed and disappointed. 'Sorry, I don't think it's working . . .'

'Even when you fall on your face, you're still moving forward,' encouraged Shiryu, retrieving the *wakizashi* for him.

Persuaded to carry on, Jack started more slowly this time.

But, despite his initial success, his *kata* moves remained stilted, the *wakizashi* feeling heavy and cumbersome in his altered grasp.

'Let the sword float in your hand,' advised Shiryu with sharp observation. 'Just as with a brush, a gentle grip is required for the precise and pure motions of a samurai.'

Only now was Jack aware that he'd been tensing his hand muscles to compensate for his little finger. As soon as he relaxed his hold, the *kata* began to flow more freely. His *wakizashi* cut the air in perfect unison with his *katana*. By his fifth run-through of the *kata*, he achieved the final move without a single mistake.

Shiryu quietly applauded his success. Jack bowed his appreciation in return.

'You could even reverse the *wakizashi* in your grip,' suggested Shiryu with a wry smile. 'That would *really* confuse your opponent.'

Jack grinned back at his new sensei. It was a radical idea, but one that might just work.

Two weeks passed undisturbed, during which Jack practised hard. The new hold soon became familiar as an old glove, while the reverse grip proved to be a formidable and revolutionary sword technique. Although less powerful and more limited in range, the reversed blade enabled him to execute hidden slashes, unexpected stabs and full coverage deflections. He could even strike to the rear and, combined with his *katana*, perform devastating double cross-cuts that the traditional Two Heavens style wouldn't allow.

Yet, despite this progress, Jack was mindful that the new technique would only work in certain close-quarter situations. So he trained himself to fluidly switch between forward and reverse grips.

A clever tiger hides its claws, the Grandmaster had once said in reference to a ninja's tactical use of surprise. Jack knew it was important that he saved this secret technique for the right moment.

At the end of each training session, Jack joined Shiryu in the pavilion for a *Shodo* lesson. The old master had explained, 'A samurai warrior well versed in the arts of peace is strong for the arts of war. *Shodo* cultivates a strength of mind and composure that will allow you to respond more instantly to an opponent's attack. By removing the hesitation in your brushstroke, we'll remove any hesitation in your sword strike too.'

The 'spiritual forging', as Shiryu liked to call it, lasted until nightfall . . . or else Benkei complained for lack of company in the house. Each lesson began with a fresh sheet of rice paper and a new set of *kanji* to learn. Jack would kneel beside Shiryu, copying the brushstrokes for each character, memorizing their order and attempting to put 'rhythm' and *ki* into them. He would repeat the characters over and over, focusing on quietening his mind so that he could become one with the brush, ink and paper. Familiar with meditation as a result of Sensei Yamada's Zen philosophy lessons, Jack found this aspect the easiest to master. But the essence of *Shodo* – stillness in motion – eluded him.

Nevertheless, by the end of the first week, Shiryu had been

impressed enough with Jack's progress to ask him what *kanji* characters he'd like to learn next. Without a second thought, Jack asked for the Five Rings:

地　　水　　火　　風　　空
Earth　Water　Fire　Wind　Sky

Shiryu smiled appreciatively. 'A powerful set of *kanji*,' he remarked, pointing to a scroll hanging from the eastern beam of the pavilion. Upon it, Shiryu had inscribed a poem in *kanji* in his exquisite hand:

> If we always look at the earth,
> we do not see the sky.

'A *Shodo* master often seeks the Ring of Sky as a means of connecting to the energy of the universe,' he explained.

Jack tried to contain his surprise at the idea of a *Shodo* master using ninja techniques to write.

'The element of Sky inspires our creative nature,' Shiryu continued, 'and nourishes our ability for self-expression.'

With a flourish, he inked the strokes for Sky. The *kanji* was so charged with energy, it seemed to soar off the page.

He invited Jack to follow his movements. Jack loaded his brush and tried to imitate Shiryu's work. He produced an admirable likeness, but spotted an incomplete stroke and without thinking went back to touch up the character. Shiryu immediately stopped him.

'Just as a mistake in a sword duel results in death, in *Shodo* all mistakes are final too.'

He handed Jack a blank sheet.

'Start afresh. Remember, a *Shodo* artist endeavours to succeed before the brush even touches the paper, in much the same way that a skilled samurai will spiritually win *before* drawing his sword.'

Nodding, Jack pictured the *kanji* for Sky in his head before committing brush to paper. Only when he could see the whole form in his mind's eye did he begin. This time the strokes were faultless.

Within a few days, as a result of Shiryu's excellent tuition, Jack had mastered all five of the elements. He finished the *kanji* for Wind with a small flick of the brush, then handed his work to Shiryu for inspection.

Shiryu raised his eyebrows appreciatively, then glanced at Jack.

'A word of warning: never let an enemy observe you write. By studying your *Shodo* form, they could uncover your inner sword techniques and defeat you. That little flick told me a great deal about how you finish a cut.'

Jack was taken aback. He'd never realized there was so much to the art of *Shodo*. Its knowledge seemed to be as limitless as the sky itself.

26

A GOOD DEED

Jack's brush hovered over the paper, uncertain how to begin. Shiryu had presented him with the most difficult and complex *kanji* yet:

躊躇

The two characters meant 'Hesitation', which was exactly what he was doing now.

Gently taking his hand, Shiryu steadied the tip of Jack's brush.

'In *Shodo*, the body reflects the mind,' he said, his voice soft as a stream. 'A shaking brush not only makes it difficult to paint stable *kanji*, but it also indicates a nervous mental state. As you prepare to write, the tip of your brush *must* be still.' He let go of Jack's hand. 'It's the same for the sword. If you notice your opponent's *kissaki* begin to tremble, this indicates *suki* – a break in composure and concentration. And *that* is your opportunity to attack.'

Taking a deep calming breath, Jack refocused. After two weeks of constant practice, the brush was becoming as familiar in his hand as his *katana*. With a loud *kiai*, he put brush to paper *without* hesitation. The tip danced across the surface, moving from stroke to stroke with effortless grace. Jack felt his *ki* flow through the bamboo and into the ink. For a moment, his soul seemed rooted in the *kanji*, the characters suddenly clear and precise in his mind. With a last out-breath, he inked the final stroke.

Shiryu knelt forward and admired Jack's work with quiet astonishment. '*Dochu no sei*,' he uttered.

Jack gave a humble and surprised bow, his *kanji* somehow having attained 'stillness in motion'.

'The student is only as good as his teacher,' he said.

Shiryu laughed. 'No,' he corrected. 'The teacher is only as good as his student. And there's nothing more I can teach you that time and practice won't.'

'Am I glad to hear that!' cried Benkei, strolling over the bridge, only a slight limp visible. 'No disrespect, Shiryu, but I've got cabin fever. And I'm not a bird that can stay caged for long.'

'With your peacock feathers, I can see why,' replied Shiryu, eyeing Benkei's unconventional kimono with wry amusement.

'No bird flies too high, if he soars with his own wings,' Benkei shot back in good grace, flapping his wide sleeves and jumping in the air as if to take off. 'Thanks to you, I can fly again.'

'Benkei's right,' said Jack. 'Grateful as we are, we need to move on. Not only for your safety, but we have a journey to complete.'

Shiryu nodded. 'All birds must leave the nest at some point.'

Jack and Benkei stood at the gate that had opened so unexpectedly two weeks before and saved their lives. And it was here that they said their goodbyes to the old *Shodo* master. Shiryu had prepared a fresh bag of supplies for their journey and given Jack a new straw hat to wear. Jack pulled the brim low to shield his face. Finally, Shiryu bowed and handed him a small scroll.

'Something to remember me by,' he said, 'and remind you where to look for inspiration.'

Jack carefully unrolled it. At the top a perfect *enso* had been drawn, as round as the midday sun. Below was Shiryu's poem of Earth and Sky. Jack smiled, the significance of the gift not lost on him. He stowed the scroll in his pack next to the *rutter* and bowed his thanks to Shiryu. 'My father used to say, good friends are hard to find, difficult to leave and impossible to forget. I'll always remember your kindness, Shiryu.'

With a final bow, Jack and Benkei headed into the forest. Shiryu remained in the gateway until they rounded a bend, then the old man disappeared from view.

As they followed the main trail south, the morning sun glimmered through the canopy, dappling the ground with golden leaves of light. A soft breeze played among the branches, giving the impression that the forest was breathing in the new day, while birds fluttered from tree to tree, singing brightly to one another.

'Feels good to be walking again!' said Benkei, skipping along the track.

Jack was glad to be back on the road too. Every step took them a little closer to Nagasaki and the possibility of home. But he remained wary. Although Shiryu had assured him that the search parties had moved on, he still kept an eye out for any signs of a patrol. Kazuki may have lost their trail, but his rival was tenacious and Jack had no doubt that their paths would cross again.

'Do you know where we're going?' asked Jack as they followed a zigzagging trail down the valley side.

Benkei nodded. 'Shiryu suggested we head towards Ōzu, then follow the Shira River to the castle town of Kumamoto.'

'We want to avoid such towns, if we can,' said Jack, anxious at the thought of entering a samurai stronghold.

'Not much choice, I'm afraid,' replied Benkei, leaping over a log. 'That's where we have to catch the ferry across Shimabara Bay. But then it's only a hop, skip and a jump to Nagasaki.'

Benkei enacted each of the actions as he spoke, dancing down the slope.

Shiryu's herbs certainly did the trick, thought Jack, amazed by his friend's recovery and boundless energy.

'How long will it take?'

'A week at most.'

Heartened by this news, Jack couldn't help but bound alongside his friend. They reached a dirt road running through the forest. It appeared to be well used, so they kept to one side just in case they heard any samurai approaching and needed to hide.

Heading west, they stopped by a stream for an early lunch of cold noodles before continuing on their way. Jack was eager to press on and take advantage of the deserted road. But by mid-afternoon Benkei's limp had become more pronounced and their pace slowed.

'Ōzu shouldn't be much further,' announced Benkei, pausing on the road.

Jack noticed him massaging the stiffness from his thigh and suggested, 'Let's rest there for the ni–'

A piercing scream interrupted him.

'That's the sound of trouble,' Benkei hissed and dived into the bushes.

Jack joined him as another scream broke the forest silence. A girl's scream.

Moving swiftly, Jack headed in the direction of the cries. His feet barely made a noise as he trod lightly between the bracken and twigs. But Benkei, who didn't know the ninja art of stealth-walking, ploughed through the undergrowth like a startled pheasant. Jack turned and put a finger to his lips, urging his friend to be quiet. They crept the last few paces in silence. Remaining hidden behind a tree, they peered round to see three rough-looking men on the road, surrounding a defenceless girl.

'Come on!' grunted one of them, a bear of a man with bushy eyebrows and a beard that looked like he'd had a fight with a thorn bush and lost. 'Dance for us!'

The girl, maybe sixteen, with brown eyes, rose-red cheeks and shoulder-length dark hair, was in tears, terrified for her life. She wore a green silk kimono that was torn at the shoulder and a string of jade-coloured beads that hung from her hair. With as much composure as she could muster, the girl began a formal dance, moving her arms in graceful arcs and shaking her head so that the beads jingled.

The two other men, one portly, wearing a dirty red bandanna, and the other a scrawny runt with a ponytail, laughed at her efforts. Ridiculing her, they started throwing sticks and stones. The girl squealed in pain as the missiles pelted her legs and feet.

'Dance faster!' ordered the bearded man.

Sobbing, the girl continued to twirl like a wounded butterfly.

'Bandits!' spat Benkei in disgust.

Jack reached for his sword. Bandits were the curse of the countryside – low-life criminals and dishonoured warriors who pillaged defenceless villages and robbed innocent travellers. As a samurai, Jack couldn't just stand by and watch this poor girl be assaulted . . . maybe even killed. But a hand upon his arm held him back. Benkei was furiously shaking his head.

'You can't risk getting involved,' he warned under his breath.

'Shiryu took a risk to save us,' reminded Jack. 'And one good deed deserves another.'

27

HERO WORSHIP

'I'm bored with this dance,' declared the bearded bandit. 'I think we should cut her out of the show, don't you?'

Grinning at his nodding associates, he drew a rusty blade from his belt and approached the girl. Before she could run away, the bandit with the ponytail grabbed her by the hair. The girl struggled in his bony arms as the bearded bandit raised his knife to her bare neck.

'Let her go!' ordered Jack, stepping out from behind the tree.

The three bandits spun round to see who their challenger was. Mindful to keep his face hidden, Jack nonetheless ensured the men noticed the two samurai swords on his hip.

The bearded bandit laughed. 'Honour isn't dead then? A noble samurai come to the rescue of a damsel in distress!' he mocked.

'There's no need for bloodshed,' replied Jack, taking his time to assess his opponents and work out the best tactics. 'Release her and go on your way.'

The bearded bandit considered this for a moment. 'Of

course . . .' he replied, throwing the girl to the ground. 'But we *won't* be going anywhere.'

The three bandits seized their weapons. The scrawny one picked up a staff leaning against a tree, while the portly bandit took out a pair of short-handled *kama*, the sickle-shaped blades sharpened into deadly points. The bearded leader swapped his knife for a *chigiriki*. He swung the short flail in tight arcs, making the spiked iron weight at the end of the chain whistle menacingly through the air.

Jack stood his ground, yet to draw his swords. Benkei remained hidden behind the tree, wide-eyed at Jack's boldness.

The portly bandit scraped his *kama* blades together as if preparing to slice up *sushi*. 'We eat young samurai for lunch,' he warned.

'Well, I eat old bandits for breakfast,' replied Jack.

Exchanging an amused look, the three men grunted with laughter at Jack's retort. Then they attacked.

Jack had decided not to resort to his swords, unless forced to. He planned to incapacitate the bandits, save the girl and quickly move on. Leaving evidence of a bloody fight might draw the attention of a samurai patrol. So Jack's intention was for the encounter to be quick and painless . . . *painless for him at least*.

Before the bandits got close, he threw the rock concealed in his right hand. With sharp accuracy gained from his *shuriken* training, he struck the scrawny bandit in the centre of his forehead. The stunned man stopped dead in his tracks and collapsed face first in the dirt. Next, Jack kicked up the earth at his feet, sending a clod into the eyes of the *kama*-wielding bandit, stalling his attack. As the bearded bandit took a swipe with his *chigiriki*, Jack dropped into a crouch, the flail passing over his head, and rolled towards the blinded *kama* bandit. He performed a spinning sweep kick, knocking the man's legs from under him, and followed up with an axe kick. His heel struck the fallen bandit's solar plexus like a blacksmith's hammer, cracking a couple of ribs. Wheezing for breath, the bandit let go of his lethal *kama* to clutch his crushed chest.

Jack dived away as the bearded bandit lunged for him again. The *chigiriki* whipped through the air, just missing his shoulder.

'I'll pound you into a pulp, samurai!' vowed the bandit, bringing the flail down as if he was beating a drum.

Jack leapt aside. With lightning speed, he roundhouse-kicked the bandit in the thigh. The man staggered under the blow, but kept his feet. Jack had judged this one would be his toughest opponent and kicked him again. Howling in pain, the bandit foamed at the mouth as he swung his flail in furious swipes. The *chigiriki* shot towards Jack's head. He ducked at the last second, the iron tip rocketing past and clipping the bark of a nearby tree. Chunks of wood flew in all directions.

Roaring in frustrated fury, the bandit swung again and again. Jack was forced on the retreat, the *chigiriki* whipping either side of him as he dodged to left and right. There was no chance to retaliate – just survive. Then, in an overzealous attack from the bandit, the spiked weight of the flail became wedged in the fork of an overhanging branch. With the weapon temporarily out of action, Jack charged at him with Demon Horn Fist. His head collided with the man's gut and the bandit staggered backwards, losing his grip on the *chigiriki*.

Jack then launched a barrage of punches and body kicks. Yet however hard Jack hit him the man wouldn't go down.

The bandit front-kicked Jack in the chest, sending him barrelling into a thorn bush. As Jack fought to untangle himself, the bandit rushed back to the tree and yanked out his *chigiriki*. He whirled the weapon above his head and strode towards Jack, intent on fulfilling his deadly promise. Jack still struggled to free himself.

The bandit was about to crack his skull in half when there was a surprised grunt of pain. Then he toppled forward to land with a heavy *thud*.

Benkei stood over the bearded bandit, a broken branch in his hands.

'What took you so long?' asked Jack, breathless from the fight.

'I was waiting for the right moment,' replied Benkei, resting his foot triumphantly on the back of the unconscious bandit.

At this, the girl came running over and prostrated herself in front of them.

'*Arigatō gozaimasu,*' she sobbed and began to repeatedly bow her head to the floor in gratitude.

Realizing she might never stop, Benkei asked, 'What's your name?'

'Junjun.' She glanced up at him with eyes still red from tears.

'Well, Junjun, there's no need to cry any more . . . or bow,' reassured Benkei. With a flick of his wrist, he conjured up a pink flower and handed it to her. 'You're safe with us.'

The unexpected appearance of the blossom brought a shy

smile to Junjun's face. She stared at him with a combination of relief, thankfulness and awe.

'I'm Benkei the Great,' he announced, clearly enjoying the hero worship.

'You *were* great!' she breathed, unable to take her eyes off him.

More than happy for Benkei to receive the credit and attention for the rescue, Jack used the moment to adjust his hat and keep his face hidden from the girl.

'What were you doing in the forest on your own?' asked Benkei.

Junjun, clasping the flower to her chest, replied, 'I was returning from an errand . . . promoting our *kabuki* show in Ōzu.'

'*Kabuki?*'

Junjun nodded enthusiastically. 'It's a new style of dance and drama from Kyoto. Okuni, our troupe leader, is the founder of the style. It's proving *very* popular.' She pointed down the road. 'We're holding a show this evening in town. Perhaps you'd like to join us as my honoured guests.'

'A dancing troupe!' exclaimed Benkei, his eyes twinkling with excitement. 'We'd love to –'

'That's very kind of you,' cut in Jack, 'but we have to move on.'

Benkei turned to Jack, his expression one of protesting dismay.

Junjun tried to hide her disappointment. 'Well, if you change your mind, we're performing in the market square. Now I must get back for rehearsals, otherwise Okuni will worry. Thank you for coming to my rescue.'

Junjun bowed her farewell, then scampered off down the road.

'Be careful!' Benkei shouted after her. Then he glared at Jack. 'Why can't we see the *kabuki* show? Life shouldn't be all fight and no play. We're staying the night there anyway. And Junjun seemed lovely . . .'

Jack regretfully shook his head. 'I'd be easily spotted and you certainly stand out in a crowd. It's an unnecessary risk.'

'And fighting three bandits isn't a risk?' shot back Benkei.

Jack didn't reply. He'd suddenly noticed the scrawny bandit with the ponytail was missing.

28

SWORD TEST

'Time to go!' said Jack, retrieving his pack from behind the tree.

Their dispute forgotten, Benkei picked up the supply bag and they both hurried down the road in the direction of Ōzu. But they hadn't gone twenty paces when a group of men stepped from the forest and blocked their path. Jack and Benkei turned to head back the other way, only to discover they were surrounded.

'That's the samurai who attacked us!' whined the scrawny bandit, a nasty red welt marking his forehead.

The bandit gang, armed to the teeth, closed in on Jack and Benkei.

'I told you we should have gone with Junjun,' said Benkei, unnerved by the lethal array of weapons that now encircled them: serrated knives, studded clubs, samurai swords, spiked chains and barbed spears.

Jack unsheathed both his *katana* and *wakizashi*. This time there would be no avoiding a bloody confrontation.

'I'll cut a path through,' he hissed under his breath, 'then we'll make a run for it.'

Benkei nodded his agreement at the plan. But, as Jack raised his swords to attack, a net dropped from a tree above. Its weight knocked them to the ground and the mesh entangled their limbs. Jack fought to cut through the ropes, but the bandits leapt on them in an instant, quickly disarming him.

'The samurai is a . . . *gaijin*!' exclaimed the scrawny bandit in shock as Jack's hat became dislodged.

The gang crowded closer to gawp at their remarkable catch. Then they stepped away as a brute of a man barged his way to the front. Shaven-headed with a thick scar across his right cheek, he was dressed in a mismatch of stolen samurai armour: a red and white breastplate, brown shoulder pads and black shinguards. In his right hand, he carried a bloodstained battle-axe. From the fearful respect shown by the other bandits, he was evidently the leader of the outlaws.

'I hear you ruined the entertainment, *gaijin*,' he snarled.

'Your men didn't appear to be enjoying the show,' replied Jack, secretly trying to work his hand into his pack so he could retrieve a *shuriken*.

The leader stepped on his wrist. '*Don't* try any games with me.'

Jack gritted his teeth as the bandit leader twisted his foot and crunched the bones in Jack's hand.

'You're a very sought-after individual,' he continued. 'I've never known so many samurai patrols in this forest. And to think that *I* found you –'

'Give that back!' cried a bandit.

The leader fumed as two of his men began arguing over the possession of Jack's *katana*.

'I got to it first,' spat the other bandit, steadfastly holding on to the handle.

A tussle broke out between them and punches were thrown.

'Enough!' declared the leader, bringing his axe crashing down. The two men jumped apart a split second before the axe head cleaved them in half. 'The sword's now mine.'

He snatched the *katana* from the bandit's grasp. Inspecting its gleaming blade, his eyes lit up at the name etched upon the steel.

'A *Shizu* sword!' he uttered in astonishment. 'These are legendary. I've heard they can slice through three warriors in a single stroke!'

'Impossible,' declared a potbellied bandit with a drooping moustache. 'No blade can do such a thing.'

'If it's sharp enough, it could,' said a bandit with buck teeth.

'Never. At some point, the sword would get stuck in bone.'

An argument erupted among the bandits as they debated the possibility of such a feat.

'*Quiet!*' shouted the leader, his face purple with rage at his men's disorder. 'There's only one way to prove the legend. We need to test these swords . . . properly. By *tameshigiri*.'

The suggestion was greeted with enthusiastic shouts. A moment later, Jack and Benkei were hauled from the net and laid upon the ground. Held down by several strong pairs of hands, they were helpless as their ankles and wrists were bound with rope. Jack was then staked to the earth, Benkei thrown on top and his body tied to Jack's.

Neither of them could believe what was happening.

'If I'd known he was going to test swords on *us*, I'd have

swallowed stones to stop the blade,' muttered Benkei, humour his only defence against his rising panic.

Jack struggled to free his hands. He'd been quick enough to tense his muscles when the bandits had bound him, so he now had a little slack in the knots. Working his wrist back and forth, he tried to pull out a hand. But the rope was still viciously tight and he felt his skin scraping off as he yanked at the bonds.

'But we need one more body,' said the buck-toothed bandit.

'Of course,' agreed the leader, grinning. 'Where's that dancing girl?'

Two bandits dragged a screaming Junjun from the forest and began to lash her to Benkei.

'No!' pleaded Benkei, his eyes wide in shock at seeing the dancer recaptured. 'She's done you no harm. Let her go.'

'I would if I could,' sighed the leader in mock sympathy. 'But we need to *prove* the legend.'

'Then put her beneath us,' urged Jack, realizing Junjun would have the greatest chance of survival there. He also hoped if the bandits changed their positions, he might get an opportunity to fight his way free.

'Such gallantry when facing certain death,' remarked the leader, nodding approvingly. 'You are a true samurai.'

Ignoring their pleas, he took several practice swings with the *katana*. The blade whistled through the air, its razor-sharp edge glinting like a guillotine. Junjun fell silent with fear, her tearful eyes following the steel as it rose and fell. In her hand, she still clasped Benkei's flower.

'What about the reward for the *gaijin*?' asked the potbellied bandit. 'Shouldn't we keep him alive?'

The leader shook his head and smirked, 'Dead or alive, the order said. Besides, the Shogun might double the reward if I cut him in half!'

The bandit gang laughed heartily at their leader's joke. But Jack didn't find their predicament funny in the least. They were bound to stakes, at the mercy of a brutal bandit. Try as he might, he couldn't untie his hands and soon all three of them would be slaughtered like pigs.

The bandit leader stood over them, contemplating his cut. 'Should I aim for the chest, stomach or hips?'

'The stomach,' advised the buck-toothed bandit. 'Less bone. Only their spines to chop through.'

Nodding in agreement, the leader lined up the *katana* with Junjun's bellybutton, then raised the sword above his head. 'Let's hope for your sake, *gaijin*, the legend isn't true.'

At that moment, Jack pulled his right hand free, but it was too late. The *Shizu* blade was already slicing down.

29

FOREVER BOUND

Junjun screamed as the *katana*'s razor edge scythed towards her stomach. A spray of blood and gore splattered Jack's face. He tensed, waiting for the steel to cleave through him too.

But the searing cut never came.

Instead, he heard a strangled guttural cry from the bandit leader. Blinking away the blood, Jack saw an arrow embedded in the man's throat. His eyes bulging in shock, the leader dropped the *Shizu* sword and clasped his pulsating neck. His fingers ran red and he spewed up more gobs of blood.

Above Jack, Junjun was sobbing yet alive, the *katana* blade never having made contact.

With the attack so sudden and swift, the other bandits merely stared open-mouthed as their leader collapsed to his knees. Then more arrows flew and the gang of outlaws broke into a wild panic. Not knowing which way to run, they barged one another out of the way in a desperate bid to escape with their lives. The scrawny bandit fled for the cover of the trees, but an arrow struck him in the back. The potbellied bandit, tripping over him, hit his head on a rock and ended up sprawled in the earth, before being trampled by the other bandits.

'Someone's ruffled their feathers!' said Benkei, glancing at their fallen leader, who was now quivering on the ground in his death throes.

Amid the chaos, Jack fumbled at the knots binding his left hand. From his position staked to the ground, he could only see the stampeding feet of the bandits. But there was no question in his mind that a samurai patrol had ambushed them. And he didn't want to be around when they finished massacring the outlaws.

Then Jack spotted a lone samurai thundering down the road astride a white stallion. Clad in a turquoise-blue suit of armour with a bronze face mask, the warrior wielded a formidable Japanese bow and was unleashing arrow after arrow with deadly accuracy. Jack, Benkei and Junjun watched in amazement as the warrior laid waste to the bandit gang. Jack had rarely witnessed such archery skills, especially on horseback.

'Wait, it's only *one* samurai!' cried the buck-toothed bandit, furiously waving his spear for attention.

He managed to rally a few men and they rushed to intercept their attacker. Two were felled by arrow fire before they got anywhere near. But the other three met the warrior head on. Now at close quarters, the mounted samurai switched from bow to sword. The bandits each tried to land a blow, but the samurai was too quick. Blade met blade, every attack blocked and lethally countered.

They tried to surround the samurai and attack from opposite sides, but the stallion – coaxed by a tug on the reins – reared up and lashed out with its hooves. The bandits scattered . . . but were a fraction too slow. One was kicked in the chest.

Another was trampled under hoof and barely managed to crawl into the bushes with his life.

The buck-toothed bandit alone kept his distance. He thrust his spear at the samurai. But, with a single sword swipe, the warrior cut the shaft in two and its barbed tip clattered to the ground. The samurai then heel-kicked the bandit in the face. There was a sickening *crunch* as his nose imploded and his two front teeth were knocked out. He staggered backwards, howling in agony and spitting blood. Glancing at the useless stump of spear in his hand, the toothless bandit turned tail and ran off down the road.

With all the outlaws dead, wounded or fleeing, the samurai warrior dismounted the white stallion and strode over to Jack and the others. Still staked to the ground, the three of them were powerless to escape.

'I hope this samurai doesn't want to test any swords!' whispered Benkei.

Jack frantically stretched his fingers for his *katana* lying on the earth beside the dead bandit leader . . . but the red leather handle was just out of reach.

Staring at Jack, the warrior picked up the sword and held it aloft. In two quick swipes, the blade cut through their bonds. The three of them rolled off one another with relief.

While Benkei helped a trembling Junjun to her feet, Jack warily approached their saviour.

'Thank you,' he said, bowing yet not taking his eyes off the warrior. 'But who do we have the honour of thanking?'

The samurai removed the turquoise helmet and bronze mask. A cascade of jet-black hair unravelled past the warrior's shoulders. A girl's face was revealed, eyes dark as ebony, skin like cherry blossom, and with a smile that warmed Jack's heart like no other.

'AKIKO!' he gasped.

With complete disregard for Japanese formalities, he embraced his friend. 'Is it *really* you?'

Akiko returned his hug and whispered into his ear, '*Forever bound to one another*.'

30

OKUNI

With Akiko in his arms, Jack felt time stand still. All his pain and worries melted away. It was as if the *ensō* inside him was whole again. He now repeated their vow – the one they'd made on the battlefields of Tenno-ji, when the bond between them had become unbreakable.

'*Forever bound to one another,*' he whispered back.

But how could Akiko be here in Kyushu? She was supposed to be in Toba, caring for her mother. After all, they'd said their final heart-wrenching farewells in the Iga mountains the previous year. Her appearance now was like a dream to him.

For a moment, they simply gazed into each other's eyes, their breathless silence expressing more than words ever could.

A polite cough interrupted their embrace. 'I don't wish to break up this happy reunion,' said Benkei, an urgency to his voice, 'but the bandits are coming back.'

Akiko stepped away from Jack, suddenly self-conscious of their display of affection.

'And there's a samurai patrol not far behind me,' she revealed, regaining her composure and handing Jack back his *katana*.

This double threat impelled them all into action. Jack retrieved his *wakizashi* from the dead leader, while Benkei gathered their belongings. Junjun, however, appeared to be in a state of severe shock. She stood unmoving, her large brown eyes fixated on Jack, the trauma of the *tameshigiri* evidently too much for her.

'Y . . . you're . . . the *gaijin* samurai,' Junjun finally managed to stutter. 'And it's true . . . your hair is *golden*.'

Jack's hand went to his head, his straw hat missing. He realized that Benkei's advice not to get involved in the girl's predicament may have been hardhearted, but it had been prudent. Now Junjun might tell the samurai patrol.

'Well, I don't see any *gaijin*,' Benkei stated, shooting her a conspiratorial wink as he plonked Jack's hat back on his head. 'Do you?'

For a moment Junjun crinkled her nose in puzzlement, then it dawned on her what he was implying.

'No,' she replied earnestly. 'I *never* saw any *gaijin*.'

Angry shouts warned them that the bandits were getting closer.

'Let's go,' urged Akiko, mounting her stallion and taking up the reins.

With Junjun offering to guide them to Ōzu, they hastened down the road. A few well-aimed arrows from Akiko kept the outlaws at bay as they made their escape. After two more fell by the wayside, the bandits ceased their pursuit and raided their slain comrades for weapons and spoils instead.

'Bandits have *no* honour!' exclaimed Akiko, disgusted by their immoral behaviour.

But Jack was just relieved the gang had given up the chase.

Yet this was no reason to slow down. 'How close is that samurai patrol?' he asked, running alongside Akiko's horse.

'In the last village, a little way up the valley,' she replied.

'Were they still searching for me?'

'The whole of Japan is looking for you.'

'Well, I'm glad it's *you* who found me first,' said Jack, grinning up at her.

'And not a moment too soon,' added Benkei, hurrying along beside them. 'Any later and we'd have been sliced and diced like *sushi*!'

The forest had given way to paddy fields and the road now followed a broad lazy stretch of the Shira River. Further along, a small town hugged its banks and spread out like the fronds of a pond from the water's edge. Even from a distance, Ōzu was evidently busy. A steady stream of foot traffic crossed a wooden bridge at its centre.

'It's market day,' explained Junjun, pointing to an open field on the opposite bank filled with stalls, farmers and local townsfolk.

'We should avoid the town, if we can,' said Jack, searching for a path across the paddy fields.

'That might look suspicious,' said Akiko. 'Besides, we can't afford to waste time. If you walk by my side, with your head down, people will think you're my retainer and not give you a second look.'

Trusting in Akiko's judgement, Jack kept close to her horse's flank. They entered Ōzu, Benkei taking the weight off his aching leg with a strong forked stick Junjun had found for him in the forest. The tea houses and shops were thronged with visitors and farmers from the neighbouring villages. So much so that no one paid Jack and his friends any attention.

As they crossed the town's bridge to the market itself, they heard the twang of a *shamisen* and the *clack* of wooden clappers coming from a tented encampment. Two rectangular marquees with red and white vertical stripes were pitched inside a circular camp curtain. As Junjun stepped through a gap in the curtain, Jack spotted a wooden stage upon which two young women were dancing – their flamboyant movements like two birds-of-paradise competing in a courtship ritual.

'Junjun! There you are!'

The music stopped and a beautiful woman in a purple and green kimono came running across. Her hair was styled into a curving bob that perched on her head like a black falcon with folded wings. Her flawless face was painted white as snow with her lips stained the colour of rubies. Black and red make-up rimmed her eyes and her brows had been redrawn like the fine strokes of a *Shodo* brush. She reminded Jack of an exquisite porcelain doll.

Despite her delicate appearance, the angry look on her face told a different story.

'*Where* have you been?' demanded the woman. 'Rehearsals started ages ago.'

'Sorry, Okuni,' said Junjun, looking apologetically down at her feet. 'But I was attacked by bandits. These samurai saved me.'

With formality and practised grace, Okuni bowed her respects to Jack and Akiko. She smiled openly at Benkei, whose colourful appearance seemed to garner her approval.

'It's heartening to discover there are still *true* samurai in this land,' she said, addressing Akiko. 'Junjun is one of our star performers; we'd be lost without her. Please honour us by being our guests for this evening's *kabuki* show.'

'I'm sorry, but we cannot stay,' replied Akiko.

'It's not to be missed,' insisted Okuni with evident pride in her voice. 'We perform in towns and festivals all over Japan, and even for *daimyos* and the Imperial Court.'

'Another time perhaps. I'm afraid we have an urgent engagement in Kumamoto.'

'But it's late already,' she protested, indicating the sun sinking low on the horizon. 'You won't get there tonight. Why not rest here?'

The sound of pounding hooves caused them all to turn. A patrol of six mounted samurai thundered down the road on the opposite bank. Jack fought the urge to run. They had to appear unconcerned by the patrol's arrival. Akiko casually pulled on the reins of her horse to leave, although the apprehension in her face belied the approaching threat.

Junjun whispered urgently in Okuni's ear. The woman's eyes widened, her shock accentuated to dramatic proportions by her make-up.

'And *this* samurai saved your life?' Okuni asked again, reassessing the hatted warrior before her.

Junjun nodded emphatically.

'Then we are in his debt.'

She bowed once more to Jack and the others. 'Do not worry, my girls will distract the patrol.'

Okuni clapped her hands and beckoned her performers. A group of young ladies, all dressed in colourful robes and their faces painted white, scurried out.

'We have potential patrons,' she announced, indicating the

mounted patrol. '*Ensure* they stay to see this evening's perfor-mance.'

Giggling and fluttering their fans, the *kabuki* troupe crossed the bridge to head off the samurai.

'Junjun, you need to get changed for rehearsals,' reminded Okuni sternly.

Bowing a final goodbye, and with a lingering look towards Benkei, Junjun hurried inside the curtained encampment.

'Like the cherry blossom in spring, she disappears again!' sighed Benkei.

'You're a poet?' queried Okuni, with the protective tone of a mother.

'No, a conjuror.'

Okuni seemed pleased by this answer. 'Perhaps one day you can show us your talents? We're always looking for new acts.'

'I'd very much like to –'

'Come on!' urged Jack.

Offering an apologetic smile, Benkei hobbled after Jack and Akiko as they lost themselves in the throng of the market. The patrol reached the bridge and paused, their eyes drawn to their glamorous welcome party. The six men stood little chance against the charms and attention of so many beautiful girls. Like sailors bewitched by the song of the sirens, they dismounted their horses and allowed themselves to be led into the tented enclave.

With the patrol hopelessly distracted, Jack, Akiko and Benkei left the market and disappeared down the road towards Kumamoto.

31

NO BUTTERFLY

Benkei sat astride the white stallion. Akiko had offered her saddle to him so he could rest his leg following their escape. And although he'd never ridden a horse before – such a privilege being reserved for the samurai class – he was clearly enjoying the experience. Settling in the saddle, he patted the horse affectionately and announced, 'This is the *only* way to travel!'

Jack and Akiko walked on ahead, leading the horse by its reins. With evening drawing in, the dirt road to Kumamoto was deserted and Jack and Akiko were able to talk freely. Lost in each other's company, they barely heard Benkei as he continued to expound the virtues of riding to the only companion now listening – the horse. '*No more aching feet, no more muddy sandals . . .*'

'How did you *ever* find me?' asked Jack, still reeling from Akiko's surprise arrival.

'I knew you were headed for Nagasaki, but it was mostly luck,' she explained, then raised her eyebrows in a teasing accusation. 'Not that you were too difficult to follow given the trail of destruction you leave behind!'

Jack held up a hand to protest his innocence. 'I'm just trying to get home. And I left some clues on purpose.'

'I know, and you've made some very loyal friends on the way too,' she added with a smile. 'Shiryu sends his regards, as do Yuudai and Hana.'

'Hana?' exclaimed Jack, fondly remembering the girl thief who'd helped him recover his stolen swords and possessions. 'So she made it safely to Toba?'

Akiko nodded. 'Along with my brother.'

As she said this, her eyes lit up and her face seemed to radiate happiness. Jack realized how important her brother's homecoming was to her. Kiyoshi had been kidnapped by the ninja Dragon Eye when he was just five and Akiko had spent years searching for him. By pure good fortune, Jack had discovered her brother living among a ninja clan, hidden in the Iga mountains. He'd managed to reunite Kiyoshi with his sister, but their meeting had been brief – the ninja clan forced deeper into the mountains for safety, and Kiyoshi going with them.

'My mother is beside herself with joy at seeing Kiyoshi again,' explained Akiko. 'And he and Hana agreed to stay and look after her, while I came looking for you.'

'But didn't Hana warn you about Kazuki?'

'Of course. She told me the danger you were in.'

'But so are *you*,' insisted Jack, alarmed that his warning had gone unheeded. 'Even more so now you're with me.'

'I'm no defenceless butterfly, Jack,' Akiko replied, laying a hand upon her bow and narrowing her eyes with steely determination. 'If Kazuki wants to find me, let him come. But he'll discover I'm the bee that stings him first.'

Jack had to admire Akiko. She was as brave as she was beautiful. But Jack also knew that Kazuki was as devious as he was deadly.

'Kazuki's not an enemy to be underestimated,' he reminded her. 'He has the help of his Scorpion Gang and a thirst for revenge. By leaving a trail, I've been trying to lead him *away* in order to protect you.'

Akiko's expression softened. 'I know you strive to be the "English gentleman", Jack. But I'm the daughter of a samurai. I'm a trained warrior and know how to look after myself. Besides, *together* we stand a greater chance of defeating Kazuki.' She took his hand in hers, this time not caring if Benkei saw.

Jack realized her plan made sense. He began to wonder why fate had ever parted them in the first place. They were *meant* to walk this road together.

Akiko let out a small gasp of shock.

'Who did this to you?' she asked, for the first time noticing his missing fingertip.

'Sensei Kyuzo,' said Jack, touched by the tender way she examined his injury.

Akiko's eyes widened in disbelief. 'NO! He wouldn't dare . . .'

But she saw the cruel truth in Jack's eyes. She sorrowfully shook her head. 'The Shogun has much to answer for. His rule is destroying the very spirit of *bushido*. It's a dark day when a sensei turns against his student.'

They walked on in silence, their shadows following hand in hand, stretched thin and long across the road by the dying light of the day.

'Can we stop, please?' moaned Benkei, his face grimacing

in pain with every jolt of the saddle. 'My rear's bruised black and blue!'

Spotting a copse of trees, they turned off the road to make camp. Benkei stiffly dismounted and stroked the stallion's mane.

'Thanks for the ride, horse, but I think I'll stick to walking tomorrow.'

While Akiko tended to her stallion and unpacked their provisions, Jack and Benkei went off to collect firewood.

'So what's the story with you and the samurai girl?' asked Benkei, as he picked up a dead branch and passed it to Jack.

'We trained at the *Niten Ichi Ryū* together.'

'Looks more than that to me!' pressed Benkei, giving him a knowing wink.

'Akiko's just a good friend,' Jack insisted, feeling his face flush.

Benkei suppressed a grin. 'Of course,' he replied and continued gathering wood.

Once Jack's arms were full, they returned to camp and built a fire. Akiko wrapped several handfuls of rice in a cloth, soaking the bundle in water before burying it beneath the fire to cook. Among the supplies Shiryu had given them, Benkei found a couple of dried fish and Jack cut these into strips to eat with the rice.

As the sun dipped behind the mountains and darkness closed in, they gathered round the fire. The tinder-dry wood cracked and popped, sending sparks like fireflies into the night sky.

'Did you know the reward is now twenty *koban*?' said Akiko, digging out the cooked rice and sharing it between them.

Jack shook his head in disbelief; every month the Shogun seemed to double the price on his head.

'Twenty *koban*!' exclaimed Benkei, almost choking on his fish. 'That's enough gold coin to feed a man for a lifetime!'

'You're not thinking of turning me in, are you?' asked Jack, grinning playfully as he tucked into his rice.

'I could do with a new kimono,' replied Benkei in all seriousness and began inspecting his tattered patchwork of robes. Then he noticed Akiko glaring at him. 'I wouldn't dream of it, Akiko! The *nanban* saved my life. He's my friend.'

Akiko smiled cordially, but Jack could tell she didn't fully trust Benkei. His explanation of how he'd met the conjuror caused her to question Benkei's integrity. In her opinion, anyone found buried up to his neck in sand and who made a living tricking people wasn't to be trusted. But in the time Jack had known Benkei he'd more than proved his loyalty.

As soon as the meal was over, they turned in for the night. Akiko unclipped a blanket from the saddlepack on her horse and spread it on the ground.

'Three's a crowd!' remarked Benkei, giving a wide, obviously feigned, yawn. 'I'll let you two catch up. See you in the morning!'

Finding a grassy patch and a rock for a pillow, he lay down, wrapped his kimono tightly around him and closed his eyes. Within moments, he was snoring away. Jack didn't mind if Benkei was faking sleep; he just appreciated the gesture of privacy.

Akiko settled on the blanket and invited Jack to join her. For a while they sat in silence, the chirps of the crickets sounding all around them, the flickering light of the fire dancing off their faces.

'So tell me,' whispered Akiko, 'did you *really* save an entire village from bandits?'

Jack nodded.

Akiko gazed at him with wonder and admiration, but also a touch of sadness. 'Your good heart will get you killed one day.'

Jack prodded the dying embers of the fire with a stick, unable to meet her eye. 'And my friends.'

'What do you mean?'

Holding his head in his hands, Jack tried to pluck up the courage to tell her. 'They're dead . . . Yori . . . Saburo . . . Miyuki.'

Akiko went visibly pale at the news. 'No . . . they can't be!'

'All drowned at sea . . . and it's *my* fault.'

Jack tearfully recounted their escape from Pirate Island, the devastating storm that struck their tiny boat and his failure to sail them safely to shore. Akiko listened without interruption or judgement. When he'd finished, she laid a hand on his arm to comfort him.

'It was an act of nature. You mustn't blame yourself. '

Jack swallowed hard, trying not to let grief overwhelm him once more. 'But I do. If I hadn't agreed to them coming with me, they would *still* be alive.'

'Jack, it was their choice. They were willing to risk their lives to help you get home. They *wanted* to be with you . . . just like I do.'

Akiko gently kissed Jack on the cheek, then lay down. 'Get

some rest. We need to make an early start to stay ahead of the patrol.'

Despite his exhaustion, Jack continued to coax the fire a while longer. He fought sleep, not wanting to close his eyes, in case he woke the following morning to find Akiko's arrival was all just a dream.

32

KUMAMOTO CASTLE

'The hop's done – only a skip and a jump left!' declared Benkei, pointing to Shimabara Bay in the hazy distance.

With the morning sun at their backs, Jack and Akiko joined him on the rise and gazed across the grassy plain. The Shira River meandered like a silver thread before passing through the city of Kumamoto to join the glistening waters beyond. Across the bay, its summit shrouded in cloud, the volcanic peak of Unzen-dake could be seen brooding on the far reaches of the horizon.

But what drew Jack's eye was Kumamoto Castle. Set atop the only high ground on the floodplain, the fortress dominated the skyline. Built on epic proportions, the complex even challenged Osaka Castle in size – and *that* had been a city in itself. The stone walls boasted over fifty turrets and the battlements stretched for almost a mile in each direction. From what Jack could make out, the formidable fortifications enclosed a grand palace with majestic arching roofs, several gardens, a proliferation of courtyards, rows of barracks, at least four tree groves, a small lake and, at its heart, a black-and-gold keep that looked like an armoured eagle poised for flight. Beyond the castle walls, Kumamoto city itself fanned out across the plain, the dwellings clustered like dutiful servants in the shadow of the fortress.

'Kumamoto is the stronghold of *daimyo* Kato,' warned Akiko, as they set off towards the city. 'A fiercely loyal supporter of the Shogun, he rules this province with an iron fist – even prides himself on the brutality of his samurai to keep law and order. So we must stay vigilant.'

'Nothing like putting your head into the lion's mouth!' remarked Benkei drily.

'Sometimes that's the best place to hide,' said Akiko, 'since it's the *last* place they'll look.'

Despite her words, Jack was bracing himself for a rough ride. Kumamoto was likely to be the most dangerous part of their journey. The streets would be crawling with samurai and *metsuke*, the Shogun's spies. One false step and there'd be nowhere to run or hide. But he accepted that the risk was necessary. Kumamoto was the only realistic crossing point to Shimabara. The alternative was to trek round the inland Ariake Sea, which would add weeks to their journey – as well as increasing the opportunities for being spotted. But once on the ferry and across the bay they would be home free – Nagasaki less than two days' travel. With such a gain, they'd all agreed the gamble was worth taking.

They reached the city outskirts towards late afternoon. The streets and alleyways bustled with travellers, merchants, samurai, craftsmen plying their trade and *ronin* looking for work . . . or trouble. Jack kept his head down, walking obediently alongside Akiko's horse and fulfilling his role as the faithful retainer. The steady stream of foot traffic was both a danger and a cover. Every pair of eyes threatened to discover his identity. Yet most people were too busy going about their daily business to pay a samurai retainer much attention.

As the three of them made their way through the winding streets, they passed the outer perimeter of the castle. Jack risked a glance up and was astounded by the sheer scale of the fortifications. Up close, the immense walls rose above them like a tidal wave of rock. The smooth curving stone-block construction raked at such a steep angle that no one could possibly climb it. And even if, by some miracle, an invader did manage such a climb, then they would be faced by the perilous overhangs of the battlements. Hatches in every section threatened to release an avalanche of rocks, boiling oil and other lethal deterrents.

If any castle can be described as impenetrable, this is it, thought Jack.

They carried on down a street lined with stalls selling fried noodles, *yakitori*, *ramen* and many more mouthwatering dishes, as well as a few less savoury items like candied crickets and pickled pigs' ears. Strips of meat and slices of fish sizzled on little grills and the spicy aroma of cooking eventually became too tempting. Having not eaten since breakfast, Akiko gave Benkei the money to buy three steaming bowls of *ramen*. Sitting on a wooden bench beside the noodle stall, the three of them ate ravenously.

All of a sudden, cries of alarm broke out and the people in the street scattered. A unit of samurai in black-and-red armour, a white circular *kamon* on their breastplates, marched four abreast down the road. As they advanced, a ripple of fear seemed to pass through the crowd. Like toppling dominoes, the inhabitants bowed their heads or prostrated themselves on the ground, according to status.

'Stay calm,' urged Akiko, putting down her bowl. 'And bow like everyone else.'

Jack did as he was told, pulling his hat lower, yet keeping his eyes alert.

The samurai unit headed straight for them. Jack's hand twitched for his sword. He noticed Akiko reaching for hers at the same time. The sound of marching feet drew closer and Jack grasped the handle of his *katana* ready to do battle.

But the unit stopped short outside a tea house. With a nod from the commanding officer, two of his samurai strode inside and dragged out the owner. Dumping him in the middle of the street, they set to beating him with sticks. The dull *thud* of wood on flesh was unnaturally loud amid the fearful silence of the onlookers. There was a harsh *crack* as a bone broke and the man screamed in agony. A shrieking woman rushed out of the tea house and tried to intervene, but she was kicked to the ground. Then she too was beaten unmercifully.

Jack was sickened by the savage violence against two defenceless individuals. He felt compelled to intervene, but knew such a move would be suicidal.

The beating stopped.

'Let that be a lesson to you . . . both,' snarled the officer, before giving the order to march on, the reason for the beating never declared.

The unit of samurai left the semi-conscious man bleeding in the gutter and the woman sobbing beside him, one side of her face cruelly puffed up. When the samurai were gone, the street returned to normal and everyone went on their way. But no one approached or helped the battered couple.

'We need to get out of here as soon as we can,' whispered Akiko. 'This is an unforgiving place.'

'My thoughts exactly,' said Jack, hurriedly finishing his broth of *ramen*.

Leading the horse on foot, Akiko guided them down the road. But the city was so overwhelming in its size, they soon lost their bearings. Facing a bewildering number of streets and alleyways, Akiko stopped to ask an old woman for directions to the harbour. With a polite bow, the woman gestured down the road then said something Jack didn't catch, before going on her way.

Akiko turned to Jack and Benkei, her expression grim.

'She says to follow this street until we come to a bridge, cross the river then take the main road west. *But* there are no ferries until tomorrow morning . . . and we'll need travel permits.'

33

THE INNKEEPER

'So it's the long way round to Nagasaki, after all,' said Jack, as they ducked down a side street to avoid another unit of samurai marching by.

'Not necessarily,' said Benkei, a crafty twinkle in his eye. 'There are ways and means of getting permits, especially in a city like this.' He rubbed his fingers, making the gesture for money. 'We just need the means.'

'Will this be enough?' asked Akiko, holding up a string of silver and copper coins.

Benkei grinned. 'Definitely. We're good to sail!'

'But what are we going to do until then?' asked Jack. 'We can't keep dodging patrols like this.'

'Certainly not after dark,' Akiko agreed. 'That will look even more suspicious. We must find an inn, one with a stable.'

'I know where to go,' said Benkei. 'Follow me.'

With the plan agreed, they crossed the bridge and took the main road west. Wooden slatted buildings crowded the street on either side. They passed several well-to-do establishments with views over the Shira River, but none of these met with Benkei's approval. He turned down a side street, and Jack and Akiko followed him into what appeared to be a less prosperous area of the city. The inns along this stretch showed signs of wear and tear; loose roof tiles held down with stones, crooked guttering, unrepaired rips in *shoji* doors. Empty *saké* bottles were piled high in crates, still awaiting collection, and the signs above various businesses were chipped and weather-beaten. The clientele hanging around outside and wandering through the streets mirrored the rundown appearance of the neighbourhood. Their clothes were travel-worn, their weapons more prominently displayed, and polite bows were replaced with hard stares and hostile scowls.

Benkei stopped outside the shabbiest-looking inn.

'Here?' exclaimed Akiko, turning up her nose.

'A place like this will ask fewer questions,' explained Benkei, 'and be more likely to know where to acquire permits.'

'I suppose beggars can't be choosers,' said Jack.

'As long as the stable is satisfactory,' agreed Akiko, stroking her horse's mane, 'and they've got a hot *ofuro*.'

Benkei pulled on the bell. It gave a dull clang, its ringer broken. He banged on the door.

They waited a moment. Then the door slid open a crack.

'Yes?' demanded a wrinkle-faced man with hangdog eyes and a left ear that stuck out like a sail.

'We need a room for the night,' replied Benkei.

The innkeeper eyed the mismatched threesome with suspicion: the elegant and well-armed girl samurai and her valuable white horse, the spiky-haired and gangly lad in the rainbow-coloured kimono, and the mysterious samurai retainer with a straw hat pulled too low over his face.

166

'*One* room?' he asked, rubbing his bristled chin thoughtfully.

'Two,' corrected Akiko. 'My retainers will share.' She indicated her stallion. 'I presume you have a stable?'

The innkeeper grunted. 'Out back . . . but I may not have a vacancy.'

'I think you *might* find one,' stated Benkei, glancing meaningfully at Akiko, who produced the string of coins.

The innkeeper's manner instantly changed at the sight of the money. 'I've just had a late cancellation. Go round the back.'

Shutting the door in their faces, he was then heard bawling, '*Momo, get up! We've guests.*'

'That's warm hospitality for you,' remarked Akiko as she led the stallion down the side alley.

The innkeeper opened up a gate and ushered them into a rear courtyard.

'Take your pick,' he said, pointing to three dilapidated stalls that were the inn's excuse for a stable.

Akiko peered in, frowning in disgust at the state of them.

'At least the hay is fresh,' she muttered, tethering her horse in the first stall and removing his saddle.

'Two rooms . . . breakfast . . . plus stabling and hay . . . one night . . .' The innkeeper licked his lips as he counted off his fingers. 'That'll be ten *mon*. Payment in advance only.' The innkeeper bowed graciously and held out his hand.

'*How much?*' queried Akiko, her face registering shock.

'They are our two *best* rooms,' he said, offering his most ingratiating smile. 'And they guarantee *privacy*.'

The innkeeper glanced at Jack as he emphasized the last

word – the clear implication being that his silence did not come free.

With reluctance, Akiko handed over the ten copper coins. 'The *ofuro* had better be *hot*.'

'*Momo!*' shouted the innkeeper over his shoulder. 'Stoke up the fire.'

Pocketing the money, the innkeeper led them inside. As they passed down the lamplit corridor, the warped wooden floorboards creaking beneath their feet, Jack and Akiko exchanged doubtful looks at Benkei's choice of establishment. But to their surprise the rooms, though small, turned out to be clean with *tatami*-matted floors, low wooden tables and pristine white *futons* neatly rolled in one corner. The *washi* paper walls were even decorated with colourful screen paintings depicting hunts, festivals and theatre scenes.

'As I said, our best rooms,' remarked the innkeeper, noticing Akiko's approval. He glanced at Jack, who now looked even more conspicuous wearing his hat indoors. 'May I take that for you?'

Jack shook his head.

'He was beaten in a duel and lost face,' cut in Akiko. 'The shame of it!'

'Ahhh . . . the famous samurai pride,' replied the innkeeper, accepting the answer but clearly not believing a single word. 'Perhaps I can get you some green tea instead?'

'That would be nice,' said Akiko, taking off her sandals and entering her room.

'*Momo! Green tea!*' hollered the innkeeper. He bowed low, though less out of courtesy and more out of curiosity to catch a glimpse of Jack's face. However, Jack bowed quickly back and foiled his attempt.

'Have a pleasant stay,' said the innkeeper as he shuffled off.

'I'll ask where to buy the permits when he returns,' said Benkei, stepping into their room and dumping their supply bag.

Jack slipped off his pack too and rubbed his shoulders. The journey that day had been long and tiring. He was looking forward to a good night's rest in a soft bed. Laying down his swords, he began to take off his hat, when the *shoji* shot open.

'Your tea!' announced the innkeeper, walking in and placing the tray on the table.

'Thank you,' acknowledged Benkei. Without giving the innkeeper the chance to linger further, he asked, 'May I have a word?'

The innkeeper nodded and the two of them left the room.

Once the door was closed and he was certain the innkeeper had gone, Jack removed his hat and relaxed. Pouring himself some tea, he sat down and, with nothing else to do, gazed at the screen painting in his room. It portrayed a vibrant theatre scene with men and women dancing upon a stage. One panel was devoted to a lithe woman singing and playing a thirteen-string *koto*. The figure was almost full-size and exquisitely painted, the work so lifelike the woman's eyes appeared to be staring right at him.

'Jack!'

He almost jumped out of his skin. But it was just Akiko whispering through the thin *washi* paper wall.

'Benkei's taken some money for the permits,' she said.

'Seems my opinion of your new friend was mistaken. He's proving very useful.'

'If anyone can get them, Benkei will,' Jack reassured her. 'He's got a silver tongue.'

'Good. I'm going to take a bath now. Then I'll arrange for some dinner.'

Jack thought he could do with an *ofuro* too. Three days had passed since his last wash at Shiryu's house and his skin felt grimy. He smiled to himself; back in England he'd have considered three months still too soon for a bath!

While he waited for Akiko and Benkei to return, Jack passed the time cleaning his swords. He used a cloth to wipe off any dirt, then polished the steel to a high gleam. Once satisfied, he put the blades aside, laying them by his *futon*, and rummaged in his pack for his father's *rutter*. Carefully laying the logbook on the table, he unwrapped the protective oilskin covering and flicked through the pages. The sea charts, compass bearings, travel logs and observation notes were like familiar friends. Thanks to his father's instruction, he could decipher the coded passages as easily as if they'd been written in plain English. Jack even remembered his father inserting many of the entries in the logbook during their long voyage to the Japans; the memories were so distinct that, as he turned the pages, Jack could almost imagine his father by his side.

All the while he read, Jack couldn't shake off the feeling that he was being watched. Yet when he looked around the room, there was no one there . . . only the *koto* woman's eyes upon him. He put this down to nerves from the fraught day and went back to studying the logbook. In a few days he'd be sailing for home – perhaps as a pilot like his father – and the idea of using this information to help navigate a ship back to England filled him with excitement.

When he heard Akiko return from her bath, Jack closed the *rutter* and stashed it back in his pack before slipping it under his *futon* for a pillow. It had become habit for him to sleep on top of his most prized possession. He couldn't be too careful.

Glancing up at the little window to his room, he noticed that dusk was fast approaching. Benkei still wasn't back and Jack began to worry. He was about to call to Akiko, when the corridor floorboards softly creaked. Jack now realized his concerns were unfounded – Benkei was returning.

Then Jack registered multiple footsteps. He reached for his swords. But, before he could get to them, the *shoji* burst open and ten of *daimyo* Kato's samurai charged in.

34

THE DOHYŌ

Bound and gagged, Jack was dragged through a twisting, turning and baffling complex of passageways to reach the inner bailey of Kumamoto Castle. He struggled in his captors' grip across the courtyard, his hobbled feet scoring two lines in the grey gravel behind him. All ten samurai had pounced on him when they'd barged into his room. He'd thrown the first three off and broken the arm of the fourth before they managed to pin him to the floor. With a knife held to his throat, Jack's hands were tied behind his back and his ankles fettered. Powerless to resist, he'd been forced to listen to a violent tussle next door, Akiko screaming then falling silent. For several long seconds, he feared she was dead. Then they'd hauled her in, half-conscious, between the shoulders of two burly soldiers. Her lip was split and there was a vicious red welt across her temple. Jack's blood boiled at seeing Akiko in such a state and, fighting against his bonds, had vowed retribution the first chance he got. The samurai had all laughed in his face before the lead officer had shoved a gag in his mouth. Then, glaring up at Akiko's two attackers, Jack had felt a small surge of satisfaction when he noticed one sported a freshly broken nose and the other walked with an awkward limp. *At least Akiko had been able to put up a fight as well*, thought Jack.

Now they were both being escorted through the enormous castle for an audience with *daimyo* Kato. Akiko, having regained consciousness, stumbled along behind. Tied to a short length of rope, she was barefoot and bound like Jack. The two samurai delighted in manhandling her across the gravel. A sharp pull on the tether sent Akiko sprawling.

'Not so feisty now, are you?' said the samurai, his voice muffled by his broken nose. He dragged the grazed Akiko back to her feet.

'And you're not so pretty,' she retorted defiantly, before being yanked onward.

The black keep of Kumamoto Castle loomed closer. Its seven arched roofs with its golden eaves soared into the sky like a colossal multi-winged beast, its entrance a gated mouth that seemed to swallow all who entered. And, in the deepening twilight, its barred windows flickered orange with burning oil lamps, transforming the fortress into a mythical dragon with a hundred fiery eyes.

But the samurai patrol took them past the forbidding tower and over to a grand hall on the other side of the courtyard. Two massive wooden doors peeled back on their approach, and Jack and Akiko were led inside. A highly polished wood-block floor stretched out before them like a glassy sea. Stout oak pillars, stained black, stood to attention in a regimented line down either side and supported an ornate panelled ceiling high above. Around the walls a vast collection of weapons was on display – *katana, bokken,* spears, *bō* staffs, spiked chains, studded clubs and a host of other lethal implements.

The hall was the largest and best-equipped *dojo* Jack had ever laid eyes on. Similar to the *Butokuden* at the *Niten Ichi Ryū*, there was a ceremonial throne set within a curving alcove midway down the hall. Two carved eagles, their wings gilded and their eyes blazing with emeralds, perched atop the alcove's entrance and stared down with the keen watchfulness of vengeful guardians. Beneath their protective gaze sat a slim man in a dark green kimono and black *kataginu* jacket.

Daimyo Kato, Jack presumed, as they were escorted in his direction.

The samurai lord was seated upon a tiger-skin rug, the animal's head still attached and fixed in a snarling growl. He held an iron-edged fan, which he tapped upon the palm of his hand. His face was young yet severe, his eyes sharp and intense, and his posture straight as an arrow. With his pate neatly shaven and the remaining hair tied into the traditional topknot, the *daimyo* looked every inch the samurai warrior and gave the impression he could spring into action at a moment's notice.

Yet *daimyo* Kato paid them no attention as they approached. His entire focus was on the *sumo* wrestling ring – a *dohyō* – that took prominence in the centre of the *dojo*. The *dohyō* consisted of a raised square platform of hard-packed clay, its surface covered with a thin layer of brushed sand. A circle of rice-straw bales were partly buried in the clay and two white lines scored, parallel to one another, in the middle. Above the ring, suspended from the hall's rafters, was the pitched roof of a Shinto shrine with coloured tassels – blue, red, white and black – hanging from each of the corners.

Standing at the edge of the ring was a small man in a purple silk outfit. He wore a peaked hat and carried a wooden oval war-fan. The man was dwarfed by two gargantuan warriors, whose chests were bare, their lower halves wrapped in loincloths. They were each the size of elephants, their bodies a combination of blubbery fat and bulging muscle. At the command of the purple-clad referee, the two combatants mounted the *dohyō*. Facing out, they clapped their hands loudly, then turned to each other and stomped the ground in a ritual to drive the evil spirits from the ring.

Jack watched all this as the patrol dumped him and Akiko unceremoniously opposite the razor-toothed tiger's head. The samurai soldiers forced them both into a kneeling bow and waited patiently for their lord to acknowledge them. But *daimyo* Kato's eyes remained firmly fixed on the *sumo* bout.

The two wrestlers, having stepped from the *dohyō* to rinse their mouths with water, now returned and squatted, hands on knees, either side of the white lines. They glared at one another, clapped their hands for a second time, then spread them wide to show neither of them carried weapons. Still they did not fight. Rising back up, they strode over to their respective corners and grabbed a handful of salt from a wooden box. In the manner of a farmer scattering seed, each of them tossed the salt on to the ring to purify it. Once this sacred rite was concluded, they crouched beside the white lines again and stared each other down.

Jack waited for the attack but it never came.

Instead, after glaring at one another, the two warriors returned to their corners. They repeated the salt rite and the staring contest twice more, before both wrestlers placed their fists on the ground. Then all chaos broke loose.

The two juggernauts sprang up, colliding mid-ring with

the force of charging bulls. The *smack* of flesh against flesh echoed through the *dojo*, as they slapped, pushed and grappled one another for dominance. One seized his opponent's loin-cloth, trying to topple him sideways, but the other sidestepped the attack, spun and tripped his rival up. The *sumo* wrestler crashed heavily to the sand, tumbling out of the designated ring. The referee brought the match to a halt and held up his fan to declare the champion.

Following the slow drawn-out ritual of preparation, the bout itself lasted a matter of seconds.

The winner bowed his respects to *daimyo* Kato, who applauded the man's victory. Then the samurai lord at last turned his attention to Jack and Akiko.

'Good work,' said *daimyo* Kato, addressing the officer of the samurai unit. 'Ensure the informant is handsomely rewarded. Such loyalty to the Shogun is deserving of special consideration.'

'As you command, *daimyo* Kato,' said the samurai officer, bowing.

Akiko glanced at Jack, her eyes telling him all: *Benkei had betrayed them.*

Jack couldn't . . . *wouldn't* believe it. The informant had to be the innkeeper. But the suspicious old man hadn't managed to see his face, so how could he have known Jack was the *gaijin* samurai? A tiny seed of doubt was sown. Maybe twenty *koban* was too much for *any* person to resist?

Daimyo Kato's gaze raked appreciatively over Akiko and he tutted at her injuries.

'That's no way to treat a lady,' he remarked. 'Untie her.'

'I wouldn't advise it,' said the officer. 'She's a wildcat.'

The *daimyo* laughed. 'Like this tiger?' he said, tapping the skin of the dead animal with his fan. He caught Akiko's eye. 'I killed this tiger in Korea . . . with just a *tantō*. If you try anything, I'll snap your neck in two. Do you understand?'

Chilled by his murderous tone, Akiko offered a submissive nod.

Confident he'd broken her will, the *daimyo* smiled and indicated for her bonds to be cut.

'And the . . . *gaijin*?' queried the officer with hesitation.

'Is he as dangerous as they say?'

The officer nodded his head. 'It took all ten of us to subdue him. He *broke* the arm of one of my men and threw others around like they were toys.'

Daimyo Kato rested his chin upon the end of his fan, his expression one of marked interest rather than concern.

'A spirited fighter!' he said, regarding Jack with a hint of admiration. 'Let's put that warrior spirit of yours to the test.'

35

SUMO

'*Sumo* is combat at its purest,' declared *daimyo* Kato, gesturing towards the *dohyō* with his fan. 'Two mighty forces confronting one another. Yet the battle is rarely won on strength alone. The true conflict takes place in the mind. The conqueror and conquered decided in the blink of an eye.'

He clapped his hands. '*Gyōji!* Summon Riku.'

The *sumo* referee bowed and turned to one of the many armed retainers, who stood unnoticed at the edge of the hall. The retainer hurried out and returned a few moments later accompanied by a hulking young man. With the body of an ox and legs like tree trunks, the wrestler clomped across the *dojo* floor to the central ring.

'Riku is our youngest champion,' explained the *daimyo*. 'What he lacks in girth compared to his opponents, he more than makes up for in skill and mettle.'

In Jack's eyes, Riku looked as huge and intimidating as the other two wrestlers, but he wasn't going to argue with the *daimyo*. In fact, he couldn't – even if he'd wanted to – the gag was still in his mouth.

'I wonder,' mused the *daimyo*, a playful grin on his lips, 'can a *gaijin* survive a *sumo* bout?'

With a wave of his fan, he commanded the officer to unbind Jack.

Glad to be free, Jack swallowed the dryness from his throat and rubbed his raw wrists. He glanced over at the man-mountain that was Riku. The young wrestler was pounding a fist into a fleshy palm, the message clear: he would beat Jack into a pulp.

'I'm not here to entertain your whims,' said Jack. 'What reason do I have to fight your champion?'

Daimyo Kato considered this a moment – then glanced at Akiko. 'For her life.'

Jack felt as if all the breath had been knocked out of him. He knew their situation was desperate, but the *daimyo*'s statement brought home the grim truth. As prisoners of a loyal supporter of the Shogun, they were destined to die. Yet a chance, however slim and uncertain, had been offered to save Akiko's life.

'He's just playing a cruel game with us,' whispered Akiko.

'You're right. But what a prize to win,' said *daimyo* Kato, his hearing keen as a hawk's. 'While all traitors *must* be punished by death, clemency is possible in certain circumstances. I've considerable influence with the Shogun. Defeat my champion, *gaijin*, and, I assure you, your lady will live.'

Although Akiko urged him to refuse, Jack nodded his acceptance of the challenge. Akiko's welfare was all that mattered now. And he would fight till his last breath to save her.

The officer led Jack at sword point over to the *dohyō*. Two attendants stripped him to the waist, then shoved him into the ring. The samurai patrol eagerly crowded round the edge to watch the spectacle. Akiko remained kneeling with one of the samurai guarding her closely. She offered Jack an encouraging smile, but her eyes couldn't disguise her concern. The inevitable result of the forthcoming bout was impossible to ignore as Riku stood on his slab-like feet, an immovable mound of flesh and muscle, waiting to destroy him.

Nonetheless, Jack took up position behind his white start line. The referee in the purple robes turned to him. Although he was a great deal shorter, the man somehow managed to look down his nose in distaste at Jack when he spoke. 'The winner of the bout is the first wrestler to force his opponent out of the ring, or make him touch the ground with any part of his body other than his feet,' explained the referee. 'It is *against* the rules to use fists, pull hair, or choke your opponent. Is that clear?'

Jack nodded. Despite never having fought *sumo*-style before, he had trained in *taijutsu* and was familiar with a number of wrestling techniques. Almost every day at the *Niten Ichi Ryū*, Sensei Kyuzo had tested their throwing and grappling skills.

Break their balance, break the opponent! That was what Sensei Kyuzo had drilled into them.

Jack rapidly assessed his opponent. There was no way he could match Riku's brute strength or sheer weight, but he did have the advantage of agility and a longer reach. If he timed his movements so that Riku overcommitted to an attack, he might be able to use the wrestler's immense power against himself. He would only have one chance at this, so he had to make it count. Adjusting his feet for the best stability, Jack felt the coarse sand between his toes and the hard unyielding clay beneath. He dropped into a crouch, his knuckles on the line, and readied himself for the charge.

Glaring at Jack, Riku raised his left leg high and stomped the ground. Then he lifted his right leg and brought this crashing down. Each time his foot pounded the clay, Jack felt the whole *dohyō* shudder. The wrestler was like an earthquake about to happen and Jack was directly in its path. Then Riku broke away and stepped out of the ring. He drank a ladleful of water from a bucket before drying his lips with a piece of rice paper. Returning to his white line, Riku squatted, clapped his hands and spread them wide . . .

In his determination to win, Jack had forgotten about the *sumo* rituals that preceded the actual bout. He now mirrored Riku's gesture, opening out his arms to show he held no weapons. Satisfied, Riku returned to his corner and scattered a handful of salt. With the ring purified, he crouched once more in front of Jack and locked eyes with him. To Jack, it was like staring into a fathomless pit – Riku's stony gaze giving nothing away.

Daimyo Kato had spoken the truth when he said *sumo* was a battle of the minds.

Riku's glare continued to bore into him and Jack shifted uncomfortably. At that tiny lapse in concentration, Riku charged. The speed of his attack was inconceivable for his size. Jack barely had time to raise his arms before Riku almost pulverized him. Meaty forearms slammed into Jack's chest. Hands like rocks slapped at his face. As the avalanche of muscle and flesh bowled into him, all Jack's tactics crumbled like a castle made of sand.

He numbly felt the edge of the ring with his back foot and in a last-ditch effort tried to stall Riku's charge. But the wrestler, rather than going for a final push, grabbed Jack by an arm and a leg and lifted him high above his head. Flailing helplessly in Riku's grip, Jack was then slammed into the clay ring. The impact was bone-shattering; Jack's skeleton rattled like a child's toy, even his brain seeming to shake inside his skull. Yet through the pain all Jack could think of was that he'd failed to save Akiko's life.

'Disappointing,' remarked the *daimyo*, as Jack gave an agonized groan and curled up in the foetal position on the *dohyō*. 'I expected more from the infamous *gaijin* samurai.'

Although Jack's body throbbed as if a stampeding bull had thundered over him, he wasn't defeated. With an immense effort of will, he pulled himself back to his feet and gasped, 'I demand . . . a rematch . . . now I understand the rules. Best out of three!'

The *daimyo* raised his eyebrows in surprise. 'I do admire your fighting spirit, *gaijin*. On your head be it.'

Splashing water in his face with the ladle, Jack revived himself and took up position at the white marker. *Daimyo* Kato dipped his fan to indicate to the official to commence the match. Riku re-entered the ring and faced off against Jack.

'I'll break *every* bone in your body, *gaijin*,' warned Riku, loosening his neck with a crack.

'I'll do the same to you,' replied Jack, 'if I can find any!'

Riled by the insult, Riku began stomping the ring.

This time Jack followed all the rituals of *sumo*: clapping his hands, stamping his feet and tossing the salt. If Riku was offended or thought Jack was ridiculing him, he didn't show it. He remained as stone-faced as before. As they crouched opposite each other, his hard and glassy stare focused on Jack, Riku gave no ground on their mental battlefield. Yet neither did Jack. This resulted in a second round of staring. On this occasion, Jack played to Riku's overconfidence and feigned a flash of doubt. Riku registered it but broke away without charging, trying to hide the smug grin of certain victory on his face.

They both returned to the ring, Riku tossing salt. Taking up their fighting positions, the battle of wills reached its peak. The moment both fists touched the sand, Riku exploded into a charge. But, like a spitting cobra, Jack flicked the salt he still held into the eyes of his opponent. Riku was momentarily blinded, allowing Jack to neatly sidestep him. Sweeping his right foot across, Jack knocked Riku's legs from under him. His balance taken, the wrestler tumbled head first into the sand. His own momentum drove him forward and over the edge of the raised *dohyō*. Riku landed like a beached whale on the woodblock floor below. A muffled crack and cries of pain filled the hall: not just from Riku, who rolled around like a defective Daruma Doll, the force of the drop having broken several ribs, but also from the two samurai who'd captured Akiko. They lay pinned beneath the mammoth wrestler, Riku's immense weight crushing the breath from them.

Payback for Akiko!

Dusting his hands of the salt, Jack locked eyes with Riku. 'Seems I did find a bone or two to break!'

36

BID FOR FREEDOM

With Riku struggling to rise for a third bout, even with the help of two attendants, Jack turned to *daimyo* Kato and declared, 'Final match is forfeit. I win.'

'No!' said *daimyo* Kato firmly. 'You cheated.'

'I used tactics,' corrected Jack. 'You said the conqueror and conquered are decided in the blink of an eye. Riku blinked.'

Outfoxed, *daimyo* Kato fumed, his face contorting in silent rage. His hands gripped his fan so tightly it was on the verge of snapping in half. Then the referee stepped in.

'The *gaijin* is disqualified,' he announced, 'for being over his start line.'

'I wasn't —'

'The referee's decision is *final*,' cut in the *daimyo*, with an imperious sneer, as the *sumo* official turned his back on Jack's protests and left the ring.

Jack realized the samurai lord *had* been playing a cruel game with him, one that he'd had no intention of letting Jack win. Incensed, Jack glanced at Akiko held prisoner at the feet of the smugly smiling *daimyo*. *Forever bound to one another*, he mouthed to her, then leapt from the *dohyō*.

The samurai patrol, clustered round the defeated wrestler and their crushed comrades, were too distracted to notice Jack's bid for freedom. As he touched down on the *dojo* floor, Jack targeted the neck of the nearest samurai with a knife-hand strike. The man collapsed like a puppet whose strings had been cut. Jack swiftly unsheathed the *katana* from the samurai's *saya* as he fell.

The patrol officer, suddenly realizing what was happening, rushed to draw his own sword. Jack floored him with a spinning elbow strike to the jaw. He took out the next samurai using the brass pommel of his *katana*'s handle, embossing the man's forehead with the dragon design that adorned the end. The five other samurai finally pulled themselves together and drew their weapons. In a frenzied attack, Jack charged into them, knocking one samurai over the writhing body of Riku and attacking another with his sword.

At the same time as Jack was decimating the patrol, Akiko dropped forward as if to bow to the *daimyo*, then mule-kicked the guard behind her. The samurai went flying. He landed unceremoniously on his backside and skidded across the polished woodblock floor. Leaping cat-like to her feet, Akiko raced to help Jack. But the two *sumo* wrestlers from the earlier bout charged to intercept her. As they converged on either side, determined to crush her between their bloated bodies, Akiko sprang into the air and somersaulted away. The two titans collided head first. There was a sickening crack of skulls and they collapsed in a fleshy useless heap.

Jack fought furiously, but with only a single *katana* to keep the four samurai at bay he was in mortal danger. As he deflected a blade slicing for his chest, he heard the ominous *whoosh* of a sword cut from behind. With no hope of avoiding it, Jack anticipated the icy sensation of razor-sharp steel scything through his flesh. But the blade missed and the sword clattered to the floor as his attacker let out a pained grunt and crumpled where he stood.

Akiko had destroyed the samurai with a flying side-kick. Snatching up the dropped *katana*, she joined Jack at his side and engaged the remaining three samurai. Executing an Autumn Leaf strike, she disarmed one and took another down with a spinning hook kick, the heel catching the man's jaw with a concussion-inducing crunch.

'What's the plan?' she asked as Jack fended off the final samurai.

'*Plan?*' exclaimed Jack, disabling his attacker. 'I hadn't got that far.'

'Then we'd better get out of here *fast*.'

Together, they raced for the double doors. Jack glanced over his shoulder to check on any pursuers. *Daimyo* Kato, rather than looking alarmed by the situation, merely observed their escape with the enthralled amusement of a man watching a sporting match. The *daimyo*'s quiet confidence unsettled Jack, but that was the least of his worries as the armed retainers now rushed from their stations around the hall to head them off.

Jack and Akiko fought their way through, edging closer and closer to the double doors. Attacks came from all directions, but by battling back to back they managed to hold them off.

The double doors were now almost within reach . . .

Like a crack of thunder, *daimyo* Kato clapped his hands

together. The noise silenced the hall and all his samurai retainers withdrew. Jack and Akiko were left panting for breath, bewildered by the sudden retreat.

'I stand corrected, *gaijin*. You certainly don't disappoint,' stated *daimyo* Kato. 'You remind me of the legend of the Furious Frog. Unfailing courage against impossible odds.'

He looked around at the profusion of groaning and unconscious bodies littering his *dojo*.

'My men could learn a great deal from your fighting skills,' he admitted with begrudging admiration. 'But, as diverting as your little bid for freedom has been, I must quash your hopes of escape.'

He rapped the iron edge of his fan against a bronze gong, the shimmering ring filling their ears. The doors to the hall burst open and the *dojo* flooded with troops. Within seconds, Jack and Akiko were encircled by a ring of steel-tipped spears.

Daimyo Kato offered Akiko a pitying look. 'I warned you not to try anything.'

37

WRAITH

Three torturous days . . . three painfully long nights . . . with neither sight nor sound of Akiko.

Jack had barely slept for worry. Had *daimyo* Kato killed her? Snapped her neck as he'd promised? Or was he torturing her? Making her pay for their defiance. After all, unlike Jack, she was of little value to the *daimyo*. The best he could hope for was that she was languishing in another foul cell like his, perhaps crouched in a damp filthy corner worrying about *his* fate. Jack pictured her sitting in the only light that came from a pale crescent moon, barely glimpsed through the bars of a tiny grate high in the wall. There was a chance she might be still alive, looking at that same moon. For three whole days Jack had clung to that dream. But now he felt it slipping from his grasp, a nightmare consuming every flicker of hope.

Daimyo Kato rules with an iron fist . . . prides himself on the brutality of his samurai . . .

In their situation, a quick death might have been the most merciful option. Jack shifted his position on the dirt floor and groaned, rubbing his bruised and battered ribs. The guards checked on him twice a day: to bring him food – a thin rice gruel – a jug of slimy water and, at the end of every visit, a fresh beating. Nothing that would permanently damage him for his presentation to the Shogun, but enough to make his stay in the cell as painful and unpleasant as possible.

A rat scuttled in the darkness and Jack batted it away with his foot. The creature had squeezed itself under the door and was looking for anything to eat. Jack shuddered at the thought that he might fall asleep, only to wake and find vermin gnawing on his hands or bare toes. He couldn't afford to lose another finger.

On the first night, Jack had explored every inch of his cell for a way out – a loose bar in the grating, a weak panel in the door, a crumbling area of plaster in the wall. But his prison was secure, mostly below ground level at the base of the keep, the tiny grate his only view of the world outside.

Music now drifted down from the upper storeys of the fortress. Jack strained his ears to listen to the insistent *twang* of a *shamisen*, accompanied by the percussive beat of *tsuzumi* drums and the *click-clack* of wooden clappers. Every so often he'd catch bursts of laughter or applause, the joyous sounds seeming to mock his pitiful state. Judging by the night's frivolity, Jack guessed that the Shogun's samurai must have arrived and were being entertained by *daimyo* Kato. The samurai lord would be buoyant in the knowledge that he could demonstrate his loyalty to the Shogun in the highest possible manner – by successfully capturing and delivering the infamous *gaijin* samurai.

Jack surrendered himself to despair. He'd been in many difficult and desperate situations before, when escape or salvation had seemed impossible. Yet, with the help of his friends, he had survived and overcome each one of those challenges and obstacles. But *this* time he realized there would be no one saving him – no courageous last stand, no miracle escape. Because there were *no* friends to rescue him.

All of them were dead, destined to die or long gone.

Jack felt tears run down his cheeks in the darkness. There was no one here to see him cry, so he let them come – all his grief, anger, frustration and sorrow in a single flood. The faces of his late friends swam before his eyes and he begged for their forgiveness. Although the Shogun was truly to blame, Jack felt responsible for leading them to their deaths – for not *insisting* that he took his perilous journey alone.

As his sobs subsided, he thought of his little sister. He could see her now, standing on the Limehouse Docks in London to welcome him as his ship sailed in.

'I'm sorry,' he whispered, 'but I won't be coming home.'

Yet the Jess in his mind refused to hear him. She beckoned him on.

Although all logic told him to give up, it seemed as if his heart wouldn't let him. Jack composed himself. In honour of his friends' memories, he *had* to confront his fate like a true samurai. For the sake of the love he held for his family – and needing to return home in his father's honour – he *had* to be strong.

Wiping dry his tear-stained cheeks, his thoughts now turned to Benkei – the friend who'd apparently betrayed them. Despite Akiko's conviction, Jack still found this notion hard to believe, especially after all they'd been through together.

The conjuror might be a con artist, possess a silver tongue and be as slippery as an eel, but Jack was convinced he wasn't in league with the Shogun and his followers. Yet, even if Benkei was loyal, what could he do to help? Jack wouldn't blame Benkei if he was a hundred miles from Kumamoto and still running. It would be foolhardy for him to attempt any sort of rescue. He was a conjuror, not a trained warrior. He'd have more chance of flying to the moon and back. With its towering walls, complex of winding passages and vast garrison of samurai, Kumamoto Castle was an impregnable fortress. Jack couldn't see how anyone could breach the castle's defences – not even a ninja.

With his head in his hands, Jack racked his brains for a way to escape. But he always came back to the same conclusion as before. Confined to his cell, it was only a matter of time before the Shogun's samurai took him away to Edo . . . where he was condemned to die.

The door to his cell swung open.

Resigned to his fate, Jack waited for rough hands to grab him and haul him to his feet – either to be beaten yet again or dragged off to face the Shogun.

But no guards appeared.

Instead, out of the inky darkness, a white-faced wraith floated into the room – lips red as blood, eyes black as midnight, pale sea-green robes shimmering like ghostly waves in the barred moonlight.

Jack's breath caught in his throat. A tremor of shock rippled through him like a chill breeze. But it wasn't fear that seized him. It was *recognition*. The face of the apparition was one he now saw only in his dreams, its restless spirit forever destined to haunt him.

'I . . . I . . . *tried* to save you,' pleaded Jack. 'Save you all . . .'

'Save *me*?' queried the wraith, the corner of its red mouth curling into a smile. 'Jack, I've come to rescue *you*.'

38

KABUKI GIRL

The wraith took a step closer, concern etching its ashen face.

'Are you all right, Jack? The guards didn't *seriously* hurt you, did they?'

With a methodical yet familiar touch, the wraith carefully checked him over for injuries. Up close, Jack could see the waxy white make-up and thick layer of rouge on its lips.

'*You're alive!*' he gasped.

'Of course I am,' said the wraith, satisfied Jack was still in one piece, if a little battered. 'Now stop your mad act and let's get out of here.'

'But . . . *Miyuki* . . . you drowned,' Jack spluttered, unable to comprehend her miraculous resurrection.

'Do I *look* drowned?' she said, giving him a tender yet impatient smile.

Shaking his head, Jack stood and embraced her. 'I thought I'd lost you forever.'

'It'll take a lot more than a storm to lose me,' she whispered, hugging him with equal affection. 'Now get dressed.'

She grabbed a pile of clothes from the doorway and laid them at his feet. Still in a daze, Jack picked up the first garment – a pretty pink *obi* with a cherry-blossom pattern. He rummaged through the rest of the items. A rose-coloured underslip, a bold red kimono with yellow and magenta chrysanthemums and long dangling sleeves, a set of white gloves, several ornate hairpins, a large ivory haircomb, two white *tabi* socks and a pair of wooden *geta* for his feet.

'But these are *girl's* clothes!' he exclaimed.

'Exactly,' said Miyuki, producing a black wig and fitting it on to his head. 'The perfect disguise for a ninja. You already know the art of *Shichi Hō De*, "the Seven Ways of Going". Well, this is the eighth! A *kabuki* girl.'

Miyuki held up the rose-coloured underslip for him to wear and averted her eyes. 'Hurry! We don't have long.'

Jack began to dress, then stopped. 'We *have* to find Akiko first . . . if it's not too late.'

He bolted for the door, but Miyuki grabbed him.

'I already did,' she revealed.

'Then why isn't she here?' asked Jack, beginning to expect the worst.

Miyuki looked at him as if the reason was obvious. 'Because she's putting on her make-up.'

For a second Jack thought Miyuki was joking. Then it dawned on him Akiko was safe. Jack's heart almost burst with joy at the news. Only a short while before he'd been drowning in despair. Now he'd discovered both Miyuki *and* Akiko were alive and well. He grabbed his new clothes, impatient to be reunited.

'I found her in the first cell I looked in,' explained Miyuki as she helped Jack into the rest of his costume. 'She's just finishing off her disguise.'

'The kimono's rather . . . tight,' complained Jack, stiffly moving his arms.

'I'm afraid Okuni didn't have anything larger in her wardrobe.'

'*Okuni?*' gasped Jack, as Miyuki tugged hard on the *obi* around his waist and tied it off in a willow knot.

Miyuki nodded. 'She and her *kabuki* troupe are upstairs performing to the *daimyo* as we speak.'

'They're helping us escape?'

'You've become a folk hero to them after everything you did to save their star performer,' she revealed, inserting the pins and comb into his black beehive of a wig. 'Next, we need to do your make-up.'

Miyuki took out a wooden box from her sleeve pocket and opened it to reveal a number of compartments. Each was filled with a different coloured powder or paste. Beside this, she placed a small jar of milky-coloured wax, several bamboo brushes, a piece of charcoal and a bowl into which she mixed some white powder and the remains of Jack's slimy water.

'Close your eyes,' she instructed, warming a dollop of wax between her hands and rubbing a thin layer over his face and neck. Then she loaded a bamboo brush with the white make-up and painted his exposed skin until it was as featureless as a snowdrift.

'That's the foundation layer done,' Miyuki explained, blotting the excess moisture with a sponge. She picked up the piece of charcoal. 'Don't move or even blink. I can't afford to make a mistake here.'

Jack sat still as a statue as she redrew his eyebrows, high on his forehead, in an expression of permanent astonishment –

which was exactly how he felt at seeing Miyuki again. He was bursting with questions, desperate to know how she had survived, how she had found him and, most importantly, whether she knew the fate of Yori or Saburo. But he understood there'd be time for answers later, once they had escaped *daimyo* Kato's clutches.

Jack gasped as he remembered the *rutter*.

'Stay still,' tutted Miyuki, trying not to smudge the charcoal line.

Although he hadn't seen *daimyo* Kato presented with his pack, the *rutter* was undoubtedly in the samurai lord's possession. And, in a castle this size, Jack could have no idea where it was being kept. With a sinking heart, he realized he had no choice but to leave his father's precious *rutter* behind.

'Keep your head up,' instructed Miyuki, carefully outlining his eyes in black.

Chewing on her lower lip as she worked, Miyuki then selected a thin rabbit-hair brush and highlighted the corners in a garish red hue.

'Purse your lips like this,' she told Jack, forming her mouth into a pout and looking like she might kiss him.

Jack mirrored her pose and she laughed.

'Not so fast, English boy,' she teased, dipping the brush in the same deep red paste and painting his mouth into the shape of bee-stung lips.

Dressed in girl's clothes and plastered in make-up, Jack had to admit he was feeling a little self-conscious. But, as a means of escape, he realized Miyuki's plan was both daring and their only chance. With so many sentries posted on the castle walls, Jack had to be invisible – or, at least, unrecognizable.

Miyuki took a step back to admire her handiwork and grimaced at what she saw.

'What's wrong?' said Jack.

'I'm afraid that'll have to do,' she sighed.

A burst of giggles made them both turn round. Akiko stood in the doorway, dressed in a glorious mauve kimono with an ivory-coloured design of herons in flight. Like Jack, her face was painted white, her delicate features highlighted in black and red. But, unlike Jack, she looked divine.

Clapping a hand to her mouth, Akiko tried to suppress her laughter.

'*Shh!*' warned Miyuki, shooting her an annoyed look as she hurriedly repacked the make-up box.

'Sorry,' Akiko whispered, 'but I've never seen Jack look so . . .'

'Pretty?' suggested Jack, tilting his head to one side and batting his eyelids.

'Pretty ugly more like!' smirked Miyuki. 'But as it's dark you should fool the guards.'

Jack squeezed his feet into the wooden *geta* and clip-clopped over to Akiko. 'I was so worried. I thought the *daimyo* had . . .'

Akiko took his hand, squeezing it reassuringly. 'The guards didn't lay a finger on me. The *daimyo* had other plans for my fate. I was more worried about you.'

'And *everyone* will be worried about us, if we don't get moving,' interrupted Miyuki, purposefully passing between them to reach the door. 'The *kabuki* show must be almost over by now.'

Akiko stiffened slightly at Miyuki's ill-mannered barging, but said nothing. Though neither girl liked the other – the rivalry of samurai and ninja running deep – they at least shared a healthy respect for each other's skills.

Alert to the danger they now faced, the three of them cautiously made their way down the darkened corridor. Four unconscious guards lay sprawled on the floor. Half-drunk cups of *saké* were discarded on the stone slabs next to their lifeless hands.

'A sleeper drug,' explained Miyuki as she cleared away the evidence.

A ninja's presence should be like the wind – always felt but never seen, thought Jack, remembering their training together under the Grandmaster Soke. Miyuki's cunning, expertise and thoroughness were only some of the reasons why he admired her so much.

They hurried along to the bottom of the stairwell, Jack tottering on his wooden clogs. The tight kimono restricted his movements and he stumbled over a stone slab. Akiko and Miyuki caught him on either side and they both exchanged a look of concern.

'Let's just hope we don't have to make a run for it!' remarked Miyuki.

39

MIE

'You're cutting it fine,' said Okuni under her breath, as Jack, Akiko and Miyuki joined her at the edge of the stage. She arched her painted eyebrows at Jack's vastly altered appearance, but made no comment. 'The final act's about to go on.'

Junjun and six other girls, dressed in a collection of flamboyant kimono, waited in the wings for the previous act to finish. Jack peeked through a gap between two side screens. *Daimyo* Kato and his guests reclined on silken cushions in the keep's main reception room. It was a magnificent chamber with a gold-panelled ceiling of painted flowers and silk-screen walls adorned with exquisite scenes of blossoming trees and mist-shrouded mountains. The samurai lord took prime position in the centre of a large raised dais. He clasped his iron fan in one hand, tapping to the rhythm of the music played by three musicians on the stage. Ten high-ranking officials, their silk robes as grandiose as their status, sat either side of him. Four bore the *kamon* of the Shogun – a trio of hollyhock leaves in a circle. And, around the chamber, another thirty armed samurai of the Shogun's personal guard knelt watching the show.

Jack thought he couldn't go any deeper into the lion's mouth without being swallowed whole.

Taking centre stage, a juggler in a multicoloured robe was performing the climax to his act. Juggling five eggs at once, he tossed them so high into the air that they almost hit the precious gilded ceiling. As he caught then threw one of the eggs, it miraculously transformed into a tiny sparrow that fluttered away. Each consecutive egg did the same until the room was filled with the sound of twittering birds.

'I don't believe it!' exclaimed one of the officials. 'He turned the eggs into *suzume*!'

The audience burst into astonished applause. Even *daimyo* Kato put down his fan to join in the clapping. The spiky-haired performer gave a flourishing bow, then bounded off the stage.

'You were *amazing*!' fawned Junjun. 'How on earth did you make that happen?'

'A good conjuror never reveals his tricks!' he replied, grinning from ear to ear at his enthusiastic reception.

'*Benkei*!' whispered Jack, both delighted and relieved to see his friend safe and sound. He wasn't a traitor after all. He was one of their saviours.

Turning, Benkei did a double-take, then laughed, 'You scrub up well, *nanban*.'

'Careful what you say!' hissed Miyuki. '*Anyone* could be listening.'

Benkei immediately sealed his mouth, pretending to sew his lips together with a finger, as the musicians struck up a new song and Junjun and her dancers swanned out on to the stage for the finale.

'You *have* to watch this,' urged Benkei, too excited to keep quiet. 'Junjun is simply outstanding.'

Encircled by the other dancers, Junjun began to twirl and twist as if performing a Buddhist prayer dance. The *shamisen* twanged to the intense beat of the *tsuzumi* drums and the wooden clappers accentuated her movements. Floating in short dainty steps around the stage, she bobbed and weaved like a feather caught in the wind. Her hands flowed in complex patterns, seeming to press and lift the very air around her.

'I hope this dance is short,' mumbled Miyuki under her breath. 'We're living on borrowed time.'

Like the rest of the room, Jack was dazzled by Junjun's display, but he also felt Miyuki's agitation. Their breakout could be discovered at any moment – a change of guards, a spot check, or even the alarm being raised if one of the comatose samurai recovered.

Junjun continued to flutter across the stage, teasingly exposing her wrists and displaying her painted neck. At the height of the music, she struck an unexpected pose. Stamping her left foot powerfully to the floor, she stood stock still, her right hand outstretched and flat towards the ground and her left pointing directly skywards. Her red-tinted eyes were opened so wide, they seemed to fill her doll-like face. The effect was so sudden and overpowering that many of the officials gasped in shock. Jack had never seen anything like it. Nor, apparently, had *daimyo* Kato and the other samurai. They all sat transfixed, their mouths hanging open like stunned goldfish.

'Junjun has cut a *mie* pose,' explained Okuni in hushed

tones. 'I created the technique to draw attention to the emotional climax of the dance. This is what makes my *kabuki* show stand out from all others.'

The *shamisen*, drums and clappers reached a fever pitch, then ceased abruptly. The silence that followed was almost as deafening. While Junjun hesitantly bowed, the audience remained thunderstruck. The samurai all awaited the reaction of the *daimyo* to this dramatic and sensational display. Then, just as the lack of reaction was becoming unbearable, *daimyo* Kato smiled and began clapping and the whole room exploded into fervent applause.

Junjun gave another bow before Okuni joined her on stage and presented her star performer to the *daimyo* himself. After the necessary formalities, Okuni and Junjun took their leave and joined the rest of the troupe backstage. Junjun was immediately swamped by well-wishers, but Okuni shooed them away and set everyone to work packing up the show's clothes and props. To blend in with the troupe, Jack, Akiko and Miyuki did their best to help, while Benkei spent most of his time engaged in charming Junjun.

'How much longer do you think we have?' Jack whispered to Miyuki.

'Depends,' she replied, hurriedly folding up a kimono. 'Those sleeper drugs can last all night, or . . . just a few hours.'

Once Okuni had settled her business affairs with the *daimyo*'s treasurer and apologized for their need to leave for a booking in Shimabara the next day, she led her troupe from the reception room. Jack tottered along between Akiko and Miyuki. He kept his head down as they paraded past the *daimyo*, who gazed longingly at the departing Junjun. This worked in their favour, and he and Akiko slipped from the chamber unnoticed.

Descending several flights of stairs, the *kabuki* troupe exited the keep and crossed the gravelled courtyard that only three days before Jack and Akiko had been dragged over as prisoners. They approached the courtyard's inner gate. A unit of eight samurai stood sentry. Flaming torches lit the entrance, banishing the night and exposing anyone who passed beneath to their unforgiving glare.

Jack felt himself trembling with nerves. This would be his first real test. Could he really pass himself off as a *kabuki* dancer? He was taller and stockier than the others. His wooden *geta* clumped on the stone path, seemingly louder than all the girls put together. Perspiring heavily, he now worried that his make-up might be running. Miyuki had been crazy to believe this disguise could work. Any guard worth his salt would be able to tell that he wasn't a girl!

But it was too late to turn back now. Okuni was showing her castle pass to the guard. Satisfied, the guard beckoned the troupe through. Jack shuffled forward. The unit of samurai eyed each of the dancers. But they weren't looking for an escaped *gaijin*. They were simply admiring the girls. And Jack was quickly ushered through, none of them giving *him* a second glance.

Astounded to have made it past, Jack breathed a sigh of relief . . . until Miyuki whispered, 'One down, six more to go.'

With each gate, however, Jack became more and more confident of success. The samurai soldiers, distracted by the beauty of the troupe, relaxed and lowered their guard. All the men were eager to please rather than be obstructive. With

Okuni and Junjun leading the way, they breezed through each checkpoint.

'Last gate,' Miyuki whispered to Jack as the *kabuki* troupe proceeded along the road to the castle's main entrance. A full detachment of samurai guarded this gateway. Armed with swords and spears, they lined either side two deep. Beyond them lay Kumamoto city and freedom. For Jack, the temptation to run was almost overwhelming. But he forced himself to maintain a steady pace. The last thing he wanted to do now was trip over.

The guards leered as the troupe promenaded by, the girls smiling demurely and giggling with all the attention. Okuni at the head of the group handed over her castle pass to the chief guard, a hairy man with a bristling beard, heavy jowls and bulbous eyes. He gave the scroll a cursory glance and waved her through, more interested in her protégée than any paperwork.

Akiko and Miyuki stuck close to Jack's side, hoping to shield him from direct view. Jack kept his eyes demurely to the ground, while making every effort to walk in tiny feminine steps. Ahead, Benkei was already through the gate. Another ten paces and Jack would be too –

'STOP THERE!' ordered the chief guard.

A criss-cross of steel spear tips forced Jack to a startled halt. The spears separated the troupe in half. His heart hammered in his chest as the chief guard strode straight over to him.

With his bulging eyes, the man looked Jack up and down. 'What's your name?' he demanded.

Flustered, Jack offered what he hoped was a coy sweet smile as he thought of a suitable name. Then, remembering Benkei's birds, he replied in a high-pitched, squeaky voice, 'S . . . S . . . Suzume.'

The chief guard thumbed the hilt of his sword as he considered this name. Out of the corner of his eye, Jack noticed Miyuki reaching into the folds of her kimono sleeve, where she concealed a knife. He felt Akiko tense, ready to pounce too. They would have to make a break for it.

The chief guard leant in close to Jack's face. 'Well, my little sparrow,' he breathed into his ear, 'you certainly caught *my* eye.'

Jack yelped as he felt his bottom get pinched.

'Fancy visiting my nest one day?' the man asked, grinning like the fat slimy toad he was.

'Certainly not!' Jack replied with as much grace as he could muster. 'This little sparrow's flying south for the winter.'

Acting offended by the proposition, he boldly clip-clopped past the chief guard and parted the crossed spears with his gloved hand.

'Come back soon, my little sparrow!' called the chief guard, admiring his departure from behind.

Not likely, thought Jack, hurrying out through the gate as fast as his wooden clogs could carry him.

40

REUNITED

'We made it!' exclaimed Benkei, giving a little skip as the *kabuki* troupe turned a street corner and the castle gate disappeared from view.

Miyuki shook her head gravely. 'We're not out of trouble until we're on-board the ferry and halfway to Shimabara.'

'I still can't believe your escape plan worked,' said Jack, grabbing hold of Akiko's arm to steady himself as they kept up their hurried pace. Okuni led them through the deserted city streets towards the harbour. Dawn was still a few hours off, but they needed to ensure they were on the first boat out of Kumamoto.

'It almost didn't when that guard took a liking to you,' said Akiko, shaking her head in disbelief.

'Some men have very unusual taste!' remarked Miyuki. 'Anyway, I can't take all the credit for the plan. Benkei was the one who suggested using the *kabuki* troupe for cover.'

'Then we owe you our lives, Benkei,' said Akiko, bowing her head, repentant for having doubted his loyalty.

He acknowledged her praise with a humble shrug. 'All in a day's work for Benkei the Great!'

The *kabuki* troupe crossed the bridge over the Shira River and turned down a side street.

'But how did you and Miyuki meet each other in the first place?' asked Jack.

'I recognized your friends, of course,' said Benkei, grinning like a Cheshire cat and pointing down the road.

Jack and Akiko both came to a stunned halt. Tethered outside one of the inns was Akiko's white stallion. Beside the horse stood a rotund young samurai with bushy eyebrows and a beaming smile. And next to him a small boy in monk's robes carrying a *shakujō* ringed staff. Their shadowy appearance in the darkened street made them look like ghosts.

'*Saburo . . . Yori . . .*' gasped Jack, almost too scared to say their names out loud in case the spell was broken.

Arms open wide, Jack ran towards his friends, and promptly fell flat on his face as one of his *geta* tripped him up. Rushing over, Saburo and Yori helped him back to his feet.

'Steady there, young lady,' smirked Saburo, trying to stifle his laughter at Jack's comic tumble and feminine appearance. 'These streets can be dangerous at night. Never know who you might meet!'

Jack looked from Saburo's face to Yori's and back again, still not quite believing his friends were real.

'Akiko!' cried Yori in delight, as she now joined the unexpected reunion.

'It's *very* good to see you too,' she smiled, bowing to them both. 'Jack told me you'd died at sea.'

'We almost did,' said Saburo, a grim look passing across his face.

'So how *did* you escape the storm? Or even find me?' asked Jack.

'Time for all that later,' cut in Miyuki, collecting her pack from a pile beside the inn's entrance. 'First let's catch that ferry.'

'After our last experience, I hope there aren't any pirates this time!' said Saburo, handing Akiko the reins to her horse and picking up his own bag.

Akiko tenderly stroked the stallion's mane, tears welling in her eyes. 'I never thought I'd see Snowball again. Thank you, Saburo.'

'It's not me you should thank. Yori was the one to recognize him.'

'I spotted your family's *kamon* on the saddle and thought Benkei had stolen your horse,' explained Yori.

'But I hadn't!' Benkei interrupted, hastily defending his honour.

'Then what were you doing with all their belongings, high-tailing it out of Kumamoto?' challenged Saburo.

'Keeping them safe,' he replied, offering Jack and Akiko his most sincere smile. 'After getting the travel permits, I returned to the inn and saw the samurai patrol on the doorstep. So I hid in the stables. Once they were gone and the innkeeper was busy celebrating his future reward, I sneaked back into our rooms.'

'So it was the innkeeper who betrayed us,' said Akiko in disgust, 'even though we paid him off!'

Benkei shook his head. 'It was actually his wife, Momo.'

'I *knew* I was being watched,' said Jack, recalling the too lifelike eyes of the *koto* player in the screen painting.

'Anyway, I grabbed all our packs, your swords and bow, and made off on the horse. I wasn't thinking where I was going, just trying to –'

'You got my pack?' interrupted Jack. 'I thought the *daimyo* had taken everything.'

Yori stepped forward, cradling the bag with its precious cargo. 'I've been looking after it for you.'

'Then it's been in safe hands,' said Jack, smiling at his dear friend as he felt the reassuring weight of the *rutter* inside.

Reunited, he gazed in turn at Yori, Saburo, Miyuki and Akiko. His circle of friends was complete – as if another perfect *ensō* had been drawn in his life. 'It's so good to see you all . . . alive!'

'Are you coming?' urged Okuni, who'd been waiting anxiously with her girls. As leader of the troupe, she was only too aware of the danger she'd put them in by aiding the escape of a sworn enemy of the Shogun. Now they'd finished loading their belongings on to two handcarts and were keen to depart.

Saddling Akiko's horse with their packs, Jack and his friends rejoined the *kabuki* troupe and headed west along the main road out of Kumamoto. Still in disguise as a dancer, Jack couldn't be seen to carry any weapons, so his swords were also strapped to the saddle. Akiko and Miyuki walked alongside him to prevent any further mishaps, while Saburo and Yori followed behind, leading the horse.

The harbour was some distance beyond the outskirts of the city. So by the time they'd navigated the streets, avoiding the night patrols, and reached the mouth of the river, the early glow of dawn was visible on the horizon. Jack could hear the gentle wash of waves, as the velvet-black sky retreated to reveal the rippling bay before them. The silhouettes of four large wooden ferries were visible alongside a line of fishing boats moored to a broad stretch of dock. As they approached the harbour, a checkpoint loomed into view. A bamboo barrier straddled the road, beside which sat a reed-covered hut and a small wooden bunkhouse.

'What about travel permits?' Jack asked Benkei. 'Are the ones you got still valid?'

'Afraid not, but there's no need to worry,' Benkei replied confidently. 'Travelling performers don't need them. We should pass straight through without too much question.'

As the procession reached the barrier, a bleary-eyed harbour guard emerged from the hut.

'Halt!' he growled. Unshaven and with hangdog jowls, the man leant wearily upon his spear and gave a huge yawn.

Inside the bunkhouse, Jack could see at least a dozen other samurai snoring away. All were heavily armed, even if they weren't yet awake.

'Why are you all up so early?' the harbour guard demanded gruffly. 'The sun's not even risen!'

'I need to guarantee places for my whole troupe on-board the first ferry,' replied Okuni brightly, introducing her girls with a flourish of the hand.

But the bleary-eyed harbour guard failed to be impressed. 'You're performers, eh? What, *all* of you?'

Okuni nodded. 'You may know of us. My dance troupe performs *kabuki* all over Japan.'

The harbour guard snorted. 'Never heard of such a style. You'll have to prove your talents. You, girl, show us what you can do.'

He gestured with his spear, but no one moved. Jack wondered why the performer hadn't begun her dance. Then his stomach knotted into a ball of shock as he realized the harbour guard had pointed at *him*.

'Suzume is a little shy . . . she's still learning the routines,' said Okuni hurriedly. 'How about Junjun? She's our best dancer.'

'A *shy* performer?' queried the harbour guard, ignoring Okuni and eyeing Jack suspiciously. 'The girl had better dance well or *none* of you will be on that ferry.'

41

JIG

The harbour guard stood unsmiling, arms crossed, waiting for the show to begin. The other samurai now emerged from the bunkhouse to see what the commotion was all about. They blinked in heavy-eyed surprise at the presence of so many girls, before gathering round in anticipation of the early morning performance.

Jack swallowed nervously as the troupe's three musicians unpacked their instruments and waited for his cue to begin. Akiko and Miyuki reluctantly stepped away from him, wondering what he would do. A refusal to dance would arouse further suspicion and stop them boarding the ferry. Retreating to Kumamoto simply wasn't an option. And drawing their weapons to fight the samurai could only be a last resort since it would risk the lives of the entire troupe.

Jack had no choice but to dance.

Slipping off his *geta*, Jack took his position in the middle of the road. He gave a hesitant nod and the music struck up. Its rhythm and melody were strange to his Western ears. He couldn't distinguish any definite beat and the song seemed to unfurl with no obvious breaks or repeat of theme.

As he stood swaying uncertainly, at a loss how to even begin, he felt the eyes of the samurai boring into him.

'If this is *kabuki*, you can keep it. My dog dances better than this girl!' the harbour guard grumbled.

Jack realized he had to attempt *something*, however lame. He couldn't hope to reproduce Junjun's spellbinding performance, but since none of the samurai had ever seen *kabuki* before it didn't matter what he did, as long as it was convincing. And Jack knew only one type of dance – a sailor's jig.

Taking up his long sleeves in his hands like hankies, he began to skip to the music. Waving his arms backwards and forwards and jumping in the air, he tried to remember the moves Ginsel, the Dutchman on-board the *Alexandria*, had taught him. He twirled one sleeve then the next. He bobbed up and down. Spun on the spot with his hands planted on his hips. Kicked out with his left foot. Hopped on his right. In his head, he imagined the lively tune of a fiddle and whistle and pranced enthusiastically before the harbour guard, with a fixed grin on his face.

Okuni and her dancing troupe watched his performance with a mix of shock, fascination and utter bewilderment. Akiko and Miyuki both smiled encouragingly, but their expressions were strained to the limit. Saburo shook his head in doomed despair, while Benkei was barely able to conceal his mirth. Only Yori tried his best to clap along, acting as if he knew the dance.

But the harbour guard and his men observed the performance in stony-faced silence.

Jack now threw himself into the jig with an almost desperate energy. Jumping around like a firecracker, he slapped his thighs, clapped his hands, tapped his feet and circled his sleeves above his head. The samurai grew even more dumbstruck by this flailing attempt at a dance. Even the musicians trailed off as his crazy jig distracted them from their playing.

Panting heavily, Jack pirouetted to a stop, then bowed with a dramatic flourish of the sleeves.

A deathly silence hung in the air. The harbour guard cocked his head to one side and looked Jack up and down.

'We're as good as dead,' whispered Miyuki, reaching for the throwing knife hidden in her kimono sleeve.

Of the same opinion, Akiko stealthily edged towards her horse to grab her weapons.

Then a wide-mouthed grin creased the harbour guard's face and he roared with laughter, a full-throated guffaw bending him double. He was quickly joined by the other samurai, who all began belly-laughing at the spectacle they'd just witnessed. Wiping the tears from his eyes, the harbour guard chortled, 'That's the . . . *funniest* dance . . . I've ever seen! No wonder your troupe is so famous!'

Almost helpless with laughter, he raised the bamboo barrier and ushered them through.

For a moment, Jack simply stood there, stunned by the samurai's reaction to his earnest efforts at a dance. The jig wasn't supposed to be funny.

Unable to believe their good fortune, Miyuki urged him onwards and the troupe hurried through the checkpoint and into the harbour.

'Well done, Jack,' praised Yori. 'I never knew you could dance so well.'

Jack smiled wryly at him. Yori was a loyal friend but a terrible liar.

'That wasn't dancing,' remarked Benkei. 'That was a lethal form of martial arts – death by laughter!'

'Remind me never to ask *you* for a dance, Jack!' quipped Saburo.

'Who says I'd even accept!' Jack shot back, feigning offence at the jibes.

'Good or bad, your performance saved us a fight,' said Miyuki, glancing over her shoulder to check none of the harbour guards were following them. 'And we certainly don't want to leave any trail for *daimyo* Kato to follow. As far as he's concerned, you two could have escaped in any direction.'

'Do you think he knows by now?' asked Yori, his staff jingling as they made their way along the harbour side.

'Possibly. But if not, he soon will. They change the guards at dawn.'

'Then let's find this ferry and get out of here,' urged Akiko.

The dock was relatively quiet, with just the local fishermen at work this early in the morning. In no time at all, they found the ferry that was leaving first. Although the captain had barely woken, he was only too keen to have such glamorous passengers on-board his vessel. Lowering the gangplank, he welcomed each of the girls personally and offered them prime seats near the prow. The ferry was a large open-decked ship with room for some sixty passengers plus cargo. The crew helped transfer the troupe's belongings on-board and there was even a stall for Akiko's horse. As the girls made themselves comfortable, Jack had a quick glance round the vessel and was relieved to discover that not only did it possess a large canvas sail but a dozen burly oarsmen sat ready to power the ferry. That meant they wouldn't be reliant upon the wind to depart – which could be an essential factor if they needed to make a quick getaway.

Once settled, the troupe could do nothing but wait for the ferry to cast off. But that wouldn't happen until the captain had enough passengers. Jack and his friends sat in silence, aware that every passing minute further endangered their lives. A steady trickle of travellers and merchants began arriving and the captain's crew busied themselves loading the cargo hold with rice, salt, ceramics, bamboo and various other goods for shipment to Shimabara. But their progress towards departure seemed painstakingly slow.

The sun poked its head above the horizon and its golden rays clipped the top of Kumamoto Castle. At that moment, the peace of dawn was shattered by the sound of clanging bells.

42

FERRY

'Wakey-wakey, *daimyo*!' said Benkei with a grim smile. 'Your guests are gone.'

Jack and his friends exchanged uneasy looks at the continuing klaxon of noise.

'I doubt they welcome in the dawn like this every day,' said Saburo.

'We've still a little time before any patrol gets here,' reminded Akiko, glancing up the road in the direction of Kumamoto. Clusters of travellers queued for the checkpoint, but there were no samurai charging down to the harbour . . . not yet anyway.

'The ferry's almost full,' said Yori hopefully. The crew had finished loading the cargo and the captain was welcoming the last few groups of passengers on-board as the alarm bells rang on.

'Doesn't matter,' replied Miyuki. 'The harbour guard's bound to stop any ships leaving now.'

'They've already closed the checkpoint,' Akiko noted with growing concern.

Jack leant over the side of the ferry. 'There's a small fishing boat moored next to us. We could try to escape in that.'

'Not after last time!' pleaded Saburo, his face turning decidedly green at the prospect of another bout of seasickness, pirates and storms.

'The fishing boat might be our only option,' said Miyuki, directing everyone's attention back to the road.

In the distance, a unit of samurai were marching double-time towards the harbour.

The captain caught sight of the patrol. 'Not *another* military drill,' he moaned. 'Cast off now, otherwise we'll be stuck here all day.'

Drawing in the gangplank, the crew raised the anchor, set the main sail and unhitched the ropes from the dockside. The offshore breeze proved too light to move the ship, so the oarsmen took up their positions and dug their paddles deep into the water. But the fully laden vessel was slow to pull away from the quay. Meanwhile, the samurai were drawing nearer and nearer.

Jack was reminded of the race between the tortoise and the hare. But this time the hare was going to win.

As the oarsmen got into their stride, the ferry gained momentum and headed for the mouth of the harbour. The samurai, seeing the ship depart, were now running down the road. Jack silently willed the oarsmen to row harder, each stroke promising them freedom. The patrol reached the checkpoint and interrogated the harbour guard. He appeared to shake his head, then could be seen attempting to dance a jig. The patrol leader pushed past him and ran on to the dock, gesturing for the captain to turn back, but by this time the ferry was out of the harbour and beyond hailing distance.

Jack and his friends sat down and breathed a collective sigh of relief. They'd escaped by the skin of their teeth. Sensing this was a moment to celebrate, the musicians took out their instruments again and started to play. The music inspired some of the girls to dance and they launched into an impromptu performance – much to the delight of the crew and passengers on-board.

But Jack experienced a growing sense of unease. He wondered whether they had *really* escaped scot-free. The harbour guard had evidently been convinced by his dance. But would *daimyo* Kato, when his samurai reported back to him, suspect the *kabuki* troupe had been involved? Or did he already believe they were? The troupe's appearance at his castle and the simultaneous breakout of his prisoners could arguably be coincidence. There was no obvious connection between the two. But, in the eyes of an astute and cunning *daimyo*, a well-planned subterfuge might be seen. Whatever the case, Jack would feel happier once he was out of the *kabuki* costume and there was no clear link to Okuni and her troupe.

While the impromptu show continued, Jack scanned the wide expanse of bay that marked the bottleneck of the inland Ariake Sea. No boats pursued their ferry, which could only be a good sign. And the stretch of water before them was clear all the way to their destination on the opposite side. Maybe they *did* have a reason to celebrate . . .

Once out in open water, the breeze stiffened and the ferry powered steadily through the waves towards Shimabara. The castle port shimmered on the horizon, overshadowed by the mountainous and scarred Unzen-dake. The menacing cone-shaped volcano rose out of the water like a devil's fang, its smouldering peak biting into the clear blue sky and spitting out sulphurous clouds.

An ominous feeling seized Jack, as if something, not necessarily the volcano, would soon erupt with devastating consequences.

'This voyage had better be short,' said Saburo, holding his head in his hands and groaning.

'Still haven't found your sea legs then?' replied Jack, dragging his eyes away from the brooding volcano.

'I must have lost them during that storm!' He attempted a smile but failed miserably.

Jack gave an involuntary shudder as he recalled the ferocious tempest that had nearly killed them all. Despite the favourable conditions in the bay now, being at sea again brought the nightmare vividly back. He looked at his friends. 'I truly thought you'd all drowned.'

'We thought *you* had drowned,' said Yori, sitting close by his side on the rough wooden deck. 'When you disappeared beneath that wave, I . . . I . . .' He was unable to finish the sentence as emotion choked his voice.

Jack laid a comforting hand on his friend's shoulder. 'I understand. I felt the same way when I washed up on the beach and found the three of you gone. So how *did* you survive?'

'Your decision to tie us to the skiff saved our lives,' explained Miyuki. 'Even though exhaustion and the cold nearly killed us, when the storm had passed a fisherman spotted our capsized boat. He hauled us on-board and took us back to shore. For the next few days, we recovered in his fishing village. We believed you were dead until we heard the stories of the Golden-Haired Devil of Beppu.' Miyuki grinned. 'We knew that could *only* be you!'

'But I've been on the run ever since. How did you find me here?'

As he asked the question, Jack realized he already knew the answer: she was sitting right opposite him.

'Miyuki tracked you, of course!' replied Yori, his tone expressing respect and awe at her skills. 'Your arrest in Yufuin. The missing prayer flag. The cut rope bridge. The search parties around Aso –'

'I lost your trail after that,' admitted Miyuki. 'I guessed you were going to Kumamoto; it was the most obvious crossing point for Nagasaki. But there was no sign of you there, even after a few days of searching.'

'You must have gone ahead of me,' said Jack, thinking of the period he and Benkei had taken refuge with Shiryu.

'That's the conclusion I came to, so we began to double back. We were taking the road out of Kumamoto, when Yori spotted Akiko's horse and we bumped into Benkei, who was "looking after" your belongings.'

She raised her eyebrows dubiously at such a notion, but Benkei brushed aside her insinuation with a wave of his hand. 'And lucky they did, *nanban*, otherwise your friends would never have found you in time. Nor would they have been introduced to Okuni and her *kabuki* troupe when they arrived in Kumamoto to perform for the *daimyo*.'

'I have to admit that was a stroke of good fortune,' said Miyuki. 'We'd never have got inside that castle otherwise.'

'We have a lot to thank them for,' said Jack, watching Junjun dance across the deck.

Her performance came to an end and the passengers broke into rapturous applause. Okuni and her dancers were bestowed with so many tokens of appreciation that their passage on-board the ferry was paid for twice over.

Akiko glanced wistfully across the bay towards Shimabara. 'You're almost home free now, Jack.'

'Not quite,' he replied, a shadow falling across his face. 'Kazuki's still out there.'

Yori's eyes widened in shock. 'But I thought he'd given up. Especially after almost dying in that flood.'

'That only made him more determined,' said Jack. 'Kazuki's vowed on his life to hunt me down . . . and kill me.'

For a moment no one said anything, the only noise being the flap of the sail, the wash of waves and the splash of oars.

Akiko turned to Miyuki. 'Did you come across Kazuki's path while tracking Jack?'

Miyuki shook her head.

'Then he's ahead of us and waiting to pounce.'

Miyuki's gaze dropped to Jack's injured hand. 'Did Kazuki do *that* to you?' she asked, her dark eyes narrowing in anger.

'No, that was Sensei Kyuzo,' Jack replied, and told them about his harrowing encounter. Yori could hardly believe a teacher of the *Niten Ichi Ryū* would commit such a betrayal. And when Jack came to the moment the Akita dog ate his fingertip, Saburo's seasickness took a turn for the worse and he heaved over the ferry's side.

Miyuki could barely contain her rage. 'So long as I live, I won't let *anyone* harm you again.'

'Nor will I,' stated Akiko, with equal determination.

'None of us will,' assured Yori.

Jack didn't know what to say. Once again, he was over-whelmed by his friends' loyalty and courage.

43

SHIMABARA

The ferry docked at Shimabara just as the sun reached its zenith. The voyage had been smooth and for once uneventful, giving Jack and his friends the opportunity to recover from the night's fraught escape. After a much-needed breakfast of cold rice and dried fish from their supplies, Jack had slept deep and long, comforted by the familiar pitch and roll of the boat. His friends had taken turns to keep watch, but now, as they disembarked, everyone was on full alert to negotiate the unknown threats of the bustling port.

Akiko guided Snowball down the gangplank and resaddled him, while Jack and the others helped the *kabuki* troupe load their belongings back on to the handcarts. Once everyone was ready, they headed for the checkpoint. The port was teeming with travellers, merchants and dockhands, the hectic atmosphere providing useful cover as they approached the barrier.

Four harbour guards were stationed at the exit, meticulously checking permits.

Jack braced himself for another performance. As the line cleared, Okuni stepped up and introduced herself and her troupe. Noting the guards' obvious interest in the arrival of so many girls, Okuni offered them front-row seats at the *kabuki* show that evening. The subtle bribe brought broad smiles to the men's faces and they welcomed the troupe through the checkpoint unquestioned.

'Easy as falling off a log!' said Benkei, giving Jack a wink.

Jack wished he shared his friend's confidence. But he knew from bitter experience that the moment they dropped their guard would be the moment an enemy attacked. And the smouldering volcano of Unzen-dake did nothing to raise Jack's spirits. It loomed over Shimabara like a brooding monster. Trapped between the volcano and the full glare of the sun, the town sweltered in the summer heat, the ocean breeze doing little to alleviate the discomfort. Townsfolk wafted to and fro along the main road, fluttering their fans like a flock of frantic butterflies. Samurai stood on every street corner, observing the passers-by and slowly broiling in their armour. Jack wondered if the intense heat had anything to do with being so close to a volcano.

'I've got a bad feeling about this place,' whispered Jack to Miyuki.

'Me too,' she replied, anxiously thumbing the hilt of her hidden knife.

As they neared the centre, the town suddenly disappeared into rubble, every building razed to the ground. At first, Jack thought the volcano must have erupted, a lava flow destroying this section of the port. But on closer inspection he could see the huge swathe of land had been cleared – houses and whole streets purposefully demolished to make way for a new construction.

A castle.

Samurai guards were stationed all over the site, keeping a watchful eye on hundreds of men, women and children, all in ragged clothes. They laboured like a swarm of ants over the broken ground. Bare-chested men, smeared in dirt and sweat, dug out a vast moat, while exhausted women and sunburnt children hauled out endless buckets of earth. The trench was wide and deep enough to dry-dock a Spanish galleon and extended for at least a mile northwards and half a mile inland. Within its vast boundaries, immense stone walls were being laid boulder by boulder and watchtowers built at key strategic points. At the heart of the site was a partially constructed fortress. Made of pure white stone, it stood in stark contrast to the black-and-gold keep of Kumamoto.

'How can a small port warrant a castle this size?' exclaimed Saburo, gasping in disbelief.

'The *daimyo* must be power hungry and very rich!' said Benkei.

'And a ruthless ruler,' added Yori as he spotted two samurai beating a man who'd dropped his shovel. 'The workers are being treated like slaves.'

'We need to get out of here as soon as we can,' urged Akiko.

No one argued with her. They hurriedly followed Okuni and her troupe to a field on the outskirts of Shimabara, where the performers pitched their tents. Within one tent, out of sight of prying eyes, Jack, Akiko and Miyuki washed off their make-up and changed back into their own clothes. The cloying heat of the day made it impractical for Akiko to wear full armour, so she kept to a simple breastplate and a pair of shoulder guards over her dark-green silk kimono. The rest of her armour she stored in Snowball's saddlebags. Miyuki wore an unassuming cotton *yukata*, dyed indigo and tied off with a plain white *obi*, to blend in with the local people. As she wrapped her belt around her waist, she took care to conceal several *shuriken* within the folds. Hidden in the sleeve pocket she stowed her knife, and into her black hair she slipped a decorative brass pin, the tip sharpened into a lethal point.

'How do I look?' she asked Jack, putting the final touches to her hair.

'Deadly,' he replied with a grin and they both laughed.

At that moment, Akiko returned from packing her horse. 'I hope I'm not interrupting anything,' she said, glancing uncomfortably between the two of them.

'No, of course not,' replied Jack, sensing she was upset.

'The others are ready to go,' she added, then abruptly left the tent.

Jack didn't know what to make of Akiko's uncharacteristic brusqueness. 'We'd better make a move,' he urged Miyuki.

Picking up her *ninjatō* and stashing it in her bag, along with her *shinobi shozoku* outfit, she replied, 'I'll see you outside,' then strode from the tent, a smile curling her lips.

Jack watched her leave. Akiko and Miyuki were like two sides of a coin: made of the same metal, but with different characters. They were both loyal, courageous and highly skilled warriors. Each was quick, intelligent and shrewd. But Akiko's true nature was gentle, caring and warm-hearted; whereas Miyuki was more playful, spirited and fiery in her attitude to others. He valued both their friendships and dearly wished they'd become firm friends with one another too – not that such a thing was likely between a samurai and a ninja.

'Come on, *nanban*!' called Benkei. 'Or are you still doing your make-up?'

Slipping on his sandals, glad they now fitted like his blue kimono, Jack picked up his pack and swords. As he eased the red-handled *katana* and *wakizashi* into his *obi*, he felt a surge of strength and confidence return to him. Without these Shizu swords, he realized he'd felt vulnerable and open to attack. But now he was a warrior again, ready for the final push to Nagasaki.

Adjusting the straw hat on his head, he emerged from the tent. Okuni, Junjun and the rest of the dancers were waiting to say their farewells.

Jack bowed low. 'I appreciate the great risk you took for us.'

'And we appreciate you risking your life for Junjun,' replied Okuni, bowing in return. 'Another time you must show me that jig of yours. I'm keen to include it in our show as a comic interlude.'

Jack didn't know whether to take that as a compliment or an insult to his dancing ability, but after all she'd done, he didn't mind either way. 'Are you sure you want to? If your girls all looked like me, you'd never get any bookings!'

Okuni laughed, then turned to Benkei. 'If you want to stay, there's a place in our troupe for you.'

Benkei appeared torn by indecision. He looked longingly at Junjun – who returned his gaze – before regretfully shaking his head. 'I promised to guide Jack to Nagasaki. And I'm a man of my word.'

Junjun's eyes welled slightly with tears as she nodded in acknowledgement of his duty.

'And I, a woman of mine,' replied Okuni, noting the exchange with a smile. 'So the offer is always open.'

Bowing their farewells, Benkei led Jack and his friends out of the camp and along the main road. With one last look back in Junjun's direction, he forged ahead, yelling, 'Nagasaki, here we come!'

On the edge of town, the road divided in two.

'Which way?' Akiko asked Benkei, bringing her horse to a halt.

'We can take either,' he replied. 'North follows the coastline round the peninsula. It's flat, but the route's much longer. West skirts the base of the volcano. It's tougher going, but only two days' travel at the most.'

'West it is,' said Miyuki, riling Akiko who'd been about to reply.

'Don't you think we should ask the others first?' said Akiko.

'We need to keep off the main road,' argued Miyuki.

'But mountainous routes are prime bandit territory.'

As the two girls began bickering over the direction, Benkei and Saburo exchanged bewildered looks while the squabble grew in intensity. Jack was about to intervene, when Yori threw his *shakujō* into the air. The staff landed with a jingling clatter on the ground, silencing Akiko and Miyuki. They both stared at the discarded staff, its brass tip pointing towards the left fork.

'Fate says we go west,' declared Yori, picking up his *shakujō* and striding off up the road.

Jack had to admire Yori. His friend knew how to settle an argument quickly and fairly. Accepting the decision, Akiko spurred her horse on. Miyuki followed behind, not quite triumphant but pleased nonetheless.

The road wound steeply up the slope, leaving the port of Shimabara behind. As they climbed, they approached a small plateau with a tea house overlooking glorious views of the bay.

'We should stop here,' suggested Saburo, panting from the heat and exertion.

'I don't think we have a choice,' replied Akiko, as five men emerged from the tea house.

Armed with swords and clubs, they formed a line across the road, blocking their path.

44

RONIN RECRUITS

The five men had travel-worn appearances, their kimono slightly threadbare and their faces unshaven. They each held weapons that were chipped and stained with the dried blood of old battles. No *kamon* or other insignia were visible on their clothes. The gang were all *ronin*, masterless samurai.

Jack and his friends had no way to avoid the *ronins'* blockade. The tea house sat upon the lip of the plateau which rapidly dropped away down a rocky slope. The other side of the road met a steep bank of forest. The only route they could take was *through* the line of samurai and they weren't shifting.

'We've been waiting for you, Benkei,' said the apparent leader, a warrior with bulging arms like knotted ropes and a chest as solid as a battering ram.

'Me?' said Benkei, alarmed.

'Is there something you haven't told us, Benkei?' asked Akiko, her hands subtly reaching for her bow.

'I've never seen these men in my life!' he protested.

Saburo raised a questioning eyebrow at him. 'But he knows your name.'

'So do a lot of people.'

'Could you have tricked them at some point?' asked Jack, keeping the rim of his hat low over his face.

Benkei took a good look at the five men. Along with the leader was a thin samurai with a scar down his right cheek; a heavily bearded warrior with fists like boulders carrying a studded club; and the last two appeared to be brothers, they shared the same crooked noses and pencil-thin mouths. The only difference was that one was missing an ear.

'I . . . don't think so,' said Benkei, slowly shaking his head. 'I would've remembered men this ugly.'

'Well, we know *you*!' snorted the bearded *ronin*, slapping his club in one meaty hand. 'And I'll make you pay for that insult . . . in blood.'

Benkei shied away, moving behind Jack for protection.

'And I think we've found the *gaijin* samurai too!' exclaimed one of the brothers, pointing at Jack. 'Look, his *daishō* have red handles.'

Jack now glanced up, his identity discovered.

'It *is* the *gaijin* samurai!' confirmed the other brother, rubbing his hands together in delight. 'We're going to be very rich indeed.'

'But I thought there were only supposed to be two of them. Not six,' said the thin samurai, the scar on his cheek wrinkling like a snake as he spoke.

'No matter,' replied the leader, launching a gob of spit at the ground. 'They're just *young* samurai.'

He drew his sword, a mighty *nodachi*, the blade twice the length of a usual *katana*, and advanced on them. The other *ronin* took up battle formation on either flank. Jack and his friends seized their weapons as the samurai rushed towards them. With effortless calm, Akiko selected an arrow, nocked it on her bow and took aim. In the blink of an eye, she let it loose towards the brother with the missing ear. The arrow struck him in the shoulder with such force he was thrown backwards into the tea house and pinned to the wall. Howling in pain, he struggled to free himself.

Enraged by the attack on his brother, the other sibling charged at Akiko before she could fire off another arrow. He swung his *katana* to cut her down from her horse, but Saburo blocked the attack with his sword. Then he roundhouse-kicked the man in the stomach and sent him staggering backwards. Yori was waiting for him and thrust his staff between the brother's legs. He rolled once before disappearing over the edge of the plateau. A rattle of rock and scree receded into the distance as he tumbled head over heels down the slope.

At the same time, the bearded warrior attacked Benkei. He wielded his club in lethal arcs, forcing Benkei to dive out of the way. Jack leapt to his defence, using his *katana* and *wakizashi* to drive the *ronin* towards Miyuki. Like a cat, she pounced on the bearded *ronin*'s back and buried her hairpin into a nerve point on his neck. The man's eyes rolled in his head and he collapsed like a felled tree, unconscious before he even hit the ground.

Taken aback by the ease with which the young samurai had dispatched three of his men, the leader of the gang now went for Jack, his *nodachi* raised high to slice him in half. Akiko fired off a second arrow. The steel tip buried itself in the man's chest. But the leader was strong as an ox. He merely grunted and tore the arrowhead out before swinging his massive sword again at Jack's head. Jack deflected it with his *wakizashi* then retaliated with a cross-cut. The tip of his *katana* missed the man's neck by a fraction. The lethal length of the *nodachi* meant Jack couldn't get close enough to inflict a damaging blow.

But Miyuki could. She threw a *shuriken*. It embedded itself in the man's right bicep and he howled in pain. The distraction allowed Jack to disarm the leader with a double Autumn Leaf strike and the *nodachi* clattered to the ground. The leader roared in fury and charged headlong at Jack. Akiko tugged on the reins of Snowball and the horse turned and kicked out with its hind legs. The hooves caught the leader in the chest and sent him flying over the lip of the plateau to join the other *ronin*.

Only the scarred samurai was left. He made a last-ditch effort to kill the *gaijin* samurai. But his sword skills were no match for Jack's. With a simple Flint-and-Spark strike, Jack knocked the samurai's blade aside and cut up at the man's face. The steel tip of the *katana* sliced across his left cheek to leave a thin red line of blood.

'Now you have a matching scar,' said Jack. Standing in a Two Heavens stance, one sword held high, the other low, he gave his opponent the opportunity to reconsider his chances of survival.

Outskilled and outnumbered, the samurai dropped his sword, turned tail and fled down the road. He was running so fast, he left a dust trail in his wake.

'We need to get moving before he tells *everyone* in Shimabara about you,' said Akiko, securing her bow back on the saddle-bag.

Jack nodded in agreement and sheathed his swords to leave.

But Miyuki picked up a rock and flung it after the fleeing samurai. The rock sailed through the air and struck the man in the back of the head. He took one more faltering step, then collapsed face first in the dirt.

'That should give us a little more time,' said Miyuki, arching an eyebrow at Akiko.

Akiko nodded a stiff acknowledgement, while the others stared at her, astounded by the accuracy of her long shot.

'How did you do that?' said Saburo.

'I'm a ninja,' stated Miyuki, her tone matter-of-fact.

Then Yori cried in alarm, 'Where's Benkei?'

Jack and the others looked around, but he was nowhere to be seen – not on the road, not beside the tea house or even down the slope. Then Benkei's head popped out from behind a tree. 'Is it safe to come out yet?'

Jack smiled and nodded.

'Well, you're a brave one!' mocked Saburo.

'I didn't want to get in the way,' replied Benkei, unashamed by his obvious self-preservation. 'Besides, when you all fight so well together, you don't need Benkei the Great spoiling your flow.'

'What I want to know is how they recognized you and me in the first place,' said Jack.

'Why don't we ask the *ronin*?' suggested Akiko, pointing to the brother still pinned to the tea house.

'Release me . . . please!' the man whimpered, feebly tugging at the arrow shaft.

'As soon as you tell us why you were lying in wait for Benkei and Jack,' demanded Miyuki.

'A samurai . . . hired us,' he gasped. 'Told us . . . to look for someone in a multicoloured kimono . . . and a warrior in a straw hat with red-handled swords . . .'

'What did this samurai look like?' asked Jack, already fearing the answer.

'Black armour . . . a golden helmet . . . the crest of a red sun . . .'

'Kazuki!' spat Saburo in disgust.

'I bet you he's recruited *ronin* all the way to Nagasaki,' cursed Miyuki.

'That means *no place* is safe,' said Yori as they all turned to depart.

'Wait . . . the arrow . . .' groaned the *ronin*, clutching at his wounded shoulder. 'Take it out . . . you promised.'

'Of course!' said Akiko. She ripped the shaft out of the man's shoulder with a single sharp tug. The *ronin* gave a startled scream as the barbed arrowhead tore his flesh.

'I need it back anyway,' she remarked as the man passed out in shock.

45

FUMI-E

Ascending the foothills of Unzen-dake, Jack and his friends left the tea house behind and continued west. Pine trees clung to the slopes in an evergreen blanket that rapidly unravelled near the summit to expose a barren cone of rock. Clouds of sulphurous steam swirled around the craggy peak and Jack was glad to be skirting the volcano on this occasion rather than going over it. The thunderous mountain was like a permanent shadow in the sky and he was anxious to put as much distance between it and them as possible.

As they travelled further from the coast, the mountain air became cooler and less humid. So even when the road gave way to a rutted track, they continued to make good progress. With everyone keenly aware that Kazuki might have hired an army of *ronin*, they kept up their vigilance. Benkei guided from the front with Akiko on horseback as first lookout, Yori walked beside Jack, and Miyuki and Saburo took up the rear. But they encountered few other travellers along the route.

'What will be the first thing you do when you return to England?' asked Yori, almost taking two steps for every one of Jack's.

'Find my sister,' replied Jack.

'Of course, but what then?'

A smile curled Jack's lips as almost forgotten memories of home crowded his heart. 'I'll eat beef pie dripping in gravy . . . Drink fresh cows' milk . . . Listen to the bells of St Paul's Cathedral . . . Walk across London Bridge . . . Explore Cheapside market . . .' His smile faded as a mournful look entered his eyes. 'I'll pay my respects at my mother's grave . . . maybe bury my father's memory there too.' He sighed heavily at the thought. 'Then I'll go home to Limehouse with Jess, if we still have one after all this time.'

'I'm sure you will,' said Yori, who began to chew his lower lip as if he might cry. 'Jack . . . I'll miss you when you're gone,' he admitted.

Jack turned to his friend, surprised by such a personal expression of feelings.

'You always stood by me at the *Niten Ichi Ryū*,' Yori continued. 'Believed in me, when no one else did.'

'Sensei Yamada believed in you,' Jack reminded him.

'Yes, but he was my teacher. You're my friend. And I only realized how great a friend you are to me, when you were gone . . . when we thought you'd drowned. I know you have to leave . . . but I don't want you to.'

'You could always come with me,' said Jack, half serious.

'Really?' said Yori, the idea cheering him up no end.

'That's if you could stand two years at sea cramped into a dirty cabin with only a lice-ridden hammock to sleep on!'

'Two years?' replied Yori, the prospect not seeming to dampen his enthusiasm. 'That's a good deal of time for meditation.'

Jack laughed. In every cloud Yori somehow managed to find the silver lining.

The track emerged from the forest and cut across an upland plain. The plateau and its lower slopes were divided into a jumble of terraced paddy fields. A small village, no more than a cluster of flimsy straw buildings, sat amid the dried-out beds.

As they drew near, Jack and the others could hear the sounds of weeping.

Entering the village, they passed thatched farm huts in various states of collapse. A wooden handcart with a broken wheel was propped up against a ramshackle barn. A few scrawny chickens ran loose in the road. The place was clearly impoverished – and virtually deserted. There were signs of a struggle: several doors kicked in; a broken hoe; the remains of a fire, the ruin still smoking. And a large patch of blood-caked earth drying in the sun.

An old man in a ragged kimono was crumpled in a heap beside the entrance to a dilapidated house. Bony fingers covered his face as he sobbed loudly. At their approach, he glanced up fearfully, his half-starved body trembling all over. His face was worn with time and tears, his eyes bloodshot and sunken with grief.

Yori knelt beside him and asked, 'What's happened?'

Recognizing the robes of a monk, the old man calmed a little. He swallowed, seeming to find it hard to speak, then spat out a name as if it was poison. 'Matsukura! The *daimyo* of Shimabara.'

'A *daimyo*?' queried Akiko, dismounting from her horse. 'But he should be protecting farmers like you.'

The old man shook his head. 'Our previous lord, Arima,

certainly did. But he was exiled last year by the Shogun for his Christian beliefs. Now we're under the rule of a tyrant . . . and he's hell-bent on persecuting us Christian Japanese –' The old man suddenly clammed up, realizing he may have said too much. 'Who are you people?'

From what the old man had revealed about himself, Jack decided to take a risk and removed his hat. The man's eyes widened like saucers when he saw Jack's face.

'You're a foreigner! A . . . Christian?' he asked, almost hopeful.

Jack nodded his head. 'You can trust us. My name is Jack.'

'I'm . . . Takumi,' the old man hesitantly replied, and bowed his head.

Now he opened his heart to them.

'You must have seen the monstrous new castle in Shimabara?' he began, wiping his nose with his sleeve. 'Matsukura cleared an entire Christian district just to make way for it. All those he evicted he forced into slavery to build his prideful fortress. And to pay for his folly he's doubled the rice tax on all farmers . . . yet he still demands more!'

'So his samurai came to take the rest of your rice?' said Saburo.

'No, we've very little left,' sniffed Takumi. 'It's not enough for him to tax us to death. One of his patrols visited our village and we were forced to perform *fumi-e.*'

'*Fumi-e?*' questioned Jack.

Takumi nodded. 'We must . . . *trample* . . . on a picture of our Lord Jesus Christ,' he explained, his face contorting from horror to revulsion at the memory of such a sacrilegious act.

'But why?' asked Saburo.

'To prove we *aren't* Christians. If anyone – man, woman or child – refused, they were taken away to be executed on top of Unzen-dake.'

'So why did they leave *you* behind?'

Takumi's expression now became guilt-ridden. 'I . . . I performed *fumi-e*.'

He rose to his knees, hands clasped in desperate prayer.

'*Oh Lord, please forgive me for my sins*. I only did it to save my family . . .' He now turned to Jack, almost pleading. 'But my daughter wouldn't . . . and now she and my granddaughter are . . .' He broke into wailing sobs.

'I know your God will forgive you,' said Yori, trying to console the broken man.

Takumi stared up at Jack again, his eyes wild and lost to grief.

'Go now!' he cried. 'Leave this Hell, young foreigner, while you still have a chance.'

'That's good advice,' said Benkei, already taking the lead down the road.

'I can't walk on by,' said Jack. 'Not when fellow Christians are suffering like this.'

'A rescue mission? We can't risk that,' Miyuki argued. 'Matsukura's samurai must be on our trail by now. And this *daimyo*'s got an axe to grind with foreigners like you. With the Shogun and Kazuki already baying for your blood, you don't need another enemy.'

Jack pointed to the hellish peak that had haunted him since their arrival. 'But there are innocent women and children up there being tortured and killed, purely for their beliefs!'

Akiko looked torn by the situation, her heart and her mind

at odds with one another. 'You can't save every Christian in Japan, Jack,' she said eventually. 'Our priority must be to get you safely to Nagasaki and on your way home. You're the one Christian we *can* save.'

'But isn't this exactly what a samurai is supposed to stand up for? Honour, Benevolence and Rectitude.'

'It's not about *bushido*. It's about what's possible. There are just six of us against a *daimyo* and his entire army. What difference can we make?'

As harsh as the decision was, both Saburo and Miyuki nodded their heads in agreement with her.

Yori now piped up. 'A tsunami once washed ten thousand fish up on the shores of Japan,' he began. 'A monk went down to the beach, saw the fish flapping on the sand, and one by one started to pick them up and throw them back into the sea. A samurai sitting nearby saw the monk and laughed at him. "Foolish monk! There're miles of beach and thousands of fish. What difference will that make?" The monk picked up a gasping fish and tossed it back into the sea. With a knowing smile, he replied, "It made a difference to that one."'

46

LORD'S PRAYER

They crouched at the lip of the volcano and peered into its depths. The immense crater was a desolate bowl of black ash and grey rock smeared with patches of sickly yellow clay. Vents torn into the earth bled sulphurous clouds of steam, while lurid ponds and bubbling mudpools blistered the ground like grotesque boils. As wafts of vomit-inducing steam passed overhead, a shrill screaming filled the ghastly air.

'Sounds as if we're already too late,' choked Saburo, his voice muffled behind his hand in a vain attempt to block the stench of rotting eggs.

The constant screeching, like ragged fingernails down slate, set Jack's teeth on edge. Yori was forced to cover his ears, the anguished cries of the dying too much for his sensitive soul.

'That's just the noise of the "Great Shout" *jigoku*,' croaked Takumi, having guided them up Unzen-dake to *daimyo* Matsukura's favoured place of execution. He pointed a gnarled finger towards the seething Hell at the base of the crater, where steam rocketed out like a dragon spitting fire.

Beside the boiling Hell pool, a unit of samurai stood guard over a group of cowering villagers. Not that any of them could put up much of a fight. They were all emaciated, many were women, some old men and the youngest a mere babe-in-arms.

'The steam's so dense I can hardly see them,' remarked Akiko.

'For a ninja that's an advantage, *not* a problem,' Miyuki replied pointedly. 'It'll cover our escape.'

'But how are we going to free them in the first place?' said Saburo. 'There must be at least thirty soldiers.'

Jack looked around the boulder-strewn crater, trying to devise a plan. There were too many samurai for a full frontal attack. They would have to rely on stealth and ninja tactics to overcome such a force. He was about to ask Miyuki for ideas, when –

'DO YOU RENOUNCE YOUR FAITH?' boomed a voice that seemed to emanate from the very depths of Hell.

'That's Matsukura!' cried Takumi, shrinking back in fear.

The samurai lord was dressed in purple and red robes and wore a coal-black helmet crowned with stag antlers. His face was a knot of fury as he glared at the scrawny farmer trembling before him. At the man's feet, cast upon the pitted ground, was a stone tablet into which was carved the image of Christ on the cross.

'Stamp on your god or DIE!' demanded the *daimyo*.

With a single shake of his head, the farmer knelt before the effigy and put his hands together in prayer. Incensed by such a blatant act of defiance, *daimyo* Matsukura backhanded the man across the jaw. The farmer's head rocked with the force of the blow. A thin stream of blood seeped from his mouth, but he kept praying.

'BOIL HIM ALIVE!' yelled *daimyo* Matsukura.

Two samurai seized the farmer by his bony shoulders and dragged him towards the steaming *jigoku*. The farmer now prayed out loud, '*Our Father who art in heaven hallowed be thy –*'. They threw him into the scalding Hell. The farmer plunged beneath the super-heated waters and came up howling the Lord's Prayer '*– on EARTH as it is in HEAVEN. Give us –*'. His agonized cries were drowned out by a screech of steam. Scrabbling for the bank, he was pushed back by the spear of a samurai. '*FORGIVE those who trespass against us –*' he gasped. The *daimyo* watched with a fiendish glee as the farmer writhed in agony. '*– deliver us from evil –*' The man's skin was peeling off in flakes, his flesh turning red raw. '*– thine is the kingdom –*' Then the tortured farmer's voice faded towards the end of the prayer '*– forever and ever –*' before he slipped beneath the bubbling surface.

'*AMEN!*' cried the condemned villagers, finishing the prayer for their fellow worshipper. Tears streamed down their faces as they chanted '*AMEN!*' over and over again.

The *daimyo* glowered at this defiant protest to the Shogun's outlawing of Christianity.

'NEXT!' he bellowed, now apoplectic with rage.

A young woman and her daughter were shoved forward by the samurai guard. The girl looked too young to even understand what was going on. She just clung to her mother's leg, quivering with fear.

Beside Jack, Takumi gasped and fell to his knees, clawing at the black ash around him. '*Those are my girls!*'

Sickened by the gruesome scene he'd just witnessed, Jack knew in his heart he'd been right to risk his life for these innocent farmers. He couldn't allow such an atrocity to happen again.

Jack unsheathed his *katana*. There was little time for stealth now. 'We'll have to gamble everything on a surprise attack.'

'Wait! I've a better idea!' said Saburo. 'Yori and Benkei, come with me. Jack, you go with Akiko and Miyuki. Get close to the samurai. Then, when I give the signal, free the prisoners and run as fast as you can.'

'What's the signal?' asked Jack as Saburo raced off with Benkei and Yori in tow.

'You'll know it when you see it,' he replied with a roguish grin.

Leaving Takumi to pray for his family, Jack, Akiko and Miyuki darted over the lip of the crater. They sprinted from boulder to gully to rock, using the cover of steam to hide their movements. But the billowing clouds were as much a curse as a blessing. Although they concealed their approach from the samurai, they also hindered their progress. It was hard to see where they were going – twice they lost sight of their target and once Akiko even stumbled. Jack just hoped they could reach the little girl and her mother in time.

They hunkered down behind a black boulder. They were now so close they could hear the terrified mutterings of the villagers. Some were praying, others begging and many sobbing. The young woman and her daughter faced the *daimyo*.

'Stamp on your god or die!' ordered the *daimyo*.

'We can't wait much longer,' said Akiko in a tense whisper. 'What's Saburo up to?'

Through the swirling steam, Jack caught a glimpse of Saburo and the others behind one of the larger boulders along the crater rim. 'I'm not sure. But whatever he's planning, he'd better be quick about it.'

In response to the *daimyo*'s command, the little girl had picked up the effigy of Christ and was hugging it to her chest. *Daimyo* Matsukura snatched the stone tablet from her grasp.

'Throw this evil child and her mother into Hell!' he ordered.

Two samurai grabbed the woman by her hair. A third picked up the little girl around her waist. Kicking and screaming, she and her mother were borne towards their deaths.

Unable to hold off any longer, Jack and Akiko rose to their feet, while Miyuki pulled a *shuriken* from her belt. Then an ominous rumbling was heard above the screech of the *jigoku*. The clouds parted briefly to reveal shale trickling down the crater sides, rapidly building into a flood of stone, clay and ash. Leading the charge, a huge boulder came bouncing down the crater slope towards the samurai and villagers, gathering speed as it went.

'*That* must be the signal!' cried Miyuki in disbelieving horror.

47

LANDSLIDE

Daimyo Matsukura glared up at the thundering avalanche. He neither ran nor showed any fear. His expression was one of utter outrage, as if indignant that the volcano would dare to interrupt his executions. His samurai guard, however, panicked upon seeing the lethal landslide. They scattered in terror, scrambling up the crater's opposite slope, leaving the shackled villagers directly in its path. The two soldiers, who were dragging the mother by her hair, let go and fled for their lives. But the samurai with the little girl remained determined to toss her into the boiling *jigoku*.

Jack sprinted from his hiding place to stop him, his feet crunching on the brittle ash as he powered towards the murderous samurai. But he knew all his efforts would be in vain – he was just too far away to save the little girl's life.

He flinched as a flash of light shot past his shoulder. His mind registered the glint of steel at the same time as the *shuriken* struck the samurai in the neck.

Miyuki!

The throwing star embedded its point deep into the samurai's throat. With a gargled scream, he dropped the girl to the stony ground and yanked out the *shuriken*. Lurching in pain and shock, blood spurting out, he tripped. A scalding hiss greeted him as he tumbled head first into the boiling waters of the Hell.

Dashing over, Jack scooped up the little girl in his arms and carried her away from the infernal *jigoku*. She stared up at him with big round eyes.

'I knew you'd come!' she said, tiny fingers clasping a strand of his blond hair.

'You knew?'

'I prayed for you, Jesus, to save us.'

'I'm not Jesus,' he quickly corrected her. 'I'm Jack, from England.'

But the little girl merely gave him a knowing smile.

The girl's mother crawled over on her knees, weeping.

Jack pulled her to her feet. 'This way!' he ordered as the landslide surged in a relentless torrent down the slope towards them.

Amid the chaos, Akiko had darted over to the villagers and cut their bonds. Rounding them up like sheep, she cried, 'Follow me!'

The villagers obediently scurried through the mist after her. Miyuki took up the rear guard, ensuring none were left behind and that no samurai tried to stop them.

Jack raced after his friends, the girl in one arm, her mother pulled along in his other hand. The avalanche now roared in their ears like a thunderous waterfall. They had but seconds before the first rocks ploughed into them.

Out of a swirling steam cloud, a pair of stag antlers materialized like the crooked horns of Satan. *Daimyo* Matsukura stood blocking their escape.

'*Your head will roll for this,* gaijin*!*' he bellowed, raising a mighty double-edged *katana* to smite him down.

With both hands occupied, Jack couldn't draw his swords in time. *Daimyo* Matsukura swung his cruel *katana* to take Jack's head from his shoulders in a single slice. As it whistled towards his neck, the steel blade parted the wafts of sulphurous steam, cleaving a clear trail in its wake. Jack went to duck beneath the blade, when *daimyo* Matsukura and his sword disappeared before his eyes. The mother screamed as a colossal boulder tore by, inches from them, crushing the samurai lord and taking his sword with it.

No, your head was the one to roll! thought Jack, resuming their mad dash for safety.

As the landslide overtook them, it was like trying to dodge a stampeding herd of oxen. Boulders bounced like oversized cannonballs, rocks flew like missiles, ash billowed around them in blinding clouds. The ground constantly shifted under their feet. With every step, they were in danger of being sucked along with the cascading debris and swept into the hellish *jigoku*.

But suddenly they were beyond the worst of it and scrabbling up the ash-covered lip of the volcano. Hands reached out and pulled the three of them to safety. Jack lay gasping on the crater's edge, the girl still in his arms.

'Maiko! Rimika!' cried Takumi, first embracing his daughter, then reaching for his granddaughter.

Jack let Rimika go and she ran into her grandfather's arms.

'We were saved . . . by Jesus!' she said, her eyes mesmerized by Jack's hair.

'Thank the Lord!' sobbed Takumi, his prayed-for reunion overwhelming him. 'Thank the Lord!'

'Or you could just thank *us*,' said Saburo, jogging over with Benkei and Yori.

Jack sat up. The landslide had rumbled to an uneasy stop, but smoke and ash still swelled up from the crater's base like a poisonous mushroom.

'Your plan worked a treat!' Benkei declared, slapping Saburo on the back.

'A little too well . . .' coughed Jack, clearing his lungs and struggling to his feet.

Saburo offered him a hand and an apologetic smile. 'I didn't plan such a *large* landslide.'

'You idiot! You almost killed us all!' Miyuki yelled, charging over and knuckle-punching a nerve in his arm.

'Ow!' cried Saburo.

'I thought dodging a landslide would have been child's play for a ninja,' remarked Akiko as Saburo tenderly rubbed his dead arm.

'And you *weren't* worried?' shot back Miyuki.

Akiko appeared about to deny this, then stopped herself. Instead she offered Miyuki a conciliatory bow of the head and admitted, 'To be honest, I was *terrified*!'

Then she knuckle-punched Saburo's other bicep.

'Ow!' groaned Saburo, now rubbing both his arms. 'Is that *all* the thanks I get for saving the day?'

'YES!' said Akiko and Miyuki together.

'At least the two of you can agree on something,' remarked Yori, suppressing a grin.

Jack looked over at the flock of dazed villagers. Almost unable to believe their miraculous escape, they fell to their knees and bowed as one to Jack and his friends.

'We thank the Lord for delivering us from evil and sending us his angels of mercy,' praised one of the farmers, making the sign of the cross.

'Amen,' chanted the villagers in unison.

As they bowed again, expressing their gratitude both to God and their samurai saviours, Jack noticed the black ash around them shifting. Then the ground beneath their feet started to tremble.

48

A MINOR ONE

'Saburo . . . what *have* you started!' accused Akiko, peering into the crater's depths.

Below, the steam and dust had settled and they saw that Saburo's landslide had blocked the main vents of the Great Shout *jigoku*. With no way of escape, the super-heated waters snaked through the earth, seeking out other routes. The back pressure rapidly building, the crater floor began to fracture along its fault lines before their very eyes . . .

'RUN FOR YOUR LIVES!' shouted Jack as Unzen-dake awoke from its grumbling slumber.

Sweeping Rimika into his arms again, Jack and his friends herded the villagers in a frantic race down the mountainside. Saburo carried one of the elderly men on his back. Yori had given his staff to another. Akiko and Miyuki worked together, shouldering a lame woman between them. The rest of the villagers, half-starved as they were, proved to be hardier than they looked. With the sure-footedness of mountain goats, they scrambled down the rocky slope.

'This way!' cried Benkei as the volcano rumbled and loose shale and stones clattered past, seemingly determined to beat them in their flight. Their pace slowed dangerously as they wound a circuitous path through the gullies and ridges of old lava flows. Far below in the valley, the haven of the village seemed to be getting no closer.

All of a sudden a huge explosion shook the ground. The earth pitched like the deck of a storm-tossed ship and all of them were thrown off their feet. Knees and hands were scraped bloody and raw as they tumbled out of control down the slope. Clutching Rimika tightly to his chest, Jack skidded to a painful stop.

'Are you all right?' he asked her, brushing ash from her hair.

She nodded brightly. 'I'm safe in your arms.'

Jack only wished that was really true. He staggered onward with the others. The volcano was belching out an apocalyptic pall of smoke and ash. The sky darkened, a sinister twilight smothering the land as the sun was eclipsed behind the billowing inky cloud. The heavens began to hail shards of rock, and ash fell like black snow on to the ripped earth.

Jack followed Benkei and the others into the treeline. The pine trees swayed wildly, as if trying to tear their roots from the earth and run free. Splintering cracks and woody groans filled the ashen air in the forest's angry protest against its inevitable devastation. A huge tree trunk split apart and toppled into their path, almost flattening Benkei. He jumped aside with a startled yelp. Then, recovering, he beckoned the villagers onwards, guiding them past obstacles and through the perilous forest, his multicoloured robe a beacon in the dim light.

Jack levelled with Saburo, who was puffing and wheezing from the old man he bore on his back.

'You don't seem . . . scared . . . by the eruption,' he was gasping to his passenger.

The old man nonchalantly shook his head. 'I've seen far worse in my time.'

'Really? Ever been . . . this close to one?'

'No, neither do I want to be. So stop your yabbering and get moving!' he scolded, cajoling Saburo with an impatient pat on the head as if he were a mule.

Saburo's indignant face turned purple at the farmer's lack of respect towards a member of the samurai class, but fear for their lives outweighed his desire to correct him. Jack would have laughed at the exchange, if he too wasn't terrified out of his wits. Having been caught in an eruption once before, he'd vowed not to repeat the experience. The volcano was a foe that could never be beaten, only survived.

And, as the mountain roared again, their very lives hung in the balance.

The ground trembled, a shock wave rippling through the earth and scattering the villagers like leaves. Jack forced himself to keep moving. The further away from the volcano they were, the better their chances. Yori urged everyone on, offering words of encouragement even when terror held him in its icy grip. Akiko and Miyuki staggered through the gloomy forest, still bearing the lame woman between them. As they fled, Jack lost all track of time. He was just running, blindly following Benkei and carrying Rimika like the most precious jewel in his arms. Then all of a sudden they were out of the forest and dashing across the plateau of paddy fields.

Exhausted, scratched from rock, filthy with ash, they hobbled into the village. The volcano continued to grumble, smoke still pouring from its devil-fanged cone of a mouth. But fortunately only steam, not lava, flowed from the gashes in its sides and the tremors had all but died down.

'Told you, the eruption was a minor one,' said the old man as Saburo dropped to his knees in the road.

'Get yourself a new horse!' replied Saburo through gritted teeth.

'Thanks for the ride,' the man said with a toothless grin. Dismounting, he stretched his legs and tottered off.

Saburo's jaw fell open, incredulous, as he watched the farmer go, perfectly able to walk.

'Now there's a wily old trickster!' remarked Benkei with admiration. 'I could learn a thing or two from him.'

The villagers gathered together and Jack returned Rimika to her mother.

'How can we ever thank you?' said Takumi, bowing his head deep with respect.

'Seeing Rimika safe is thanks enough,' replied Jack humbly.

Rimika beamed at him.

'But there must be something more we can do?' insisted Maiko, ruffling her daughter's hair.

'How about a bath?' suggested Akiko, glancing down at her soot-stained kimono.

Takumi and Maiko lowered their gaze, embarrassed.

'Unfortunately, *daimyo* Matsukura's samurai destroyed the only tub in the village,' Takumi apologized. 'But there is a natural hot spring further along the road, near where a stream crosses. I trust that will do.'

'Sounds perfect,' said Akiko, not wishing the villagers to feel ashamed of their lack of means.

'Perhaps a meal before you leave?' Maiko offered graciously.

Jack glanced around at their devastated village with its ramshackle homes and empty rice barn. Whatever food they had left, he realized, would be their last. And these villagers were willing to give everything they had by way of thanks. This only reaffirmed to him that the risk they'd taken had been worth it to save such good people.

'Just pray for my safe return home,' said Jack.

'We will. We certainly will,' replied Takumi, putting his hands together.

'And with *daimyo* Matsukura dead,' added Akiko, 'you should be more free to do so.'

The joy in Takumi's face died and he gravely shook his head. 'I'm afraid the *daimyo*'s son and heir is equally cruel.' He gave a heavy sigh at the burden they bore. 'But we have time to gather what little we have and start afresh in a more Christian-friendly province.'

Jack wished them well, but wondered what real chance they had, given that the movement of farmers was tightly controlled and the Shogun had outlawed Christianity throughout Japan.

'We should go,' said Miyuki, looking up at the sun, now a fiery eye in the smoke-laden sky. 'We want to be as far from here as possible by sunset.'

Collecting her horse from the barn, Akiko and Jack followed the others out of the village. As they headed down the road, Jack took a final glance back. The villagers were already on their knees, praying. Behind, looming over them like a belligerent god, the volcano rumbled away.

'Did we *really* save them?' asked Jack, thinking of the twin threats posed by the *daimyo*'s son and the Shogun.

Yori nodded sagely. 'None may know what tomorrow brings, so each day is a gift to be treasured. And you've given them that gift.'

END OF THE ROAD

'Less than a day's walk and you'll be in Nagasaki, *nanban*!' announced Benkei, polishing off his breakfast of rice and fish, which Miyuki had steamed over a hissing vent from the hot spring.

They'd spent the night camped beside the volcanic pool and everyone was much revived from the combination of a good night's sleep and an invigorating soak in the spring's warm waters.

'It's almost the end of the road for you,' remarked Saburo with a cheery smile.

Finishing his rice, Jack nodded in acknowledgement. It was true his journey would soon be over. He couldn't quite believe that he'd made it this far – alive. But now he was so close to his destination, he was filled with trepidation. Would Nagasaki deliver all that he'd hoped for – a ship bound for England? Or would the countless risks he and his friends had taken all be for nothing?

But if fortune did favour him with an English or Dutch boat, Jack now considered what he might be leaving behind. There was the Shogun and his threat of execution, of course, as well as Kazuki and his obsession for revenge. These he'd be glad to see the back of. But he'd also be losing a valuable and irreplaceable part of his life: his friends.

Jack gazed around the hot spring with its rock pools and the lush vegetation hanging like silken curtains from the trees. Within this idyllic encampment was almost everyone he cared for. Benkei, only known for a short while but whose wild antics and exuberance would be hard to replace. Saburo, whose jovial and big-hearted nature would be sorely missed. There was Yori, ever faithful, understanding and kind. Jack wondered if he'd meet anyone in England who could offer such calm wisdom and selfless friendship. There'd certainly be few English girls to match Miyuki for her cunning, devotion or deadliness. Then there was Akiko . . . Jack knew he could sail the Seven Seas for the rest of his life and never find a girl like her again.

And very soon he'd be saying a final farewell to her; to *all* his friends.

Saburo was right. It was the end of the road – in more ways than one.

'Time to go,' announced Akiko, tying the last of their packs on to her horse.

Jack stood. But his feet refused to move. Despite the obvious peril he faced by staying in Japan and the pressing need to be reunited with his sister, he *didn't* want to go on.

There was a jingle of metal rings next to his ear. Yori smiled up at him, the Buddhist staff held firmly in his hand.

'When climbing a mountain, the push for the summit can be the toughest part,' he said, sensing the conflict in Jack's heart. 'You never know if you have the strength to complete what you started. Or what view awaits you when you reach the peak. But know this, your friends will be with you every step of the way.'

Yori tapped his staff on the ground three times to underscore his point, the metal rings jingling, beckoning Jack on. Encouraged by his friend's wise words yet again, Jack realized to stop now would be to betray his friends and abandon his sister Jess. That was something he could never do.

Putting one foot in front of the other, Jack headed down the road, Yori at his side, Saburo and Miyuki guarding from behind, and Akiko and Benkei taking the lead. None of the friends talked much as they walked west through the forested foothills of Shimabara peninsula. They too felt the end coming.

Though immersed in his own thoughts, Jack noted Miyuki was being extra vigilant, her eyes scouring the trees for the slightest sign of danger. Akiko kept tugging anxiously at the feathered flights of the arrows in her quiver, occasionally glancing back at him. And Saburo's hand never left his *saya*. Even Benkei was relatively quiet for once.

As they rounded a bend, Akiko held up her hand, silently bringing everyone to a halt. A cloaked figure sat upon a rock. His head was bowed and covered by a cowl. He leant upon his staff, still as a statue. With no one else on the road, his presence so early in the morning was disconcerting.

50

BAIT

'One of Kazuki's *ronin*?' whispered Jack as they retreated out of sight from the mysterious figure.

'Could be,' replied Akiko under her breath.

'I suggest we double back and find a more stealthy route through the forest,' said Miyuki, keeping her eyes trained on the surrounding trees.

'He's only one *ronin*!' said Benkei.

'Then why don't *you* challenge him?' suggested Saburo pointedly.

'Me?' exclaimed Benkei, alarmed at the proposition. 'Shouldn't someone more qualified do it?'

'Don't tell me Benkei the Great's scared,' Saburo mocked.

'Of course not, I simply value my life higher than yours!'

'Then you'll be more careful with it than Saburo,' said Miyuki, impatient at their boyish posturing. 'Now go and find out whether he's a *ronin* or not. If he recognizes you, then we'll know.'

'You're using *me* as bait!'

'I'll have you covered,' Akiko replied, drawing an arrow from her quiver.

'Here, take one of my swords,' Saburo added helpfully, passing Benkei his *wakizashi*. 'Just in case.'

With great reluctance, Benkei accepted the *wakizashi* and slid it into his *obi*.

'Other way up,' corrected Saburo, twisting the *saya* so that the blade would emerge cutting-edge to the sky. 'And try not to cut yourself.'

'Superb advice, O great sensei!' replied Benkei sardonically, bowing with a flourish of his hand.

Jack had serious reservations about the plan, but before he could object Saburo sent Benkei on his way.

Approaching the stationary figure, Benkei called nervously, 'Good morning . . . are you a *ronin*?'

No reply.

'You don't recognize me, do you? Not that you should . . .' Benkei quickly added. He took a tentative step closer and bowed to get a glimpse of the stranger's hooded face. He turned back to the others and mouthed, 'It's all right. He's asleep!'

All of a sudden the figure sprang to life, grunting loudly. Panicking, Benkei lashed out with Saburo's sword. He drew the blade so fast, and without any real aim, that the sword sliced the man's staff in two.

'No!' cried the figure, cowering at Benkei's feet. 'Please don't kill me!'

His hood slipped off to reveal a scrawny middle-aged man with thinning hair and a long stringy moustache. He blinked, bleary-eyed in shock, at his rainbow-robed attacker.

'Who are you?' demanded Benkei, his panic now turning to bravado at the sight of his opponent.

'I'm just a lamp-oil salesman,' the man replied hurriedly, gesturing to a bamboo-framed backpack containing an immense ceramic jar with a cork plugging the top.

Benkei whistled through his teeth. 'Rather you than me carrying that load!'

The oil salesman nodded wearily. 'I've had to travel this road three times this week alone. That's why I was resting. And I need a staff . . .'

He glanced down in despair at the severed pieces scattered on the ground.

'Don't worry, there's plenty more where that came from,' said Benkei, gesturing with a sweep of his hand at the surrounding forest. He offered the man a rueful grin and pretended to look for a replacement staff.

Satisfied there was no threat, Akiko spurred her horse and led everyone along the road. Passing the despondent salesman, Yori handed him some copper coins. 'For a new staff. A decent one,' he explained.

The salesman just stared at the coins, amazed by the young monk's generosity.

Benkei clapped the man on the back. 'Clearly you're a pious man for the gods to respond so quickly in your hour of need!'

Leaving the bewildered salesman on his rock, he hurried after the others and round the next bend.

'Congratulations! Benkei the Great defeated *Ronin* the Merciless!' laughed Saburo, applauding him as he trotted up to them. 'Now I know who to call upon when I need some firewood chopping!'

'As long as I can use your sword,' retorted Benkei, holding the *wakizashi* aloft and cutting through a branch overhead.

Twigs and leaves cascaded on to Saburo's head.

'Give that back!' he cried, snatching the sword from Benkei's grasp. 'Before you do some *real* damage.'

Gradually the trees thinned out as the road left the foothills and dropped down to a slender neck of land that tethered the Shimabara peninsula to the Kyushu mainland. To the north, the waters of the Ariake Sea could be seen glistening in the bright morning sunshine. To the south, the rolling waves of the East China Sea beat against the shoreline, throwing up a silvery haze over the pebble-strewn beach. A narrow ridge of higher ground ran along this southern stretch, while northwards the land flattened out into a coastal floodplain, parcelled up into neat rectangles of paddy fields.

The road they were on split, offering the choice of either the ridge or the floodplain. Benkei paused, wiping his brow and trying to decide which direction would be the best to take.

'They both eventually end up at the same village,' he said. 'It's your choice.'

'We should follow the ridge,' called Miyuki from behind.

'If I was Kazuki, then the ridge would be the most obvious route to take,' called back Akiko.

'But on the floodplain we'll be exposed to attack.'

'True, but at least we'll be able to see them coming.'

'On the ridge, we have the advantage of higher ground,' insisted Miyuki with an exasperated sigh.

Just as Jack and the others expected the discussion to break down into another quarrel and for Yori to throw his staff into the air again, Akiko said, 'That's a fair tactical point. The ridge it is.'

Miyuki was taken aback by Akiko's ready agreement. 'Excellent . . . Of course, your reasons were also sound.'

Akiko nodded politely, acknowledging the magnanimous spirit of her reply.

Perhaps there is hope for a friendship after all, thought Jack.

They followed the ridge, keeping their eyes peeled for danger. Each time they crested a rise, Jack half expected to see Kazuki, his Scorpion Gang and an army of *ronin* waiting for them, armed to the teeth.

But, surprisingly, neither Kazuki nor any band of hired warriors appeared on the road.

Jack began to wonder if they'd managed to slip past his old school rival – that by some sheer stroke of luck, they were now home free all the way to Nagasaki. An odd sense of disappointment washed over Jack. He realized that he *wanted* Kazuki to find him; that he himself had half sought that final confrontation. In truth, he couldn't leave Japan without resolving their rivalry. If Kazuki wasn't dealt with before Jack departed for England, then Akiko would always be in danger. Jack recognized that Akiko could handle herself, but he'd never sleep soundly again without knowing – with absolute certainty – that she was safe from Kazuki's vengeful spite.

Jack wondered if Nagasaki would be their ultimate battleground.

The road left the ridge and passed through grassland before re-entering the forest.

Around noon, they came to a winding river, where a narrow wooden bridge led into a sizeable village. Surrounded by paddy fields and thorn bushes, the settlement was a criss-cross of wooden buildings and rice barns. A large pond fed by the river stretched along the eastern side of the village, its waters undisturbed in the stifling heat of the day.

'Not far now,' said Benkei, bounding over the bridge. 'By tonight we'll be dining in Nagasaki!'

Only when they were passing the first few houses did Jack and the others notice something strange.

His *shakujō* jingling loudly in the unnatural silence, Yori asked, 'Where are all the people?'

51

PINNED DOWN

Jack's eyes scanned the buildings and paddy fields surrounding them. There was no one in the street and no farmers working the fields. A lone watchtower stood at the centre of the community like a redundant guardian. Some of the closely packed dwellings had their windows wide open to let in what little breeze there was. Several doors were also ajar, as if awaiting the imminent return of their owners. The faint aroma of boiling rice and the taint of woodsmoke wafted through the air. The village even boasted a small inn, but this was shuttered up. It was as if every villager had been spirited away.

Still, Jack had the unnerving feeling of being watched.

Miyuki felt it too. She was already reaching into her bag and pulling out her *ninjatō*. 'Back to the bridge. Right now!'

Akiko tugged on her reins, wheeling Snowball round, when an arrow shot out of nowhere. Its barb struck her in the chest, the impact knocking her from her horse.

'Akiko!' cried Jack, running to her aid.

'No, Jack!' shouted Miyuki, shoulder-barging him to one side.

Another arrow whistled past, a hair's breadth from Jack's neck. He sprawled into the dirt, dust choking his mouth. He crawled over to Akiko and tried to shield her from further attack.

More arrows whizzed past like angry wasps. Snowball stood over them, as if sensing his mistress was in danger. He whinnied and reared up as a steel-tipped shaft pierced his flank, but he held his ground.

'Get Akiko into cover,' instructed Miyuki as she desperately tried to pinpoint the source of the attack.

Saburo was by Jack's side in an instant and together they dragged their injured friend into a narrow alleyway. Once sheltered between the two buildings, Jack propped Akiko against a wall.

'Akiko, speak to me,' he pleaded as he examined her wound.

'It's not . . . too bad,' she gasped, her face pale from shock. 'The breastplate . . . took most of the impact.'

Mercifully, the arrow had missed her heart, penetrating just below the left shoulder. Yet blood still poured out at an alarming rate. Jack tore a strip from his kimono sleeve and tried to staunch the flow.

Crouching beside them, Miyuki peered out into the street. She whipped her head back – *thunk!* – as an arrow embedded itself in the wooden pillar next to her.

'I can't locate the archer!' she snapped in frustration.

'Where's Yori?' asked Jack, suddenly realizing there were only four of them in the alley. 'And Benkei?'

Saburo looked across the street. 'Over there!'

Yori and Benkei were huddled together behind a large water butt. Yet it provided scant cover for two and they were in a perilous position. An arrow cracked into the barrel, water spurting out in a fountain on to the sunbaked ground.

'Can you see anyone?' Miyuki called to them.

Benkei shook his head, too scared to even risk a glance. Yori peeked over the top of the barrel.

'In the watchtower!' he cried, pointing to a flicker of movement behind the defensive panels surrounding the raised platform.

'We have to get Akiko to safety,' said Jack, his fingers wet with her blood.

'As long as we stay clear of the tower, we can retreat into the forest,' Saburo suggested.

'There isn't just *one* archer,' said Miyuki, studying the pattern of arrows that peppered the ground. 'See how they're stuck at different angles. Other archers must be hidden on the roofs.'

'We can't stay pinned down here forever,' said Jack.

'You're right,' replied Miyuki. She looked to the other end of the alley, only to find it blocked by a spiked fence. 'We've no choice but to make a run for the bridge.'

She turned to Akiko. 'Can you make it?'

Akiko nodded. 'It's my shoulder, not my legs, that's the problem!'

'We'll soon fix that.' Miyuki rifled in her bag for her ninja pouch. She pulled out a vial with a cork stopper and a couple of field dressings. Taking hold of the arrow shaft in both hands, she snapped off the feathered flights.

Akiko gasped in pain.

'Careful!' said Jack, holding Akiko steady.

'That is me being careful,' replied Miyuki. 'We need to get to the wound.'

Unclipping Akiko's breastplate, she eased it away and inspected the injury.

'Good, it's not deep,' she muttered and gripped the remains of the broken arrow. 'I'll try to be quick,' she told Akiko.

Nodding, Akiko bit down on her lower lip as Miyuki teased the arrowhead out of her punctured flesh, but shrieked as the barb came free. More blood flooded out. Miyuki soaked this away with one of the dressings, then uncorked the vial.

'This might sting a little,' she warned, sprinkling white powder over the open gash.

Akiko's eyes flew wide open as if Miyuki had just set fire to her shoulder.

'The pain means it's working,' explained Miyuki, allowing Akiko to clasp her hand tightly. 'It'll stop the bleeding and prevent any infection.'

'It had better do!' panted Akiko, a sheen of perspiration on her brow. 'Thanks, anyway.'

'What are friends for,' replied Miyuki with a smile.

Jack hurriedly wrapped the spare dressing over the wound as Miyuki repacked her pouch.

'Where's Snowball?' asked Akiko, the pain easing slightly.

Jack risked a glance into the street. In that split second, an arrow speared his straw hat and pinned it to the wall. But he managed to spot Snowball. The horse had jumped one of the high thorn hedges and was now galloping across the fields. 'He's fine. But he's taken our packs and your bow with him,' said Jack, wondering how he'd ever retrieve his *rutter*.

Akiko saw the concern on his face. 'Don't worry, he won't go far. And I still have my swords to fight with,' she replied, managing a valiant smile and patting the *katana* and *wakizashi* on her hip.

Jack tied off the dressing and clipped her breastplate back into position.

'Are you ready to go?' asked Miyuki, having signed to Yori and Benkei their plan to run.

Nodding, Jack slipped an arm round Akiko and helped her to her feet. Miyuki checked the watchtower and village roofs one last time. 'On my signal . . . three . . . two . . .'

'Wait!' exclaimed Saburo. 'We *can't* retreat.'

Jack and his friends stared in dismay as the wooden bridge burst into flames.

'This is an ambush!' said Miyuki, her tone grave. 'And a well-planned one at that.'

52

DEATH TRAP

The absence of the villagers; the fortified watchtower; the spiked fence blocking the alley – and now the sabotaged bridge. In hindsight, it was all so obvious. They'd walked straight into a trap.

'What are we going to do?' asked Saburo.

'We fight our way free,' Akiko replied, clenching her teeth against the pain and drawing her *katana*.

'But *who* are we fighting?' said Miyuki, her eyes sweeping the deserted street. 'They're hidden like ninja!'

Jack knew of only one person who could be responsible for such devious planning.

The roof above them creaked. They looked up to see an archer glaring down, an arrow targeted on Saburo. The archer drew back his bow, his task as easy as shooting fish in a barrel. A *shuriken* spun upwards, slicing through the hemp bowstring. The metal star lodged in the archer's chest as the huge bow sprang apart in his hands and the arrow dropped harmlessly to the ground. Losing his footing, the injured archer tumbled head first into the alley to land with a bone-snapping crunch.

'Get the bow!' said Akiko. 'He should have a spare string in his quiver.'

Jack rushed over, but the bamboo shaft had cracked on impact. Instead, he wrenched Miyuki's *shuriken* from the dead archer's chest. They'd need every weapon they could get their hands on to survive this battle.

He checked the man's kimono for a *kamon*, but found no identifying crests. But he did find a knife.

'What's Benkei up to?' exclaimed Saburo, directing their attention to the other side of the road.

Benkei had tipped over the wooden butt, emptying out the remains of the water. Yori was crawling inside, swiftly followed by Benkei himself. They righted the barrel and began to shuffle across the street, Yori poking the end of his *shakujō* through the bunghole.

'They're crazy!' uttered Saburo, as arrows rained down, blasting the barrel in a hailstorm of death.

Splinters flew in all directions, but Yori and Benkei were cocooned safely inside. Or so Jack hoped. He could see some of the arrows had penetrated almost halfway up their shafts. They heard a muffled yelp and the barrel shuffled faster. Sections of it began to disintegrate under the relentless onslaught and Jack caught a glimpse of a pair of terrified eyes. By the time the water butt reached the alleyway, it had a coat of arrows so thick that it looked like a swollen porcupine.

Tossing off their improvised and crumbling armour, Benkei and Yori dived into the alleyway. Benkei lay on his front, clasping his rear, a red patch staining his kimono.

'Next time I suggest an idea like that, Yori,' he groaned, 'tell me to shut up!'

'Don't worry, I will,' Yori replied, several drops of blood marking his face and arms where the tips of the arrowheads had pierced him.

'That's some acupuncture treatment!' said Saburo, handing Yori his *shakujō*.

Jack pulled Benkei to his feet, giving him the knife he'd found. 'And for your next trick can you magic us out of here?'

'I wish I could, *nanban*,' said Benkei, swallowing uneasily as he stared over Jack's shoulder.

The dread in his eyes made Jack turn to the street. The road was no longer empty. A band of samurai, five warriors wide and four deep, stood battle-ready with weapons drawn.

'It looks as if the arrows were just to soften us up!' remarked Saburo.

Miyuki frantically searched for another way out, but the windows overlooking the alley were all barred shut from inside. She tried to scale the spiked fence and cursed as she cut her hand.

'It's covered in thorns,' she cried, blood dripping from her palm. 'This place is a death trap!'

'Six against twenty,' said Jack. 'That's better odds than when we fought those bandits in Tamagashi.'

'But that time we had a whole village helping us,' Saburo argued. 'And these *ronin* are trained samurai.'

'So are we,' reminded Yori. He bent down and took an arrow from the dead archer's quiver. He snapped it in half. 'A samurai alone is like a single arrow.' He now took six in his hand. 'But together we're strong and unconquerable.'

The significance wasn't lost on Jack or Akiko, both of whom recalled Sensei Yamada's morale-raising lesson prior to the Battle of Osaka Castle. A slight trembling in Yori's hand betrayed his true feelings, though. Jack grasped the six arrows with him and steadied his hand.

'Where there are friends, there's hope,' he said, repeating the same words he'd used to comfort Yori moments before that terrible battle on the Tenno-ji Plain.

Yori smiled bravely up at him. Jack had to admire his friend. Out of all of them, Yori was the most afraid of fighting, yet he displayed the greatest courage in overcoming that fear.

Akiko now held the arrows too. Her gaze met Jack's, their heartfelt vow passing silently between them.

Forever bound to one another.

Saburo placed his hand on top and looked at Jack. 'Only twenty samurai, you say? I agree, far better odds.'

Miyuki joined Jack at his side. She clasped the arrows just below his hand. 'To the death!'

Benkei was the last to grab hold. 'I *hate* to feel left out,' he said, even managing a nervous grin.

They all knew what had to be done. As the samurai closed in on their dead-end alley, they threw the arrows into the air and let out a mighty battle cry. Then, drawing their weapons, the six young warriors charged out into the street.

53

CUT OFF

Taking up a fighting formation across the road, Jack and his friends confronted the enemy head on. Their boldness brought the advancing samurai to a halt.

'This is your last chance to surrender!' shouted Miyuki. 'Put down your weapons and we'll spare your lives.'

The samurai turned to one another, incredulous at such an absurd demand. A low chuckle rose from one of the *ronin*. He was soon joined by the others as he exploded into a bellyful of laughter.

'*Surrender?*' he guffawed. 'Are you serio—' His amusement was cut short by a *shuriken* piercing his throat.

'Deadly serious,' said Miyuki.

The laughter from the other samurai quickly died as their comrade collapsed to his knees, blood spurting from his torn neck.

'Nineteen left,' said Saburo. 'The odds are improving.'

The band of *ronin* roared in anger and thundered forward. Jack took up a Two Heavens 'Rising Sun' stance, both *katana* and *wakizashi* held high and wide. The seemingly open and unguarded posture was actually a powerful offensive technique, drawing in the unwitting challenger before destroying them in a double sword swipe. Two samurai rushed Jack at once, but their sword attacks were no match for the Two Heavens. Nor were the quality of their blades equal to the steel forged by the legendary swordmaker Shizu. Jack's red-handled *katana* and *wakizashi* scythed through his opponents' weapons, shattering their blades. The two samurai stared in shocked disbelief at the sword stumps in their hands. Jack side-kicked one of the men in the chest, cracking his ribs. Then he whipped round, striking the other in the jaw with the brass pommel of his *wakizashi*. The man was knocked out cold in an instant, not even aware of hitting the ground.

Akiko fought furiously, the rush of combat flooding her with adrenalin and masking the pain in her shoulder. As nimble as a dancer, she wrong-footed her first attacker and drove the tip of her sword into his left shoulder.

'Now we're even!' she said, before spin-kicking him in the head.

Miyuki was faced with a mighty warrior wielding a battle-axe. Twice her size, he loomed over her.

'Don't hurt me,' she pleaded, cowering to the floor.

The warrior grinned maliciously. 'Don't worry, you won't feel a thing,' he promised. 'Well, not after I've finished with you.' He raised the axe to cleave her in half.

Snatching a handful of dust from the road, Miyuki threw it into the warrior's eyes. Blinded, the man didn't see Miyuki leap to her feet and aim a front kick squarely between his legs. With a high-pitched yelp, the warrior collapsed in an eye-watering heap, before dropping the axe on his own head.

'You were right. I didn't feel a thing,' Miyuki replied, wiping the dust from her hands in triumph.

Without a sword, Yori valiantly kept his opponent at bay by repeatedly thrusting the iron tip of his *shakujō*. After the third successful strike against him, the *ronin* grew furious and frustrated. Yori hit him again, but this time the *ronin* was prepared for it and grabbed the staff, wrenching it out of Yori's grip.

'What are you going to do now, monk boy?' he laughed.

'This,' replied Yori, sucking in a deep breath and yelling. '*YAH!*'

For a moment, the *ronin* simply looked stunned. Then he keeled over backwards as if he'd run into a stone wall.

Jack tried not to laugh as his friend nonchalantly retrieved his staff from the comatose man. Yori had clearly perfected his *kiaijutsu* to a fine art. Sensei Yamada would be proud of his protégé.

'Eight down, twelve to go,' shouted Saburo, despatching another *ronin*.

Benkei stood behind everyone, the knife in his hand, boldly threatening anyone who got past Jack and the others. Not that any did. With the adjusted grip suggested by Shiryu, Jack was wielding his swords as fluidly as ever. No attacker could get near him without lethal consequences. At this rate, they would soon conquer the *ronin* and leave this fateful village far behind.

Then a second wave of samurai appeared: twenty in front and at least that many again behind them.

'We're surrounded!' Yori cried in alarm.

'Time to get out of this death trap,' said Miyuki, checking between each of the buildings as they drove the first wave of samurai back up the street. But every alleyway and path had been blocked off with spiked fences. Behind, the samurai were closing in fast. In moments they'd be overwhelmed.

'Down here!' called Benkei, beckoning them towards an open alley he'd spotted.

Disarming his attacker with an Autumn Leaf strike, Jack raced over to Benkei and the others. The route led to the village pond. They charged along the narrow alley, Benkei leading the way, Miyuki taking up the rear. As they fled out the other side, they passed beneath an overhanging section of roof spanning the alley. Jack didn't think anything of it until it was too late. Without warning, a bamboo grille dropped down and Miyuki was cut off, leaving her to face the samurai alone.

54

LAMP OIL

Sheathing his swords, Jack ran back to help Miyuki raise the grille. Straining every muscle, he cried, 'It *won't* move.'

Saburo and Yori now joined them. Even with their combined strength, they couldn't shift the bamboo frame.

'The grille's locked in place from above,' observed Akiko.

Miyuki glanced up, seeking another way out. The bamboo bars met flush with the overhanging roof and building walls, leaving no gap to climb through. She was boxed in like a mouse in a trap.

The samurai now entered the other end of the alley, one by one. The *ronin* in front was a bearded monster with a battle-chipped *katana*. He took his time, knowing that his quarry had nowhere to run to.

'*NANBAN!*' shouted Benkei, suddenly realizing the others weren't following. 'We have company. Lots of it!'

Looking over his shoulder, Jack saw that the second wave of samurai had doubled back and was now at the lower end of the village pond near the river. Strewn with clumps of reeds and a couple of willow trees hanging from its banks, the large expanse of muddy water blocked any direct route to the fields beyond. They'd have to run round it. And, with the samurai charging up both sides of the pond, they had no time to lose.

'Get out of here,' said Miyuki. 'Save yourselves while you can.'

'No, I won't leave you behind,' Jack replied, still desperately trying to lift the grille.

'You don't have any other choice.'

Saburo and Akiko prepared to engage the frontline of attackers in a brave, but ultimately futile, attempt to hold off the tide of samurai. In the alley, the first of Miyuki's assailants closed in.

Miyuki looked intently through the bamboo bars at Jack, her midnight eyes resolved to her fate. 'I always knew what sacrifice I might have to make for you, Jack. And I do so with all my heart.'

She tenderly touched Jack's hand, savouring one last moment of goodbye. Then she turned to confront the first *ronin*.

'NO!' said Jack, shaking the bars as Miyuki clashed blades with the first of her attackers. '*No one* should sacrifice them-selves for me. We'll find a way to save you.'

'Come on!' urged Benkei, heading along the bank towards a large rice barn and the fields beyond.

Jack felt Yori's hand on his arm, pulling him away. He resisted.

'Don't let her sacrifice be in vain,' said Yori, his voice break-ing at having to make such a harsh choice. Like Miyuki, he recognized everyone's chances of survival were rapidly dwind-ling the longer they delayed. And, with no realistic hope of rescuing her in time, they *had* to leave her behind.

Yori dragged Jack away, but Jack despised himself for every step he took. He felt he was betraying his ninja friend, abandoning her to her fate. Miyuki was swallowed up by the mouth of the alley, his final glimpse of her a flash of steel as she fought to the death.

'GO! GO!' cried Akiko, running up behind them.

'Where's Saburo?' asked Yori.

'He's holding off the samurai,' she panted.

Jack looked further down the bank to see Saburo swinging his sword in wide defensive arcs. Eight samurai tried to fight their way past him, but he held his ground.

'We can't let him fight alone,' protested Jack.

'He said . . . the odds were good,' replied Akiko, but the sorrow in her eyes told another story. 'And as soon as we reach that barn, he's promised to join us.'

They sprinted up the bank, realizing every second counted. On the opposite side of the pond, the other samurai were racing to head them off. Just as Benkei levelled with the rice barn, they heard Saburo cry out. One of the *ronin* had got through his defence and shoulder-barged him to the ground. They were both locked in combat, Saburo throttling his attacker who was trying to plunge a *tantō* into his heart. Rolling over and over, the two of them tumbled down the bank into the pond, before disappearing beneath the water with a huge splash.

'Saburo!' gasped Yori, stopping in his tracks.

Jack waited a beat for Saburo to come back up – but neither he nor the *ronin* did. Only an ominous pool of blood rose to the surface.

'No! NO!' sobbed Yori, struggling in Jack's arms.

'It's too late . . . to save him,' said Jack. With the samurai hot on their heels, it was Jack that now pulled the distraught Yori along with him. But he was no less distressed. The cruel loss of *another* loyal friend was like an iron punch to the gut – one that Jack didn't think he would ever recover from.

They skirted the edge of the pond towards the fields. But the samurai on the opposite bank got there first.

'Which way now?' Benkei cried as the two groups of samurai converged on them, closing off all escape routes.

'Through the rice barn,' said Jack. 'There has to be a back door.'

They dived inside. The barn was surprisingly empty of rice, yet full of straw.

'There!' shouted Akiko, pointing to a stable door in the rear wall.

Hurrying over, Jack grabbed the handle to slide it open. But the door had been nailed shut. Jack furiously yanked on the handle. The door wouldn't budge.

'Why aren't they following us inside?' Yori asked, noticing the samurai had formed a semi-circle outside the main barn doors.

Letting go of the handle, Jack's palm came away slick and greasy.

Lamp oil.

Looking around, Jack now saw the whole barn was doused in it – the walls, the straw, the floor all glistening with splashes of oil. Before he could warn his friends, a burning torch was tossed inside the barn. There was a ferocious *whoosh* as a straw pile caught alight. The blaze spread through the barn as if it was alive, tendrils of orange-red fire shooting in all directions across the floor and tongues of flame licking up the walls. More bundles of straw exploded like blinding fireworks. Jack and his friends shielded their faces from the sudden and intense heat.

'We're going to fry!' exclaimed Benkei, making for the main door.

Akiko grabbed hold of him. 'They'll cut you down as you run out.'

'Better than burning alive.'

But Benkei stayed with them as Jack began to furiously kick at the rear door. His whole leg jarred on every impact, the wooden panels solid and unyielding. He kicked again and again, favouring a side-kick for power. Akiko joined in the attack, coordinating back-heel strikes with his side-kicks.

The fire now roared all around them, smoke billowing in the air and choking their lungs. Jack could smell his hair singeing and feel his skin blistering. The barn was going up like a tinderbox.

Jack clenched his teeth, driving his foot like a battering ram into the wood. But the door wouldn't give. Akiko kicked with all her might. Nothing moved. Still, they kept up the relentless pounding as the roof turned into a swirling sky of flame.

Benkei and Yori huddled in the middle of the barn, keeping as far as possible from the burning walls.

Jack was about to give up hope when one of the door panels splintered. Akiko struck out and it cracked. Then, with a final side-kick, the panel burst apart.

'OUT!' shouted Jack above the roar of the flames.

He pushed Akiko through the narrow opening first. Benkei made a mad dash for it and dived through. Jack urgently beckoned Yori to go next, his friend almost lost from view amid the choking smoke and red-hot sparks. A horrendous *crack* made them both look up. Flaming chunks of wood and burning thatch rained down, forcing Yori to jump out of the way. As whole sections of the roof fell at Jack's feet, he had no choice but to dive through the door for his own life.

Landing on the hard-baked earth, coughing and spluttering, he immediately looked back inside for any sign of Yori. He spotted a small shimmering figure in the centre of the inferno. His friend stood motionless, eyes closed, his hands clasped in prayer.

55

SNATCHED

Jack was in a state of total shock. He'd lost three of his closest friends in as many minutes. He knelt in the dirt, head bowed, black smoke and sparks swirling around him.

The barn continued to burn with Yori inside. And there was nothing he, Akiko or Benkei could do about it. The gap in the door was now blocked with flaming debris, the fire too fierce for them to enter. And on the other side, waiting like vultures, stood the band of murderous samurai.

'I *really* liked Yori,' croaked Benkei, his bloodshot eyes brimming as he stared glumly at the blaze.

Jack's grief was beyond tears. His hurt ran so deep that it was his heart, not his eyes, that wept for Yori. His friend had always been the still small voice of reason, the rock he'd counted on in the storms of life. And, now Yori was gone, Jack felt as lost and drifting as a rudderless ship. Miyuki, Saburo and Yori *all* dead — it was too much for him to cope with. He understood that the Way of the Warrior was to fight and die in the name of Honour and Loyalty. But *his* life wasn't worth such sacrifice. He was no samurai lord. He was simply trying to get home. And where would this slaughter end? In the death of Benkei? His beloved Akiko? No sense of loyalty was worth that high a price.

'We have to leave,' said Akiko, equally traumatized by the tragic turn of events, yet somehow managing to hold her nerve.

Jack nodded numbly, but still didn't move.

'*Seven times down, eight times up*,' she whispered, a tear running down her soot-stained cheek as she laid a gentle hand upon his shoulder.

The remembrance of Yori's wise words from the *Taryu-Jiai* three years before – his lesson in never giving up – finally spurred Jack into action. He forced himself to his feet and stood beside Akiko. He noticed her kimono sleeve clinging to her left arm, its green silk now stained an ominous red. 'Are you all right?' he asked.

'I'll live,' she said wearily. 'The arrow wound's just opened up again.'

Concerned for her deteriorating health, Jack snapped back to the harsh reality of their situation. They *had* to survive, if only for the memory of their fallen friends. He looked around. No samurai had yet discovered their escape. The back of the barn met with one of the high thorn boundary hedges, preventing access to the fields. They could either head to the pond and risk being spotted, or work their way through the village and flee via the main road towards Nagasaki. Peering round the corner of the barn, Jack saw that the samurai were still engrossed in the fire, celebrating their victory.

There was a patch of open ground to reach the nearest alley, but Jack decided this was still the best option. They waited until a pall of smoke came their way, then Jack, Akiko and

Benkei darted across. They raced up the alley, Benkei taking the lead. It switched left, passing a stack of empty *saké* barrels, and ran behind the village inn.

'There may be more samurai ahead,' warned Akiko, pausing to rest. 'So stay alert.'

Nodding, Benkei slowed his pace. Jack looked over his shoulder to check if any *ronin* were following. The alley remained clear. He heard a scuffle and a door slam. When he turned back, Akiko had disappeared and Benkei was lying on the floor, clasping his bleeding nose.

'Deh dook her!' he said, pointing to a studded door in the wall of the inn.

Jack could barely believe they'd snatched Akiko so easily. He shoulder-barged the door, grunting in pain as he bounced off. In a fit of fury, he kicked at the hinges, but the door had been barred shut from the other side.

'*Akiko!*' he cried, but there was no reply.

Dragging over an empty *saké* barrel, he clambered on top and reached for the tiled lip of the wall. Pulling himself on to the tiles, he then stretched out his hand for Benkei. 'Quickly!' he urged.

Scrambling over, they landed in a courtyard garden.

The unexpected peace and tranquillity was in stark contrast to the chaos of battle and burning buildings. Wooden walkways weaved between manicured bushes and artfully placed rocks. A large hollowed-out stone rippled with water, the constant trickle from a bamboo pipe sounding like evening birdsong. At the centre, surrounded by a thick cushion of green moss, was a cypress tree, its upper foliage bent over providing welcome shade from the beating sun. And set upon a flat bed of rock was a *washi*-walled tea house, located in prime position to enjoy meditative views of the serene garden.

Jack cautiously trod the walkway leading to the inn's main building. He kept his eyes peeled for any clue to Akiko's whereabouts. Benkei followed the path that circled the cypress tree towards the tea house.

Jack was the first to spot a fresh drop of blood on a rock; then another on the boards at his feet.

'This way,' he said, increasing his pace.

Suddenly there was a *whump* and a crash of branches, as if a bird had been startled. Jack looked round for Benkei, but he was gone.

Shading his eyes against the sun, he glanced up. His friend swung helplessly, upside down, from the top of the cypress tree, its branches no longer bent now that the snare had been triggered. Benkei dangled unconscious high above the garden.

'Alone at last!' declared a figure, silhouetted within the tea house.

56

A HAND FOR A HAND

Jack spun towards the tea house, his *katana* unsheathing in the blink of an eye. 'Where's Akiko?' he demanded.

The *washi* screen drew back to reveal his rival. 'All in good time, *gaijin*,' said Kazuki.

'No, this ends here and now,' said Jack, advancing on him.

Kazuki held up his black-gloved hand in warning and Nobu appeared at his side, cracking his knuckles threateningly. 'If you want to see your precious Akiko alive, don't *dare* take another step!'

Jack froze where he was, hating the control his rival wielded over him.

'I intend to relish this moment to the full,' announced Kazuki, taking a sip from a steaming cup of green tea. '*Everything* has gone according to plan. I really don't know why I didn't think of this before. It would have saved all that pointless chasing.'

Jack's eyes scanned the inn's garden. If Kazuki and Nobu were here, then the other members of the Scorpion Gang had to be too.

'I realized you'd have to pass through this village on your

way to Nagasaki,' explained Kazuki, revelling in his own clev-
erness. 'There's no other route from Shimabara. All I had to
do was hire a bunch of *ronin*, set a few traps and wait patiently,
like a tiger for its prey. In fact, I'm surprised you made it this
far.'

'You killed my friends!' Jack seethed, clenching his *katana*
handle so tightly his knuckles turned white.

A fiendish grin lit up Kazuki's face as he delighted in Jack's
torment. 'I promised that I'd destroy you, *gaijin*. That means
not only killing *you* but anyone who's helped you and in
particular those you *love*.'

He sneered at the word, then clicked his fingers. The inn's
main *shoji* overlooking the garden slid open. Akiko was on her
knees, bound and gagged, a wooden block in front of her.
Hiroto stood behind, wrenching her head back by her hair, a
knife held to her throat. The hulking Raiden was beside them,
his formidable *nodachi* sword unsheathed.

Jack glared at Kazuki. 'You vowed not to harm Akiko,
remember? In return, I saved your life.'

'That's true, *gaijin*.' Kazuki stroked his chin thoughtfully.
'And I'm a samurai of my word. That's why *I* won't lay a finger
on her.'

He nodded towards Raiden and Hiroto.

'But I can't say the same for my companions.'

Hiroto cut the rope binding Akiko's right arm. Seizing her
wrist, Raiden forced her hand on to the block and held it
firmly in place with his foot. Despite her obvious pain and
discomfort, Akiko's expression remained defiant.

'A hand for a hand – that's fair, don't you think?' said
Kazuki, massaging his black-gloved claw.

'Stop!' begged Jack, throwing down his *katana*. 'I surrender. I'll do anything you want. I'll even commit *seppuku*. Just leave Akiko alone.'

Kazuki laughed. 'What I want is for you to *watch*, *gaijin*.'

Raiden raised his *nodachi* over his head to sever Akiko's hand. Akiko screwed her eyes shut, bracing herself for the agonizing cut . . . There was a flash of steel and a sickening howl of pain. Raiden's *nodachi* clattered to the ground as he clasped his bleeding face in both hands. Between his fingers, the sharpened point of a *shuriken* gleamed.

Snatching up his *katana*, Jack charged along the walkway to rescue Akiko. His surrender had been nothing but a ruse to allow him to grab the *shuriken* he'd taken from the archer's body. In one fluid movement, he'd slipped the star from his *obi* and flicked it with deadly accuracy at Raiden's right eye. As he now dashed across the garden past the cypress tree, Akiko held up her hand, signing for him to stop. But it was too late. A blade scythed out of nowhere. On instinct alone Jack ducked, the sword slicing so close it shaved off a lock of his hair.

'Not so fast, *gaijin*,' Goro snarled, his blade coming round for a second attack.

Jack blocked it with his *katana* and the two blades sparked off one another. He kicked Goro in the chest. Goro stumbled backwards but kept his feet. He slashed low with his sword. Jack jumped the blade and brought his *katana* down on to Goro's head. Goro's sword met the *katana* halfway. The two weapons jammed, and Jack and Goro became locked in a power struggle through the garden.

As Jack fought for his life, Akiko drove herself upwards and threw her head back. There was a dull crunch as Hiroto's recently healed nose imploded once again. He collapsed to the floor, sobbing with pain. Akiko seized his knife with her free hand and drove the blade through his shoulder, pinning him to the floorboards. Hiroto writhed like a harpooned fish.

Half-blinded and maddened with pain, Raiden now tried to stamp-kick Akiko where she lay. Still bound by the ropes, Akiko was in no position to fight off the monstrous young samurai. She frantically rolled across the inn floor, trying to free herself before Raiden could land one of his skull-crushing kicks.

'Leave the *gaijin* to me, Goro,' Kazuki ordered, leaping from the tea house. 'Go and help Raiden *kill* Akiko.'

Goro immediately disengaged and headed for the open *shoji*. Jack chased after him, but Kazuki blocked his path.

'Revenge is long overdue, *gaijin*,' he declared, pointing his black-handled *katana* at Jack. 'But it'll be all the sweeter for it.'

57

REVENGE

As his rival advanced on him, Jack drew his *wakizashi* and took up a Two Heavens stance. He realized this would be a fight to the death. No more running. No lucky escapes. Their feud was destined for a bloody end, one way or the other.

'Can you still do the Two Heavens with a fingertip missing?' Kazuki smirked.

'Why don't you find out for yourself?' challenged Jack, impatient to reach Akiko before it was too late.

Kazuki's cut was so fast that Jack barely had time to deflect it with his *katana*. The razor-sharp steel whistled past his ear like a lightning bolt. As Kazuki pulled back, Jack felt a bee-like sting across his cheek.

'Clearly not,' gloated Kazuki, flicking Jack's blood from his blade.

A thin red line ran along Jack's face where Kazuki's blade had caught him. The cut wasn't deep, the pain yet to fully register, but first blood had been drawn – and laying claim to the opening victory meant *everything* in the battle to come.

'I'm going to bleed you like a stuck pig,' Kazuki declared. 'Cut by cut.'

Then he attacked with a vengeance, his blade slicing in a series of deadly arcs. Jack had to apply all his skill just to defend against them. Although he had the advantage of two weapons, Kazuki was a supreme swordsman. Even with his injured right hand, Kazuki had adapted and become more lethal. Moreover, he knew how to evade and counter every Two Heavens technique. Whatever Jack tried – Running Water strike, Lacquer-and-Glue, Monkey's Body – Kazuki foresaw and retaliated with devastating consequences. He cut Jack across the forearm with a switchback slice. Then he avoided Jack's attempt at an Autumn Leaf strike, feigning a thrust and turning it into a diagonal cut to his shoulder. Jack drove forwards to deliver a Flint-and-Spark strike, their blades scraping fiercely against one another. But Kazuki masterfully deflected the thrust and sliced through Jack's kimono, leaving a nasty gash across his chest.

Wincing in pain, Jack was forced to retreat. He was exhausted from the previous battles, worn out from their frantic escape, and his strength was further sapped with every cut Kazuki inflicted.

This *wasn't* how he'd envisaged their final duel.

Kazuki prowled towards him, his sword dripping with Jack's blood. 'You seem distracted, *gaijin*. Didn't Sensei Hosokawa teach you *fudoshin*?'

A samurai must remain calm at all times – even in the face of danger.

But how could Jack remain calm and focused when Akiko was in such peril? He glanced anxiously in her direction. She'd managed to shed her bonds, but was now cornered by Goro and Raiden. Weakened from her arrow wound and without a weapon, she was doomed to die.

Kazuki smiled. His ploy had worked. With Jack's attention briefly on Akiko, he clenched his gloved hand into a fist. The secret blade inside his kimono sleeve shot out. Rushing forward, he drove the deadly weapon at Jack's heart.

Realizing his potentially fatal error, Jack leapt away. The steel tip ripped through his jacket, just missing his skin by a whisker. He smashed the blade aside with his *wakizashi* and retreated once more.

'You don't catch me twice with that trick,' Jack panted, recalling the first time Kazuki had revealed his secret weapon.

'How about a third time?' replied Kazuki, cocking his head to one side.

A pair of meaty arms clamped down on Jack from behind and held him like a vice. Jack struggled, but Nobu's grip was crushingly strong. Kazuki held up his secret blade and gave a triumphant grin.

'Time to gut you, *gaijin!*'

He drew back his arm to thrust the razor-sharp steel into Jack's defenceless stomach. At the same time Goro and Raiden closed in for the kill on Akiko. Jack fought wildly to free himself, but deep down he knew all was lost.

The end had come.

Then there was a *crash* of doors as a dripping wet Saburo burst through the inn's main entrance. His arrival was followed by a yell from above that made Jack, Kazuki and Nobu all look up.

Plummeting down like a multicoloured angel of death, Benkei dropped from the tree. Stood directly beneath, Nobu panicked and let go of Jack, who dived aside as Benkei crashed on top of Nobu, flattening him like a pancake. Nobu groaned weakly, then lay still. Benkei rolled off and got unsteadily to his feet, one ankle still tethered to the snare where he'd cut it with his knife.

'Thank goodness for a soft landing!' said Benkei, patting himself down for injuries.

While Benkei dropped from the tree to save Jack, Saburo had rushed to Akiko's aid. He'd charged at Goro, their swords clashing, and driven him backwards into the half-blind Raiden. His surprise attack had given Akiko the opportunity to steal Hiroto's *katana* and she was now battling Raiden and his *nodachi*.

Sensing his long-awaited revenge slipping from his grasp, Kazuki roared in rage. 'You will *die*, *gaijin*!'

It was now Kazuki who'd forgotten the principle of *fudoshin*. 'It's your fault! All your fault my mother died,' he spat. '*Gaijin* are a disease. A plague that must be wiped from the face of this earth. And *I* will destroy you!'

His anger consumed him, his hunger for revenge overwhelming all rational thought. His *katana* and hand blade became a whirl of steel as he attacked Jack with the brutal fury of a man possessed.

Jack fought back with equal passion. Encouraged by Saburo's miraculous survival and Akiko's fighting spirit, he'd regained his warrior's sense of control. The two of them battled through the garden, their blades ringing like deathly tolls as the steel struck, blocking and countering one another. Neither could break through the other's defence.

Panting from exhaustion, Jack and Kazuki circled one another, their eyes locked in a battle of wills. Jack had drawn upon all his reserves to fend off his rival, but he knew Kazuki was the stronger in this duel – and so did Kazuki.

From within the inn, Raiden cried out as his *nodachi* rolled across the floor and he clasped what remained of his severed hand. With one eye gone and an arm disabled, Raiden had had enough and fled from the inn. His desertion didn't go unnoticed by Kazuki. Although he didn't break his stare, Jack spotted the tip of Kazuki's sword tremble ever so slightly.

'*Suki – a break in composure and concentration. That is your opportunity to attack*,' the *Shodo* master had said.

Realizing his opportunity, Jack flipped his *wakizashi* in his hand, deftly swapping to the reverse grip he'd mastered with Shiryu. Spinning on the spot, he knocked Kazuki's sword aside with his *katana*, then drove the tip of the *wakizashi* backwards. Caught totally off-guard by the unconventional technique, Kazuki was skewered through the side. The blade penetrated all the way through, pinning him to the trunk of the cypress tree behind.

Kazuki gasped in agony, his eyes widening in shock. '*That* wasn't the Two Heavens!'

Disbelief registered on his face as he looked down at the shaft of steel piercing his right-hand side, just below the ribs.

But Jack wasn't finished with him. Letting go of the *wakizashi*'s handle, he followed through on his spin, whipping his *katana* round, ready to decapitate his rival and end their blood feud for good.

58

ALL IN VAIN

'NO, JACK!'

The blade stopped a hair's breadth from Kazuki's neck, Jack's killing stroke stayed by a voice from the grave.

'Revenge has no more quenching effect on the emotions than salt water on thirst,' said Yori, entering the garden.

Jack couldn't believe his eyes. Yori's robes were singed at the hem, the tip of his *shakujō* charred black, and he walked with a slight limp. But his friend was *alive*. 'Yori . . . you survived the fire! *But how?*'

Yori smiled serenely up at him. 'The same way we survived the Way of Fire at the *gasshuku* – the Heart Sutra meditation. Part of the barn wall burned down and I walked out through the flames.' He lifted a foot, the skin of his sole blistered red raw. 'But I admit I've yet to perfect the technique.'

Kazuki groaned in pain, a bloodstain blossoming where the *wakizashi* impaled him to the tree.

Jack still held the *katana* to his throat, the urge to follow through almost overpowering. After the years of torment and suffering Kazuki had inflicted upon him and his friends, he surely deserved to die.

'Let him live,' said Yori. 'There's no place for anger or rage in *bushido*.'

'But Kazuki's responsible for Miyuki's death!' argued Jack, his sword hand trembling in its desire for justice.

'Completing your journey would be the best revenge,' Yori replied calmly. 'Honour her sacrifice not through hate and killing, but through triumph and mercy. Remember, the Way of a Warrior is not to destroy and kill, but to foster life. To protect it.'

Jack was struck by Yori's words. They were exactly the same as Sensei Yamada's three years before, when his Zen master had spoken with him about his desire for revenge against Dragon Eye. 'But why *should* Kazuki survive? If I'd been the one to die, Miyuki wouldn't hesitate to end his life. I owe it to her.'

'Then you must decide whether you're a samurai or a ninja, Jack.'

Yori turned his gaze upon Kazuki. 'But think on this: a far greater punishment than a quick death would be a long life lived in the knowledge that his efforts were all in vain. That he'd *failed* in his duty as a samurai to the Shogun. The loss of face would be unbearable.'

Kazuki scowled at Yori, the truth of his words cutting deeper than any sword.

Jack pressed his *katana* against Kazuki's throat, drawing a thin line of blood. It would be so easy to end this feud. But would he be any better than his rival if he killed out of revenge? Sensei Yamada's counsel came once more to his mind: *Rectitude, your ability to judge what is wrong and what is right, is the keystone to being samurai.*

Kazuki glared up at Jack, daring him to push harder.

With immense willpower, Jack withdrew his blade. He of all people knew that revenge didn't heal the wounds of the heart. The death of Dragon Eye had brought him little comfort; he still deeply missed his father and no day passed when he didn't think of Yamato. So why would executing Kazuki be any different? Whether his rival was dead or alive, the loss of Miyuki would haunt Jack forever.

But, by showing compassion at least, he could hold his head high and know his rival suffered too.

He pulled out his *wakizashi* with a sharp jerk. Kazuki collapsed to his knees, clutching his wounded side, blood seeping through his clasped fingers.

'I despise you . . . *gaijin*,' he spluttered, pure malevolence in his eyes.

'And I . . . forgive you,' replied Jack, the words hard to say, but even harder for Kazuki to accept.

The bitter shame of defeat and Jack's unexpected mercy crushed him. In a last-ditch attempt to save face, he turned his secret blade upon himself. But Jack stamped on the steel, snapping it from its fixings, and kicked the blade away into the bushes.

Curling up in a ball, Kazuki sobbed in frustration, 'You won't even let me die an *honourable* death! Curse you, *gaijin*!'

From inside the inn, Goro spotted Kazuki at Jack's feet, bowed and defeated. Immediately he broke off his fight with Saburo and bolted out of the inn's entrance. Akiko stood over the pinned Hiroto, his *katana* clasped in her hand.

'Please . . . don't kill me,' he pleaded.

Bending down, Akiko pulled the knife from his shoulder

and, with a kick to his rear end, sent him on his way. He blundered after Goro.

'When the tree falls, the monkeys scatter,' observed Yori with a wry smile.

Saburo and Akiko joined them beneath the cypress tree. Although Akiko looked pale, their victory had given her renewed strength and she strode over without help from Saburo.

'You arrived in the nick of time, Saburo,' said Jack.

'But we saw you die,' said Yori, overjoyed to find his friend safe.

'Then I must be a ghost,' he teased, wringing the water from his kimono sleeves.

'So how did you survive?' asked Akiko.

'As we rolled down the bank, I managed to twist the *tantō* round. The *ronin* impaled himself on his own knife. I knew the other samurai would slaughter me if I surfaced, so I used the ninja method of breathing through a reed, just like Miyuki had once shown me . . .'

He trailed off, keenly aware of her absence, and a deep grief consumed the five surviving friends.

After a moment's silence, Akiko asked, 'But how did you both find us?'

Saburo managed a smile. 'I spotted Benkei hanging from the tree!'

'And it was a good thing that I *dropped* in too,' jested Benkei, popping his head out from behind a bush. 'Without me, you'd be dead by now.'

'True,' said Jack, glancing at the unconscious Nobu. 'And you hit the bullseye!'

He turned back to Kazuki, crumpled on the ground, then looked at Akiko. 'What about Kazuki's vendetta against you?'

Akiko shook her head, untroubled. 'With all his gang abandoning him, he's a scorpion without a sting.'

A low, weak chuckle bubbled from Kazuki's lips.

'What's so funny?' demanded Jack.

'*Your* efforts – not mine – are all in vain!' he said, giving Jack a hard cold stare. 'The Shogun's samurai are on their way.'

59

PALANQUIN

Four samurai in gold-and-black armour stood over Miyuki's lifeless body. A trail of corpses led from the alleyway to where she'd fallen in battle in the middle of the street. Jack and his surviving friends hid within the entrance to the inn.

'We should have gone back to save her,' said Jack, his vision blurring with tears.

'How could we?' said Saburo. 'We were all fighting for our lives.'

'And we wouldn't be here now,' Akiko reminded him, 'if Miyuki hadn't been so brave.'

'The blossom may fall, but the tree survives,' said Yori, planting his staff between them.

Following Yori's gesture, Jack, Akiko, Saburo and Benkei gripped the *shakujō* as one and bowed their heads in silent prayer.

The sound of horses' hooves made them look up.

'We'd better go,' said Akiko as more of the Shogun's samurai arrived at the burnt-out bridge.

With one last grieving look in Miyuki's direction, Jack followed his friends through the inn and across the garden. As they headed for the back gate, he spotted a gardener's straw sunhat and grabbed it.

'You can run, but you can't hide, *gaijin*,' wheezed Kazuki, a malicious glint in his eyes.

'Save your breath for living,' replied Jack and closed the gate on his rival, who they'd left bound to the cypress tree along with the dazed Nobu.

Keeping low, they evaded any patrolling *ronin* and escaped the death-trap village. Once they were a safe distance, Akiko whistled twice and Snowball galloped from the fields to reunite with them. Much to Jack's relief, his pack and its precious contents were still tied to the saddle.

Exhausted, injured and bleeding, they embarked on their final dash for Nagasaki, praying they could reach the port before the Shogun's samurai caught up with them.

'How much further?' asked Jack, breathing hard as they raced along the dirt road.

'If I'm right, the main road from Fukuoka should be over that next hill,' Benkei panted, hobbling slightly from the arrow wound to his rear. 'And then it's no more than five *ri*.'

Jack rammed the straw hat on to his head; it was proving too small for him and threatened to fall off. He grimaced as he lowered his sword arm. His injuries from the duel were mercifully only flesh wounds, but still painfully raw and seeping blood.

Yori limped alongside him, aided by his staff. He winced with every step of his blistered feet, but made no complaint. Akiko, the most gravely injured among them, trotted behind on the back of Snowball. Saburo followed last, keeping a lookout for any sign of their pursuers. Since leaving the inn, they'd paused only to apply a fresh bandage to Akiko's shoulder, eat the last of their supplies and drink from a stream. Ragged and battleworn, they looked like refugees of war. And, as they passed farmers in the fields and other travellers on the road, they were greeted by barely suppressed gasps of astonishment and given a wide berth.

But being noticed was the least of their concerns now. They simply needed to make a run for it.

Joining the main road to Nagasaki, they encountered more foot traffic as the route wound through the last knot of hills and valleys towards the coast. Akiko led the way. Her samurai status and the fact she was on horseback cleared a path through the stream of farmers, pilgrims and merchants headed for the port. On either side of the road, tea houses sprang up at each milestone and small food stalls offered welcome refreshments to the weary travellers. With the blazing sun giving no respite from its glare, the establishments were doing a roaring trade.

But Jack and his friends didn't dare stop to eat or rest again. Hounded by the unseen force of samurai, they pressed on.

As they crested a rise, the view opened out into a long, narrow bay. The large natural harbour was bounded on either shore by a ruckle of steep green hills and the late afternoon sun shimmered like silver across its still waters. A busy port filled the flatlands of the bay before fanning out into the tucks and crevices of the surrounding hills.

'Nagasaki!' exclaimed Jack, unable to believe they'd actually made it.

Protected from storm and wave, the bay was a haven for ships of all kinds – large and small, fishing and merchant, ocean and coastal, Japanese and Chinese and . . . European. There were so many different boats nestled in the harbour that Jack thought an armada had arrived. Only a few were ocean-going galleons, but one of them *had* to be English.

His pace became urgent. But Akiko pulled on her reins and brought Snowball to a sudden halt.

'There's a checkpoint ahead,' she said.

At the end of the road, a wooden-gated entrance marked the port's boundary. A unit of guards was meticulously checking permits.

'How will we get past *them*?' said Yori.

Jack looked towards the surrounding hillsides, but any such approach would easily be spotted by a sharp-eyed guard, and then there was the high boundary wall to negotiate. Their only other alternative was to wait until nightfall, but the Shogun's samurai were bound to reach Nagasaki and find them before dusk came.

'Why don't we carry Jack through in style?' Benkei suggested, pointing to a palanquin parked outside the last tea house.

The enclosed wooden seat, mounted on two poles for carrying, was fancy and ostentatious. Decorated with black lacquered wood and gilded with flowers and birds, the palanquin clearly belonged to an aristocrat of some importance. Inside were soft plush cushions, but the seat was empty, its owner dining within the tea house. The four bearers were fast asleep under a tree, exhausted from the heat of the day and their exertions. Despite wearing just loincloths, their bronzed bodies still glistened with sweat.

'Palanquins are for high officials only,' reminded Akiko.

'Exactly,' Benkei replied with a grin. 'And they *don't* need travel permits.'

Jack and his friends immediately grasped Benkei's plan.

'We can't *steal* from a high official,' exclaimed Yori.

'Technically, it's not stealing,' Benkei assured with a wink. 'Just borrowing.'

'But how are we going to carry it? We won't pass as bearers,' said Saburo.

'Perhaps we can help?' said a familiar voice.

Jack and the others spun to discover the old farmer Takumi standing unexpectedly behind them. He was accompanied by four younger men from the Christian village they'd saved.

'What are *you* doing here?' exclaimed Jack.

Takumi bowed. 'We prayed as you asked and the Lord spoke to us. He told us to follow.'

'A god who foresees need is a powerful one indeed,' remarked Yori.

'Our prayers were answered when you came to our rescue.' Takumi smiled. 'True faith can move mountains.'

'Well, can it move a palanquin?' said Benkei, hurriedly beckoning them over to the tea house.

With no time to waste, Jack clambered inside the palanquin and slid the ornate door shut. The four farmers, having stripped to their waists, lifted the seat by its poles and hurried down the road before any of the official bearers awoke. Once again Akiko took the lead, her samurai armour and horse adding status to the ragtag entourage. Yori, Saburo, Benkei and Takumi brought up the rear as loyal followers.

Hidden inside the swaying palanquin, Jack peeked through

a gap in the door. They were approaching the gate. Everything now relied upon the impression of high status.

A guard held up his hand. The farmers slowed to a stop.

'What happened? Where's the rest of your escort?' the guard demanded, peering suspiciously at the palanquin.

'We were attacked by bandits,' Akiko explained, indicating her wounded shoulder. 'Many lost their lives, but thankfully our master is safe.'

The guard nodded gravely at such honourable sacrifice.

'What are you waiting for?' challenged Akiko. 'Send out a detachment *immediately*!'

She gave the command with such authority that the guard jumped.

'And be warned,' she added, 'the bandits are disguised as the Shogun's samurai.'

The guard's eyes widened in shock at this news. He bowed in acknowledgement of the order, then waved them on. The farmers bore the palanquin through the gate and into the port.

60

FLAG

Jack had finally arrived.

After more than a year of running, hiding and fighting for his life, he'd reached his destination. Nagasaki. He just hoped that it would offer the salvation he'd been praying for all this time.

As he peered out from the palanquin, he caught glimpses of the bustling port. They were heading along the main street towards a bridge that spanned the Nakashima River. Women in brightly coloured kimono hurried to and fro. Traders called out their wares – exotic spices from Java, ivory from India, silk from China and foods from all four corners of the known world. There was a lively, relaxed atmosphere to the place, as if the outside influence of foreigners had diluted the traditional Japanese formality and injected a vibrant, almost rebellious spirit. Jack even spotted a Catholic church, although its doors were boarded up.

'That was clever of you, Akiko,' remarked Saburo. 'If we're lucky, that ploy should delay the Shogun's samurai.'

'It might even give *us* a chance to escape once Jack's on-board his ship,' said Benkei with a grin.

'Don't speak too soon,' replied Akiko, hearing a shout from behind.

'STOP! THIEVES!'

A portly aristocrat with four panicked bearers came lumbering down the hill towards the gate.

'THAT'S MY PALANQUIN!'

The gate guards spun round and glared at the disappearing entourage. Several immediately gave chase.

'GO!' cried Saburo.

The farmers pumped their legs, clattering across the wooden bridge. Jack was thrown around inside the palanquin as they barged through the crowd. But the streets were thronging with people, and, even with Akiko on her horse, their progress was hampered. The guards, on the other hand, wielded their swords with abandon, scattering the crowd and clearing a path through.

'Get out, Jack!' Akiko ordered, quickly dismounting Snowball, realizing she was too visible.

The farmers dumped the palanquin on the ground and Jack leapt out. 'Thanks for your help,' he said.

'Don't worry, we'll draw the guards away,' said Takumi.

'Then take Snowball to attract their attention,' Akiko suggested, handing Takumi the reins as Jack and the others snatched their packs from the saddle. 'But I'll be back for him.'

Bowing a hurried farewell, Takumi and the four farmers disappeared down a side street with the stallion in tow. In an attempt to throw off the guards, Jack and his friends went the opposite way, taking to the warren of alleys that circled the harbour. They switched right, then left, before cutting across another bridge. Behind, their pursuers were shouting for them to stop. They passed beneath a fire-red gateway, golden dragons adorning its green-tiled eaves. Hundreds of yellow lanterns festooned with red streamers floated above their heads. As they ran, Jack noticed all the inhabitants in this district were Chinese. Their eyes widened in shock as the five fugitives careered past.

Akiko broke left and darted inside a temple. The chaos of the port was suddenly replaced by the tranquil chime of bells, heady wafts of incense and the incantation of praying monks. Respectfully avoiding the central shrine, the five of them dashed through to a backstreet. They crossed a small stone bridge out of Chinatown and headed for the harbour. But the alley they chose came to an abrupt end. Backtracking, they heard the shouts of their pursuers drawing closer. They ducked inside a darkened warehouse and waited for them to pass.

No one spoke, their hearts racing and lungs burning.

The guards shot by.

Bolting from their hiding place, Jack and his friends took the opposite alley, then bore right. A few turns later, they emerged by the harbour side. The quay was crammed with fishing boats, Chinese junks and cargo ships. Warehouses swarmed with deckhands and port workers loading and unloading barrels. The hubbub of activity meant that their sudden appearance went unnoticed. Jack's eyes scanned the port for the galleons. The enormous multi-decked ships were easy to spot. Their distinctive castle-like design, heavy cannon and square-rigs set them apart from the Eastern-style flat-keeled boats with their batten sails. Jack spied three galleons in the bay almost immediately.

But his heart sank like a stone. None flew the British flag.

They all boasted the stark white rectangle and golden coat of arms of his country's sworn enemy, Portugal.

Jack collapsed to his knees in despair. Benkei had been right. *Only* the Portuguese traded out of Nagasaki. He was doomed. All his friends' efforts and sacrifices were for nothing, his dream of returning home to Jess no more than that – just a futile dream.

'What's wrong?' asked Akiko, kneeling beside him. 'They're galleons, aren't they?'

Jack nodded. 'But they fly the Portuguese flag,' he explained. 'They'd sooner take me prisoner than take me home.'

Yori looked out beyond the mouth of the bay towards the distant sea. 'An English ship will turn up soon, Jack . . . I'm sure of it.'

'Yes,' Saburo agreed readily. 'And we can protect you until one arrives.'

Jack turned to his friends, their unwavering belief in him only highlighting the cruel truth.

'That could be years,' he said, resigning himself to his fate. 'This is the end of the road. You got me here, alive, and I'm grateful for that. But you can't hide me from the Shogun's samurai forever. And I can't allow you to keep risking your lives for me.'

'No!' exclaimed Yori, defiant tears brimming in his eyes. 'We'll find another way. Another ship –'

'What flag's that?' interrupted Benkei, pointing towards a mast at the far end of the quay.

Protruding above the roofline of a large warehouse were four tall masts – another galleon. Atop the main fluttered a banner with red, white and blue horizontal stripes.

Jack stared in astonishment. *How could he have missed it?*

'That's a Dutch flag!' he cried, jumping up and hugging Benkei with joy. 'That's a Dutch flag!'

He raced along the harbour, his friends following in his wake. As they rounded the warehouse and came alongside, they slowed to a halt, awed by the sheer size of the colossal ocean-going vessel.

'This floats?' said Saburo, utterly astonished.

'A ship like this can sail around the world. All the way to England!' Jack declared, heading towards the gangway.

'*Ahoi, aan boord!*' he cried, recalling the Dutch he'd learnt from his fellow seaman Ginsel.

A crewman with a sunburnt face, thick beard and sharp blue eyes leant over the side. '*Wie ben jij?*'

Jack threw off his hat to reveal his blond hair. '*Mijn naam is* Jack Fletcher. *Ik ben Engels!*'

The crewman looked astonished. '*Kom aan boord! Kom aan boord!*'

Jack and his friends hurried up the gangway and on to the deck before any of the gate guards appeared. The bearded crewman and several other sailors greeted them with bemused expressions. They were unsure what to make of the kimono-clad, sword-bearing English boy and his bizarre retinue of a Japanese warrior girl, a young samurai, a tiny monk and a patchwork clown.

'*Kapitein!*' called the bearded crewman.

A tall Dutch man emerged from the main cabin and approached. Despite the heat, he was dressed smartly in a brown leather jacket, waistcoat and linen shirt with a lace collar. He wore wide black breeches with knee-length white socks and polished buckle shoes. His light auburn hair was a thick carpet of tight curls and he sported a trimmed beard and moustache.

'I'm Captain Hendrik Spilbergen of the *Hosiander*,' he announced in slightly accented English. He looked Jack up and down. 'And whom do I have the pleasure of meeting?'

'Jack Fletcher of the *Alexandria*,' he said, bowing.

The captain's face blanched slightly, as if he'd seen a ghost. 'The *Alexandria*?'

'*Hai* . . . I mean yes,' replied Jack, nodding. He was so used to speaking Japanese that it was a shock to converse in English after so many years.

The captain shook his head in disbelief. 'We believed you all to be dead.'

61

PASSAGE HOME

'You needn't worry, Jack,' assured Captain Spilbergen, raising a crystal glass of red wine to his lips, 'you're safe on-board the *Hosiander*. This is Dutch territory.'

Jack was greatly relieved to hear this and told his friends the good news. They sat round a large oak table in the captain's quarters. Upon his insistence, they'd all been tended to by the ship's doctor before joining him and his officers for dinner. Akiko now looked more her normal self, having regained some of her colour and had her arrow wound dressed properly and her bloodstained kimono changed for a fresh one. Jack felt better too, the worst of his cuts stitched and bandaged. Yori had soaked his blistered feet in brine, while the only medicine Saburo required was food. Benkei had passed the time making friends with the ship's cat and she now sat on his lap, purring loudly.

The setting sun spilled in through the gallery windows and bathed the table in golden light. There was a feast of coarse bread, dumplings and pottage. His mouth watering, Jack wondered what his Japanese friends would make of the thick steaming stew; they were already bemused enough by the conversations in English.

He shifted in his seat. It felt strange to be on hard wooden chairs after being used to sitting cross-legged on floor cushions for so long.

'I met your father once,' revealed Captain Spilbergen. 'John Fletcher's regarded as one of the greatest pilots to sail the Seven Seas.'

Jack felt a flush of pride at his father's memory.

'Which is why the Dutch East India Company – who funded both your father's and my trade expeditions to the Far East – was so surprised that his ship didn't return. After a few years, we could only assume you'd all perished.'

'The *Alexandria* was shipwrecked in a typhoon,' Jack explained. 'But my father navigated us safely to shore.'

'So where's your father and the rest of the crew now?'

Jack shivered at the dark memory. 'All dead. Killed by *wako*. My father too.'

Captain Spilbergen nodded solemnly. 'I'm grieved to hear that. You certainly look like you've been through the wars. How have *you* survived all this time?'

Jack looked to Akiko, then at Yori, Saburo and Benkei. He thought of Yamato and of Miyuki.

'I have my friends to thank for that.'

Over dinner, he gave a brief recount of his adventures since landing in Japan: his rescue and adoption by the swordmaster Masamoto; his training as a samurai warrior in Kyoto; his deadly clashes with the ninja Dragon Eye; and his escape from the Battle of Osaka Castle. The captain and his officers listened rapt, alternating between disbelief, shock and admiration. While Jack spoke, Saburo devoured his stew and polished off the dumplings. Akiko and Yori were slightly less enthusiastic about the European-style meal, not being familiar with such rich and fatty foods. But, like Benkei, they ate as much as they could, encouraged by hunger and good manners, before discreetly passing the remainder to Saburo. Every so often Captain Spilbergen would ask a question and Jack would reply, taking the time to translate for his friends' benefit. The captain and his officers were astounded by his fluidity in the impenetrable language.

'You possess valuable skills, young Jack,' remarked the First Officer, raising his eyebrows in high regard. 'We could have done with your help when trading. They're a shrewd lot, these Japanese.'

Jack was encouraged to continue his story. He went on to explain the Shogun's edict banishing all foreigners and Christians from Japan. Then, as Jack recounted the troubles he'd faced on his perilous journey from Toba to Nagasaki, Captain Spilbergen and his officers exchanged concerned glances.

'We've heard tales of persecution, but didn't know what to believe,' said the captain. 'Here in Nagasaki, the Japanese are civil to us. But perhaps that's only because of the trade we bring them.'

'And the fact that we don't force our religion on them, like the Jesuits,' remarked the First Officer in distaste. 'It's their own fault they've been banished. Just this week the Portuguese had their trade privileges revoked by the local *bugyō*. That's why they can no longer dock at the quay.'

'You're extremely lucky, Jack, to have arrived in Nagasaki when you did,' continued the captain. 'We're due to set sail in a few days, as soon as the trade winds pick up. It'll be a year before the next Dutch ship arrives.'

Jack decided this was the moment to ask. 'I have a request. I need passage home to England.'

Captain Spilbergen considered this. 'Then I have a question for you. Are you as competent a sailor as you're a samurai?'

Jack gave a confident nod. 'My father taught me the skills to be a pilot. It's in my blood.'

'Dare I ask if you have *all* his knowledge?' enquired the captain, leaning forward and steepling his fingers in anticipation. 'It was rumoured he possessed an accurate *rutter*.'

Jack hesitated. His pack containing the precious logbook was just outside the captain's door. But could he trust this man?

'No matter,' said the captain, leaning back in his chair. 'I'd acquire your services with or without it. But you'll be a very sought-after young man if you do have it still. The Dutch East India Company is desperate for reliable pilots.'

'So you'll take me home?' asked Jack tentatively.

'Why, of course!' said Captain Spilbergen, breaking into a smile and opening his arms in welcome. 'If you're half the pilot your father was, then we're in safe hands.'

Jack was speechless. All that he'd strived for these past four years, every obstacle he'd overcome, every sacrifice he and his friends had made, had been for this very moment. He was so overwhelmed, he didn't know whether to laugh with joy or cry with relief.

'What did the captain just say?' asked Akiko in Japanese, concerned by the look of shock on Jack's face.

'I'm . . . going home,' he replied.

For a second no one said anything, then Yori clapped in delight. 'Praise the gods!'

'Praise *us* more like,' said Benkei, grinning wider than the cat in his lap, and they all began to celebrate the good news.

After dinner, the midshipman showed Jack and his friends to their quarters for the night. Akiko was given her own cabin, courtesy of one of the officers, while the others were offered berths on the lower deck. The crew had slung several spare hammocks from the beams. Benkei clambered into one and promptly fell out the other side, much to everyone's amusement.

'I prefer the floor anyway!' said Benkei, massaging his behind and pulling his pack over for a pillow. The ship's cat curled up next to him and purred contentedly. 'As you can see, it's far more comfortable.'

With practised ease, Jack rolled into his hammock. Saburo and Yori struggled with theirs, before giving up and joining Benkei on the floor. Exhausted from the battles of the day, they were soon fast asleep.

Clasping his hands behind his head, Jack settled back, still unable to believe his good fortune. As the hammock gently swayed back and forth with the lapping of the waves, he too was lulled to sleep. His last thoughts were of his sister, Jess, and his return to England.

62

GUNPOINT

Jack stared into the muzzle of a gun.

Woken by a prod to the ribs, he'd opened his eyes to find the First Officer holding a flintlock pistol to his face. Next to him stood Captain Spilbergen.

'I'm sorry, Jack,' said the captain. 'I've been given no choice.'

'But . . . you said we're protected on-board the *Hosiander*.'

'Even if you were Dutch, I couldn't save your life,' he sighed. 'The *bugyō* of Nagasaki has threatened to revoke all our trade privileges. He's also arrested several of my crew. They're as good as dead . . . *unless* we turn you over to the Shogun's samurai.'

Jack glanced round to discover his friends also held at gunpoint.

'Can't you just hand *me* over?' he begged.

Captain Spilbergen shook his head regretfully. 'I'm afraid it's a life for a life. And my duty is to my crew first. Do understand this is not personal.'

Jack dropped from his hammock. His pack and swords had already been seized. Still, there'd be little point in trying to fight their way free. The captain's hand was being forced. It wasn't his fault.

Surrendering to their fate, Jack and his friends were taken up to the main deck. Blinking in the bright morning sunshine, Jack spotted Akiko beside the main mast, her head bowed, a resigned expression on her face.

'So close to going home,' she whispered as they were directed towards the gangway. 'I'm sorry we let our guard down.'

'Don't be,' he replied. 'To come this far with you is closer than I could have ever dreamed.'

At the bottom of the gangway, dressed in gleaming gold-and-black armour, a detachment of the Shogun's samurai awaited them. The forty troops glared up at their elusive quarry, eager to have the traitors in their clutches at last. In front of them, five Dutch crewmen were on their knees, swords held to their throats.

'What a cheery start to the morning!' Benkei remarked, scratching his wayward hair and yawning.

Captain Spilbergen led Jack and his friends down the gangway and on to the quayside.

The *bugyō*, a short man with waxen skin, hollow cheeks and a thin preened moustache, greeted the captain.

'I'm so glad you could see matters our way,' he said with an ingratiating smile.

Giving a wave of his hand, he allowed the five Dutchmen to be released.

Captain Spilbergen grunted and handed over his captives. The Shogun's samurai stepped forward and seized Jack and his friends, roughly escorting them away.

63

STAKE

The blistering sun beat down, the air hot and humid. Even the breeze coming off the bay gave no relief.

A bead of sweat rolled down Jack's brow. But he couldn't wipe it away. His hands were bound, along with the rest of his body, to a wooden stake. A row of them had been erected along the harbour front earlier that morning. They'd heard the hammering from their prison cell as the stakes were driven into the hard ground. Akiko was lashed to the one on his left, Yori to his right. Benkei and Saburo were being tied to the final two stakes.

Dressed in a purple *kataginu* jacket and gold ceremonial kimono, the waxen-faced *bugyō* oversaw the preparations with an enthusiasm that went beyond his duty as a magistrate. He personally checked each of their bonds, ensuring they were all painfully fastened. Once satisfied, he directed the Shogun's samurai to form an arena round the execution site, quashing any hopes of escape . . . or of rescue.

Bound and helpless, Jack could only look to the heavens for salvation. But the merciless sun stared blankly back at him, while in the distance dark clouds gathered over the sea as if heralding the tragedy to come.

Encircling the five stakes, a growing pile of wood was dumped at their feet. Their execution had been publicly proclaimed throughout Nagasaki and the local inhabitants instructed to bring their own contributions to the fire. By the early afternoon, the pyre was knee-deep and a vast crowd had gathered on the quayside – merchants, samurai, farmers, monks, and even families with children. A burning at the stake promised to be quite a spectacle and no one wanted to miss it.

'Please forgive me for getting you into this mess,' Jack begged his friends. 'I never imagined it would end this way.'

'A samurai is born to die, Jack,' replied Saburo, bravely holding his head high, despite the tremble in his voice.

'I suppose it's better to burn out than to fade away!' jested Benkei, forcing a smile. But this quickly disappeared as another bundle of wood was stacked against him.

Yori craned his head to look at Jack. 'There's always more beyond the horizon than you can see. This is *not* the end.' He turned to the others, trying his best to offer them spiritual reassurance. 'Sensei Yamada once told me, *Don't be afraid of death, be afraid of a life unlived.*'

Meeting Jack's eyes, Akiko whispered, 'If I only live one life and die by your side, then it's been a life worth living.'

Jack didn't know what to say to this. Yet again his friends astounded him by their courage and loyalty. But just looking at Akiko made his heart burst. He didn't want her to die – or any of his friends. Not when they had so much still to live for.

'*Forever bound to one another,*' he declared, desperately wanting to reach out to Akiko.

A single tear rolled down her cheek. '*Forever . . .*'

The *bugyō* stepped forward and announced to the crowd, 'The Shogun, supreme ruler of all Japan, commands that these traitors are punished for their crimes and burned alive!'

A chorus of approval accompanied his declaration. Jack felt an uncontrollable shudder of fear as the executioner lit his torch and approached. The crowd's excitement grew to fever pitch. Men jeered and threw stones. Women heckled their disgust at such treachery. Kids watched wide-eyed in anticipation. Jack couldn't believe their suffering would bring such entertainment to the masses.

But, as Jack scanned the crowd, he saw that a number stood silent and grave-faced. Some mothers had covered their children's eyes and refused themselves to watch. A group of monks in straw hats had their heads bowed in mournful respect. Then Jack recognized Takumi and the four farmers among the throng. Tears streamed down their faces as they silently mouthed a prayer for Jack and his friends' souls. Jack realized not everyone craved their deaths and drew some comfort from this.

However, his solace was short-lived as he spotted another face in the crowd – one he'd hoped never to see again. Pale and full of spite, Kazuki pushed his way to the front, a blood-soaked bandage wrapped around his waist. He took up prime position before Jack's stake.

'You're going to burn, *gaijin*!' he cried. 'BURN IN HELL!'

64

THE MESSENGER

The crowd fell silent as the executioner held the torch over the pyre, awaiting the *bugyō*'s command to set the traitors ablaze. Not wanting his last moments to be consumed with his rival's gloating face, Jack turned to Akiko. She held his gaze, her eyes no longer brimming with tears but with love and friendship. In those final dying seconds, Jack felt a moment of peace.

The *bugyō* drew in a breath to issue his command. A startled cry from the back of the crowd distracted him as a horse thundered on to the quayside, scattering people aside. The Shogun's samurai parted for it to gallop into the centre of the arena and a cloaked messenger leapt from its back.

'STOP!' he bellowed at the executioner.

'What is the meaning of this?' demanded the *bugyō*, striding towards him.

The messenger presented the magistrate with a scroll bearing the formal seal of the Shogun. The *bugyō* snatched it from his grasp and broke the wax seal.

The baying crowd had become deathly quiet. Only the lapping of the waves and the crackle of the burning torch could be heard. Jack and his friends waited with bated breath, their lives hanging in the balance.

The *bugyō* looked up, stunned.

In a dry voice, he declared, 'With great sorrow and regret, I must inform you that Shogun Kamakura, our supreme leader, the Light of the East, passed away at the Hour of Serpent, on the fourth day of the seventh month of the Year of the Rabbit.'

A collective gasp rose from the gathered crowd.

'Our Shogun is *dead*!' wailed a woman, collapsing to the ground in grief.

The whole quayside now fell to its knees, the crowd prostrating themselves as they mourned their deceased leader. The former Shogun's samurai laid down their swords and bowed their heads in deep respect.

Jack was equally shocked by the news and looked to his friends, wondering what this would mean for them. The executioner still held the burning torch over the pyre.

The *bugyō* continued. 'All power now lies with the Council. And in their esteemed judgement they've appointed *daimyo* Takatomi to be Regent of all Japan until the Shogun's heir, Hidetada, comes of age and takes his rightful place as our ruler.'

While the crowd still lamented their great loss, Jack and his friends found cause to smile – and even entertain hope of salvation. *Daimyo* Takatomi was the former lord of Kyoto, master and friend of Masamoto Takeshi, and benefactor of their old samurai school, the *Niten Ichi Ryū*. Jack had even saved his daughter's life, Emi, during the Battle of Osaka Castle. The new ruler of Japan was their ally. The question was whether he had the authority to overrule the exile of foreigners and Christians. More importantly, would his influence stretch to protecting their lives in their hour of need?

The *bugyō* scrutinized the scroll once more, its parchment fluttering in the stiffening onshore breeze. He appeared unable to believe what he was reading. 'The Regent's first act in office is to . . . *pardon* the following individuals of all crimes: the foreign samurai Jack Fletcher . . . Akiko Dāte . . . Yori . . .' He trailed off, dismissively waving the scroll in the direction of the staked prisoners. 'Free them. Free them all.'

Jack and his friends were as astounded as the Shogun's samurai were dismayed at their last-second reprieve.

Benkei whooped loudly. 'If I didn't have my legs bound, Jack, I'd dance a jig!' he laughed.

Saburo hung his head and let out a huge sigh of relief.

'I've never prayed so hard,' sobbed Yori, 'or been so grateful to the gods.'

Jack beamed at Akiko. Life seeming more precious than ever, he vowed to cherish every moment with her.

'We live to fight another day,' she said, blinking away tears of joy.

Jack nodded. But there would be no need for more fighting. They were no longer fugitives. And he was free to go home.

'NO!' shouted Kazuki, breaking through the line of mourning samurai. 'They're traitors!'

Limping over, Kazuki seized the flaming torch out of the executioner's hand. And, before anyone could stop him, he tossed it on to the pyre.

65

THE RING OF SKY

The bone-dry tinder caught immediately. Crackling and popping, the fire spread its tendrils through the piles of wood like spitting snakes. Fanned by the strengthening sea breeze, the flames rushed to engulf Jack and his friends in a hellish blaze.

Kazuki laughed as they struggled against their bonds. 'Squirm, *gaijin*, squirm all you like!'

Benkei desperately blew at the approaching fire. Saburo wiggled his feet to shift the bundles of wood away from him. Akiko tried to prise open her knots. Yori began praying again, while Jack slammed his body into the stake, attempting to loosen it from the ground. But the Shogun's samurai had done their job too well. Their efforts to free themselves proved futile.

Takumi and the farmers in the crowd started screaming for the samurai to save the pardoned prisoners. But none made a move, either too afraid to approach the deadly blaze or secretly pleased to see the fugitives burn.

Kazuki was to have his revenge after all.

Jack bowed his head in defeat. Only a miracle could save

them now. For some strange reason, Shiryu's *kanji* poem popped into his thoughts:

> If we always look at the earth,
> we do not see the sky.

Jack looked up. Above the bay the clouds had gathered and grown darker. 'With true mastery of the Ring of Sky,' the Grandmaster had once told him, 'a ninja can even control the elements of nature itself.' Jack had been witness to just such a miracle. *But could he encourage a storm like the one Zenjubo had invoked in the mist of the Iga mountains?*

At this time, anything was worth a try. Despite his hands being bound behind his back, Jack spread out his fingers, the index and thumbs touching, and feverishly uttered the mantra for *Zai*: '*On chirichi iba rotaya sowaka . . .*'

He focused his mind on the clouds, becoming one with the sky and beckoning the storm on. The heat around him rose and the crackle of flaming wood filled his ears. He risked a glance. The fire was raging towards his feet. But the clouds definitely seemed to be drawing closer . . . *or was it his imagination?*

Jack concentrated harder, the mantra tumbling from his lips in an unending chant. He looked up again. But this time, the clouds appeared no nearer. He realized then he was just fooling himself, sheer desperation making him believe the impossible was possible. He was no ninja Grandmaster. No god. He couldn't bend the elements to his will.

The fire encircled him and his friends entirely, the blasts of heat so intense that all oxygen was seemingly sucked from the air. Jack could only gasp in scorching lungfuls of smoke and ash as the failed mantra died on his lips. Coughing and spluttering, he felt the first of the flames lick at his feet, searing his flesh. At the same time he heard Yori scream as the fire burned him too.

Then a crack of thunder split the sky and all of a sudden the heavens opened. A tropical storm broke over Nagasaki in one torrential downpour. The fire spat angrily as the flood of rain doused the flames, killing the blaze within seconds.

'Talk about the luck of the gods!' cried Benkei, shaking his sodden mass of hair in joy.

The others began laughing too, their tears of relief mixing with the welcome rain.

Jack lifted his face to the billowing sky, relishing the cool drops of water as they washed over him. Soaked to the skin, he felt reborn.

Was it pure luck the rain had fallen? Or had he really harnessed the Ring of Sky?

Such an idea seemed too great to believe. A miracle.

Then through the deluge his eye was caught by the group of praying monks in the crowd. Each of them had their hands spread out in front, just the thumb and index finger touching. And above the patter of rain, Jack heard a familiar incantation, '*On chirichi iba rotaya sowaka . . .*' The lead monk glanced up from beneath his straw dome hat, seemingly aware Jack was looking in his direction. Clasping his hands together, the monk entwined his middle fingers, then extended both thumbs and little fingers into a V shape. Jack blinked in surprise. But, when he looked again, the monk and his fellow brothers had vanished among the crowd.

Yet Jack was certain of what he'd seen – the *Dragon Seal*. The secret hand sign of the ninja. Now Jack knew, beyond a doubt, the rainstorm had nothing to do with chance.

The Ring of Sky had saved them.

Thwarted from roasting Jack and his friends alive, Kazuki gave a great howl of fury. He drew his *katana* and limped forward to run Jack through with the blade.

'Now *you'll* feel the edge of my steel,' Kazuki growled, aiming for Jack's stomach.

Still bound to the stake, Jack was powerless to avoid his rival's vicious attack. But the cloaked messenger leapt between them before Kazuki could make his thrust.

'Get out of my way!' snapped Kazuki, his face twisted in rage.

The messenger held his ground.

'I'll run you through as well.'

'Will you?' questioned the messenger, pulling back his hood to reveal the shaved head of a man in his late forties. He had a small trimmed beard and amber eyes that demanded total respect. But his most distinguishing feature was the crimson scarring that marked the left-hand side of his face.

66

BON FESTIVAL

'Masamoto-sama!' gasped Jack, stunned by his guardian's miraculous appearance.

His friends stared in equal disbelief. None of them had believed they'd ever see their old swordmaster again.

Kazuki somehow stood his ground, but his *katana* visibly trembled in his hand. 'You were exiled! You've no power here. Whereas I'm an *ōmetsuke* of the Shogun. Stand aside.'

'Lay down your sword, Kazuki,' ordered Masamoto, flicking back his rider's cloak to reveal the black silk handles of his *daishō*.

Kazuki tensed. Jack could see his rival summoning up the strength – and possibly the courage – to attack. Masamoto remained motionless, his right hand relaxed by his side. The swordmaster's unwavering calm in the face of such a threat to his life was unsettling. He merely stared at Kazuki, daring his ex-student to strike.

But even in his arrogance and anger Kazuki recognized the futility of duelling the founder of the Two Heavens. He dropped his sword, the steel clattering on the quayside.

Masamoto took a step towards him. 'By virtue of the power

invested in me by Takatomi-sama, the Regent of Japan, I hereby strip you, Oda Kazuki, of all samurai status.'

He seized both of Kazuki's swords and ripped the sun *mon* from his kimono before throwing it on to the smouldering fire.

'Arrest this traitor,' Masamoto commanded the *bugyō*.

The magistrate, clearly aware of the swordmaster's reputation, immediately ordered four of the samurai guards to apprehend Kazuki.

With the Oda family name so publicly dishonoured, Kazuki hung his head in shame as he was shackled and led away to a life in prison. Staring morosely at the ground, he never even glanced once in Jack's direction. Jack realized his rival's spirit was truly broken. Kazuki would never pose a threat again – not to him and, more importantly, not to Akiko.

Jack walked openly and freely through the streets of Nagasaki. He had nothing to fear with his guardian by his side. Three days had passed since Masamoto had averted their execution and in that time Nagasaki had been transformed into a boisterous celebration. The inhabitants were marking the annual *Bon* Festival – a Buddhist custom honouring the spirits of their ancestors. Yori had explained that the Japanese believed the spirit lives on after the death of the body, returning periodically from the mountains and other sacred places to the land of the living. To welcome the spirits back, Nagasaki was traditionally decorated with pennants and flickering candles. The narrow alleys were filled with colourful paper lanterns hanging overhead, and the townsfolk spilt into the streets, visiting temples and burial sites on the hills to invite their ancestors to come and eat with them. All over the port, people chatted, drank and ate with imaginary spectres. Fireworks lit up the night sky and music and dancing filled the harbour.

'I hear you've learnt a new trick or two with your swords,' remarked Masamoto as the two of them made their way through the partying crowd. 'A *reverse* grip?'

By the tone of his voice, Jack wasn't certain whether his guardian approved of him modifying the Two Heavens. Bowing respectfully, he held out his hand to show the missing fingertip.

'I was forced to make a few changes to my technique,' Jack explained in his defence.

Masamoto smiled, a rare occurrence as only one side of his face reacted to the expression. 'You must teach me the grip,' he said.

Jack's jaw dropped open at the suggestion. *What could he teach the greatest swordsman in Japan about combat?*

Noting Jack's stunned expression, Masamoto continued, 'No sensei ever stops being a student, Jack-kun. If a sword style doesn't evolve, then it becomes redundant and dies. As you know, the essence of the Two Heavens is the *spirit of winning*. And in order to accomplish this, the style must constantly adapt and overcome each and every situation.' He glanced at Jack's injured hand. 'Which I see you have done. Sensei Kyuzo sends his apologies for his grave mistake in carrying out *yubitsume*.'

Jack studied his little finger. 'It's a little late for apologies,' he replied.

'It's a bit late for many things,' said Masamoto with a heavy sigh. 'The past is behind us, so we must learn from it. And

Sensei Kyuzo won't *ever* make such a misjudgement again. He's committed *seppuku*.'

Jack turned to his guardian in shock. He knew the two were firm friends and saw a deep seam of sadness in Masamoto's eyes. 'But why?'

'Out of shame for his actions.'

Jack suddenly felt a wave of guilt. *He* was the reason Sensei Kyuzo had killed himself. Although he understood that such an act of ritual suicide by a samurai was considered to wipe away all previous transgressions and restore their honour, it didn't make him feel any better.

'I'm sorry . . .'

'Why should you be?' said Masamoto firmly. 'He volunteered. It was the right thing to do.'

Jack bowed his head in respect. 'Then I accept his apology and will remember Sensei Kyuzo for his courage in the Battle of Osaka Castle.'

Masamoto nodded with approval. 'I'm proud to call you my son, Jack-kun. At the *Niten Ichi Ryū*, I taught you all you need to live this life. And you've proven you can apply those skills not only for your own sake, but for the benefit of others too. *Bushido* is in your blood. You are a true samurai.'

67

LANTERNS

Peals of temple bells filled the night air as the harbour side swelled
with revellers. Many were gathered beside a wooden tower built
near the water's edge for the festival. On top of the main platform, a group of musicians and singers were performing a jaunty
song. *Shamisens* twanged loudly and *tsuzumi* drums beat out the
rhythm as three girls sang a soaring melody to the crowd. A circle
of people danced a series of choreographed moves in unison
around the base. Leading the dance were Okuni and her *kabuki*
troupe. They'd arrived the previous night and their shows had
been a great hit with the locals. The young girls now swayed and
twirled to the music. In their hands, they flourished bright red
fans that fluttered like a flock of birds through the night.

Jack spotted Benkei at the front of the admiring crowd, his
eyes transfixed upon Junjun. He'd been as delighted as Junjun
at their reunion. Nearby, Saburo was tucking into a slice of
watermelon and licking his lips contentedly. Yori was tapping
his staff to the beat of the music, while Akiko was browsing
a street stall selling a colourful array of paper lanterns. With
his friends no longer deemed traitors to Japan, they were all
at ease and enjoying the celebrations to the full.

'You should join them,' Masamoto urged Jack. 'If I learnt anything during my exile, it's that friends and family are what matter most in life. Treasure the moments you have left here.'

Jack bowed graciously to his guardian. 'You *are* my family.'

Masamoto laid a hand upon Jack's shoulder with firm affection. For a moment, the great warrior seemed choked with emotion. Then, with a nod of the head, he sent Jack on his way.

Jack headed across the harbour, aware of his guardian watching him all the way. As he walked towards his friends, a hatted figure slipped from the crowd and matched his stride. Jack's hand instinctively reached for his sword, but he relaxed when he saw the face. '*We* made the rain fall, didn't we?'

The ninja smiled enigmatically. 'Tropical storms are common this time of year.'

Jack knew he'd get no more from Zenjubo, the ninja characteristically terse. Yet he was surprised to see one of Miyuki's clan in Nagasaki at all. 'What are you doing this far south?'

'Searching for you, and recovering the fallen.'

'You mean . . . Miyuki.'

Zenjubo nodded. 'That was some battle by the looks of it. She defeated ten samurai before succumbing to her wounds.'

'I'm sorry,' said Jack, his heart heavy with grief and guilt. 'I should have done more to save her.'

'Don't be,' replied Zenjubo. 'She died a ninja's death. Feel only pride at her valour.'

He palmed an object into Jack's hand. 'Miyuki would want you to have this.'

Jack opened his hand to find one of her silver throwing stars. The steel gleamed like a jewel in his palm, and he felt a lump form in his throat as the tragic loss of Miyuki was brought home to him once more.

'Thank you,' he managed to reply. But, when he looked up again, Zenjubo was gone.

Wiping away a tear with the back of his hand, Jack tucked the precious *shuriken* into his *obi* and joined Akiko, Saburo and Yori at the water's edge.

'You look sad,' said Saburo. 'This should be a time for a celebration. We're *all* free!'

'I was thinking of Miyuki,' replied Jack, attempting and failing to manage a smile.

Yori bowed his head in respect and recited:

> 'Among flowers, the cherry blossom;
> Among men, the samurai;
> Among shadows, the ninja;
> And among stars, Miyuki.'

Jack was almost overwhelmed with emotion when he heard Yori's dedication to their lost friend, and Akiko gently took his hand in comfort.

'Like Yamato, Miyuki made the ultimate sacrifice for us,' said Akiko, passing Jack a paper lantern set upon a wooden float. 'We should honour her.'

Jack studied the lantern where Akiko had inked two *kanji* characters:

美雪

Beautiful Snow. The meaning behind Miyuki's name.

'The *Bon* Festival ends with *Toro Nagashi*,' explained Akiko, indicating the crowds gathering around the moonlit bay. 'Lanterns are floated down rivers and out to sea to guide the spirits back to their own world. And Miyuki deserves a light of her own, one that burns bright.'

Jack nodded, touched by Akiko's thoughtfulness. Taking a smouldering taper from Saburo, he lit the candle inside. And with a silent heartfelt prayer he placed the lantern upon the water and pushed it out into the harbour. Then he lit a second lantern for his father, while Akiko launched one in memory of Yamato.

The four friends stood in silence, side by side, and watched the three flickering lights bob across the bay to join the growing stream of lanterns that slowly and peacefully floated out into the distant sea. An endless line of candlelit spirits, gone but never to be forgotten.

68

FAREWELL

The *Hosiander* sat low in the water, its hold packed to the gunwales with the finest silks, silverware and several tonnes of supplies for the long voyage ahead. While her crew made the last checks to the sails and rigging, Captain Spilbergen completed the necessary formalities with the *bugyō* of Nagasaki.

Jack stood on the dockside with his friends, bathed in the golden glow of the rising sun. They'd gathered for a final farewell, but no one wanted to begin the goodbyes. After four years of training, fighting and surviving together, the idea that their paths were to separate forever was as unimaginable as it was heart-rending.

'You're welcome to stay as much as you're free to go,' Masamoto declared to Jack. 'The Regent has bestowed you with the rank of *hatamoto*. This guarantees your safety throughout Japan. And now you're of age, Jack-kun, as a samurai in the service of the Regent, you'll receive an income and some land. Your future here is assured.'

But Jack had already made his decision.

'I appreciate the honour, but I must go home,' he replied. 'With my father dead, my sister needs my protection.'

Masamoto bowed his head, as much to acknowledge Jack's duty as to conceal the sadness at his adopted son's departure. 'Then this is my last lesson to you, Jack-kun. *Saya no uchi de katsu* – victory in the scabbard of the sword.'

Jack looked down at his *katana*, bemused.

'During my exile, I was enlightened that the ultimate Way of the Warrior is to achieve victory without fighting,' explained Masamoto. 'To win a conflict without unsheathing the sword.'

'Even though you could take down your opponent with one cut?' said Jack, surprised that such a benign philosophy was being proposed by a swordmaster.

'Absolutely. That is why I let Kazuki live,' replied Masamoto. 'True victory lies in forgiveness and understanding.'

Jack bowed deeply to his guardian, the lesson both understood and recognized to be Masamoto's official goodbye to him.

Saburo was next in line. His friend started to bow, then throwing all Japanese decorum aside, he opened his arms and embraced Jack in a bear hug.

'Take care, my friend,' he said, the words catching in his throat. 'And if you ever find yourself in the Pacific again, make sure you stop by. My-my-my . . .'

'Hey, no tears, big boy!' cried Benkei. 'This is a happy time. Jack's going home at last.'

Wiping his eyes and sniffing, Saburo let go of Jack. 'Not much of a fearless warrior, am I?'

'Saburo, you're the bravest and most loyal samurai I know,' said Jack earnestly. 'Your father will be proud of you.'

'I really hope so. I've done enough courageous deeds on this *musha shugyō* to last me a lifetime!'

Reluctantly parting from Saburo, Jack bowed his gratitude to Benkei. 'Without your guidance and scheming, I'd never have made it to Nagasaki.'

'The pleasure's all mine!' exclaimed Benkei with a grin. 'Boiled, stabbed, punched and almost burned alive. We must do it again some time!'

Jack couldn't help but smile. 'And to think when I met you, you were only going to be buried alive.'

Benkei laughed and with a flick of his wrist produced a fresh *mikan* fruit out of thin air. 'For the journey. Don't want you going hungry!'

Accepting the fruit gratefully, Jack noticed Yori standing quietly, awaiting his turn to say goodbye. He gazed up at Jack, his wide eyes pleading for him not to leave.

'Good friends . . . are like stars,' Yori managed to say, clasping his *shakujō* tightly. 'You don't always see them, but you know they're always there for you.'

Jack now felt the tears welling in his eyes and pulled his dear friend into a hug. 'You've *always* been there for me, Yori. I'll miss you greatly.'

'Me too,' he sniffed.

'Time to set sail, Jack,' called Captain Spilbergen, waiting for him at the bottom of the gangway.

Nodding, Jack finally turned to Akiko. This was the one goodbye he'd dreaded the most. The first in Toba had been painful enough. The second in the Iga mountains had been almost unbearable. This third time would break his heart forever.

Their eyes met. But they said nothing, words incapable of expressing what either of them truly felt.

A single tear ran down Akiko's cheek. '*Sayonara*,' she whispered. 'Don't forget us.'

'How could I forget *you*?' said Jack, wanting to hold her and never let go.

Akiko looked away. 'There'll be a world between us. Just like snow melts in the spring, so memories fade with time.'

'But we're *forever* –'

Akiko put a finger to his lips. 'Don't say what can never be.'

Jack felt an invisible gulf open up between them – one that he could never sail across, however strong and favourable the wind. This was their final parting and they both knew that their paths might never cross again.

With a heavy heart, he picked up his pack, his father's *rutter* secure inside. Bowing, he took Akiko's hand and kissed it, cherishing the touch of her soft skin one last time. Then, fighting the tears that threatened to come, he headed towards the gangway without looking back.

69

SETTING SAIL

Captain Spilbergen greeted Jack with a broad smile. 'Welcome back on-board. I promise, no guns this time. You're officially one of my crew.'

'That's reassuring to hear,' replied Jack.

He stepped on to the wooden gangplank then stopped, one foot still on the quayside. He felt caught between two worlds. One he knew that he must return to and the other he no longer wished to leave. Japan might have taken everything from him – his father, his future and his hopes – but it had also given him a guardian, new skills, fresh hopes and, above all, friends. This last bond was so strong that even now Jack questioned his decision to leave. He simply couldn't fathom a life without his friends by his side. Without Akiko.

'Forgotten something?' queried Captain Spilbergen.

'Yes,' replied Jack, and whispered a private request.

After a moment of serious consideration, the captain nodded once. 'I owe you that much.'

Jack turned back to his friends. Benkei, Saburo, Yori and Akiko returned his gaze, confused as to why he wasn't boarding.

'It's time for me to say goodbye,' he finally said. 'Unless . . . you want to come with me to England?'

For a second, no one spoke. Their expressions were a mixture of astonishment and uncertainty, none sure if he was serious or not.

Benkei broke the silence first.

'I'd really love to,' he said, 'but I've accepted Okuni's offer to join her troupe. And I've also made a certain promise to Junjun.' He threw Jack a roguish wink.

Jack nodded his understanding, pleased that Benkei had finally found where he belonged. He now looked to Saburo who, to his dismay, regretfully shook his head.

'It's a tempting offer, Jack, but, as I said, I've had enough heroism to last me a lifetime. And two years of seasickness would be the end of me! Besides,' he added with a grin, 'I've heard the food in England is terrible.'

'At least we cook ours first!' Jack retorted, and they both managed a laugh.

With two refusals, Jack wondered if he'd overstepped the bonds of friendship in even suggesting they leave their homeland. He'd be putting his friends in the same situation as his own in Japan – a stranger in an alien world. But he'd be their faithful guide and ensure their safety, just as they had protected him. So perhaps it was etiquette or duty, or the law of the land that forbade them from leaving.

Yori stepped forward, the metal rings of the *shakujō* jingling.

'I'll come with you,' he piped up, his eyes sparkling with excitement. 'Sensei Yamada's always telling me to expand my horizons.'

'You'll certainly do that on the voyage,' remarked Jack, welcoming his friend to the *Hosiander*.

That only left Akiko.

Jack felt his mouth go dry as he waited for her response. He was keenly aware that she was duty-bound to her mother, and realized it was beyond hope that she could come . . . even if she wanted to.

Akiko glanced in Masamoto's direction, then she slowly approached. As she stood before Jack, her head bowed, the corners of her mouth curled into a smile. 'I thought you'd *never* ask.'

Jack felt his heart skip with joy. 'But what about your mother?'

'Kiyoshi's with her now,' she explained. 'They knew I might not return. My mother even gave me her blessing. And Masamoto-sama, as my uncle and guardian, has done so too.'

Jack looked over Akiko's shoulder at his adoptive father, who was finding it hard to suppress a smile.

'Take good care of Snowball for me,' Akiko called to Saburo as she retrieved her pack, bow and arrows from her horse's saddle. Giving the stallion a final affectionate pat, she followed Jack and Yori up the gangway.

Once on the quarterdeck of the *Hosiander*, Jack instantly felt the call of the sea. The crew couldn't raise the mainsail fast enough in his mind. And when the captain gave the command to cast off he shouted an almighty *kiai* in celebration.

As one journey ended, another now began. A new voyage, one potentially as perilous and uncertain as his days as a fugitive of the Shogun. But Jack had the skills of a samurai, the guile of a ninja and the knowledge of a sailor to help carry him safely across the Seven Seas back to England. More importantly, he had his friends by his side.

He might be leaving Japan, but a part of Japan was leaving with him too. The wisdom of the East in his firm friend Yori, and all that he'd come to know and love about Japan in Akiko – its grace, its beauty and its strength of spirit.

Find your heart and you'll find your home, the Riddling Monk had said to him the year before.

Glancing at Akiko beside him on the deck, her hair billowing in the sea breeze, Jack realized that he was already home.

HAIKU

The murmuring of the summer grass
All that is left
Of the warrior's dream

NOTES ON THE SOURCES

The following quotes are referenced within *Young Samurai: The Ring of Sky* (with the page numbers in square brackets below) and their sources are acknowledged here:

1. [Page 37] 'When it is dark enough, you can see the stars.' By Charles Austin Beard (American historian, 1874–1948).
2. [Page 127] 'No bird soars too high, if he soars with his own wings.' By William Blake (English poet, 1757–1827).
3. [Page 300] 'Revenge has no more quenching effect on the emotions than salt water on thirst.' By Walter Weckler (1905–69).
4. [Page 325] 'Don't be afraid of death, be afraid of a life un-lived.' By Natalie Babbitt (author, b.1932).
5. [Page 350] *Haiku*. By Bashō (1643–94).

ACKNOWLEDGEMENTS

With Jack's journey in Japan finally coming to an end, so has mine. And it has been a *musha shugyō* of epic proportions. The original idea was first born in 2006, with the first book, *The Way of the Warrior*, written in the spring of 2007 and published the following summer in 2008 (UK). Six years have passed since that spark of an idea. Eight books have now been released in the series: 636,208 words written in total. Jack's adventures have been published in twenty-five countries and eighteen foreign languages (so far). They've been nominated for more than sixteen book awards (and won some!). And I've toured ten countries, twenty book festivals, more than 500 schools, and performed live to over 100,000 fans and almost a million as part of the Biggest Book Show On Earth online festival. Yet none of this could have happened without the support and belief of the following people . . .

Charlie Viney, my agent, who recognized the idea for its potential and had the unwavering belief to make it happen.

Sarah Hughes at Puffin Books for seizing the *Young Samurai* sword before anyone else could; swiftly followed by my editor, Shannon Cullen, who bravely took up the sword from Sarah and sharpened it to perfection over the years. Also, Lola Bubbosh at Disney and the ever-faithful and fantastic Puffin team, including Wendy Shakespeare, Helen Gray, Julia Teece, Jayde Lynch, Sara Flavell and the cover designer Paul Young.

Pippa Le Quesne for her early guidance in the art of writing. Tessa Girvan, Franca Bernatavicius and Nicki Kennedy, my overseas agents at ILA, for taking *Young Samurai* round the world.

My martial arts instructors – Steve Cowley, David Ansell and Peter Brown – for their expert tuition, knowledge and support.

My friends – Karen, Rob and Thomas, Geoff and Lucy, Matt, Hayley, to name only a few – for their constant encouragement and feedback.

My family – Sarah, Zach, Mum and Dad, Sue and Simon, Steve and Sam, Ann and Andrew, Laura – who have been with me every step of the way, carrying me through the toughest of times and celebrating with me at the best of times.

And, finally, a huge heartfelt thanks must go to my readers. This book is dedicated to you, and here are just a handful of the most ardent supporters:

Adeeb Nami, Guilherme Merched Salomão, Charlie Harland, Hannah Lim En Hui, Paul Nelson, Koh Xuan Hong, Tyler Thompson, Cross Lee Jun Ye, Gabby Bolderstone, Tee Yew Ping, Andrew Whetherly, Nick Ritter, Nathaniel E Whiles, Lorraine Whiles, Cameron Clarke, Joel Monroy,

Alexander De Potter, Rhiona O'Brien, Mon Yeu Chan, Natalija Damjanovič, Laura Colussi, Tom Horton, Shevy Oakly, Siddhant Ganguly, Liam Moir, Daniel Baryshnikov, Elmiga Herbst, Gracie Millett, Victoria Fröberg, Matthew Apps, Philip Morgan, Charlie Baker, Low Chuan Wei, Aidan Bracher, Kirby Phillips, Marco Rivolta, George Griffiths, Tiwa Ethan Adelaja, Nur Zarifah Mohd Zafrullah, Callum Dunlop, Seth Alexander James Turquand-Cook, Nirmit Dhanani, Thean Li-Yang, Robert Mitchell, Li Chao, Anurag Kumar, Elliott Daly, Isabelle Monteiro, Chloe Anne Dervey, Soon Jia Yi, Isaac Roe, Mu'ammar Theba, Mohammad Dainish Jabeen, Nicholas Mitchell, Thibaut Revers, Nathaniel L. Williams, Emilie Elizabeth Carroll, Anisur Rahman, Shelbert Creech III, Shelbert Creech IV, Bishal Bahadur Sanmani Magar, Instructor Steve McCormick, Shazaan Nadeem, Hank Kiser, Simranjit Cheema, Zoe Oakes. Lande Fourie, Banti Debnath, Colby Wolfer, Edward Bennett, Oliver Morley, Millie Tillman, Oliver Hall, Matthias Moosburner, Sian Maiden, Matt Selesky, Jivjyot Singh, Daphne Ooi, Kevin Haex, Daniël Altena, Shray Bhandary, Ishaan Kumar, Byron Paterson, Sarah Aschmann, Jonathan Kaname Sison, Dmitry Alyohin, Noah Benoit, Dion Birney, Thomas Leyton Sidney, Dawn Sidney, Robbie Cannon, Janis Lim Hui Qin, Andy Honrado, Jessica Morgan, Luke Wolfer, Ozzie Teschler, Tim Hoogstoel, Harrison Facey, Zac Wakamatsu, Roman Frenkenberg, Sam Buss, Nate Kimball, Gabriel Kemble, Mark Butterworth, Brock Burnett, Jonathan Paul Walkotten, M. Salman Khan, Joseph Baross, Órla and Cíara Murphy, Axel Revin, Harry Woodley Luneth Calibur and every other Young Samurai fan (sorry I couldn't include all of your names!) . . .

Remember, keep waving the sword — the battle may not yet be over!

But as one journey ends, another now begins. I am embarking on a new adventure, the modern equivalent of the samurai warrior: the BODYGUARD. This past year I've been training in the art of close protection and I'm now primed to deliver an action-adventure story that will be as thrilling and exciting as the Young Samurai series.

I do hope you, my reader, will join me on this brand-new journey . . .

Chris

JAPANESE GLOSSARY

Bushido

Bushido, meaning the 'Way of the Warrior', is a Japanese code of conduct similar to the concept of chivalry. Samurai warriors were meant to adhere to the seven moral principles in their martial arts training and in their day-to-day lives.

Virtue 1: *Gi* – Rectitude
Gi is the ability to make the right decision with moral confidence and to be fair and equal towards all people no matter what colour, race, gender or age.

Virtue 2: *Yu* – Courage
Yu is the ability to handle any situation with valour and confidence.

Virtue 3: *Jin* – Benevolence

Jin is a combination of compassion and generosity. This virtue works together with *Gi* and discourages samurai from using their skills arrogantly or for domination.

Virtue 4: *Rei* – Respect

Rei is a matter of courtesy and proper behaviour towards others. This virtue means to have respect for all.

Virtue 5: *Makoto* – Honesty

Makoto is about being honest to oneself as much as to others. It means acting in ways that are morally right and always doing things to the best of your ability.

Virtue 6: *Meiyo* – Honour

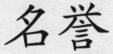

Meiyo is sought with a positive attitude in mind, but will only follow with correct behaviour. Success is an honourable goal to strive for.

Virtue 7: *Chungi* – Loyalty

Chungi is the foundation of all the virtues; without dedication and loyalty to the task at hand and to one another, one cannot hope to achieve the desired outcome.

A Short Guide to Pronouncing Japanese Words

Vowels are pronounced in the following way:
'a' as the 'a' in 'at'
'e' as the 'e' in 'bet'
'i' as the 'i' in 'police'
'o' as the 'o' in 'dot'
'u' as the 'u' in 'put'
'ai' as in 'eye'
'ii' as in 'week'
'ā' as in 'far'
'ō' as in 'go'
'ū' as in 'blue'

Consonants are pronounced in the same way as English:
'g' is hard as in 'get'
'j' is soft as in 'jelly'
'ch' as in 'church'
'z' as in 'zoo'
'ts' as in 'itself'

Each syllable is pronounced separately:
A-ki-ko
Ya-ma-to
Ma-sa-mo-to
Ka-zu-ki

arigatō (gozaimasu)	thank you (very much)
azuma no yabun hito	Eastern barbarian
bō	wooden fighting staff
bōjutsu	the Art of the *Bō*
bokken	wooden sword
bugyō	a magistrate or governor
bunbu ichi	the pen and sword in accord (also

	Bunbu Ryodo – the duel path of pen and sword)
bushido	the Way of the Warrior – the samurai code
Butokuden	Hall of the Virtues of War
chigiriki	a Japanese flail weapon with a wooden shaft and a spiked weight on the end of a short chain
daimyo	feudal lord
daishō	the pair of swords, *wakizashi* and *katana*, that are traditional weapons of the samurai
Daruma Doll	small wooden egg-shaped doll with no arms or legs, which is modelled after Bodhidharma, the founder of Zen; one eye is filled in with black ink while making a wish or goal, and the other is filled in when the wish or goal is attained
dochu no sei	stillness in motion
dohyō	the ring in which *sumo* wrestling bouts are held
dojo	training hall
dōshin	Edo-period police officers of samurai origin (low rank)
ensō	a circle and a concept strongly associated with Zen
fudoshin	literally 'immovable heart', a spirit of unshakeable calm
fusuma	vertical rectangular panels that act as sliding doors or room dividers
futon	Japanese bed: flat mattress placed directly on *tatami* flooring, and folded away during the day

gaijin	foreigner, outsider (derogatory term)
gasshuku	martial arts training camp
geisha	a Japanese girl trained to entertain men with conversation, dance and song
geta	traditional Japanese sandal with an elevated wooden base
gyōji	a referee in *sumo* wrestling
hachimaki	headbands, sometimes reinforced with metal strips
hatamoto	literally 'under the banners'; a samurai in the direct service of the Shogun
hayanawa	a short rope used for restraining prisoners
hikyaku	'Flying Feet' (a courier)
ippon seoinage	one-armed shoulder throw
jigoku	Hell pool
jutte (or jitte)	an iron truncheon or rod with a short pointed hook
kabuki	a classical Japanese dance-drama
kama	sickle-shaped weapon
kamon	a samurai family crest (also *mon*)
kata	a prescribed set of martial arts moves
kataginu	a Japanese-style jacket with stiffened shoulders like wings
katana	long sword
ki	energy flow or life force (Chinese: *chi* or *qi*)
kiai	literally 'concentrated spirit' – used in martial arts as a shout for focusing energy when executing a technique

kiaijutsu	the Art of the Kiai (shout)
kimono	traditional Japanese clothing
kissaki	tip of sword
koban	Japanese oval gold coin
koto	a thirteen-string zither-like instrument
kuji-in	nine syllable seals – a specialized form of Buddhist and ninja meditation
kunai	a farming tool, which resembles a masonry trowel and can be used as a weapon
kyusho	vital or nerve point on a human body
mabiki	a farming process of weeding out the rice seedlings; also a term for infanticide
menpō	protective metal mask covering part or all of the face
metsuke	technique of 'looking at a faraway mountain'
mie	a powerful and emotional pose struck by an actor during a *kabuki* performance
mikan	satsuma, orange citrus fruit
mikkyō	secret teachings
mochi	rice cake
mon	a round copper coin with a hole in the centre, common currency of Japan until 1870; also can be a samurai family crest
musha shugyō	warrior pilgrimage
nanban	southern barbarian
ninja	Japanese assassin
ninjatō	ninja sword

ninjutsu	the Art of Stealth
Niten Ichi Ryū	the 'One School of Two Heavens'
nodachi	a very large two-handed sword
obi	belt
ofuro	bath
ō-metsuke	a spy of the Shogun, reporting directly to the Council of the Shogun
onsen	natural hot springs used for bathing
ramen	a noodle dish
ri	traditional Japanese unit of distance, approx. 2.44 miles
ronin	masterless samurai
rotenburo	open-air hot spring bath
saké	rice wine
sakura	cherry-blossom tree
samurai	Japanese warrior
sankyo	a wrist lock in aikido that is termed 'third teaching'
sashimi	raw fish
saya	scabbard
Saya no uchi de katsu	victory in the scabbard of the sword
sensei	teacher
seppuku	ritual suicide
Sha	ninja hand sign, interpreted as healing for *ninjutsu* purposes
shakujō	a Buddhist ringed staff
shamisen	a three-stringed plucked lute
Shichi Hō De	'the Seven Ways of Going', the art of disguise and impersonation
shinobi shozoku	the clothing of a ninja
Shodo	the path or way of writing; Japanese calligraphy

Shogun	the military dictator of Japan
shoji	Japanese sliding door
shuriken	metal throwing stars
suki	a term in kenjutsu for a break in concentration that results in flawed technique or vulnerability to attack
sumimasen	excuse me; my apologies
sumo	a Japanese form of heavyweight wrestling
sushi	raw fish on rice
suzume	Japanese name for a sparrow; also can be used as a name
taijutsu	the Art of the Body (hand-to-hand combat)
tameshigiri	a test cut to assess the quality of a samurai sword, performed on corpses and sometimes convicted criminals
tantō	short knife
Taryu-Jiai	inter-school martial arts competition
tatami	floor matting
tekubi gatamae	hyperflexing wristlock
ten-uchi	a sword technique – the arm and wrist make a twisting motion during a descending strike
torii	a distinctive Japanese gate made of two uprights and two crossbars denoting the separation between common space and sacred space, found at the entrance to Shinto shrines
Toro Nagashi	a ceremony that is carried out on the last evening of the Bon Festival; paper lanterns are floated

	down rivers and out to sea in order to guide the spirits back to their own world
tsuzumi	handheld lacquered wooden drums in an hourglass shape
uke	training partner who attacks
wakizashi	side-arm short sword
wako	Japanese pirates
washi	traditional Japanese-style paper
yakitori	grilled chicken on a stick
Yama Arashi	Mountain Storm throw – a hand-throwing technique that also uses a thigh sweep to take an opponent to the ground
Yoko Sankaku Jime	side triangle choke using the legs
yubitsume	a Japanese ritual to atone for offences by means of cutting off one's own little finger (lit. 'finger shortening')
yukata	summer kimono
Zai	ninja hand sign for sky or elements control
zazen	meditation

Japanese names usually consist of a family name (surname) followed by a given name, unlike in the Western world where the given name comes before the surname. In feudal Japan, names reflected a person's social status and spiritual beliefs. Also, when addressing someone, *san* is added to that person's surname (or given names in less formal situations) as a sign of courtesy, in the same way that we use Mr or Mrs in English, and for higher-status people *sama* is used. In Japan, *sensei* is usually added after a person's name if they are a teacher, although in the Young Samurai books a traditional English order has been retained. Boys and girls are usually addressed using *kun* and *chan*, respectively.

MEET CHRIS

HOW OLD WERE YOU WHEN YOU STARTED TRAINING IN MARTIAL ARTS?

I started judo when I was seven years old. I won my first trophy at the age of eight and have since trained in over nine different martial arts.

WHAT'S YOUR FAVOURITE MARTIAL ART AND WHY?

I have enjoyed all my styles – each one has taught me something new – but my favourite must be Zen Kyo Shin *taijutsu*, since it was the first one I earned my black belt in. The style originates from the fighting art of the ninja – my sensei was even taught by a ninja grandmaster!

HAVE YOU EVER MET A REAL SAMURAI WARRIOR?

Yes – I am a student of Akemi Solloway Sensei, who is the eldest daughter of an old samurai family, descended from the *karō* of Iwatsuki Castle (near Tokyo) in the time of Lord Ota Dokan (1432–1486). The name Akemi means 'bright and beautiful' and, because she has no brothers, Akemi has a special responsibility to keep alive the traditions of her samurai ancestors.

WHEN DID YOU START WRITING?

I've been writing all my life, but mostly lyrics for songs. I didn't start writing stories until much later, though I remember making up stories in my head as a child, especially on long car journeys to stop myself getting bored.

HOW LONG DID IT TAKE YOU TO WRITE *THE WAY OF THE WARRIOR*?

I wrote *The Way of the Warrior* very quickly – in two months! The story literally burst out of me and on to the page fully formed.

WHERE DO YOUR IDEAS AND INSPIRATIONS COME FROM?

My heart and my life. The Young Samurai trilogy was inspired by my passion for martial arts. It is the story of a young boy learning about life through martial arts. It could be about me. Equally it could be about you.

WHAT DID YOU USED TO DO BEFORE YOU WERE A WRITER?

I was a songwriter and musician. I sing, play guitar and harmonica. I have performed all over the world, appeared on TV and taught music at the illustrious Academy Of Contemporary Music in Guildford. My musical experience led me to writing my first book on songwriting (*Heart & Soul*) for the British Academy Of Composers & Songwriters.

WHAT'S YOUR FAVOURITE BOOK?

It by Stephen King. The scariest, and his best.

WHAT'S YOUR FAVOURITE PLACE IN THE WORLD AND WHY?

I've travelled to many wonderful places, but my three favourite memories are playing guitar on a beach as the sun set in Fiji, sitting in a tree house in the middle of a jungle in Laos and listening to a temple bell chime at dawn in Kyoto, Japan.

WHAT'S YOUR FAVOURITE TYPE OF FOOD?

Sushi. It's so healthy and very tasty.

WHAT'S YOUR MOST TREASURED POSSESSION?

My samurai sword. The blade gleams like lightning and whistles when it cuts through the air.

WHAT'S YOUR FAVOURITE FILM?

Crouching Tiger, Hidden Dragon. The action scenes are magical and literally defy gravity, the actors are like fighting ballerinas, and it features one of the greatest female movie martial artists, Michelle Yeoh.

WANT MORE ACTION? MORE ADVENTURE? MORE ADRENALIN?

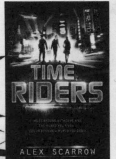

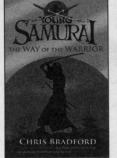

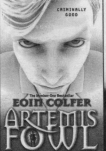

GET INTO PUFFIN'S ADVENTURE BOOKS FOR BOYS

It all started with a Scarecrow

Puffin is well over sixty years old.
Sounds ancient, doesn't it? But Puffin has never been
so lively. We're always on the lookout for the next big
idea, which is how it began all those years ago.

Penguin Books was a big idea from the mind of
a man called Allen Lane, who in 1935 invented
the quality paperback and changed the world.
**And from great Penguins, great Puffins grew,
changing the face of children's books forever.**

The first four Puffin Picture Books were hatched in 1940 and the
first Puffin story book featured a man with broomstick arms called
Worzel Gummidge. In 1967 Kaye Webb, Puffin Editor, started the
Puffin Club, promising to **'make children into readers'**.
She kept that promise and over 200,000 children became
devoted Puffineers through their quarterly installments of
Puffin Post, which is now back for a new generation.

Many years from now, we hope you'll look back and
remember Puffin with a smile. **No matter what your age
or what you're into, there's a Puffin for everyone.**
The possibilities are endless, but one thing is for sure:
whether it's a picture book or a paperback, a sticker book
or a hardback, **if it's got that little Puffin
on it – it's bound to be good.**